Readers lo
Little Godde
by AMY LANE

MW00509529

Vulnerable

"What can I say about Amy's writing that I haven't already said? Not much. She's fantastic, I love everything she writes."
—Love Bytes

"I strongly recommend you read this book, as I would hope it would please you as much as it did me. It will give you hours of enjoyment..."
—The Novel Approach

Wounded, Vol. 1

"There is much darkness in this book, but there are rays of light as well. I look forward to furthering this series."
—Prism Book Alliance

Wounded, Vol. 2

"It's another great read, so full of emotion and drama, magic and mystique."
—Jeannie Zelos Book Reviews

By AMY LANE

LITTLE GODDESS
Vulnerable
Wounded, Vol. 1
Wounded, Vol 2
Bound, Vol. 1

Published by DSP PUBLICATIONS
www.dsppublications.com

Bound

Volume One

AMY LANE

DSP PUBLICATIONS

Published by
DSP Publications

5032 Capital Circle SW, Suite 2, PMB# 279, Tallahassee, FL 32305-7886 USA
www.dsppublications.com

This is a work of fiction. Names, characters, places, and incidents either are the product of author imagination or are used fictitiously, and any resemblance to actual persons, living or dead, business establishments, events, or locales is entirely coincidental.

Bound, Vol. 1
© 2015 Amy Lane.

Cover Art
© 2015 Anne Cain.
annecain.art@gmail.com
Cover content is for illustrative purposes only and any person depicted on the cover is a model.

All rights reserved. This book is licensed to the original purchaser only. Duplication or distribution via any means is illegal and a violation of international copyright law, subject to criminal prosecution and upon conviction, fines, and/or imprisonment. Any eBook format cannot be legally loaned or given to others. No part of this book may be reproduced or transmitted in any form or by any means, electronic or mechanical, including photocopying, recording, or by any information storage and retrieval system, without the written permission of the Publisher, except where permitted by law. To request permission and all other inquiries, contact DSP Publications, 5032 Capital Circle SW, Suite 2, PMB# 279, Tallahassee, FL 32305-7886, USA, or www.dsppublications.com.

ISBN: 978-1-63476-119-2
Digital ISBN: 978-1-63476-120-8
Library of Congress Control Number: 2015931899
Second Edition November 2015
First Edition published as *Bound: The Third Book of the Little Goddess Series* by iUniverse, 2007.

Printed in the United States of America

This paper meets the requirements of
ANSI/NISO Z39.48-1992 (Permanence of Paper).

Wreathes of flowers bind me tight
As my lover takes me with care and might
My legs are bound around his hips
My mouth is pressed against his lips
I breathe because my body must
'Tis why I plunge against his thrusts
My heart has sworn its silent oaths
My body too has pledged its troths
One troth to him with whom I reign
And one to him who keeps me sane
One troth to one I keep from death
And one to the ghost with whom I've slept
As my soul is chained with silken threads
To every lover in my bed
I'm tied with love to the land I see
And those who dwell are bound to me.
My fate was made with choices free
Bound to the truth I'm bound to be.

CORY
Ou'e'hm & Due'alle

"I'VE MADE calls and put a compulsion on all of your paperwork to make sure it goes through," Green assured me earnestly, the planes taking off overhead making it difficult to hear. He was dressed in classic business sidhe—crème-colored wool suit, a dark green brocade tie, and a darker crème-colored trench coat to keep off the steady rain that made this mid-January day just a little drearier. The only thing that wasn't plain and classic about Green's outfit was the green and gold scarf I'd knitted him for Christmas and, of course, Green's hip-length braid of butter-yellow hair. As for the scarf, what else would I give an immortal sidhe lover who ruled all of Northern California and the central coastlands to boot? And maybe because he had enough magic and power at his disposal to make concrete jungles erupt into fantasy gardens, he lived simply, with clean bare wood and homemade quilts and few decorations in his room. In fact, I thought wretchedly as he searched my plain human face with his fantastically large and wide-spaced green eyes, the only indulgences Green seemed to have in his life right now were that raggedly hand-knit cashmerino scarf and me. He touched my hair restlessly with his long fingers, interrupting my thoughts. The inhumanly beautiful, clean, anime-perfect and heartbreaking lines of his face were marred by worry. I reached up—way, way up, because he was in the top half of six feet and I was in the bottom half of five—and stroked the pointed curve of his elven ear. Nobody else could see those pointed ears—only the preternatural or me, a human with preternatural gifts—and I felt an ownership of this part of him that the rest of the world couldn't have. But he was leaving, and the rest of the world was going to have him, and right now all I could do was try very hard to smile and let him know I would be all right.

"You should get right in," he was saying. "You'll be able to register by phone tomorrow, but you must take the classes we picked out or it won't work." Including Renny, Nicky, Mario, LaMark, Bracken, and me, there were six of us from Green's hill enrolling in classes at Sac State.

The commute from Foresthill was over an hour—so, in the best interest of time and gas, we scheduled ourselves through the early afternoons Mondays through Thursdays, with breaks in between to meet. Before I'd begun dating a vampire, I had been alone—a mean-spirited punk-goth bitch who hated the world. But once you've truly loved another, as I had loved Adrian, and once his family has taken you in as theirs, well, you're never truly alone again. My family and I were planning to stick close, out in the big bad human world.

I nodded to ease Green's worries, and tried to keep my face from crumpling. I'd assured Green that I'd be able to handle his traveling, because his traveling kept our people consolidated, and it kept enemies from descending on us like nightmare plagues from hell, and I didn't want him walking into those strange sidhe and faerie halls (or human boardrooms) worrying about me falling apart. However, I'd just spent four months living in another city, and it had—in a very physical, magical, and literal way—almost killed me to be apart from Green for that time, in spite of our visits back and forth. Now I was back in the foothills and I had two other men bound to me by supernatural and emotional ties, and watching him get out of the SUV and unload his luggage was still like watching my right lung rip itself out of my body to go toddling off among the vampires in play. It was excruciatingly painful, and it just plain felt wrong.

"What name is it under?" I asked, trying to be practical. My full Christian name was Corinne Carol-Anne Kirkpatrick. Since I was essentially a super-magically charged human, the elves were afraid that I was as susceptible to preternatural influences as the fey but without enough experience to know what was hostile and what was not. The general assumption was that anyone who knew my full name would have way too much power over me. Mostly, I agreed. Unfortunately, *which* name I was supposed to take had been a big fat meaty bone of contention.

"Whatever name you like," Green said gently, knowing exactly where my thoughts were headed. A part of me wished he had stepped up and claimed me, writing "Cory Green" on my paperwork with absolute authority, because he did things like that sometimes when my health or my safety was at stake. But the more grown-up part of me was glad, very glad, that he trusted me to follow my heart, and trusted that my heart would always beat for him. Still, I had never been good at lying, and my misery and indecision must have been written plainly on my face.

"Hey, Cory luv…," Green said tenderly, "I'll be back. Bracken will keep you safe, right?"

I looked over my shoulder at Bracken, my other sidhe lover, who was standing by the family's big black SUV under the rainy sky. He was a darker-haired, darker-eyed, darker-spirited, insanely tall and beautiful counterpoint to Green. Right now, in spite of the fact that I was in Green's arms and had shared Green's bed the night before, Bracken was looking at me like I was the only star in his dark-night sky and he was afraid I'd lose my gravity and fly into cosmic dust, and his entire focus was on keeping me whole.

I looked back at Green with a sad, weak parody of a smile. "It doesn't matter if it's your left lung or your right lung, *ou'e'hm*," I said after a fraught moment while I'd twisted my face trying not to cry. "It's still a part of you that you need to live, and you miss it." And with that, I lost the battle and the tears spilled over, and Green stood for a moment, stroking my shoulder-length mud-red hair and allowing me to mess up his lovely off-white coat with my mascara and my weakness and my humanity. *Ou'e'hm*, I'd called him—my leader and lover. On days like today, I wondered what in me had given me the right.

"I'll be back in two weeks, *ou'e'eir*," he reassured, making me wonder all over again, and kissing my face in a dozen places and licking the salt off my lips. "Two weeks—it's nothing, right? It's a moment. It's a heartbeat…." His words trailed off and he looked at Bracken helplessly, because his plane left in an hour and he barely had enough time as it was. Bracken came behind me and wrapped his arms around my shoulders, and Green disentangled himself from me with one last frantic kiss. In the end, it was Bracken who had to endure my miserable sniffling on his shirt, and Bracken who had to spend the next fifteen minutes in the car putting my little tiny anguished pieces back together after Green disappeared inside the airplane terminal in a flash of crème-colored coat and shockingly bright sunshine hair.

AN HOUR later, we were all standing in the lobby of the Sac State administration building, wishing we were back at Green's hill drinking hot cocoa instead. The building itself had a bright ethnic mural on its front, but inside it was as dreary and as sterile as any state building on the planet anywhere. I huddled in Bracken's oversized Sacramento

Kings sweatshirt, shifting uncomfortably as my hair, still soaked by the run from the parking structure to the building, dripped steadily onto my shoulders, and tried not to look any more uncertain than I actually felt. Bracken was about a hair's breadth away from tucking little ol' me under his arm and bolting out of the building as it was.

I had to sigh. Another semester, another school, and as much as I had wanted to leave San Francisco, and as much as I had business here in Sacramento to attend to, I was remembering once again that the bureaucracy of education sucked large.

The student in front of me—a boy a little older than me, dressed just like Bracken in a sweatshirt, denim shorts, and flip-flops on this soggy day—moved forward, and I heard Renny behind me sighing. "It's about time."

I turned my head toward her and Nicky and grinned. "What's the matter, Ren—spoiled?" The previous semester we had both been enrolled in CSUSF. Green had paid our tuition, called a few people, pulled a few strings, and voila! Instant enrollment. But Renny and I had both been grief stricken and traumatized by the deaths of our boyfriends, and coping with the day-to-day mechanics of our lives had consisted of ordering pizza we had no intention of eating so we could leave it for the sprites. Those little tiny domestic housekeepers adored Green, their leader, and doted on Renny and me. But this semester, Green was forced to travel extensively to consolidate the preternatural holdings he'd expanded (to put it mildly) at Christmas, and I'd assured him that we could take care of our own enrollment.

Nicky rolled his brown-yellow eyes—he turned into a bird in his off-hours—and his grin under his rust-and-black colored hair made him look younger than Renny or me for a moment when, in fact, he was nearing twenty-four. I'd turned twenty the past summer, after Adrian died. I'm not even sure if I had remembered the day when it passed.

"Not at all," Renny said loftily, her piquant little face assuming an easy air of superiority. "I'm just accustomed to being treated according to my status."

Nicky and I laughed, and so did Mario and LaMark, who were standing behind Renny and Nicky. Mario is five feet eleven inches of Hispanic sex appeal, LaMark a scant five feet eight of sweet dark-chocolate intelligence. They had met Green after trying to attack his people—in fact, Mario's mate was accidentally killed in the attack itself.

After four days of watching Green take care of his people, mentally and physically, they had sworn to defend us all to the death—and since they could both turn into big predatory birds just like Nicky, it wasn't an idle threat. That's just what kind of leader Green was—and the way we stood together, like a group of tourists in a foreign country, said something about how much of a family you got to be when you were of an age and not exactly human.

Bracken moved restlessly next to me, breaking my thoughts, and I reached out a hand to touch his. His fingers, long and rough and warm, wrapped around my hand, and I tried not to wince. He saw it anyway and pulled my wrist up for inspection.

"Ellis has no fucking finesse," he growled, glaring balefully at the two nasty rips over my vein, and I was forced to agree.

"He's young," I said mildly, defending the overzealous vampire in spite of my pain. He had been young when he died, around seventeen, when Adrian—my first love, my beloved, my dearly departed—had brought him over as a fellow vampire, and it had been barely a year since. Ellis was still learning that life as a vampire was, in spite of the violence of death and the bloodletting that sustained him, still much gentler than life on the streets. He was also learning that taking the blood of his queen could not, by necessity, be as rough as the games he played with his kiss mates. I was, after all, only mortal.

But Bracken was possessive, and angry at having to share me night after night, even when the sharing was bloodletting and not sex. I wasn't a vampire myself, and in order to bind the others to me, they had to know me by taste and by smell. Before Adrian had died, he marked me three times by blowing his soul through my own. I could still see a multidimensional mark on my neck glowing in Adrian purple when I looked at my reflection with power in my eyes. When the vampires took my blood, they knew what I felt and what I needed, and vice versa. And what they needed was a queen, a leader, someone who could give them a character and a personality as a group. I was their old leader's girlfriend—and when he died, I'd inherited his kiss of children.

I wouldn't have minded adopting the kiss, per se, but Bracken was bound to me by magic. If I was ever unfaithful to him without his permission, the binding would break his heart and then his body. My infidelity would mean his death. This meant that, just to be on the safe side, he was forced to watch night after night as another creature—man or woman—sank teeth into the tender, sweet flesh of my wrist. Elves as a whole are nonmonogamous, nonpossessive sorts. Green himself got his power and earned his loyalty from sex—he could arouse and heal nearly any boo-boo, physical or emotional, with a big, sexual kiss. He and Adrian had fallen in love when he had tried to heal Adrian of a miserable childhood, and they had been nonmonogamous lovers for a century and a half. That was when Adrian stumbled upon me and the three of us became....

Well, mostly we just became.

Bracken is also a sidhe, an elf with serious power, but he had been raised by lower fey parents who had loved for several hundred mortal lifetimes. He and Adrian had been brothers of the spirit and lovers of the body, and loving his best friend's girl was not a thing Bracken took lightly. And blood was, to Brack, what sex was to Green—it was the element he controlled, the element he got his power from. Having to sit and watch as others took my blood was like being aroused to the point of blue balls for him, and he worried about the drain on me as well. Bracken was not so willing to excuse the rangy, young, jumpy, undead kid who had visited my room two nights ago and asked to be bound by blood.

"He should have fed before he came," he grumbled, placing a delicate conciliatory kiss on my scabbed-over wounds. I should have asked Green to heal them, I thought mournfully—but last night we'd been making love because we loved each other, and healing had been the last thing we'd been thinking of. Besides, Ellis didn't just drink *my* blood, I got to taste *his*. Very often there were magical consequences in the bond, and something about the power exchange of the blood sharing had made the vampire bites harder and harder to heal. I ran my other hand over Bracken's face, soothing him, and smiled to lighten his mood.

"He did feed before he came," I said drolly, and my other beloved, my magically wedded mate, had to smile at that. Feeding is extremely sexual for vampires, and as a sorceress—albeit a rookie one—my blood is apparently the equivalent of eating a chocolate éclair soaked in almond liqueur and flavored with sex hormones. Watching the dark-haired, poignantly featured, beautiful vampire shudder, moan, and spill in his jeans at the simple taste of my blood had made Bracken.... Well, the vampire hadn't been the only one to come in my room that night.

Bracken's smile faded, and his eyes darted nervously around the beige tile and dirty white walls of the admin building. The actual offices, to our left, were recently remodeled and a little less depressing, but we had another half hour to go, and Bracken was getting edgy. Enrolling in college with me and the others had not been his idea—it had been Green's.

"For one thing," Green pointed out reasonably, after Bracken had spit up trail mix all over himself when it had been brought up, "at the moment, the only people besides Cory and myself with any knowledge of human business practices as well as extensive knowledge of the workings of the hill are vampires and can't function during the day, and you're third in line to lead this place." Green had told me that he'd put other creatures—nymphs, sylphs, half-elves, etc.—through school as well, but even I knew the difference between going to school for a degree and going to school for the good of the hill. Green was talking about going to school for the good of the hill, and he wanted Bracken to do just that.

Bracken's eyes had grown so big I wondered if he was choking and thought frantically that it wasn't possible to do the Heimlich maneuver on someone a foot and a half taller than you. "Am not!" he gasped in complete disbelief.

I'd stared up at Green from my place on the big white couch (between Bracken and Green, as usual) in complete surprise. "I thought Arturo was next in line," I said on a squeak, referring to Green's second-sidhe-in-command and best friend. Last summer, before Adrian had been killed, Green had showed me a list of people that his property was deeded to. It had gone from Green to Adrian to Arturo to Grace—Arturo's vampire girlfriend—and then to me. A lot had happened since then, but I was as surprised as Bracken that this change in succession was part of it.

"He was," Green said softly, "until we blew touch, blood, and song through every preternatural creature in Northern California. The touch you and I used was sex, Cory, but Bracken added blood. The power spill goes from me, to you, to Bracken, to Nicky." You'd think it would go from Green to me to Nicky, because Nicky shared Green's bed too—but the Goddess favored the powerful, and Nicky just wasn't.

"To me!" Nicky squealed from his place on the pillows at our feet. We'd been watching movies at the time, and one of the other high elves had just put in the last disc of *The Return of the King,* the extended version. "Somebody had better boink Grace and Arturo, then," Nicky blurted, "because I'm just set decoration...."

"Oh, please," Bracken snapped. "You're like fourth in line. By the time it came down to that, you'd be dead anyway." He looked at Green sharply. "So would I," he said thoughtfully. "I'm bound to Cory—if she goes, I go."

"Yes," said Green patiently. "And then Arturo *would* lead. But if I go, she's going to need someone she's bound to by magic to help her keep things running. And if you go, she stays and that's why Nicky—yes, Nicky, you do have some responsibilities to this hill besides sharing Cory's bed—and this whole discussion is beyond depressing! Bracken, you don't have any hard and fast duties besides taking care of Cory; your father is hale and hearty and will be taking care of the lower fey for many hundreds of years to come, so you don't need to worry too much about that right now. Really, the only thing you have to worry about is our beloved. And since she's going to be at school four days a week, this is the best way to take care of her."

A year before, I would have fought like hell for the right to go to my own goddamned classes. Since then, I'd been attacked, mind-raped, heartbroken, and Goddess knew what else. If Green said I needed a bodyguard to attend college, I was soooo there.

But now I looked at Bracken with sympathy. He hated the human world. He could deal with locals up near the hill with the use of glamour and in the company of other elves or vampires, but from what I'd gathered (both from Bracken and the other elves at Green's hill), Bracken's primary reason for coming out and being with the humans had been to get laid. Of course, now that he was welded to me for life, that wasn't a consideration anymore—and the idea of using his, well, limited communication skills on an almost full-time basis was as anathematic to Bracken as trying to not love the world would be to Green.

"You'll like it, *due'alle,*" I said softly as we moved up one more person in line. I used his Elvish title—it meant "male equal of my heart"—to make him happier. Green kept his people safe by using sex to bind them, so he couldn't be my *due'alle,* and I knew it made Bracken happy to have his own specific place in my life. "We can study together."

Bracken grunted, a sound that could best be described as noncommittal.

"You can come running with me!" I tried again, trying to keep my voice light. Cheering Bracken up beat the hell out of pining for Green.

Bracken looked at me as though I'd sprouted a second head that was now lecturing him on quantum physics. "I can come what?"

"Running," I said brightly. "You, me, and Renny are going to have a two-hour break between our morning and afternoon classes. I was going to go running before lunch."

Bracken blinked at me, then scowled. "You're too skinny and you have no breasts," he growled. "Why would you need to go running?"

I grimaced. I had been sick earlier in the winter—more than sick, actually. For a week I had balanced on the fine tensile nylon line between life and death, sometimes dangling so precariously over the edge that Adrian himself had offered to catch me if I fell. My body had yet to fully recover, and Green and Bracken would carry the scars of almost losing me so soon after losing Adrian for a long time.

"I need to go running for precisely that reason!" I answered back. "I got winded walking over here from the parking lot. If I started exercising, I'd get my strength back faster."

Bracken looked sideways at me, a crease forming between his eyebrows as though he were deliberating the subject.

"It's not like you can tell me no, Bracken!" I burst out. "I just thought you might like to come with me, that's all."

"You could walk with me," he said. "In the mornings."

I was so surprised I almost tripped over my own sodden sneakers. As I had discovered this last month while sharing Green's and Bracken's beds, elves needed to walk their land—to touch their (usually bare) feet to the land of their hill, to the place where they, or their leaders, drew power. It was comfort and nourishment, both physical and magical sustenance to them. When we shared a bed, Bracken often disappeared at dawn to walk the earth around the thousands of acres that made up Green's land.

I smiled softly at him, absurdly touched. It was a generous offer, and I didn't take it lightly. "It's your private time, beloved," I said, my voice rough. "I couldn't intrude on that." I tried humor. "Besides— you tend to move in hyperspeed, and I couldn't keep up." All of the Goddess's creatures could do that—it was what happened when the will of the Goddess to keep her creatures alive in God's world overrode the electricity that normally fired the synapses.

"I could carry you," Bracken replied with dignity. But he had a slight smile of his own, and I could see that he knew the impracticality of the solution.

"Someday you must," I told him seriously, bringing his big, graceful hand to my lips to kiss. "But since that wouldn't help make me stronger, for now I'll just run the track during my break."

Bracken sighed. "I'll have to watch you, then," he said fretfully. "Because if I try to run in the human way, I'll still outdistance you four laps to one."

I looked up at him—way, way up—to his carelessly cut hair and the curved points of his ears that only those of us from Green's hill could see, and to the inhumanly beautiful, stormy, and dark features of his face. "Why, Bracken," I noted. "That was almost a joke."

"Bracken made a joke?" Renny asked from right behind me.

"All things are possible," Bracken said loftily, looking down at Renny with affection in his eyes. She was fairly presentable today in black jeans, tennis shoes, a fitted white T-shirt, and a hooded jacket the color of mustard. After Mitch had died, she ran around wearing mostly one-piece dresses and nothing else because it made morphing into a ninety-five-pound tabby cat just that much easier. The fact that she was dressed in regular clothes, with her hair pulled back into a perky ponytail, meant that she had found a measure of self-possession that we had all been afraid she'd never get back.

"I'll believe it when I wet my pants," Nicky said dryly, and that did make me laugh.

"We were just talking about going running," I said brightly, making sure Mario and LaMark knew I was speaking to them too. "I wanted to start during that long break we have between classes and was wondering if anybody wanted to join me."

Four pairs of inhuman eyes regarded me silently, the thoughts behind them clearly puzzled. *Of course*, I thought, shaking my head. When you spent part of your life running or flying around in animal form with an insanely high metabolism, staying physically fit was a given.

"Never mind," I sighed. "I'll go by myself."

"But not out of my sight," Bracken said firmly, and I resisted the urge to put my face in my hands. I was young and mortal, and in spite of the fact that occasionally I shot brilliant light and tremendous metaphysical power out of my mouth or my hand or various other parts of my body, I was still much more human than the people I lived with.

"No, Bracken," I said with humor, "I'll never be out of your sight."

His arm fell lightly around my shoulders, and it seemed there was a peace in the breath of our intense and restless relationship.

And because he was Bracken, he had to completely fuck it up.

He bent down, blowing my hair away from my ear, and all I could think of was being with him, warm and dry and skin to skin. "Have you decided," he asked softly, "what name you're going to put on your forms?"

"Oh, Goddess," Renny snapped from behind me. "Not this fight again!" Elves were not the only ones with preternatural hearing.

Bracken regarded Renny with irritated indulgence. "This isn't your fight."

"It is when your argument takes over the hill," Renny grumbled, and even I with my mortal senses could hear Nicky say "Amen."

"Hush, you two," Mario said behind them, and I looked at him gratefully. He was a steady young man, and he had loved his mate with everything in him. I knew the signs of grief so well in myself that I could detect the signs of attempting to hang on to logic and sense and order so he didn't lose himself in the chaos of his own heart.

"Now see what you've done?" I asked Bracken, determined not to raise the same ruckus here in public that we'd raised at home. "You've upset the children."

"If they were our children," he grunted, "I could see why they'd be so interested in your name."

"They're interested because we screamed at each other for an hour in the middle of the living room with Green in the middle trying to break up the argument!"

"We didn't scream," Bracken denied. "We discussed." His lips quirked up. "Loudly."

"It's only for the human world," I said after a moment. "I hardly live here anymore."

Bracken sighed, and I saw his eyes dart back and forth among the tan tile and beige stucco walls. "It's your world," he said unhappily. "I want to be a part of it."

"The whole point in changing my name was to keep me under the radar," I explained patiently, unsure if I'd been able to articulate this to him rationally after he'd jumped all over me during the first discussion. "And I love you, Bracken, but I don't think Cory op Crocken is going to make me any more nondescript."

Bracken frowned and looked at me, hard. "We had that hellacious fight," he said after a moment, "and I still don't think you understand why we're changing your name." He shrugged, waving vaguely at our surroundings. "The humans can think whatever they want. They wouldn't know your value if you stood on top of that big glass building in the middle of the campus and changed the shape of the campus with a whim. And any supernatural being can see you glow from a mile away—mostly because they've had our blood pass through their skin. We're not changing your name to keep you 'under the radar.' We're changing your name so that nobody with power can call your name and make you do their bidding."

"But...," I trailed off unhappily. I looked ahead and realized that there was only one more person in the line—the good-looking kid in the shorts and sweatshirt—and my time to actually make this decision was rapidly coming to an end.

"Bracken," I said after another brief, echoing second. "Any name I take here, that's going to be my name."

"But not all your name," he said reasonably.

"It's a human tradition, not an elven one!" I exclaimed, since it was the one argument I hadn't brought up during our first "loud discussion."

"And you are human," he said calmly. "And I am tied to your mortality."

I rubbed my face with my hands. "Cory Green is the perfect name for me," I said, almost to myself. "It's plain, it's quiet—nobody would notice a Cory Green or give a shit if she passes or fails." And maybe this was the root of the whole argument in the first place, not whether or not Green had prior claim to me and my name.

"You are not a plain person," Bracken said, and for the first time since he brought it up, I heard the beginnings of anger in his voice. "You have people willing to die for you—including me. It is an old name, a good one, and it will protect you when you need it. If you don't give enough of a shit about yourself, would you at least wear my name for me?"

I felt the beginnings of tears in my eyes. I turned toward him, standing on tiptoe. "Bracken...," I whined, "I don't like to be noticed...."

"Too goddamned bad." Bracken's language was growing foul, I thought wretchedly. Not that he didn't swear, but the word he used was usually "fuck," and it was usually a verb. Here he was, swearing back at me—I was having a bad effect on him.

"Next." We had been standing close, locked in intimate conversation, and the next available registrar had apparently been trying to get my attention for some time. I sighed, touched his smooth cheek with my small, rough hand, and turned to the vacant chair at the far end of the room. Bracken, disregarding all line protocol, went to follow me, and I turned and waved him back. His face took on a thunderous look, but another registrar opened up, and we were holding up the line for everybody else, so he grudgingly turned to the window right next to mine.

The woman helping me could have been anywhere between twenty-five and forty-five. She had her extension braids pulled back into a bun, and a sweet, wry smile split her mocha-tinted face in two. She looked to where I was looking as I sat down, her gaze taking in Bracken, discomfort and unhappiness making his back ramrod straight and his beautiful face—even with the glamour to make him more human, he was beautiful—stormy and grim.

"Mmm hmm…," she harrumphed. "That is one good-looking piece of pissed-off man."

I shook my head at him and turned back to my business. "And he's all mine," I said, and even from her place on the other side of the Plexiglas, the woman could tell that there were equal parts good and bad in that statement.

"Well, you hold on to him," she said wisely. "You never know when life is going to rip a prime piece of man flesh like that right out of your hands."

An image of Adrian crossed my mind, his face sober and excited as he lowered his head for a kiss, followed by the memory of Green's profile as he turned away, swinging his yellow, yellow hair behind him. "You're right about that," I sighed, casting one last look at my intense beloved. He looked frustrated and uncomfortable, sitting in the human-sized chair that was, undoubtedly, too small for him and answering questions that were either personal or completely irrelevant to an elf who didn't even have a legitimate social security number.

The clerk—her name tag said "Liz"—smiled at me again, and then got down to business. "I'm sorry," she said apologetically, "I can't seem to read this here...." She pointed to a blank space on the registration sheet I'd handed her. Green's compulsion probably had her seeing a blur so I could decide what my name was going to be—but dammit, I hadn't come up with an answer in line.

I looked at the space with deer-shot eyes, took a deep breath, and opened my mouth, praying the name that would solve all my personal problems would just magically issue from my throat. Restlessly I touched the third finger of my left hand, where a ring would be if we'd been married the human way, and then I spoke. "Cory," I said, and I swallowed. "Cory op Crocken Green."

BRACKEN
Corinne Carol-Anne Kirkpatrick op Crocken Green

HER VOICE was still rough from being sick for so long—but I would have heard her add my name to hers if she'd still been home and I'd been stuck in this cheerless, miserable room, answering inane questions from the colorless little creature sitting in front of me.

I hate the human world.

"Cory op Crocken Green," she said again, her voice stronger, my father's name falling like smooth shiny stones from her child's mouth.

"Oh, yes," the woman across from her said. "I see it now."

"Your name, uhm, sir?" said the little translucent-blonde thing across from me. I scared her. "Bracken," I said firmly, hoping my voice would carry to Cory the way hers had carried to me. "Bracken op Crocken Green."

The rest of registration involved her punching buttons on her keyboard and me handing over Green's check, so I was able to hear the others as they sat down, and I was only mildly surprised to hear "Renny—Renny Hammond Green," "Dominic Kestrel Green," "Mario Galvan Green," and "LaMark Holden Green" come from the others as they came forward to register.

Cory caught the names too, and when she saw the surprise on her registrar's face, she said, "It's a family thing" in her laconic way as she stood up to walk toward me. Then, as her eyes—a green hazel halfway between my gray hazel and Green's emerald green—met my grateful gaze, she added, "I married in."

"Good choice," the woman said with a wink. "But you need a ring to prove it!" And then she turned toward her next victim, and I had Cory all to myself.

"Thank you," I said gruffly, touching the third finger of her left hand where, if we were human, my ring would rest. I was willing her to understand what it meant to me that she would take my name, even though I'd taken her in marriage against her will. Against both our wills, actually—but I, at least, had been planning to ask her before I'd been bespelled into the ceremony.

Her face was small, with a strong nose, a pointed chin, and wide, low cheekbones, but her plainness was never what I saw when I looked at her. I saw her heart moving gracefully over her features like clear, deep water over a rock bed. A spring flood crossed her face, and I was left, breathless, with her, waiting to see what her quick tongue would make of it.

"Thank *you*," she said simply, not meeting my eyes in that way she had when her heart was saying volumes but she was only going to allow a little bit of it to fall from her tongue. "It was... it's nice to use your family name," she said at last. What was going through her mind, I wondered. Green had told me in this last month that when he dipped into her thoughts, her words were formal and poetic. What came out of her mouth was usually colloquial and human, like she had to dumb down her words for the world to understand her. Green said it felt like a person who spoke two languages fluently, making a seamless translation from one language to the other. For Corinne Carol-Anne Kirkpatrick op Crocken Green, who, when I'd met her, said "fuck" more than any other person I'd ever met, it was habit to translate her heart's poetry into gutter spew.

"What are you thinking?" she asked, shaking her head at me. Absently she pulled her hair back with one hand, leaving it a damp, curly mess at the back of her head.

"I'm thinking you two should get out of my line," the blonde creature said humorlessly behind us, and Cory laughed at her amiably.

"C'mon, Mr. op Crocken Green," she said gaily. "Let's drag the rest of our children back into the rain."

"Did you hear them?" I asked, trying to breathe with love for her pressing on my chest like a sweet weight.

"Yeah," she said shyly. "It was... it was wonderful, wasn't it?" She smiled at me then, that whole unshuttered smile that she kept behind her wall of words so often.

"You are their queen," I said seriously, and she shrugged.

"I'm Green's girl," she responded, not comfortable with her place in our lives. Turning, she made sure the others were following us and said, "Hey—who's driving back?" as we stepped from the electronic doors into the rain.

"Not you," LaMark answered in panic. I couldn't remember her ever driving him anywhere, but it was a fact readily acknowledged by everyone but Cory that driving was on the short list of things she didn't do well.

"You whine like a mule," she quoted with dignity. "You're still alive."

"Yeah," muttered the young man under his breath, "but that's one pair of undershorts I'm never wearing again."

Mario guffawed next to him. "I *told* you!" he howled into the air. "But nooo…. You said, 'After what we survived this winter, what could be worse than Goshawk!'"

Cory turned to them, her face alight with banter. "Aw, fuck you, Mario!" she exclaimed. "What did I ever do to you?"

"Uhm, almost killed me?"

"Renny's way worse than I am!" she shot back, and I watched her, chattering with these young people who had been raised in the human world, and felt just what I knew I would feel coming with her to school—a place she'd revered since before Adrian. I felt like she was leaving me alone in this place, where the people were so ignorant she had to translate the speech from her heart in order to survive.

She'd been walking backward, exchanging friendly insults with Renny and holding my arm for balance, when suddenly her hold on my arm grew frantic and she fell to the ground, catching her fall with her elbows and then pitching her head forward to hang it between her knees.

In half a heartbeat we had gathered around her, sheltering her from the surprised eyes of the other students hurrying between the psych building and the media center, and I bent to pull her out of the water streaming from the sidewalk. I noticed that the others kept wrinkling their noses, throwing their heads around as though they had heard something unpleasant, but for the most part, our attention was focused on Cory.

"Wait," she ordered. "Just…." She squeezed her eyes, and I knew that expression because I'd held her so many times when her body had been wounded and I knew what her first line of defense was.

"Everybody out of the way," I ordered, scooping her out of the water and turning toward the big yellow trash can outside of the administration building. Her body heaved against me, and she tilted her head to be sick. She heaved again, and again and again, while I held her helplessly and the rest of our people watched in shock in the pouring rain.

Eventually her body stopped spasming. Renny said, "Follow me—there's a lounge and a bathroom in here," and she led us to one of the older squat, brick-shaped two-story buildings on the east side of the campus. We went through the door and then took a quick right into an old lounge with ugly chrome-and-Naugahyde furniture and, Goddess be praised, a couch. I laid Cory on the couch and sheltered her shivering, chattering body with my shoulders. We were all soaked to the bone, and a part of me thought miserably of the long trip home in wet clothes and how she had just gotten better and now she'd be sick again, but the more immediate part of me was wondering what in the fuck had just happened.

Renny tapped me on the shoulder and said, "We'll be right back." Then she and LaMark trotted back out into the rain again.

I nodded and pulled back from Cory for a moment to see her face. "I'mmmmmm finnnnne...," she chattered, but I ignored her. Her face was all but blue, she was so pale, and her body was one big shivering mass, like a puppy left in the rain. She'd tell me she was fine if she were missing a limb.

"What was that? And did you hear that noise?" Nicky asked from behind me. I fought a surge of irritation. He sounded peremptory, like he had a right to her. He was an accident, I thought grudgingly. His tie to her, to her bed, was an accident. He was there by her grace, because she felt bad for him, because she and Green were good enough to bed him in order to save his life. But irritating or not, it was a good question.

"Cory," I said firmly. "What hurt you?"

She shuddered and I moved hastily, because I thought she might be sick again—although there wasn't anything left in her stomach to throw up.

"It was a smell," she said through a raw throat. "A horrible smell.... Rotting bodies with black blood, bubbling in a humid sun.... Festering gangrene, boiling in piss...." She stopped and shivered some more. *Wonderful*, I thought grimly, looking at Nicky and Mario's pale faces, *now she uses her poetry*.

"It was horrible," Cory continued, her eyes glazed and blank. "It was... it was something... us." She looked up. "It was supernatural. In fact...." Her nose wrinkled, and her hands came up to the collar of the sweatshirt she'd snatched from my drawer that morning. Fitfully, fumbling, she pulled the collar down, exposing the left side of her neck. I backed up, blinking in shock.

"It's glowing, isn't it?" she asked, and the three of us nodded. We could see the three layers of Adrian's purple glowing from her skin.

"It felt like vampire," she said unnecessarily.

"In broad daylight? That's impossible, isn't it?" Mario asked. After the Avians had attacked us, one of Green's conditions on their (originally) limited freedom was that they allowed the vampires to feed. That way, the vampires would know what the Avians were feeling, and they could thwart any escape attempts. Our Avians were on good terms with the vampires now—it was one of the things that had made Cory's transition to their leader easier.

"As far as I know," I replied, surprised and shocked. *Adrian, my hero, my lover, my brother, was this something you hadn't known?*

"He was young," Cory said, catching my hand. "He was young, and he was good." She closed her eyes for a moment, yet another clench of revulsion taking over her small body. "This was evil—not ambition or greed or vengeance or jealousy... nothing explicable. This was real evil." Her eyes opened, found mine, and again, she was reassuring me instead of the other way around. "Adrian wouldn't have recognized this even if it moved at night and shook hands with him."

It looked like she might not throw up again, and she was shivering with cold in her now sodden jeans and sneakers. Abruptly I stood up from my crouch at her side and moved to her feet to pull off her shoes and ruined socks, then looked over my shoulder at Mario and Nicky. Mario got the hint, but Nicky, damn him, looked at me levelly, a determined expression on his pleasant face.

"I'm going to take off her wet clothes," I said as though to a four-year-old.

"So?" he asserted as if he had any right to be there. I felt my temper gather like a cloud. Through error and lucky accident he had earned a ticket into Cory's bed, but that didn't give him a right to her body, or to her nudity, or to any part of her that Renny or Mario or LaMark didn't have, and by Goddess he would know that before....

"So it's not date night, Nick," Cory said with humor behind me. "And we'd like a little space."

"Right. Sorry." And with that and a truly contrite look toward Cory, Nicky flushed and retreated, leaving me with my gathered temper and Cory stretching out a placating hand to touch mine.

"Tactfully done, *due 'ane*," I grunted, settling down to pulling her jeans off her hips. The jeans were big on her—otherwise they would have been harder to pull off. They left her legs bare and thin under the weak fluorescent lights.

"Bracken...," she complained, pulling the wet, oversized sweatshirt past her bare hips and bottom. "My underwear?"

Fuck. "Why do you insist on wearing them?" I asked, trying to wrestle the little cotton scrap out of her pants. There was a sound of wet tearing, and the jeans themselves ripped into two pieces because I forgot that I was stronger than human and frightened for Cory and angry at Nicky and my own strength was more than sufficient. Fuck.

Cory snorted with suppressed laughter and pulled her knees up under the wet sweatshirt, huddling in the corner of the couch like she was trying to hide. "Forget them, Bracken," she said, covering her laugh with her hand. "They sell sweats at the bookstore. I'm sure that's where Renny went, anyway."

"They don't sell underwear," I said glumly, looking at the shredded, soaking mess in my hand.

"Throw them away, beloved," she suggested. Her voice had grown dark and smoke colored, and I realized I was behaving badly and she needed something from me that I had not remembered to give. Green would have known immediately, I thought fretfully, then put it out of my mind, because we had established from the beginning that Cory would need me precisely because I was not Green.

"Throw them away," she said again, that note of indulgence still in her voice, "and come sit down next to me." And suddenly I felt like Green, because I could hear all she wasn't saying as she said it. *Forget about your stupid mistake, Bracken Brine Granite op Crocken, and come sit here and hold me. I am cold and I am frightened and I need you.*

I did what her heart asked and gathered her to me, covering her thighs with my arm and trying to protect her with my shoulders alone.

"You need to do something about Nicky," I heard myself saying and could have kicked myself, because that's not what a woman wants to hear when she's cold and frightened and thinking about a great evil in her world.

"You need to be patient with him," she admonished. "We'll settle in time."

"Tomorrow is date night?" I asked neutrally. Because of their unique situation—and the fact that Cory only loved Nicky as a friend, although she had to be with him every so often as lover or he would molt and pine and die—Cory had figured it would make everybody's life easier if Nicky spent time with Green whenever his schedule allowed and she was in my bed, and so she reserved a special night for her and Nicky. Nicky had been bound to her a little less than two months, and her second date night was coming up.

"Yeah." She suppressed a sigh, and I suppressed satisfaction that she was not looking forward to it—or so I thought. "Stop gloating," she chastised. "It's all well and good for you, you're a sidhe! Every time you have sex with someone you make the world move. I'm just me, and I'm human, and it's not easy being a disappointment."

I raised my eyebrows, legitimately surprised, and tried to resist purring when her finger crept up into my shortened hair and rubbed along the ridge and point of my ear. "How could you be a disappointment?" I asked carefully. She had been very careful to keep the men in *her* bed out of *our* bed—it was characteristic of her, I thought fondly, to think more of our feelings than we did ourselves.

"He wants Green!" she exclaimed. "Green's his other lover, and, well—you know...." She trailed off. "You've been in Green's bed. Nothing compares to Green."

"It was a long time ago, beloved," I said gently. Probably at least twenty years, but I didn't want to remind her of the sixty-or-so-year age difference between us. Although the hard truth was that Green was over eighteen hundred years old—she could probably handle seventy-five.

"He's practically a god of sweet desire," she snapped. "And I'm just me." Suddenly she blushed. "It was like 'naming of the parts' or something." Her voice took on the occasionally British tones of Green's in a fair mimicry. "This is a woman's breast, Nicky, see the nipple? Rub it more, until it's stiff. That's right. Now feel it in the palm of your hand. See how her eyes close? You're doing very well."

I felt a laugh rumbling in my chest as some of my resentment against Nicky faded away. "It sounds awkward," I said, feeling kind.

"I'm awkward," she grumbled. "I'm clumsy and silly, and I laugh at really bad moments."

"You laugh?" I was curious now.

"Condoms are the stupidest things on the planet!" Her hands were busy picking at my sweatshirt. "How am I not supposed to laugh?"

I hadn't thought of that, actually. Vampires were infertile, so Adrian, her first lover, would not have had to worry about it. And a sidhe's contraception depended only on a wish; all Green and I had to do was ask the child waiting to become to wait a little longer. Nicky would need birth control.

"You're breaking your rule," I said after smiling with her gently, wondering why she would suddenly tell me details she'd been quietly holding to her chest for over a month.

She looked at me soberly, and her hand moved from my ear to my jaw. "You're getting short with Nicky," she said, "and the vampires are pissing you off on a regular basis. You came into this relationship expecting to take a backseat to Green, and you're okay with that, but you're starting to think that I'll have to share blood or sex with the whole entire world and you'll still be in the backseat watching. You need to know that's not true. It's Green, because I love him. It's Nicky, to keep him alive. It's you, because you're my Bracken, my *due'alle,* and nobody in my life or my bed is quite like you."

I flushed. If I couldn't tell from feeling the blood rush under my skin, I would have guessed because of her delighted smile.

"Something bad is out there," I said uncomfortably. "How are we going to keep you safe again?"

She rolled her eyes. "It's not all about me, you know. For all we know, I just felt it in passing. It'll be our job to keep the rest of the world safe."

"So you're like the cosmic preternatural police?" I asked, winking.

She smiled, her in-earnest, make-men-stupid smile, the beauty of it taking my breath away. "Bracken—that was another joke!"

"No way!" Renny said, running into the lounge with her hands full of plastic bookstore bags. LaMark followed her, and behind him, wonder of wonders, an unexpected friend. "Max was at school and Bracken cracked another joke—if Cory hadn't just thrown up, I'd say it was an unusual day."

"You try smelling evil and see what your stomach does," Cory responded with feeling. Then, "Howzis, Officer Max?"

I glared at him. One more person who wanted to get into Cory's pants. Of course, he was currently dating Renny, but I could not forget that he had wanted Cory so badly he'd thought to "save" her from all of us—from Green, from Adrian, from me.

"Don't worry about the joke, Renny," Max said dryly. "He still hates my guts, all is right with the world."

"You realize that I kicked Mario and Nicky out so the whole world wouldn't be in here while she was undressed, right?" I asked pleasantly. LaMark almost skidded to a halt, he was in such a hurry to turn around, and Max had the grace to flush.

"Sorry, Cory," he apologized. "I thought I'd walk Renny in."

"All good, Max," Cory responded amiably. "But if everybody will let me and Renny change, we can let the guys back in to do the same thing."

And that got rid of Max. Renny of course stayed. She shifted skin so much that being nude in front of me didn't trouble her—and judging from the number of times we had seen Max trotting down the back stairs from the main floor to the garage, I would imagine that he had left for Cory's benefit alone.

"So," Renny asked, shucking her own wet jeans past her hips, "what was it?"

Bare-assed, she rummaged through the plastic bags and pulled out a pair of sweats that she threw at Cory and me, followed by a dry sweatshirt and a T-shirt. Then she shucked off her wet sweatshirt and dropped it in a pile at her feet with her bottoms, standing naked without shame in the middle of the lounge as she rooted through the bags. I looked at her without really seeing, trying to put Cory's report into words that wouldn't make Renny throw up, and was distracted by Cory's snort of laughter.

"What?" I asked, and she simply giggled some more.

"If you don't know, I can't explain it," she managed, and she and Renny exchanged looks that I couldn't interpret. Then Renny started laughing as well. When they were done laughing at my expense, Cory explained the phenomenon—the evil, seeking presence that had assaulted her mind—as the two of them toweled off using a new green-and-gold CSUS towel and dressed hurriedly in sweats and shirts the same colors. Whereas Renny's body had seemed as natural without clothes as a kitten's, I couldn't help but look at Cory, thin as she was, her skin translucent and pink with cold. Elves were not supposed to feel possessive—sidhe, as I was, especially so. But she was naked in this miserable, dim little room with me, and I was proud of that.

Renny saw me gazing at Cory and burst out laughing all over again, and suddenly I wished for the home of Green's hill, nearly an hour away. Abruptly I stood up and went to stalk out of the room, but Cory stopped me with a small, cold hand on my arm.

"You should change too," she urged and looked at Renny. "You got sweats for him?"

"They'll go to his knees, but yes."

"I don't mind the cold," I muttered, uncomfortable in that room where I hadn't been before.

"Change, beloved," Cory commanded, and when she used that tone of voice and called me beloved, I had no choice, no choice at all.

Eventually we were all warmer and in dry clothes, and since Renny had the presence of mind to buy vinyl rain ponchos (these too in the ubiquitous and obnoxious green and yellow) we made it out to the car much drier than we had made it to the campus. Our party split up then— Max was there, and off duty, and he and the others decided to go to a movie. I hated movie theaters (although I loved watching videos on Green's large television) and was more than happy to bundle Cory into the Suburban and take her home.

She sat sideways on the front seat, leaning her head against the rest and watching me with quiet eyes until I stopped swearing and hit I-80. It was midday, so in spite of the rain, the traffic was still not bad. Her silence had a building quality, and I could imagine her sorting through the words in her head to say the easiest, most colloquial things to me, afraid that I would laugh if it sounded too much like the poetry it was.

"You didn't grow up human," she said, "but you've met with enough town kids to know what I'm talking about here. You've got rich kids in our area, with the big houses in the new developments, and everybody expects them to go to college, right?"

I nodded. I didn't meet these people, but the young people I knew talked about them. They didn't come back and play with their old friends very often.

"And you've got the aggies, the kids whose parents inherited or bought early when it was cheap, and they grew up on big stretches of land and had to work on it with Mom and Dad, and everybody expects these kids to be waitresses or clerks in the mall or truck drivers or auto mechanics or shit like that. And a hundred years ago, that would have been perfect, because they would have been farmers, and farmers are necessary, but now they have nowhere to go." Her voice grew thick, and every nerve in my body pitched, because this *hurt* her. I realized with unhappiness that she probably felt more naked, telling me this while bundled under a stadium blanket and piles of new clothing, than she had felt in that miserable little room when she'd been bare to her pink, goose-pimpled skin.

"And which one were you?" I asked, dreading the answer.

"Well," she said slowly, "I was like the platypus of my high school—wasn't a bird, wasn't a weasel, wasn't even a fish."

I felt a smile creeping up in spite of her pain. Interpreting one's own heart into words had its uses. "What was left?"

"Me," she said simply. "When I was a freshman, I did have friends—but no one expected any of *us* to go to college. By the end of the year, a third had dropped out to have babies and a third had been expelled for drug use, and everybody who was left found nothing better to do than give me shit for keeping my grades up."

"Screw 'em," I said roughly. Fucking humans.

"Exactly," she seconded. A silence. "But it's not easy being all alone. I liked choir, but…." But her parents hadn't approved. She had a voice that would make a grown human weep, and her parents hadn't told her to sing. Unbelievable. She cleared her throat. "Anyway, so there I was. It was like the only way I could deal with the alone was to hate the world…. I was good at it."

"No," I denied.

"Let's just say humans didn't notice."

"Fucking humans," I grunted.

"Sometimes, in the privacy of their own homes," she quipped. It was our favorite play on words.

"So… the black hair dye and the eyebrow ring…."

"And the nose ring and the two tons of black mascara and the perpetual pissed-off expression… yadda yadda yadda. There I was, right when Arturo walked into the Chevron and touched my hand, right when I looked up and saw Adrian."

"You changed…," I said the obvious.

A laugh. "Nooooo, you think?" I could almost hear her eyes roll. "And suddenly I wasn't alone anymore. Last semester, Renny was there, and she was my friend. A flaky one who sometimes had to be bailed out of Golden Gate Park naked, but she was my friend nonetheless. And Nicky, who was my friend too—and I had Green to go home to on the weekends, and I thought, 'Wow! I have people now.'"

"You've got a lot more this semester," I added needlessly.

"And that's why I'm telling you all this." Her voice grew thick again, aching, sweet. "Thank you, Bracken. That's what I'm getting to. Just thanks."

"Green ordered me to," I said, embarrassed that I had complained about it.

"You didn't bitch nearly as loud as you could have," she said. There was silence in the car then, and her body, wearied by being sick for so long and so violently, pulled her into sleep.

We continued up the hill to Auburn, then took a big right off the freeway to Foresthill. I was glad she was sleeping, because although not squirrelly with curves, the Foresthill road had enough big, swinging turns to make her queasy, and her stomach was already tetchy enough. It was winter, and snow had come and receded and would probably come again, because we were just at the line where it did that—sometimes we were waist deep in it when we left Green's hill, sometimes we spent the whole winter in frigid mud. Right now it was frigid mud with greenish, overwatered grasses sprinkling the soil peeking from around the raw granite that was the face of the canyon before the road had been ripped out of the hills.

We kept going, past the span of the double bridge—the one that kept showing up in all the movies—past Lake Clementine, some more curves, and then past Scary Tree (Cory's name for it), which was looking a little darker now than it had this summer. I wondered at that—Green had once said it was some sort of preternatural barometer. I wasn't sure if the darkness was a good thing, but it was a passing notice, and I didn't remember anyone mentioning it again. Some more curves, and then we were at that curious part of the road that even those who dwelled in Green's hill forgot, and then a hidden left into a road cut into the canyon, and we were home.

We were both scheduled to work at Grace's store that evening. I would have called in sick, but Cory would have objected, and I didn't want to leave Grace shorthanded. I wanted to let Cory sleep until it was time to leave, but when I carried her into her bedroom from the car, she woke up. It was our bedroom now, actually—my parents had moved all of my clothes and personals into it after the binding ceremony. Nobody told them that the ceremony itself had not been consensual, so this had been a joyous thing for them. Now Cory slept in Green's bed when she was with Green, and in Nicky's bed on date night, and in her bed, with me, the other two thirds of her nights. There had been good reasons why Green and I had supposed she'd need another lover.

This afternoon, she woke up and smiled at me from her bed, her eyes sleepy and soft and needy in a womanly way that made my blood run hot even on this soggy day.

I started to pull away virtuously, because she was tired and I didn't want to hurt her.

"Please, Bracken, please?" she said throatily, sitting up just enough to pull my sweats down my thighs. She laughed when my cock fell forward heavily, already engorged, and licked tantalizingly. When I groaned, she popped my cock head into her mouth. As she knelt there on the bed, in a position that most women thought of as subservient, her eyes met mine over my erection and up the length of my torso. Her eyes were hazel green in the gray afternoon light and bright with passion, crinkled with humor. She hummed in the back of her throat, the sound tickling my head. My ass clenched and my hips thrust forward. She grunted and laughed, the laugh stroking me as well. I came just a little, just enough to make her throat work once, and I knew that in this position, my beloved—loving me, pulling my seed from me, making me crazy to throw her against the bed and plunge into her, hot and slick and wet and clenching around me like a slippery fist—was more powerful on her knees with me than I had ever been on my feet alone.

CORY
Dysfunction

MAKING LOVE to Bracken was a cross between cliff diving and being invaded by a returning prince who had been exiled from his home country.

The initial free fall between *I'm going to touch this beautiful inhuman* and *Oh my God, he's going to touch me* never failed to leave me breathless, suspended in air, even while I was writhing under his long-fingered, wide-palmed touch. It was a mighty wind caressing my skin, the tingle of salt air between my thighs as he spread them, being tumbled in a fantastic sensual surf where every nerve was alive when he licked and tasted and touched. And when I was screaming, unable to breathe, begging to surface in climax, he invaded.

He was gentle, because he loved this country, but he was still aggressive and, well, overarmed. He thrust into me with an intensity and concentration that forced me to hold fast to myself or I would become Bracken's second skin, a thing I dared not let happen when Green was not in the hill to control the forces that sex wrung out of my quivering body. But always, always there was an urgency, a suppressed violence in him, and I was never more aware of how delicate and fragile I was as a mortal and human than when Bracken, with his immortal sidhe strength, was trying his very best not to fuck me to a pulp. When my orgasm washed over me, the magic that strong emotion brought out tingled along my nerve endings, and although I'd learned how to control this magic with Green, whose sex grew it planet sized and leviathan strong, it was never more out of control than it was with Bracken. Maybe it was because today had been special, or because I'd confided in Bracken as I had not confided in Green. Maybe it was because Green had acknowledged that Bracken was his second as far as I was concerned, or because here, with his cock stretching me to the point I could feel it distending the lower part of my stomach, he was more at home in my body in Green's hill than he was in his own skin in the big bad human world. Whatever it was, at this instant I couldn't find a total grip on my magic. As it filled my skin, I bit his shoulder, flexing my hands and trying to grip the power, but instead it spilled over a little, onto the walls and the ceiling around us. It was a long, slow come, because I'd tried to control my orgasm, to hold on to my pleasure, and by the time the shivers in my clenching center had faded, I was keening low and insistently in my throat, trying to control the touch, the blood, and the song that had overcome me when being invaded by my beloved conqueror.

His heart was thundering in my ears, and I'm sure the other way around. We lay, body to body, his face so close to mine that I could see the haunting lack of freckles or flaws on his sidhe-pale skin and his shaggy hair sticking to his hairline in clumps. Most of his weight was resting on his forearms, and a laugh that was purely masculine hit my face with a blast of air and a little sprinkling of perspiration. Bracken could run a mile with me in his arms and not break a sweat, but face-to-face, body in body, loving me with everything inside him—that made him damp and breathless. Apparently it made something magic happen inside me too.

"You slipped," he acknowledged. In the rainy light, his sidhe-high cheekbones cast shadows against his cheeks, and his grim mouth crinkled at the corners.

"Technically, I think you slipped through me," I said back. I dreaded to look around me and see what changes I had wrought on the clean pine boards that made up my room.

Bracken raised his head, and because he was still inside me, I could feel his breath shuddering out of his body as he looked around.

"Beloved Goddess, Holy God," he said softly. "You don't ever do things in halves, do you?"

"I'm afraid to look," I said, covering my eyes, but Bracken slid wetly out of me and rolled over to his side. He pulled my hands from my eyes and forced me to look around.

Wow. It was a mural—sort of. The waxed boards weren't painted, they were… stained, saturated with rich colors, colors that bled into one another without a space between. On one side of the room was the shade of oak trees and granite surrounding a green-brown pond the exact colors of Bracken's eyes, and on the other side of the room was a meadow of multihued greens. Adrian's moon was over the shaded pond in a purple sky, and the sun was over the meadow in an azure the exact color of my power. Everybody I'd ever loved was represented in the impressionistic, darkly textured stained walls of my room, and I was the orange and the gold in the blue that gave them light.

"You think Green will like?" I asked worriedly and bit my lip because I had mentioned Green. But it's funny what Bracken will take offense to and what he won't.

"Why shouldn't he?" my stone-and-shadow lover asked. "It's...." He waved his hand, at a loss for words. "I like it," he said simply.

I shrugged, tugging the crumpled blanket around me because all I was wearing was a T-shirt, and now I really was tired and didn't feel like hunting for my sweats. "I was going to tack a poster up once and he almost had a coronary," I said uncomfortably. It was embarrassing to admit how crass I'd been when I'd arrived on Green's doorstep.

"This is much better than a thumbtack," Bracken said decisively. Then, with a deft slip, he pulled my T-shirt over my head and down my arms, then burrowed under the blankets with me, spooning me from behind so that my short, slender legs tangled with his long, thickly muscled calves and thighs.

"We are a pretty picture," I decided, not just talking about Bracken and me but too sleepy to say it all. "You're not tired," I finished with an effort, because he had settled me in with my head on top of his arm and I knew that meant he wasn't getting up without me.

"I'll just lie here and listen to you breathe," he whispered, and he sounded totally sincere. I didn't know how to take that sort of breathless, intense devotion, because I still couldn't believe any of them loved me.

"Stalker," I said, because my sense of humor is the last thing that falls asleep in my brain. It laughed with him as I drifted off to nap.

BRACKEN WOKE me up two hours later and hustled me into the shower so we could leave with Grace. The sun was down, but the light hadn't faded yet, and I had just enough time to marvel that my once unremarkable white-tiled bathroom was now the same sort of mottled mural as my pine-board room—more pond and granite-shadow colors, less green, I guess because Green never used my bathroom now that Bracken and I were bound together. Then I was out of the shower and into a new pair of jeans (courtesy of the sprites and the personal shopper Green had assigned me) and a T-shirt that had once been white and now looked exactly like my room.

"Did I do this?" I asked, looking at what was rapidly becoming my favorite piece of clothing *ever.*

"I think the sprites, once they saw the room." Bracken nodded approvingly but was completely casual—probably because he'd seen miracles like this since he'd been born.

"How do I thank them for things like this?" I asked, still overwhelmed by the thousands of flower seeds they'd planted for me after Christmas. About half of them were purple pansies, for Adrian, and the other half wild mustard flowers, for Green.

"You leave pizza in your room every Friday," Bracken argued. "I think you do enough."

"Especially since you haven't eaten pizza since you came back from San Francisco," Grace said, poking her head in my door and, after seeing that we were both dressed, coming all the way in. Grace is a tall, lanky, wide-hipped vampire with curly red hair, but shoving a roast beef sandwich in my hands and a vegetarian one into Bracken's, she was 100 percent den mother. I appreciated her more than words could say.

"Nice work!" She looked animatedly around the room. "I'll have to come in and see if I can make a quilt like this or something."

I nodded, sinking my teeth into the sandwich blissfully. There was some sort of chipotle mustard sauce on the inside that was to die for.

"Thanks—it was sort of an accident," I told her, blushing. "This is wonderful, thank you," I added with a swallow. "Grace, how do you know how to make stuff taste so good if you can't eat human food anymore?" I asked, pulling the homemade bread off my teeth with my tongue.

Grace grinned, her fangs protruding from her otherwise ordinary housewife's face. "I can't eat, honey, but there's nothing in the books that says I can't taste."

I grinned back and, after some rummaging around the messy bed, grabbed my purse and my slicker and was on my way out the door when Grace said, "Bring your knitting." So I grabbed that too.

Green's hill is in the vagueness between Foresthill, Colfax, and Auburn, and Grace's shop was right in the middle of Old Auburn sitting next to the surprising three-story mall-like building that was what tourist traps should look like, with wood and glass and twinkling lights. The store itself only stayed open till nine, which meant that by March, Bracken and I would have to come out alone and take over on the days we worked it, since Grace couldn't function in the light and it wouldn't get dark until seven.

(Technically speaking we didn't actually *have* to work for Grace, because Green would rather I didn't work at all while I was going to school, but since the reason he sent us to school was so we could help his organization, I figured that two nights a week wouldn't kill us.)

Tonight as we headed down the gently curving and occasionally icy Highway 49, I reviewed everything Grace had gone over last time we'd worked. It was mostly the standard retail crap—inventory, registers, suppliers, unloading the truck, overtime, that sort of thing. It was like the Chevron I'd worked at for two years, only classier, happier, and we got to play the music of our choice as loud as we wanted—Grace called it ambience, and I could live with that.

I enjoyed the discussion and tried to ignore how totally lost Bracken looked. Poor Bracken—he'd spent his formative years as an indulged only child, and so far, the only thing that had been expected from him had been muscle. He hated the human world so badly, I wondered how he could love me at all.

When we had turned on Lincoln Way and gone out of sight of the freeway, I remembered to ask Grace why she wanted me to bring my knitting.

"It's an icebreaker," she said happily. She liked driving and she liked conversation. "It gives you something to talk about with the customers. You seemed a little stiff last time you worked."

I blinked. And again. And Bracken started to completely crack up.

"You want me to... talk? Like to the customers?" I sounded stupid and I knew it, but....

"Is that a problem?" Grace asked, amused.

"I just...." Suddenly I felt my palms start to sweat for no good reason. "I worked graveyards at the Chevron because I'm not good with people," I said after a moment of trying to put my panic into words.

Grace spared a glance from the road to frown at me in the passenger seat. "You're fine with people."

"I'm fine with *our* people," I said, trying very hard not to make a big deal out of it. "Human beings, not so much." I shrugged, ignoring the shakiness of my breath. "It'll be fine," I finished brightly. But if Grace was satisfied with that, Bracken wasn't.

"That night I saw you in the Chevron...."

The night that resulted in vampire guts all over the walls, one of the larger, nastier scars on my body, and Adrian shoved into a car trunk to stave off the encroaching dawn? Oh yeah, that night. "I remember it."

"So do I," Bracken replied grimly. He'd almost killed me that night just by being who he was, because I was bleeding and his power pulls blood out of people's bodies. It was a bad night. "And I remember you smiled so sweetly at an old man that he wandered out of the store wondering what his own name was."

"And ended up headless and dead," I finished up for him. Did I mention it was a bad night?

"But you talked to him!" he insisted. "You were pleasant. You can talk to people. All you have to do is let them see you. You let him see you—you know, not the bitch you were trying to be back then, but you, like you are now, with your nice red hair and not that black crap, and your pretty eyes, your sweet fa— What?" He demanded suddenly, because Grace had pulled up to a stop sign and not gone when it was her turn and we were both staring at him over our shoulders as though he'd grown another head. My eyes burned fiercely, and it was hard to swallow.

"What?" he demanded again from his place in the back. Grace and I looked at each other helplessly, and Grace shrugged.

"He has no idea what that does to you, does he?" she asked softly.

"Fucking preternatural males," I forced through a tight throat. "None of them do."

A car beeped behind us and Grace pulled forward, leaving me speechless in the front seat and Bracken baffled in the back.

So that night I counted inventory and, while Bracken unloaded the delivery of yarn, fabric, and pattern books from the truck, I waited on people. Grace was right, the knitting made it easier.

"What are you working on?" a grandmotherly sort of woman asked me as I pulled the sumptuous nylon/wool bouclé through my fingers and clicked my needles in a way that never failed to completely chill me out.

"A sweater," I told her, stroking the almost completed front with my hands.

"For who, Goliath?" she asked, and I had to smile at her.

"For my… husband," I said, glancing up. My hands, though, schooled by practice and that wonderful Zen concentration that knitting induces, kept moving—knit four, purl one, knit four, purl one, reverse on the next row….

"Well"—she smiled at me conspiratorially, without even sparing a glance for my empty ring finger—"it's a good thing you're already married, because you know the myth of the boyfriend sweater, don't you?" Her brown eyes twinkled up at me from behind wrinkles and thick glasses. She was a gnomish-looking person, with curly gray-brown hair and a peach-colored leisure suit, but she was, as far as I could tell, human.

"I've never heard it," I said, curious. I looked up at Bracken, bound to me as more than a boyfriend, and more even than a husband. He was hanging the quilts Grace had brought from home on the quilt racks that loomed in display at the upper levels of the store. He was tall enough to reach without a ladder, and his sweatshirt pulled up past his lean abdomen. I wondered if he'd included cover for his two extra ribs in his glamour. Probably not, I thought warmly as he stretched and flexed with unconscious grace. I hadn't told him who the sweater was for when I was picking out the yarn and forcing him to touch it and judiciously measuring the colors with my eyes. But he had seen the mural my magic made, and the brackish, smoky violet should look very familiar.

"Well, you know," the woman was saying, eyeing my beloved with appreciation of her own, "they say that if you make a sweater for a man you're not married to, in the time it takes you to make the sweater, you'll break up."

"No!" I'd never heard that.

"Oh yes, it's true!" She added enthusiastically, "Of course, I told my husband that if he broke up with me, he'd have to give me the sweater as a parting gift."

"I take it you didn't break up."

"Well, he didn't like the sweater, but since he returned it with an engagement ring, I decided to forgive him!"

I laughed, terribly enchanted, and she laughed with me.

"But I must say," she said thoughtfully after a moment, "I don't know if it would be true if all sweaters were made with that stuff you're working with now! That's nice!"

I grinned at her and felt my work with restless hands. The fabric was so real under my fingers. I was surrounded with elves and magic and vampires, and this sweater was the only thing in my life I could talk about. "It's great, isn't it?" I affirmed. "Would you like to see it? Brack just unloaded a new shipment—we've got it in, like, eight different colors!"

And there I was, talking with a human being. I had something in common with my native species after all.

The rest of the night went well. It was actually sort of fun. I'd been talking to Grace since before Christmas about crafts—about knitting, crocheting, cross-stitching, and quilting. It was a chance to show off, to be helpful, to share knowledge. I wondered if working in the Chevron would have been quite so stifling if I had actually talked to people, or if it was sharing the same interests that made the people in A Yarning for Crafts bearable. It didn't matter, I decided as I sat at the register and bound off the front of Brack's sweater. I was happy here, and that was a good thing.

Grace came out from the back—it was the end of the month and she was balancing books—and told me to go with Bracken and get dinner before the Mongolian BBQ around the corner closed.

"Wasn't the sandwich dinner?" I was still full.

"The sandwich was lunch," she said firmly. "You've been sharing blood with the kiss, and you need to, but you haven't gained back a pound since you were sick, and you need to keep eating."

"I've gained five!" I protested, but she took my knitting firmly from my hands and placed it carefully in my quilted bag (her gift to me at Christmas), and before I could protest again, Bracken was right behind her to take me in hand.

"You have not," he said firmly, holding my slicker up with an air of no nonsense.

"How would you know? I don't think there's a single scale at home!"

"Then how would you know you have?" he returned, but our bickering was good-natured and the two of them had succeeded in their aims, because my coat was on and Bracken and I were headed for the door. It was nearing eight o'clock, and we almost ran into the woman and her two children coming inside. I took a step back and grinned at the kids—both boys—and their wide-eyed appreciation of Bracken looming behind me from his impossible height.

I looked up to their mom and blinked. "Gra...," I started to say, then looked behind me to the real Grace, but strangely enough she was nowhere to be seen. I would have thought she'd be up front, since the store was open for another slow hour. "I'm sorry," I mumbled, flushing. "You look like a friend of mine." I stood back and waited for the woman to follow her boys in, but she looked at me, troubled and almost frightened.

She was in her thirties, like Grace had been when she'd died, and her brown-red curly hair was cut a little shorter than Grace's and framed a narrower, more piquant face—with freckles the exact same color, a wide, generous mouth the same shape, and limpid brown eyes the same shade. She was shorter too, I thought, slighter, without the wide-hipped, lanky swagger—but these differences were small and superficial, and the resemblance had frightening implications.

"Grace was my mother's name," she said almost defiantly. "How did you know?"

Oh, Jesus. All of the air left my body, and for a moment I didn't think I would ever breathe again. No wonder Grace had fled to the back room.

"I didn't," I said carefully. The elves couldn't tell a lie—physically couldn't, it made them sick—and I'd made it sort of a point of honor with myself to follow their rules. I had magic from the Goddess; I never knew if or when her restrictions on lying were going to kick in for me, and I didn't want to find out the hard way. "I didn't know your mother's name was Grace," I bluffed. My hands were cold, and my face was cold too, and I wondered if I was as pale as I felt. "Uhm… can I help you? My… the… our night clerk seems to have run back for something."

Grace's daughter nodded, her eyes wide and luminous and never leaving mine. She pointed to a quilt—one of the ones that Bracken had just hung up on display.

"I need to know who made that," she asked, and if she hadn't looked like she was holding on tight to her tears, I would have said she was rude, but we both knew better. I looked at the quilt, my heart sinking.

"The owner of the store. Why?" But I knew.

"My mother… died," she said, her voice choked. Her boys were off looking at the hand-carved wooden toys the gnomes so enjoyed making, but I took a glance at them anyway. They were probably six and eight or thereabouts, smaller, freckled, sturdy, and very male for small boys. The older one had sensitive narrow hands and rubbed the carved work with a tilt to his head and an innate understanding, and the younger one watched him carefully as though taking notes.

"She died of cancer when I was fifteen," their mother continued through a tight throat, and I pulled my attention back reluctantly. I couldn't afford to escape into the world of small boys right now. "The summer she died, she made me a quilt with that exact motif. It's rare. It's really rare. The colors were different—they were…." She frowned.

"Sunnier. More yellows, more greens, not so much purple and black, and that murky oak-leaf color...." She looked at me again, that defiance in her eyes. *Lie to me,* she seemed to say. *Lie to me. I'll see it. I know the truth.* Goddess, I hoped so, I thought wretchedly. I hoped she had an inkling, because if this fell out the way I thought it was going to, the truth was going to floor her. Panic started trickling along my nerve endings, and I tried to control it, because I'd been sharing blood with half the kiss and we were tuning in to each other's brain-chatter lately. I didn't want to freak them out. And although we never talked explicitly about telepathy, the fact is, Green always knew when I was losing it—could, in fact, talk to me with words when he needed to, and Bracken and I were starting to slip into each other's brains as well. Once blooded, like Ellis, the vampires were all over my brain.

I *really* didn't want Green to hop the next flight home for what essentially boiled down to a family drama—but I couldn't help it. I was just beginning to learn how to act around human beings, but my newfound people skills were nowhere near this good.

"That's my mother's work," she said belligerently, "and I want to know who stole it."

"No one stole it," I said calmly, wondering if my eyes were swallowing my face yet. "I can swear before any god you believe in that no one stole that work."

"But it's my *mother's*," she insisted. "My best friend came in here during Christmas and bought a quilt like that one, and I saw it. I saw it up close. My mom had this knot when she finished off—she machine quilted, but she would hand sew the label, and the knot was intricate and special, and she showed it to me and my sister and made us learn it. She said she got it from her grandmother, and that knot was on my quilt and it was on my friend's quilt and I'd give money that it's on that quilt and I want to know *who stole my mother's work.*"

There was a ringing silence in the store, and Bracken's hand came up to my shoulder in what I assumed was a question. I was their leader, their queen, and I'd been known to kick some serious ass, but I did not know, could not know, how to deal with this hysterical woman, Grace's daughter, who was angry because I knew her mother and she did not.

"No one stole it," I repeated uncertainly. "It's.... The owner of the store made it. I... she's made one for me...," I trailed off weakly, because she had, and I wondered if that quilt, the one she'd made for me when I was recovering from my illness this winter, meant the same things to me that it did to this terrified, angry, grief-stricken woman. There was a fraught silence in the store then, and I prayed for someone to walk in from the street, or from the back door to the mall, or even to drop in from the sky, but no one did. In the back of my mind, I heard the flutter of one vampire mind, then two, tuning in to my uncertainty, but I was so mesmerized by the tragedy I saw here that I couldn't think to respond.

"Listen to me, you bitch," she hissed, moving up to my face in a way that would have been threatening if I wasn't sure I could take her. "You're lying to me, you're hiding something, I've never seen anyone look so scared, now *tell me what you know about my mother.*"

"She's right here, Chloe," Grace said, stepping out from behind the shelf to my left. She moved with vampiric silence and terrifying stealth, and my heart almost popped out of my chest. Even Chloe gave a little shriek. "The work is mine."

Chloe's face got even paler, if that was possible, and her freckles stood out greenly. She took a couple of shuddering breaths, and I expected a scream, or a moan, or anger—but she was Grace's daughter, and she didn't have hysterics. She spoke from the heart instead.

"You *left!*" Chloe gasped. "You were *dead.* We got your letter—Daddy found the body—you were *dead!* How could you lie to us like that!"

"I didn't lie," Grace said evenly, and she blinked hard. She didn't want to weep blood in front of her daughter, I could tell. With movement so sudden Chloe couldn't resist, Grace seized her hand and held it up to her neck. "Feel that, my darling? No pulse. No pulse, no breath, no sunlight, no redemption. I was dying. I wanted to at least see you grow up. This is the trade I made."

Chloe's breath came in short pants, and little whimpering sounds came out of her throat. I saw what was going to happen before Grace did, because I'd been there a couple of times myself. Grace, eyes shut tight against the tears, opened her mouth, her fangs extending in an obviously impossible, unmistakable way. Chloe's brown eyes, so like her mother's, rolled back in her head, and she crumpled to the ground, followed by Grace, who gathered her daughter up into her arms and sobbed like a child.

My mental shriek of panic traveled as far as Newcastle and Colfax before I could calm it down, and by then it was too late—thirty vampires were flying like, well, vampires out of Bumfuck, Egypt to save me from the bad guys, and I was too stunned to reach out and stop them.

"Oh Jesus—Bracken…," I squeaked, and Bracken, whose human skills were so obviously confined to me alone, looked equally blank.

"Before I panic and run screaming home, beloved, could you take a breath and tell me what's going on?" Green said calmly in my head, and I almost sank to the floor myself in sheer fucking relief.

I don't know how much sense I made in pictures, words, and panic, but Green started issuing calm orders in my head. My heart rate slowed, and I started listening to him.

"First off, call the vampires and tell them to calm down," Green said slowly in my mind. *"They're going to panic people."*

I tried in my head, but Grace was making a low keening sound, and the two boys saw their mother in trouble and were heading toward us, and I couldn't pull my brain together enough to feel them in my head.

"Okay…," Green said in my brain with what sounded like forced patience. There was a familiar, panting, strained overtone to his "voice." *"Okay, then, first thing, my beloved, is to move Grace and her daughter to the back room and have Bracken supervise the children."*

"Bracken?" I asked out loud, but Green's affirmative noise was short and pointed and my own panic was subsiding enough to wonder exactly what he had been doing when I'd freaked out.

"What?" Bracken answered, and I nodded my head toward the two small boys.

"Watch them," I hissed, and following Green's instructions blindly, I bent toward Grace. "Grace, sweetie…." I touched her shoulder. "Grace—we've got to get to the back room, okay? You understand?" Grace nodded, to my immense relief, and cradling her full-grown daughter in her arms like a small child, she stood and started moving to the back office.

I turned to check on Bracken in time to hear him say, "Here, little men—have you seen how this top can spin without string?" and I moved toward him while I could.

"Bracken…," I whispered, partly embarrassed, partly urgent. "In about five minutes, a whole lot of vampires are going to get here. Could you sort of calm them down?"

The look he gave me was priceless, but I gave him one of my own—embarrassed, panic-stricken, exasperated. "Well, would you rather go back and deal with Grace instead?"

"Grace?" said one of the boys at our feet—the youngest one, whose carrot-orange hair had obviously been cut by the boy himself in recent history and who had apparently had a close encounter with a permanent marker around the same time. "Grace is our grandmother's name."

Bracken shook his head in panic and turned to the boy, saying, "And it's a pretty name, isn't it? Would you like to know my favorite name?"

As I disappeared, I heard one of the boys say, "Cory—that's my best friend's stinky brother's name. Why would Cory be your favorite name?"

Inside the office, Grace was at least sitting in a chair, but Chloe's eyes were closed, and she was breathing rhythmically against Grace's chest.

"Grace...," I began, reluctant to interrupt with my complete incompetence. "Grace, Green says I have to tell the vampires that we're going to be okay. I called them, and...."

Grace looked at me, startled out of herself for the first time since she had run into the stock room after seeing Chloe walk into the store. "Why did you call the vampires?" she asked, puzzled. "Why would Green be in your head telling you not to call the vampires?"

"Oh, I don't know, Grace—maybe because I panicked?" I winced at the sarcasm in my voice, but Grace knew me and loved me anyway.

"Cory, you took down a giant bird in a public place at night with a .45 you could barely hold, you were so weak, and you didn't crack a sweat. Why would you panic?" she asked, looking bemused. She stroked her daughter's hair without thinking.

"Because you were crying," I said through a stiff jaw.

"You've seen me cry before," she replied gently. She'd told me about her family to let me see how important it was that I took Bracken's intentions toward me seriously, even though I would always love Green.

"You... you were all *you,* then." Oh yeah, that made sense. "And this time you weren't. You were falling apart... and I wanted to help you, and I didn't know how." I shrugged, trying not to make this moment about my own shortcomings. "Never mind." I heard the front bell ring, and then again and again, urgently. "I'll go tell Phillip and everybody not to lose their minds, okay?"

Grace suddenly smiled at me—a weary, sad smile, but a smile nonetheless—and reached out her hand. I took it in my own and squeezed. "Next time, Cory, sweetheart, a hug might do better than thirty freaked-out vampires, okay?" I nodded my head and took her cue to lean over her shoulders and hug her awkwardly.

"I love you, Grace," I said, meaning it. "We all love you. Anything we can do—even if it's just making sure the kids don't remember, or that they do…. You let me know, okay?"

"Love you too, sweetie," she said softly, and I pulled away, leaving her looking at her grown daughter's face with wonder and grief.

My face was hot with embarrassment by the time I hit the front of the store, and I was babbling apologies the whole way.

"I'm so sorry, Phillip!" I said as the tall, immaculately groomed, sharp-faced ex-stockbroker eyed me with grim amusement. "Marcus—I didn't mean to freak you all out!" Marcus used to be a schoolteacher before an untimely car accident. Phillip had been a stockbroker (and according to Marcus, a real prick) before Marcus found him in an avalanche and brought him over with Adrian's help. Marcus was comfortably handsome and a little shy, one-on-one; if you asked him about anything having to do with history or politics he'd talk passionately and brilliantly, but otherwise he liked to think his opinion didn't matter. Of the two men, Phillip made the more ruthless leader and Marcus made the more circumspect decision maker, which was why they'd been Adrian's seconds in the vampire world. I relied on them in the same way, and they… they revered me, in a way that was terrifying and uncomfortable. They seemed to think that I could take care of them and love them in the totally protective way Adrian had led, and I was so frightened of failure that sometimes I couldn't breathe when we were in the same room. To stumble in on them (and Chester and Bryn and Ellis and… dear *Goddess* how many other vampires were coming in?) babbling in apology could have been one of the most mortifying moments of my life.

If they had let it be.

"Is Grace okay?" Marcus asked immediately. "Bracken told us what happened—is she going to be all right?"

I swallowed and blinked. Of course. These were Adrian's vampires. Grace had led them while I'd been gone. They too had left families and loved ones to be night hunters, to be the dead. Of anyone, the vampires streaming in one after another in various states of dress (and sogginess—it was still raining out there!) would understand how traumatic this would be for Grace. They would—they *were*—all forgiving me for my panic call, because it would have been their panic call as well.

"I don't know," I said honestly. "I'm so lost with this. I think we need to let Grace decide how to proceed." The other vampires—looking around the now crowded little store I saw at least twenty of them—all nodded in understanding, and I took a deep breath of relief. Grace would deal with it, I could deal with it, human problems could be dealt with.

At that exact moment, the doors to the outside crashed open so quickly that one of the glass panes in the bottom cracked and the hinges squealed in pain as they ripped sideways. Arturo, Grace's sidhe lover, hurtled into the room with so much force from prolonged hyperspeed that I was blown backward into the cashier's stand. My head cracked against the wood, pain exploded behind my eyes, and I saw stars. Bracken was there in half a heartbeat, but I put my hand back behind my head and it came away with blood on it, so I was not going to get any cuddling from him immediately. I dragged my battered, sore, skinny ass up just as Bracken got in the face of the biggest, baddest, most physically imposing elf at our hill.

"What the fuck, Arturo! You could have killed someone!"

Arturo's eyes were whirling, his chest heaving with effort. He must have run fifteen miles in five minutes, no mean feat even if you were working on the will of the Goddess alone. "Grace," he snarled. "Where the hell is Grace?"

Of course. Every vampire in the kiss at the hill goes flying out screaming "Grace," Arturo's going to be listening to the psychic all-call, right?

"Dearest, are you all right?" Green said in my head, and I gave the equivalent of a mental grunt.

"Panicked Arturo," I summarized. *"Pissed off Bracken. Bonk to the noggin. All systems fucked up as usual."*

I heard the equivalent of a mental chuckle, but he must not have been that amused, because he kept lurking in my head, probing my wound. *"You're bleeding!"*

"Hence the reason Bracken is across the room about ready to deck Arturo. I think I need to move now."

"Grace is fine," I articulated, trying hard to see the two combatants past the darkness in my vision. "Grace is fine. Where are the boys?"

"They're in the playroom with half our inventory," Brack said smartly. Good—there was a reason we'd established a little playroom for munchkins. Little kids and craft stores sooo did not mix well. I put my hands underneath me and pushed up, then grabbed the top of the stand and hauled myself up by main force. I could stand—with wobbly knees and blurred vision, but I could stand.

"Her daughter came into the store. She panicked, I panicked. I'm sorry, Arturo," I said, still wobbling. "I truly didn't mean to send us all into a tailsp…." Oh, this was bad. I swayed on my feet and tried not to barf, and it wasn't the head wound that was making me queasy.

Suddenly, every vampire in the room went down. Five of them—the five I didn't know that well and hadn't shared blood with—simply went over backward, like felled trees or puppets with cut strings. Everybody else, including Marcus and Phillip, my pillars of support, fell to their knees and groaned. That smell was back again—that knee-leveling psychic stench of minatory corruption—and it was all I could do not to roll my eyes back in my head and join the vampires on the ground.

While Arturo was saying "What in hell?" Bracken took one look at me and said, "Oh fuck, it's back." The two boys, hearing the nasty thuds and moaning voices, popped their heads out of the playroom in the back corner, and suddenly my course of action became absolutely clear.

"Bracken, go take care of them," I barked. "Arturo, go make sure Grace is okay. This thing's bad, and it's got to go."

Green was inside my head, panicked and, from what I could tell, also otherwise engaged. *"This thing is bloody awful—you know what this is?"*

"It was at the school today. I have no idea what it's doing here, but it's after us. Can't you feel that?"

"No kidding, Corinne Carol-Anne!" Green snapped, and his voice was strained with worry for me—and with something else that was familiar and somehow inappropriate for the circumstances, which he was trying to keep from me.

"Green… what are you doing right now?"

A mental grimace. *"Bad question, beloved. What is our plan?"*

A plan. Did I have a plan? *"It's not afraid of sunshine,"* I said, a little bit afraid.

"It's never tasted yours," he answered back. *"And you have people to protect."*

A shield. "We'll need a shield," I said out loud. "A strong one. On the outside of the building—" Oh shit. "Phillip!" Phillip groaned, trying,

I was sure, not to retch up his last meal. I knew that feeling well. "Phillip, dammit—who's out there?"

"What?"

"When you guys answered my panic call—how many people that haven't taken blood from me are out there?"

Phillip shook his head, trying to pull it together, but the force that was making us all nauseous and weak gave a little surge, and not only did it send Phillip to his knees and me to the trash can to hover, just in case, it also told us that we were *running out of time*.

"*Dammit,* Phillip… who's out there?"

"Why does it matter?" he asked, his sharply handsome face nearly green with illness. "Just blast it… kill it… whatever it is…."

"Fuck it all!" I roared. "I will *not* be the source of any more innocent vampire deaths, do you hear me? You tell our people to clear out, and you tell them to clear out *now!*"

"That pretty girl said the f-word," said a small voice into the ensuing silence, and I wanted to weep. Now Grace's grandchildren were going to think I was some sort of miscreant.

"It's okay," Bracken told him back, his voice tense. "She only swears when she's trying to help people." From across the room I caught Bracken's eyes with my own eye roll—corny corny corny, and terribly frightening at the same time.

"Phillip—the other vampires!" Vampires could read thoughts, emotions, general presences, from those they had taken blood or sex from. In the first year of a vampire's life, his hungers were so huge, so all consuming, that besides needing shape-changers around to feed on—because they were harder to drain dry—a new vamp was often rolled from bed to neck to bed of his fellow kiss mates. That's why a kiss—a fully developed, well-nurtured kiss—was even better than a family. Phillip had been a stockbroker thirty years ago. By now, he'd shared blood or sex with every member of his kiss.

Phillip concentrated hard, an effort that nearly brought him to his knees, and Green murmured some more in my head. "*Beloved, that wasn't your fault.*"

"*Mine more than anyone's,*" I told him truthfully. Being insane with grief did not absolve a person from guilt, I thought with more than a hint of panic.

"We're it," Phillip was saying with an effort. Another surge of mental putridity hit us all hard, and I fell to my knees, throwing up violently into Grace's trash can. "Do it, Cory," Phillip continued on a groan. "Everybody who heard your first summons is in here."

My body hurt, my head hurt, my *soul* hurt with the stench and the nausea and the queasiness of evil, and crawling to the door was difficult and tortuous. There was shattered glass on the frame and I sliced open my palm grabbing the metal, but that pain barely impinged on my list of aches. With a whine I closed my eyes and gathered my power. The doorframe glowed, and the glow spread along the outside of the building, but it was a weak, fretful sunlight and it wasn't going to be enough.

"Green...," I called weakly, and Green was suddenly there, filling me with his scent and his mind and his *oh my God his sex....* In a flash I saw what Green had been doing while he was helping me save the world, and it was both uncomfortable and highly arousing. We were merged, so for a moment my mouth was filled with a smooth strong cock that I didn't recognize, and then I was penetrated in the only place Green *could* be penetrated, and a mouth, definitely feminine, was on a part of me that I didn't possess but that Green absolutely did, and my body was quivering on the brink of orgasm, and only my grip on the merge between us kept me from spilling into a pool of liquid sex right there on the floor, in the middle of being attacked by fuck-all whatever it was.

The impression lasted a moment—a millisecond, actually—just long enough to fill my body with sex and surprise, and then Green closed his shield down so quickly I could barely feel his embarrassment and his fear that I'd reject him for what I knew he'd left me to do. But the millisecond had worked its magic. For that moment, I wasn't susceptible to whatever it was that was leveling the vampires and me while leaving alone the elves and humans who hadn't been sharing blood with vampires. I suddenly had the strength and the power to grab the doorframe tighter, ignoring the blood trickling from my palm down the metal, and in a breath my sunshine grew strong.

Stronger and brighter, glowing yellow and azure and sunset orange and green and red. As I thought about Adrian, purposely coloring my power with something this thing, whatever it was, could understand, it began to burn purple, streaking like lightning over the flat box of storefronts and tops to the east and forming a dome of light over the glass-and-wood mall to my left. The inside of the store went from being cold, reeking of the psychic stench of gangrenous flesh and rancid antiseptic, to being warm, pleasant, and green, smelling like mustard flowers and pinks and bottlebrush under the sun.

The screech of whatever it was that had attacked us echoed through my bones and blew out the remaining glass on the doors but did not penetrate my sunshine shield. There was another scream, this one hurt, frustrated, and weak, and then suddenly whatever had started it was gone and the attack was over.

I collapsed against the doorframe with Green in my head. His presence was breathless and satiated, and I hurt and was scared and bleeding and exhausted, but I had the presence of mind to smile. *"Was it good for you?"* I asked, and I felt something in his voice give a quiver of released tension.

"As long as it was good for you, beloved." If he had stood before me, he would have been looking at me sideways from his wide-spaced green eyes, and he'd be awaiting my opinion, my censure, my response.

"It's not like I didn't know," I said kindly, in real life sitting back and leaning against the shattered doorframe in a puddle of blood and glass.

"Knowing and feeling are two different things," he said carefully.

"Nothing you do for love, pleasure, or to keep us safe would ever repel me, beloved," I said baldly, because my concentration was fading and I was going to have to deal with real life in a second, and I couldn't afford to let Green be afraid my love for him could ever end.

There was a mental kiss on my forehead, almost as warm and definitely as tender as the real thing. *"Have Marcus or Phillip lick your wounds, little Goddess,"* he said, *"and then let Bracken tend to you. Give Grace my love. I have some things to do here."*

My internal monologue gave a snark of laughter, and my external monologue barked an order. "Marcus"—because Marcus was pulling himself up to his feet and moving determinedly around to make sure the other vampires would be okay—"Marcus, you need to come here and lick my boo-boos, because I'm going to need Bracken's help, and I don't want to bleed out."

"Oh, Jesus," Marcus griped. "A head wound? I'll be spitting up hair for days...." And with that I started laughing with relief, and I couldn't stop until the slightly built vampire with the messy brown hair and kind eyes had licked my head, my palms, and my knees, stopping the blood the way vampires could do by will and touch alone. He complained good-naturedly the whole time about how humans didn't have to worry about their food wiggling around on the table in front of them.

When he was done, I called to Bracken, who brought the wide-eyed little boys out to me.

"Hey, guys," I said, looking at Grace's grandbabies. "I hope I didn't frighten you...."

"You said the f-word!" the youngest piped up.

"And you made the store glow!" the oldest added, and I laughed a little.

"Yes, that's true, I did...."

"Gavin," the older one supplied. "And my little brother is Graeme."

I hoped none of my horror showed on my face. It was like naming a baby Walter—who could look at a little wrinkled helpless baby and call him Gavin or Graeme? "Those are very good names," I lied baldly, hoping the Goddess wouldn't choose this moment to strike me with nausea and cramps for it. "But I need to ask you something—"

"What in the hell was that?" Grace said, barreling out of the back room and straight into Arturo's waiting arms. She took a moment to be embraced—if a bone-cracking bear hug could be called an embrace—before she disentangled herself gently from Arturo and took a good look at me. "Why you?" she asked bluntly. "Why is it always you getting hurt? I don't see a scratch on Bracken, Arturo's fine, vampires are dandy...." This last was an overstatement, because the ones who hadn't taken my blood were barely staggering to their feet, but that wasn't her point. "But the only one here who's mortal? Noooooo.... She's got to be covered in blood by the end of the night."

"Thanks, Grace," I returned with interest. "I was just about to ask Gavin and Graeme here if they needed their memories wiped, but I guess you just saved me from that uncertainty!"

Grace looked down at the two wide-eyed children and grimaced at me. "I guess we all need a little practice being human tonight, don't we?" she asked, and I nodded stiffly. The cut on my head was closed and the one on my palm too, but everything from my toes up to the top of my head hurt; my whole body ached from being slammed against the cashier stand and then puking up my toes for the umpteenth time that day.

"Come along, guys...," she directed. "Let's go see your mom and have a talk, okay?"

Arturo watched her go and then turned a very contrite face to me. "Corinne Carol-Anne, I cannot tell you how sorry I am," he said gently, then moved forward to take the back of my head in his hands, wincing as he did so. I was sitting meekly, looking at my lap, when suddenly I felt the buzz—the same buzz I'd first felt when Arturo had touched me almost a whole year ago and I had been drawn headlong into the world I now lived in full-time. Arturo was healing me, I could feel it, but he was not a healing elf—he was a warrior elf mostly, with some dabbling as a fertility god—and suddenly the buzzing in my skin increased to the point where it felt like the buzzing of the tattoo needle that had covered my back in December. Only a lot worse, I thought, trying not to wiggle and whine, because at least then I'd had a little preternatural anesthetic, and now my head and my palm and even my knees were buzzing with blood pain.

I had just enough time to gasp "Ouch, fuck, *jeez*, Arturo..." before the buzzing rose to a high pitch, and with a small flash of red-gold light at the parts I could see (and I'm sure the back of my skull, which I couldn't see), my wounds had closed, healed, just like that.

Arturo ruffled my hair, which was a bloody mess anyway, and patted my head kindly. "You will live, I think," he said.

"Yeah, but I like it when Green heals me better." I rubbed the back of my head gingerly, because it still felt hot and buzzy.

"But of course. Bracken, she'll live. Am I forgiven?" Arturo called—with some humor, but with some humility too, which was rare for Arturo. Of the sidhe I knew, Arturo was the most arrogant and the least likely to admit he had been wrong.

"You might be," Bracken responded in kind over his shoulder. He was standing at the door, which he had propped open, and was talking to someone standing outside in what looked like a big pool of light. He said something to the person outside, then carefully closed the door and came toward me with suppressed urgency.

"Can I touch her?" he asked, his voice betraying his worry and the strain of having to leave me because I was bleeding—just when he wanted to be near me most.

"You can always touch me, baby," I said throatily, and suddenly he was in front of me, holding my chin in his hands and examining me himself.

Bracken just shook his head and then helped me to my feet. I could tell by the tenseness of his body that he was resisting pulling me into his arms with everything in his being, and his sudden proximity reminded me of the sex that had flooded me when Green let down his shields. I was exhausted from using power, I still hurt a little from throwing up, but most pressing, I was now painfully horny.

"Swell." I leaned up next to Bracken anyway, drawing his strength into my skin like sunshine and still, still feeling that urge to have his cock in my mouth, down my throat, his mouth on my cleft, his body in my.... I shook myself, knowing that part of what I was feeling was Green—but part of it was me, too, because between Green, Adrian, and me, there wasn't much we hadn't done. I just hadn't done it like that in a very long time.

"Yeah?" Bracken asked, his arm around my shoulders drawing me tighter. "You like being healed by Arturo, you're going to *love* this."

All I really wanted right now was Bracken alone, so deep inside of me I could taste him in the back of my throat. But he hadn't been in my head with that terrifying, arousing glimpse of what Green did to keep us safe, and he obviously had something else in mind.

"What now?" I asked, keeping my self-control steady.

"The press is here. They're calling it an electricity surge. They want to talk to somebody—and Cory, you're the only one here who's not going to look damn strange on camera."

My arousal turned off like his words were a big ugly light switch, and I put my hands to my blood-matted hair. I looked over to Grace, but she was in full vampire mode, teeth and all, and was in the process of convincing her grandsons that they'd seen a power outage and nothing more. It wasn't going well, and I had time to wonder if maybe children got to remember magic when adults forgot it, but I was still taking stock so I moved on. The vampires were all on their feet, some of them shakily, but it didn't matter—they wouldn't show up on camera. The elves would, but the glamour that kept them looking human got weird and tricky on camera—only occasionally would a camera picture respect the glamour. Some of them revealed the unusual bone structure and pointy ears. Bracken was right—I was going to have to go deal with the media and, judging from the new red strobe lights outside, the police as well. The last time I'd had to deal with the police, they'd almost made me flunk out of school, and in spite of the fact that Officer Max had mellowed, I still wasn't that fond of the boys in blue. But as I looked around the store a little desperately, I realized that Brack was right. I was all they had.

Well, shit.

GREEN
Leading by Main Strength

ORDINARILY, GREEN was not a terry-robe kind of sidhe, but the sylph delegation of Marin County was in such a tizzy about the visit of their new leader that he didn't have the heart to do the towel-around-the-waist thing that Cory found so very appealing. As it was, he saw Cory's broadcast while standing tensely in front of the television in the sylph guest room with his hair dripping down the back of the lush terry cloth, oblivious to the distressed susurruses of the sylphs who felt he should be reclining in bed and letting them tend to him.

"She is very... ordinary, your *ou'e'eir*, is she not?" asked Jason, the sylph leader, while swinging his bare legs over the edge of the bed.

"Human camera, human eyes," Green said briefly, knowing that Jason hadn't meant anything negative by the comment. Sylphs as a whole were both lovely and—until sexual activity—asexual. They were attractive in order to attract other species, and they chose their gender when they chose a mate—and the very ambitious would elect to mate with their sidhe leader. For Green to have chosen a plain woman as an *ou'e'eir* meant that the joining was truly for love—no magic, no biology, no forced bindings involved. A plain lover wasn't beautiful to attract a mate, or because the Goddess made him or her that way—a plain lover was just... loved. And it meant that the binding ceremony that Green had just participated in with Jason and his other chosen leaders would truly give Jason's people the freedom they had hoped for. Green's attachment to Cory was through simple consensuality—Green had no one-way bindings that would block his bindings to as many sylphs as he wished for.

It had been a risk.

Most sidhe were bisexual. Between their longevity and their naturally sensual natures, both monogamy and heterosexuality were far too limited for a sidhe's carnal palette. This was both good and bad for the ambitious sylphs. It was good because it gave a sylph a lot more sexual freedom than his fellows enjoyed—their gender wasn't chosen by being the opposite of their mate's, it was a matter of their own choice. It was bad because, while the leader could do whomever he or she pleased, the sylph binding was for life—a sylph trying to break a bad mating would die in the backlash of breaking the mating spell. A faithless sylph was a dead sylph, and depending on how they bound themselves to their mates, both betrayer and betrayed might dissolve into a little puddle of faithless flesh. Or, in Green's case, since his power came from sex, they hopefully would not. Green couldn't afford to be monogamous, and since the binding had been with so many, the hope was that the sylphs would no longer be confined to one lover. It was a strong hope. This binding varied wildly, because the sylphs were the Goddess's levelers—they mated with any of the Goddess's species, and occasionally with God's humans as well, and everybody had their own physiological weirdness, dictating how the sylphs would live and die. It made the sylphs furtive, timid creatures, so eager to please it was almost painful.

Mist, their previous sidhe leader, had neglected the sylphs almost to the point of extinction. Those sylphs who hadn't died had emigrated, either to Green's own land or to the south of the state. Mist had been an elitist of the most offensive sort. He'd been able to use the sylphs' strength to his advantage, but refused to admit he owed them anything for their fealty. Sylphs were sensual creatures—if their chosen mate refused to love them (hell, even a good hug would do!), they faded, growing thinner and less substantial, until one day they simply didn't exist. Several of Mist's sylph leaders had wasted away from sexual apathy. One of Green's first orders of business, after Mist had died and the dust of Green's takeover had settled, had been to visit the sylph enclave and establish relations with a people he deemed quite important—and attractive—of the Goddess's get. Mist's ally, Goshawk, had been dispossessed as well, and his people, the Avians, also looked to Green now. Green was hoping to work out an agreement between the two species that would help take care of the Goddess's little limitations on both.

But it was difficult. The scene Cory had interrupted earlier had been sensual and pleasurable, but the sylphs had also been desperate, dying to please, tense with desire; this terrible need had been, partly, why there had been so many of them.

The other part had been an experiment of Green's, a hope, based on Nicky's dual binding to both Green and Cory.

"Do you think it worked?" Jason said, looking anxiously at Green.

Green barely shifted his attention from the screen. His "ordinary" *ou'e'eir* was summoning a small smile for the television crew. The title under her picture read "Cory Green," and although Green was pretty sure there was more to her new name than that, his throat tightened with pride just seeing his name there next to hers. With a sigh he spared a look for Jason. The sylph's worries were legitimate, he knew.

"I can feel the binding already—you?"

Jason nodded excitedly. "That's four of us, four sylphs bound to our leader—four sylphs who can love each other as well as you. We won't have to worry about dying, fading away...." The slightly built sylph—a very pretty young man, now that he'd chosen his gender—looked at Green with shining eyes. "Lord Green, you've saved us all."

Green spared a smile for Jason, and for Letty, Princess, and Daniel, who were sprawled, sated and naked, in the bed behind him. Tonight had been a very big night for all of them, and Green hated to dampen their happiness—and their triumph—with his own worry.

But sylphs as a whole were a compassionate people—they were meant to be nature's levelers, the perfect mates, and compassion helped guarantee that. Jason could see Green's distraction.

"It was more than a power surge, wasn't it?" he asked delicately. "It would have to be to make the news down here."

Green nodded. Cory gave one last, tense look at the camera, and suddenly her eyes caught someone she knew, someone she was happy to see, and her face relaxed, and she smiled. Next to him, Jason caught his breath just before the camera moved to Officer Max, trying to look official and in charge when he was obviously off duty. Renny was clinging to his arm, wide-eyed, so tiny she was barely in the camera's range.

"It appears to be a power surge," Max was saying assuredly. "There's a lot of broken glass, but none of the shops appear to have sustained structural damage, and we're looking into the matter now."

"She's beautiful," Jason said dazedly beside Green. "How could I not have seen?"

"It's a selective beauty," Green said. "It only shines on those she selects." He smiled, more than a little bit smug. "I see it every moment I'm with her."

Jason touched his leader's hand, looking for attention and offering comfort. "What was it, then—that thing that frightened her enough to pull you out of our play?"

Green shook his head and shuddered. "We don't know. Cory describes it as sort of a smell… a stench of evil. Sort of like vampire, but it almost overwhelmed her in the middle of the day about forty miles from where it showed up tonight."

"A vampire. In the day." Jason's voice sounded hollowly. His animation disappeared, and he sat stonelike on the edge of the bed. Behind him, Letty, Princess, and Daniel moaned and shivered, burrowing into each other for shelter and comfort, and a pit opened in Green's stomach.

"You've encountered this," he stated.

"Lord Mist was not interested in our problems," Jason said, so miserably that Green sat on the bed next to the little man and wrapped his long body around him.

"I am not Lord Mist," he replied, a certain hard edge to his voice. Mist would have a lot to answer for to the Goddess, Green thought with anger. Leadership had a price—it required integrity, compassion, and a belief that your people mattered. Mist had possessed none of those things, and now Green was left to pick up the pieces. If Green hadn't already been responsible for his old lover's death, he probably would have sought him out and killed him (or at least have had Cory kill him) for the frightened, miserable look on Jason's face alone.

Jason nodded, quivering and frightened, even as Green sought to soothe him. "It terrorized us this summer," he said, voice low. "Five sylphs between August and October, when Goshawk moved in…."

"Five sylphs what?" Green asked sharply, knowing the answer but still disbelieving and angry. Damn Mist. Damn him, damn him, *fuck* him all to hell.

Jason shrugged, even in Green's embrace. "We wouldn't trouble you with this if your *ou'e'eir* hadn't been attacked," he apologized, and Green shook his head violently.

"You'd damn well better bother me with this, Jason—all of you!" Awkwardly, because he was half dragging Jason, he pulled himself onto the bed and opened his arms, allowing the other slightly built sylphs to burrow into him and into each other.

After a moment of shivering from them and calming sounds from him, Green finally spoke, his voice serious and stern. "Listen to me, all of you. You are leaders of your people—anything that hurts your people hurts you. I can feel that from you right now, and I believe it, right?"

"Yes, Lord Green," Jason said against his chest.

"Good. You understand that the only true power I have over you is the promise of safety I gave you, right?"

No answer there. Too many years of Mist, who felt that his very birth as a power-imbued sidhe was all that was required to earn him automatic obeisance.

"It's truth," Green said, trying not to wince at their complete lack of comprehension. Then he soldiered on. "I can't help you if I don't know what happened. And my *ou'e'eir* is naked without your help. So you need to give me details, am I being clear?"

They nodded, shivering against him, but no one ventured to talk, and he sighed. They had been abandoned by their leader, bereft of love, and now, apparently, singled out and hunted by this daytime vampire. It would be, he thought with patience, a very long road convincing them that he and Cory could be their salvation.

Later, after he'd rolled the sylph leaders to sleep, he summoned sprites to tend to his snarled hair and called Cory. Her voice, when she answered, was sated and tired, but alert. She had been lying in bed with Bracken, waiting for his call.

"You look good on camera, luv," he said gently in response to her sleepy hello.

"Bullshit, Green." Even over the phone, he could hear her eyes roll. "But it's nice of you to say so."

"Seriously—is everybody all right?"

She made a growling sort of grunt deep in her throat. "Grace isn't catatonic, I'm ambulatory, and the vampires have had the fear of God put into them," she summed up. "And, wonder of wonders, Bracken hasn't put me in a glass jar to be his sexual plaything in order to keep me out of danger and away from the big scary college campus." Her words were obviously not for Green's ear alone.

"The jar's in the shop," Bracken grumbled from behind her, and Green chuckled.

"Tell him he gets no sex if you're in a glass jar," he warned.

"The cat's out of *that* bag," she replied, her sleepy voice wicked. Then her voice sharpened. "Did it work, Green?" she asked. "Are the sylphs safe?"

Green sighed. "Well, yes, the binding worked... but considering the fact that hearing about your run-in with whatever the crap-all it was scared them catatonic, I don't think 'safe' is the right word."

Even over the phone he could hear her sucking air in past her lips and teeth. "That's bad," she said sharply. "Do they know what it is?"

Green growled a little in frustration. "I have no idea what they know. One mention of it and they fell completely apart. I had to spell them all to sleep just to get them to stop shaking."

"Oooh… that *really* is bad." Then suddenly, with humor, "Bracken, stop that…."

Green laughed. "Oh, no, by all means let him continue."

"Bracken… jeez… no…. Green, you may be able to make… penetrating… insights when you're being… uhm… penetrated, but…."

Green started to laugh at her choice of words, and then more as she only somewhat successfully fought Bracken off. "Well, if you're busy…."

"No… I mean I'm trying not to be, and *dammit, Bracken, this is important!*" she finished on a note of exasperation. Bracken's low chuckle echoed in the background, but it abruptly stilled when Cory added, "The sylphs were attacked by that thing too…." A low rumble from Bracken. She translated, "Green, do we have any idea how bad the attack went?"

"I think that five sylphs lost their lives—but I'm not even sure of that."

"Wonderful," she sighed. "Well, I've already told the vampires to only travel in twos and the werecreatures not to go out of the hill without a full-grown sidhe or a vampire in escort. I had everybody talk to our people outside the hill—I told them it smells like the evil dead and travels in the day and to stay the fuck away from it, and…," she trailed off. "And that's all I could think of."

"It sounds like you've got it covered." He was impressed, but then she had always impressed him.

"Green, there's nothing really new under the sun, is there?" she asked out of the blue.

"Uhm…," he said intelligently, because she had thrown him for a loop.

"I mean, I'm a sorceress. You knew what I was as soon as you saw the power, didn't you?"

"Yes, but there's usually a reason for that power. Ancestry, Goddess blessing, something. We were just so focused on getting you to accept it that we didn't dig any deeper."

"Which is fine," she said flatly. "Because my parents' families come from your part of the world, and I'd hate to find out I was your great-great-great-great-times-a-thousand-granddaughter or something."

"Impossible, luv," Green said gently, both amused and touched by her assumption that in order for him to love her they'd have to be related in some way. "I have no living children—you're safe from the sin of incest."

"Oh...." He could hear her make the connection. No *living* children. And this was obviously something he didn't want to discuss on the phone while Bracken was playing slap and tickle with her on the other side. "That must be part of your top three bad things," she said, alluding to a conversation they'd had when he'd confessed that Adrian's death hadn't been the worst thing that had ever happened to him. Although, in his words, it had ranked in the top three. "Which we'll talk about later. I was getting to a point."

"By all means." Goddess, he loved her so much he ached with it.

"The point is that I'm not, like, a freak of the Goddess's nature. There are lots and lots of us out there, but we're not anything new." Bracken had been quiet in the background, and Green could hear him speak softly in time with his own question.

"Which means...."

"It means that this thing has a *name*. It means that *someone* has encountered it before. Someone—probably a vampire, maybe even Andres—has heard a story or knew someone or read something in some old crappy book that was burned a thousand years ago about a vampire who moves in the daylight and stinks like evil."

"Ah." The light bulb suddenly went on over his head. "So you're talking research."

"Well, besides learning from the sylphs, yeah—you are out there talking to every freaking supernatural creature in NorCal, Central and Southern Oregon...."

"And Texas."

"Texas?"

"Gas station franchises, luv—I need to keep up our source of income."

"Ewww.... A pansexual sidhe in Texas. I'm sorry."

"So am I, but you were getting to a point."

"Oh, yeah…." Her voice tipped drunkenly, and he wondered how much longer she'd be lucid. "Research. You're going to be talking to beings as old as you, and you're accepted in the vampire circles. You can do research."

"Not to sound juvenile, my dearest one, but, well, *duh*…."

Cory's seriousness broke into a giggle. "Sorry, Green."

"Not at all, luv. It is a very good point—you were just getting very…."

"Pedantic," she finished for him, and for the millionth time he wondered what it must be like for her to have those words in her brain and rarely use them.

"Too right. Anyway, you're right. I'm out and about—I'll ask some pointed questions. The sylphs were either too afraid of Mist to tell him about the attacks, or they told Mist and he blew them off."

"Fucker." The word, bitten off angrily on the other end of the line, neatly summed up Green's opinion as well.

"Yes," he agreed. "But either way, this thing may have been around. It may even have attacked the humans, and just been labeled something else."

"A serial killer or something…. Hey—you do your research, I'll do mine."

"Good thinking. But not all tonight, okay?"

Cory laughed, her voice tired, and he was reminded of all she'd done since he'd left her miserable and distraught that morning. Next to him, on the fine linen sheets, the sylphs hmmed against the incursion of his voice, and thoughts of sleep became very sweet.

"No, sweetie, I won't do it all tonight. I even got Nicky to put date night off a day. To be honest, that whole 'smell of evil' thing has me a bit queasy."

"Good thinking," he said neutrally, hoping he didn't reveal how transparent she was. They'd only had one date night so far, but her relationship with Nicky had been strained ever since, and he had no idea how to fix it. Without her physical contact, Nicky would die, and that was unacceptable to both of them. But the alternative didn't sit well on a fragile human who'd had three lovers in too short a time, but who had loved them all until death and beyond. Casual sex was not only not in her experience, it wasn't in her vocabulary—and although this was far from casual, it was intimacy with someone she only loved as a friend, and it was as hard on her as not being a true lover was on Nicky. It was hard on Nicky, it was hard on her, and he didn't have a clue how to fix it.

"I heard that," she said dryly, and he had to smile. Whether she knew it or not, she was in his head at least as often as he was in hers, only she used intuition and an almost uncanny ability to read people instead of gifts from the Goddess. "And before we get going on this subject when there's not a fucking thing either of us can do to change it, I think I should tell you that I redecorated my room."

Now *that* was a surprise. "With paint?" he asked, faintly alarmed. The panels in his home were hand carved—by him—and he was a little protective of his beloved woodwork.

"With magic" came the blurry reply. She was fading fast.

"On purpose?"

"Don't we all wish! Wouldn't that be nice? 'I want the living room done in Adrian purple, Cory.... Have some sex and cross your eyes and see what happens....'" Even blurry, her sharp tongue could make him laugh.

"Well... how does it look?"

There was a rustle, and Bracken answered directly into the mouthpiece. "It looks wonderful, Green, but our girl is practically talking in her sleep. How 'bout we grill her another day, yes?"

"Don't let her out of your or Nicky's sight, okay?"

"Like Nicky would be any help...."

"Bracken, you know that only makes it harder on her...."

"Yeah." Brack chuffed out a breath. "You're right. You're right you're right you're right, and I'm being an asshole. It's just...." There was a sound, and Green assumed he was checking to see how far asleep Cory really was. Then he heard a rustling of covers and a padding of feet, and what Green assumed was the closing of the bathroom door. "Green, I wouldn't have any problem with it if she enjoyed herself, but...."

"But she's human, and she can't chase the shame away." There was a leaden silence on the phone line that spoke volumes.

"She could do it for you and Adrian," Bracken said unhappily.

"She's doing it for you," Green pointed out kindly.

"Why can't she do it with Nicky?"

"Oh, Bracken, I'd think that answer was obvious...."

"It is," Bracken said. "I just didn't want to presume."

"Well, presume away, because she's really going to need you after her date with Nicky, and it won't help if you don't see that."

"I wasn't much help tonight," Bracken said, the bitterness strong enough to taste.

"Don't blame yourself because you're not a vampire—apparently they're the only ones this thing affects."

"I don't blame myself for not being a vampire," Bracken spat, almost against his will. "I blame Adrian for marking her that third time and not preparing her for what it would mean."

Another silence, this one so filled with pain that Green was surprised the sylphs didn't wake up drowning in it. "He was dying at the time, Bracken. I think it was one last kiss...."

"Why couldn't he have kissed you—or me, for that matter? Why did he have to mark the one person he loved who would be hurt the most?"

Green's throat tightened, and he could hear tears in Bracken's voice. This was the first time either of them had spoken aloud about the final mark on Cory's neck, and what it cost her to wear their lover's final kiss on her soul. "You know the reason for that too, my brother," he said at last. "Because as much as we loved him, he was not perfect."

"Fuck."

"Crawl back into bed, Bracken. Hold her next to your heart, and be thankful that you can do so. We'll research this threat, we'll face this enemy, and we'll protect each other. It's all we've got."

"You're all we've got," Bracken said at last. "I love you, leader. Be safe."

"You too. Good night."

I love you, leader. Be safe. The words echoed in Green's head as he lay in the strange bedroom, surrounded by the still, quietly breathing bodies of the bespelled sylphs. So many ways Bracken could feel about Green, who had been Adrian's beloved and then Cory's, and what he said from his heart was *I love you. Be safe.* He was a good man, Bracken Brine Granite op Crocken. Op Crocken *Green,* now, and that thought filled Green with pride. They had all taken his name. All his new children, all of his new *lovers,* and they had deliberately taken his name and bonded themselves into a family. It was something he had trouble getting his own people to do, with their traditions and their pride and their absolute certainty that they were the Goddess's chosen ones and that no one else could measure up. But with the addition of Cory and the death of Adrian, it was happening on a larger and larger scale. The marks that those who had fought in the city now bore on their bodies was proof of it, and those sidhe on his hill who hadn't been there to be marked had gone out and acquired their own heart's-blood tattoos to show their deference to him and to Cory as well. If Green had taught the people in his hill one thing, it was that there was safety in family, and with their triumph in San Francisco, there was pride in family as well.

There was responsibility in being the leader of such a large family, and with that responsibility came fear for them. He sighed. The four bodies burrowing into his now counted as family. And now he had an obligation to them, just as he did to his hill. And that's why he was here, and why Bracken was with Corinne Carol-Anne Kirkpatrick op Crocken Green.

I love you, leader. Be safe. And more than a little bit lonely.

CORY
Dating Skills

THE NEXT day we did very little. The store would be closed that night, because although the brownies and sprites would have the door fixed and the inventory stocked and the electricity back in a day, none of the other stores would be ready to open, and we didn't want to stand out, so none of us (and we were mostly werecreatures and midlevel fey) needed to go in. I slept in late with Bracken, and we met Max and Renny in the upper-level kitchen for a long breakfast. I'd put out some serious power the night before, something that always drained me physically, and I was ready for a nap after we had all done our time on the phone to enroll in our classes. Bracken bitched some more about that, but this time he had reason. I mean, of all things, why did six people who weren't remotely human need a human sexuality course? But all the other selections made sense, so even that was half-hearted.

Green called around eleven to tell me that he would be "otherwise engaged" with the sylphs that night—something he felt he had to do, because now that he'd mentioned the big black hanging stench of evil to the leaders, the entire sylphan enclave was trembling with abject fear. Green mentioned lots of picnic blankets and being outside, so I assumed he was going for a couple of sylph orgies in the woods to chill them out. The thought of my sidhe lover making love in the woods made everything from my nipples on down tingle, and before the nap, I made Bracken a very happy man.

The day was so kick-back that when I awoke from my nap to find it dark outside, I was a little surprised to see Grace sitting in the kitchen, staring at the phone with such intensity that I was afraid it would burst into flame. I mean, she was a vampire, and her eyes were whirling—it seemed like *something* should have been happening.

I sat next to her and stared at the phone, wondering what was up.

"Chloe said she'd call me tonight," Grace said quietly. "We tried, but we couldn't mindwipe the boys, not without really messing up their heads." She smiled. "Stubborn little goobers. But I gave her a choice whether she wanted her memories or wanted me to take it all away. She said she'd call me tonight."

Oh. Well. I looked at the phone apprehensively, waiting for it to ring and break Grace's heart.

Renny and Nicky wandered in and asked us what we were doing. "Chloe's calling back tonight," I explained, and now there were four of us, staring at the phone in quiet agony. We all loved Grace.

A group came in—Sweet and Cord, two of Green's higher sidhe lieutenants, and Leah and Anthony, werepumas. They looked at us, then looked at each other, and Sweet shook her head. "Humans," she said bemusedly, although none of us were human anymore. Then she and Cord wandered outside. Leah, a pretty dark-haired girl who had been one of the last of Adrian's saved before me, sat down next to me with Anthony behind her. Bracken wandered in and parked himself behind me in a similar way.

"What the hell are we doing here?" Leah asked casually after a few minutes of breathless silence.

"We're waiting for Grace's daughter to call," I breathed back, and to everybody's surprise, Leah started laughing.

"My God—don't you know a watched phone never rings? Do you people remember *anything* from your dating days?"

"I haven't dated in forty years," Grace retorted. "And when I was dating, it was my childhood sweetheart—the guy I married."

"On my first date ever, Adrian bit me on the neck," I said musingly. "I don't think I've ever had to wait for a phone call after that."

"We didn't count in San Francisco?" Nicky asked in mock hurt.

"Absolutely not."

"Why not?"

"For one thing, Renny was there," I answered promptly. "For another, I didn't shave my legs and you didn't pay."

"Important criteria to remember," Bracken breathed in my ear.

"My legs were shaved yesterday," I told him sweetly. "What about you, Renny?"

"If you don't count the guy my parents set me up with for the prom, my first real date was with Mitch. I spent my time giving him a blow job so intense he *had* to bite me so we'd spend the rest of our lives together," she said, so casually that she didn't see the rest of us turning our heads slowly from the phone to stare at her. "It worked, and now I'm furry." And Mitch, sweet, lost Mitch, wasn't here to share it with her.

Grace blinked at tiny, fragile-looking Renny in shock. "Renny, sweetie—if that was your first date ever, how did you know how to give that blow job?"

"Porn," Renny replied obliviously, her eyes still fixed on the phone. "Lots and lots of porn."

Our mouths slowly sank open, and about the time they hit bottom, the phone rang. Grace grabbed for it so frantically it knocked out of her hand and into Leah's lap, and Leah, in spite of her earlier mockery, picked it up quickly and with surprising gentleness put it back into Grace's hand, where it rang one more time. With a deep breath—a residual human gesture—Grace pressed the Talk button and raised the phone to her ear.

"Hello?" Breathless silence. Deep human sigh. "Hi, Chloe. Yes, it really is me."

The rest of us melted out of the kitchen like fog. On my way out, hand in hand with Bracken, I saw Nicky give me a long, considering kind of look. Then he smiled brightly, like a child with a secret. We retired to the front sitting room—Renny and I with knitting, the others with books and CD players and other diversions—and we sat quietly, like those people you see in movies like *Sense and Sensibility* and *Emma*. We talked softly or played games or read or, well, knit. Cord and Sweet came out with an ancient backgammon board, and Bracken's parents brought out a *Lord of the Rings* chess set, and soon the living room was easily busy with fifteen or so of Green's people, as it was every night we didn't have a formal banquet in the great burnished hall downstairs. Often we watched movies or television, but the second half of the TV season hadn't started yet, and tonight we just sat like family and chatted back and forth and enjoyed each other's company.

In four other parts of Green's great house that tunneled through the better part of this hill straddling the landscape change of the foothills, I knew there were similar scenes of people gathering. In the summer when this had happened, it had been in an atmosphere of anxiety, because we'd been under attack. In the fall, I'd been too hurt from Adrian's death to even come out of bed on my frantic, starved weekend visits. But since I'd come home before Christmas and stayed willingly, and in peace, I'd grown accustomed to the evening mélange of Green and Adrian's people. Green and I often visited the other family rooms like parents visiting their children's rooms at night. Or like a monarch and his lady would visit their subjects to make sure all was well.

The vampires' family room sat low in the basement of the darkling. It had a plush burgundy rug and giant leather couches the color of oxblood. The vamps tended to watch way too many horror movies for my taste, but they were always happy to see me, so they'd pause the movie and talk to me about their rising, who was sucking on whom, and who had seduced a mortal that worried the rest of the kiss.

The lower fey had two speeds—a thousand miles a minute, and passed out in the corners of their vast attic of a sitting room. Green had decorated it with ornate old furniture and lots of nooks and crannies, and if you looked very carefully you could always find sleeping (or fornicating) sprites, gnomes, pucks, pixies, little trolls, gremlins, or yunwi-tsunsdi (the Native American counterparts to all of the above). When Green and I visited, the swarm of chittering, swarming littles would stop and flock around us, telling us stories that often had no beginning, no end, and no single voice. We would nod our heads appreciatively and answer in the right places, and they would touch our faces and stroke our hair and occasionally curl up on our shoulders and coo at us until they slept, tangled in our hair.

The midlevel fey—the sylphs, nymphs, redcaps, kelpies, ogres, and the werecreatures—all seemed to hang in a room toward the middle of the middle floor. It was a vast room of dark, weathered boards and shiny brass. This room was raucous, with a pool table, a dartboard, and lots of beer—in spite of the fact that none of the species actually got drunk, and drugs had no effect on them, many of them seemed to like the taste of beer. There was arm wrestling, poker, and the occasional honest fight that ended in camaraderie and singing of old rock-and-roll songs. This was a bar like my father had gone to when he was in the mood, and like my friends had borrowed their older brothers' and sisters' driver's licenses to get into when I'd had friends in high school. Green and I would always be asked to share a table and share a drink. I wasn't twenty-one yet, and I hated alcohol. They kept soda under the bar on ice just for me.

The sidhe—including the bean sidhe, daoine sidhe, and the occasional Tuatha Dé Danann—held a more dignified court. I had tried to get Green to explain which one he was and which one Bracken was, but he had simply shrugged. "Some of the Goddess's get like to put themselves into little slots with labels, luv. Bracken, me, Arturo, even Mist and some of the others—

we just prefer to be." The ones who grouped themselves in this room may have known their station and their slot and their label, but they did not print it clearly and wear it on their foreheads. They came in all colors (as did the littles and the midlevel fey) from magenta to azure in both hair and skin, and they often sat reading poetry (mostly by mortals) and singing or playing instruments that even Shakespeare and Milton had not known of. When we visited they all stood and bowed and clasped silky, scented hands with my plain warm mortal ones. At one point, the sidhe had resented me and my place at Green's side, but Adrian's death and our subsequent victory in San Francisco had softened their vision of me, and I was treated with nothing but deference and grace. In the sidhe room, they respected my education, and I learned more about literature and history from these creatures who had lived it than I often learned from my professors who had devoted their lives to trying to know it.

But as exotic as the rest of Green's vast hill could be, my favorite place in it was still the living room with the clean light oak and white brocade where I'd woken up, scared and bewildered, the morning after I'd seen the uglier side of the supernatural world I'd entered—and had wanted it even more. Green's sitting room attracted a little bit of everybody—but then, *I* was tight with a little bit of everybody. Grace and the other vampires liked to visit here, because, hullo, I was their queen. Green and Bracken, of course, had sidhe friends who frequented this room. Bracken's parents were midlevel fey, Nicky and Renny were shape-shifters—and the sprites and littles seemed to have a *really* strong attachment to both Renny and me. They would hover about my person until Bracken or Green wrapped warm, tender arms around me or nuzzled my cheek or touched my skin, and then they'd scatter, waiting to perch again.

They hovered tonight as I sat and leaned against Bracken, knitting a sweater for him. I had grown up an only child, and my father was a trucker, and my mother waited tables at night. I think the thing I loved most about Green's hill was these quiet moments of massive, sometimes quarreling, but always bonded family. This was Green's hill. This was my home. And it was threatened once again, and now more than ever, I'd kill to defend it.

THE NEXT night was date night. Renny and Bracken sat in my room and gave wardrobe advice. Renny tended to advise toward the hot and chic—

skin-hugging, tummy-baring sweaters, low-riding jeans with lace-up sides. Bracken, for all that he'd been wearing a mullet and seducing mortals that dressed just like that, tended toward the classic—midthigh skirts, flattering, button-up blouses, lacy shawls. His gift to me this Christmas had been a handmade knit shawl made out of something glittering and silver-gold, so fine and soft and lofty that I was terrified of wearing it because it was so beautiful and so precious. He came up to me this night and wrapped it around my bare shoulders as I looked critically at the sleeveless black turtleneck and matching skirt that I'd finally settled on.

"That's perfect!" Renny breathed, delighted.

"No," I muttered, trying not to scrunch my face. I turned to Bracken and touched his proud, fine-boned jaw, and suddenly there was only the two of us in the world. "I won't wear this for anyone but you, beloved."

"Then wear it for me tonight, and enjoy yourself," he said softly. "Remember that I love you, and I love you as much for what you do to save your friend as I love you for what you do willingly with me, and don't worry about being awkward or disappointing. Go and have fun. Humans go on dates to have fun."

Have fun. Fair enough—I could do that. "Uhm...." I didn't want to ask. I had no right to ask.

"I'll be here when you get back," he said, as though suddenly he was in my head like Green. Maybe he was. Mine and Green's telepathy got stronger with time, maybe Bracken's was too. "No matter when you get back."

I nodded and managed a shaky smile. "Are you sure the makeup's okay?" I asked Renny one more time.

"How in the fuck would I know?" she shot back. "The last time I wore makeup was for my senior ball photo."

"Who'd you go with?" I asked in abstraction. I knew it couldn't have been Mitch—but she'd been living at home, and her parents had been trying to set her up with their friends' boys all through her senior year.

"Chad Collins," she said in disgust.

"Charming Collins-glass?" I asked in surprise. He'd been in my class, actually, and even I had heard of his reputation.

"Who?" asked Bracken, a little lost.

"He was the high school lothario," I replied, suddenly embarrassed. "He had sort of a reputation for...." I stopped and probably turned fuchsia. Bracken's quizzical look suddenly blossomed into a full-fledged smile.

"Of being as big around as a collins glass," Renny finished dryly. "I never found out, but not because he didn't try."

"What's a collins glass?" Brack asked, clearly intrigued now.

Renny held her tiny hands together, thumb tucked well under thumb, fingertip to fingertip to make a tube. "It's a tumbler, about this big around and about yea high."

Bracken grinned suddenly and took in my brightly colored face. He started to laugh delightedly. "Stop gloating," I muttered under my breath. I was saved from the rest of this horribly awkward conversation by Nicky's hesitant knock at the door.

So that was how I answered the door, flushed from thinking about Bracken's sex and dolled up to the nines. Nicky's eyes glowed brilliantly when he took me in, and he executed a neat little bow, taking my hand up for a kiss.

"You look amazing," he said. "And perfect for where we're going."

"Thanks," I said sincerely. "You look pretty spiffy yourself." He had on a silvery green dress shirt and gray slacks, and looked older than he had the day before yesterday in the lobby at school. "So, where are we going?"

It was a preternatural dance club, actually, tucked away behind a church on Bell Road, skirting the newly developed strip malls that kept springing up around the foothills like mushrooms. It was run by Mitch's older brother, Ray—Green had made him the manager there to give him something to do after his brother's death. And Ray, who had been lost and moving from one small-time band to another before his brother's death, had taken the show of responsibility and run with it. He called it Mitchell's Alley.

It had been magicked and spelled well, so the outside looked small, about the size of a regular ranch-style house, but the inside was huge, with vaulted ceilings and a good-sized stage and dance floor. In the darkness I could see that the walls were rough-hewn wood, and the strobe lights were as much magic as electricity. There was a bar—burnished wood with brass—and a small kitchen hidden off to the side. The interior was crowded with supernatural creatures—so much so that if I summoned even the least little bit of power, they practically made the room glow—but they were moving to the heartbeat of bass and drum like any other humans, the music was throbbing and loud, and for the first time in my life, I felt like I was on a real date.

It was actually sort of fun.

I'd never gone out dancing before—the closest I'd ever come to it was dancing to my boom box in my own bedroom. Dancing in a club, surrounded by beating bodies with a visceral commitment to the music that vibrated up from the soles of our feet, was a skin-tingly, womb-throbbing, breath-catching sort of rush. On the dance floor, it didn't matter that I didn't love Nicky like I should have. What mattered was that his hand on my midriff felt warm and possessive and *good.* What mattered was that the hard line of his front against my back was electric, and the music *forced* our pelvises to tilt, to grind, to make contact with each other. The things he said in my ear, while not crazy-sexy erotic, were funny and charming and witty, and they made me want to stay close to him with the intimacy of noise cocooning us together. The sheer joy of physical activity after a month of being sick or treated like an invalid was actually sort of a turn-on in itself—but the truth was I *had* been sick, and I had been donating blood almost nightly, and I was grateful when, after forty-five minutes or so, Ray Hammond came wading through the mass of people to tap me on the shoulder and gesture for me to follow him off the dance floor.

Back by the kitchen, there were people yelling food orders for the limited food menu, people hollering drink orders for the extended drink menu (mostly juice, but some of the weres still drank alcohol for taste), and the crash of pots, pans, glasses, and bottles, but it was *still* quieter than the dance floor. Ray had his brother's dark hair and poet-brown eyes, but he had lines of grief etched on his face and a toughness to his jaw that Mitch had never had the chance to develop. Tonight, his expression was a combination of worry, irritation, and embarrassment.

"I hate to bother you, Cory," he started out. "I mean, I know it's date night and everything."

I felt my eyes widen. Did every preternatural creature in NorCal know about date night? But Ray kept going, and my personal life faded into the background.

"Normally I'd wait until Arturo or one of the vamps made the rounds, you know—but you're here, and this…. Lady Cory, this guy is bad."

I'd gone to school with Mitch and Ray—although, admittedly, I'd been a freshman when Ray had been a senior—and ordinarily the absurdity of the "Lady Cory" would have made me laugh. But he was getting more and more agitated, and he was asking something of me that it was my obligation to give. Hey, Green's gotta get laid in the woods, I gotta kick bad-guy ass, right?

"What is he?" I asked seriously.

Ray shook his head, and because he was a werecat the gesture made it look like one of those shivery things that cats do when they wake up from a nap. "He's a were of some sort, but... there's something off about him, Cory. He's... I mean, you know how I became werecat, right?"

From the infected needle of a werecreature who hadn't yet figured out that drugs didn't work on a werecat's metabolism. Mitch had used the same needle, and *poof*, like that, no more drug problem. And a whole host of other issues to deal with—all things were a trade-off.

"Yeah, I know."

"Well, this guy—I'm sure he's using. I shot smack for two years—I know when someone's riding on something and when they're coming down. This guy, he's jonesing. I know it."

"Jonesing for *what*?" Nicky asked. He'd stayed behind me, his hand still wrapped around my waist, his body still intimately close to mine, and it hadn't occurred to me to move. "As far as I know, there's nothing out there that will get us buzzed."

"I don't know." Ray shook his head. "But he's like a drunk obnoxious customer or a junkie needing a fix in any other bar, except in this one, I don't want him to change into whatever the hell he is, because the danger of this place is that you've got hormones, pheromones, and big sex music—one strong change, in plain sight of everybody else, and this place becomes a zoo in mating season."

Swell. My own attraction for Nicky dimmed a little, and we took a mutual step away. I'd always wondered how Leda had managed to get ravished by that swan, but I certainly didn't want to see how it worked with a big predatory Avian.

"Where is he?" I asked with a confidence I didn't feel.

The look of relief on Ray's face was gratifying and terrifying at once. What if I got clobbered? Then I heard the angry voices by the corner of the bar closest to the kitchen, and all thoughts of fear disappeared.

"What in the fuck do you mean I'm cut off? I'm not drunk, bitch— where in the fuck is the manager of this shithole?"

This was Ray's place—this was *Green's* place, and nobody talked shit like that in Green's place.

"I'm sorry," I said, moving on my own past Ray to where the owner of that slurred voice stood. "Can I help you?"

"Only if you're the fucking manager." I squinted at the young man, power in my eyes, and tried to figure out why he was so... so... psychically *blurry*. He should have been a good-looking young man in his early twenties, a were of some sort, with blond hair and blue eyes. But something was off. His hair, which should have been the color of wheat, was faded—it looked like wheat-colored yarn that was more gray than gold. His eyes had once been as blue of Adrian's, I'm sure of it, but something had... faded them out. They were dirty blue now, like the sky in LA. His bone structure, his musculature... everything was shading out, like a vampire in a photograph. And judging from his swagger and his obnoxiousness, part of his personality had gone with his physical and metaphysical appearance. And to add to the faded look of the junkie, he *smelled*.

"I'm the owner's woman, sweetheart," I said absently. "And who have you been letting *feed* off of you?"

"I'm not taking no orders from no cunt banging the owner." The guy smirked, and the really obscene word (to a girl used to dirty language!) shocked me away from my speculations and right into the here and now. Without thinking about fear, I grabbed the front of the guy's oversized rap-hero sweatshirt and pulled him to me, face-to-face. My other hand went behind me, opened, and Nicky slapped his hand in mine. It's a smart man who knows when to be a friend, when to be a lover, and when to be a battery.

"That's fine, asswipe," I growled, "because this cunt isn't taking any orders from a jerkoff who doesn't know he's being poisoned and bled dry. Now tell me this, asshole, who is feeding from you?" I'd done this before with Officer Max, almost inadvertently. When you ask a question with power in your voice, with a bone-deep certainty and a lot of fucking magic at your disposal telling you that you deserve a good answer, even strong minds feel compelled to buckle.

This guy was hooked on something, someone was bleeding him to death, and his mind was nowhere near as strong as Max's.

His face went immediately slack, tears formed at the corners of his eyes, and he wobbled as he stood. "I don't know...." His voice trailed off. "I don't remember. But it feels... it feels...." His voice became dreamy, sexy, the voice of a junkie talking about a fix. "It feels sooooo good."

"Okay," I said, nodding. This was bad. If this guy couldn't remember who was poisoning him, we couldn't get to the malignant source of this disturbance. I looked up to see who the guy was with, expecting a posse of similarly dressed obnoxious scumbags, but what I saw instead was a tired-looking little werewoman, tears in her eyes, looking at the asshole in my hands with the sorrow of a loved one watching her beloved slide into madness. "So you don't know who's making you into a giant hemorrhoid. Can you tell me who made you?"

"Jon Chase," he said sadly. "He's dead now."

I blinked. I knew the names of the werecreatures who had died when Crispin and Sezan had made their moves last summer, and this was not one of them. *"Marcus."* I gave out the mental call—something I hadn't done much of yet, at least not deliberately—and got an almost immediate, startled response. *"No, no, don't panic. Who knows the roster of the weres right now?"* It used to be Adrian. The werecreatures made a convenient, friendly, renewable food supply—and just like Green took care of his people, Adrian had trained the vampires to take care of theirs.

"I do," Marcus said readily in my head. It was weird talking to the vampires like this, actually. When I pictured the vampire to talk to him, I could taste his blood in my mouth. *"Why?"*

"Jon Chase. Ring any bells?"

"Not a one."

"Well, we need to find out who he looked to. He's dead, and one of his children is here at Mitchell's Alley, and he's seriously fucked up."

"Do you need backup?"

Goddess bless him. *"No—but I do need cleanup. Send someone over here to pick this guy up and see what's poisoning him."* Sudden thought. *"And Marcus, don't let anybody feed off of him. I've got a very bad smell...."* Wait a minute.... *"In fact, I've got a really familiar smell off this guy, if you know what I mean."*

He did. There was a sudden impression in my head of four different vampires fluttering toward my location, and a reassurance that, if I brought this guy outside, he would be taken care of. *"Finish up your date, leader. We all like Nicky,"* Marcus finished, and I felt myself flushing even in my head. Everybody really did know what I was going to do with Nicky tonight, and why. Fucking beautiful.

"Okay, asshole," I said almost to myself, and the guy actually jumped. I realized that everybody—Ray, Nicky, the guy I was shoving against the bar, his girlfriend, hell, even the bartender, everybody!—had been waiting in breathless anticipation while I apparently solved quadratic equations in my head. "Don't stress, it's all good. We're going to hook you up with some real vampires, not the evil undead trash you've been hanging with, and we're going to see what you've been fucking with. But right now, I need to know two things—what's your name, and who do you look to?"

"My name?" And I suddenly ached for this guy—he really looked like he couldn't remember. "He calls me Lean Cuisine."

Oh, *ewwww.* A bad guy with a bad sense of humor. And no respect for this guy as a person, apparently.

"Well, that sucks for you, sweetie," I said with real sympathy. "But what did Mom and Dad call you?"

"I... I don't...." Mom and Dad were too far away, I guessed, either in affection or in distance, or even in the last time he'd visited.

My voice lowered, and I looked at the miserable, dark-haired, sloe-eyed woman huddling behind the guy. "Okay, sweetheart, what do you call your beloved?"

Suddenly the boy's blurry features grew solid, real, grounded. This was real, I thought. This was probably the last real thing left to him. "Ellen," he said softly. "Ellen Beth Shrick Williams."

I felt my eyes tear up, just a little. Ellen Beth Shrick Williams might have just saved her husband's life. "She took your name, didn't she?"

A sudden, sweet smile of pride. "My girl loves me."

Swallow. "Okay, Mr. Williams, we'll remember the rest later. Right now, we're going to get you the hell out of here before your madness spreads, right?"

A weak nod, and my nerveless fingers released their clench on Williams's shirt. Ray took the guy by the elbow, giving me a disbelieving stare, and Ellen Beth turned to follow. I called after her, and she turned to me reluctantly. Well, I could be a scary bitch.

"His name's Christopher," she said softly, fidgeting with her purse strap. "And he didn't used to be like this."

"What are you?" I asked, and she understood that immediately.

"Dogs," she said with a smile. "Sort of like Labrador retrievers, but taller and dappled." I understood completely—like the kitties and the Avians, they often didn't turn into any specific *breed* of their creature, but more into their own personality's interpretation of that creature. She'd said it with sort of a proud little smile, and I knew that most were-animals were proud and happy to talk about their furry sides.

"I bet you're beautiful," I said gently. Then, grimly, with purpose, "But I need to know what he's been looking like lately."

Ellen Beth shivered. "It started about a month ago. He met some guy at school...."

"Sac State?" My attention sharpened.

"Yes. Chris only had a semester to go. But ever since Christmas.... He didn't get his financial aid, he didn't reregister...."

"Did he tell you why?"

She shook her head. She couldn't have been much older than I was, but suddenly she looked aged and worn. "And his... his animal.... He's getting clear on the edges, and mean. Chris never used to be mean...."

"Does he smell different?" I asked, wondering. Only the vampires and I had been able to smell it so far.

A negative shake of the head. "No, but he... *sounds* different. His voice doesn't sound like his own. When he's turned, his breathing sets my hackles up."

Well. Vampirically evil species-specific cross-sensory stimulation.... That was no help at all.

"We'll try to help him," I said, chewing on my lower lip in worry. "But we'll need whatever else you can remember. Some vampires are going to be outside to take him with them—I want you to go too. He said someone named Jon Chase made him. Who do you guys look to?"

Ellen Beth shrugged. "No one. We come from Southern California— we all sort of just left each other alone down there. Jon came with us, but I haven't seen him in a while. He hooked up with a new... I thought it was a girlfriend, but I saw them together about a month ago. It was from a distance and he was with a man—a really good-looking guy. I didn't know Jon swung that way, but he seemed really happy. Until Chris said that just now, I had no idea he was dead." Her voice caught, thickened, as though this news had just caught up with her.

Great. "Well, we look after each other up here. The vampires care for the were-folk, the were-folk feed the vamps, the sidhe watch the vamps in the day...."

"'She'? Who's 'she'?"

"Elves? Fey? Really tall, beautiful, immortal people?" There *must* be fey in SoCal, right?

Ellen Beth laughed. "You mean like fairies?"

"That's kind of a... er... blanket term," I said, wondering if I should come up with a beginner's pamphlet in cryptozoology. Nicky shifted next to me, not impatiently, but still. I sighed. "Look—I'm on a date here, and in my world, that's more important than it sounds. I'm going to leave you with the vamps. They'll take care of you, they'll take care of Chris. They're going to roll his mind and try to get some more info, but they won't snack off of either of you, so don't panic, okay? They're going to take you to Green's hill—I'll be there later tonight. I've got school Monday morning—"

"So do I!"

"Good. You can ride with us if we don't resolve this tomorrow. Stay with us, in fact. I'll have Grace set you up a room."

"Now, wait just a minute—"

"No," I said shortly. "I really can't. Something has already attacked us—something that has apparently taken a big chunk out of your beloved's mind. You're in danger, he's almost lost, and we're the people who can take care of you and keep you safe. If you don't want our help, I can't force it on you, but your husband has no choice. He's a danger to my people the way he is, and that cannot be allowed. You can go with the vampires—and with him—or you're on your own with that big nasty whatever-the-fuck it is out there to get you too. I feel for you, you'll never know how much, but right now, those are your choices."

Ellen Beth looked at me, stunned and frightened, and I took pity on her. I felt my face—which had been in an all-hard-and-military, trying-to-prove-I'm-actually-a-leader kind of mode—soften a little bit.

"It'll be all right. You can come and go as you please—I just think you're in danger, and I know Chris is a danger to himself and to us."

She swallowed and nodded, and I gave a little mental chirrup to Marcus about what I'd just decided and got the *all's good* in return.

With Nicky at my side, we moved outside and joined Ray and his charge in a clearing beyond the parking lot, about twenty yards from the club itself. We could hear the music throbbing clearly in the crystal night, and my hips shifted. I had been free on the dance floor, I thought sadly, and now I was outside of that freedom, bound by my duty. Of course, one glance at Ellen Beth's face and suddenly the constraints of duty didn't seem like such a bad thing, and I let go of a sigh on a shiver of plumed breath. It had stopped raining this morning, so there were still big, weighty clouds scudding across the sky, but past them you could see, brilliant and close, diamond stars and purple-black void. It was a lovely night, although a freaking cold one. I had wrapped my shawl around my waist on the overheated dance floor, but now Nicky, in a show of chivalry that surprised me, loosened the knot and pulled the baby-bunny soft wool around my shoulders, and like magic I was warm again. He rubbed his hands over my arms, and I leaned back into him in gratitude.

"Nice move, Kestrel," I approved lightly.

"I've been studying up," he said in my ear.

"There's a book on this?"

"No. I've been watching Bracken and Green." He said it levelly, as though broaching a difficult subject, and I did my best to make it an easy one for him.

"Good choices, both," I replied and heard him breathe out in relief.

We stood there until the darkness started to flutter majestically and black sails obscured the moon. Watching vampires come in from a distance is like watching a movie where things get bigger in super fast-forward with a strobe light. There's a heartbeat, and I see a slight motion. Another pulse, and it's a bat. A throb of blood thunders in my ears, and it's a condor. Another crush of blood, whooshing my breath from my lungs, and it's a human-sized creature with a pale flash of skin and a sail of black trench coat—and then Marcus comes to a completely still stop only a few feet in front of me, three other vampires setting down lightly at about the same time. They all looked so imposing coming in like a black sail of doom that I was forced to giggle when Marcus gave me a casual hullo and that shy grin.

"Heya, Marcus," I said with a smile. "Where's Phillip tonight?"

Marcus grimaced. "He's found a new lunch-buddy—eating out tonight."

I rolled my eyes. Phillip and Marcus had been strictly heterosexual as humans, but that first frightening year of blood hunger and skin hunger and flesh hunger tended to make impossible bedfellows merely strange. Being so completely hetero, and forced into a position where drawing lines in the chromosome pool was pretty much impossible, had made Marcus and Phillip into a sort of Chandler/Joey pair of roommates with the occasional sexy twist. As a pair, they equaled one solid leader or two fantastic lieutenants. As a couple, they were constantly on the odds because someone was always looking for a little bit of poontang with his lunch.

"I thought he was snacking on Tasha these days," Ray asked with some curiosity. It always helped to know the ins and outs of the preternatural dating scene when you were running one of the few almost exclusively preternatural clubs in the area.

Another twist of that quietly handsome face. "Sometimes, when she's not trying to rip out his intestines with her hind claws." He turned toward Chris and Ellen Beth. "So—are these our new lost?"

I blinked. That's what they'd called Adrian's strays. "Well, they've actually already been found," I said cautiously. "Look at Williams. Does he seem odd to you?"

Marcus glanced at Chris, then blinked, and I watched his vampire come out. His eyes started to glow faintly red, and his nostrils flared to the point of changing the structure of his nose to something sharper and more predatory. His jawline extended, not fully, but enough for his fangs to emerge.

"He's not...." Marcus's voice had changed with his face, and it sounded rough and growly. "He's *faded* around the edges. And...." That inhumanly altered nose wrinkled, which looked *really* strange. "And he *smells*." Marcus turned toward me. "You're right. He smells like it— whatever the fuck it was that attacked us the other night—but faint... like the other night we were swimming in it, and now it's twenty miles away upwind."

I nodded. "His girl says it's like a sound. Nicky, do you hear it?"

Nicky nodded, his chin digging a little into my shoulder in a way that was intimate and not at all unpleasant. "When you put it that way.... The other day at school, I did hear something. Sort of like road construction on speed... and then you keeled over and I forgot all about it."

"So the vamps and I smell it, the weres hear it. When you get back, see if Bracken or the other sidhe have any sort of sensory reaction to him, and then find a way to keep him the fuck away from the rest of the household." I turned my head to see Chris Williams hanging on to Ellen Beth, weeping helplessly and swearing viciously as he clung to her, nearly dragging her down. "This is bad, Marcus. Anything that can addict a werecreature and send vampires to their knees... this is a serious threat, and we need to isolate it from the rest of the hill."

Marcus nodded. "We've got a room where we put newborn vamps—steel reinforced—it's practically a safe, with little tiny airholes for the weres who volunteer to be dinner. They're pretty comfy. We'll put him up there."

"Give his girl the option of staying with him or rooming somewhere else nearby, and brief someone who's up in the day...."

"Duh. Arturo and Bracken will know everything...." Marcus smiled reassuringly and patted the shoulder that Nicky wasn't digging his chin into, then gestured to the other vampires. In movements too fast to follow with the eye, one of them grabbed Williams, one grabbed Ellen Beth, and the three of them leaped into the air in a bound of tautly fluttering black trench coats.

"We all love Nicky," Marcus said before he took his own bound into the air. "You keep him alive, we'll do our part." And then he was gone, and Nicky and I were alone under the brittle-cold night sky.

The throb of the music reached us from the club. Nicky wrapped his arms around me and we moved together, dancing silently in the still purple night. It was not a slow song, it was pulsing and visceral—raw music. Nicky rocked back a little onto his haunches and pulled me into the cradle of his hips until I could feel the ridge of his erection nestling in the cleft of my ass. I startled, pushing myself forward, but his hands wrapped securely around my waist and pulled me back against him.

"Shhhh...," he whispered in my ear, a sensation that always made my panties flood. I'd thought it was because it was Adrian or Green or Bracken doing the whispering, and I was almost disappointed to find out it was the nerve endings in my ear and not the man. "Shhh," Nicky said again, rubbing his hands on my arms and down around my waist again, his warmth seeping into my bones. Werecreatures always ran supernaturally warm, and right now Nicky's light-speed metabolism was the only thing keeping my teeth from chattering. I relaxed just a little, the soft flesh of my now skinny bottom easing against him.

"It's okay," he said again. "We're supposed to."

We're supposed to. We were supposed to make love. Everybody knew we were supposed to make love. Bracken had given me his shawl and his blessing. Green had taken me on a walking tour of Nicky's body and had loved Nicky himself. And Nicky had been nothing if not my fellow student, my helper, and my friend. And he was warm and the music was moving my body, and it was time that I took my lover to bed.

I leaned fully against him and could feel him between my legs, separated only by the fabric of his clothing. A sound ripped out of his throat, a groan that had nothing to do with pain and everything to do with the fact that I could feel the head of his phallus, the little ridge that bordered it, rubbing at the cleft of my bottom.

I took Nicky's two hands in my own and lowered them down to the hem of my skirt and the tights on my thighs beneath, and raised them, palms down, up my thighs, slowly. His hands took over of their own volition, following a course up under my skirt until it was rucked up to my hips, and his warm, warm hands found their way to my stomach and under the elastic of the tights. My own hands reached behind me and found purchase on his hips as he smoothed his way down my abdomen. My stomach clenched in reaction, and the tights were rolled down my narrow little hips, puddling at my feet and my fuck-me shoes. With squirmy little movements I toed off my shoes, the motion bringing my now bare body up against Nicky's groin.

He groaned again, a raw, tearing sound, and I reached behind me and loosened his belt, listening for the buckle to hit the ground as it dragged his pants with it. Nicky, following the example of every preternatural man I'd ever known, wasn't wearing any underwear. And now, neither was I. The music throbbed, it beat, and Nicky's hands pulled me back into the cradle of his hips again. This time his cock slid into me as though it belonged there, and every nerve ending in my body sang. His hands came up in front of me, moving under my bra and palming my pointed little breasts. Rough fingers tweaked my nipples, and now my throat issued the shredded sound. *Oh God,* it felt good.

Suddenly my brain was full of sex words, the words Green and I didn't use, the words Bracken and I used for play because what we did in bed was so much larger than they were. *Fuck me, Nicky, fuck me... hard... fuck me with your cock, dammit. Oh, Goooooodessss, that feels....*

And then his fingers, regular-sized, slightly rough, nimble, clever fingers, found my clitoris (another sex word—blessed, blessed word to give voice to this human feeling of cock in my womb, of fingers pressing hard on my bundle of nerves, of exploding electricity shivering in my channel, along my skin, along the hair standing on end at the nape of my neck...).

"Oh God, Nicky, I'm going to come...." They were my words, rent out in puffs of breath into the chill night air, and then I was undone, shattering into fragments of sheltering stars.

Suddenly Nicky was no longer inside of me, and there was a scalding splash on my lower back underneath my skirt. He hadn't been wearing a condom, I thought wretchedly. I had forgotten that he could get me pregnant. I leaned forward, hands on my knees, bottom poking in the air, gasping for breath, and tried not to cry. We had done it. It had felt wonderful—so good in fact that I had forgotten my promise to Green, to Bracken, never spoken but made in my heart nonetheless, to have their children first. But Nicky was pulling up my tights and my panties, both of which stuck wetly to my back, but neither of us had a towel, and I would not use Bracken's precious shawl to wipe the come off my skin. Then he was pulling down my skirt, and I straightened to let him. He moved away from me for a moment on a blast of frigid air, and I heard the subtle sounds of a man doing up his pants and fastening his belt.

Nicky's arms were back around me again, and his hand, suddenly forceful when Nicky wasn't usually forceful, grasped my chin and turned my head sideways. He placed a kiss, a benediction, on my lips, and I realized that for all that we had consummated our binding, we had never kissed.

He had been so sweet, and passionate, and everything a lover should be. I closed my eyes on the thought of Green and Bracken, and how I'd almost broken faith with both of them on the promise of raw human passion with a man I was obligated to love, and kissed Nicky purely, filtering the taint of what I felt behind my eyes so he could enjoy his moment, his first best moment alone with a woman. I kissed him back, turning my body into his embrace, and the kiss deepened, became passionate, and ended, the two of us holding each other and dancing again, this time warmly, sweetly in the cold moonlight.

I don't remember the ride home, if we talked or not. I remember that Nicky escorted me up to my room with a chivalry and gallantry that made me smile, and he gave me another sweet kiss, his tongue barely brushing mine, then retreating for a chaste peck on the lips.

"Thanks, Nicky," I said softly. "It was a lovely evening."

"Any time, pretty lady." He smiled back. I held up a hand to touch his face and leaned forward to rub his cheek with my own.

"Until next month, Nicky."

I turned away then, so I wouldn't have to see the unspeakable sadness cross his pretty face with its pert little nose and little boy's freckles.

Soundlessly I slid into my bedroom and tiptoed past Bracken, sprawled fully clothed on his back on our bed. He did say he'd wait up, I thought with a tiny, weary smile.

Carefully I hung my shawl in the closet. Then, not so carefully, I stripped down, wadding up my other clothes into a sticky little ball and shoving it in the hamper, wishing I had scissors so I could shred them into tatters. Then I went into the bathroom and left the light off, avoiding looking at myself in the mirror, turned the water on so hot I could hardly stand it, and stepped under the spray.

BRACKEN
Ghosts in the Garden

SHE'D BEEN in the bathroom for more than an hour. There were several hot-water heaters in Green's hill, but I'm pretty sure none of them would keep warm for that long. I'd woken up when she'd been wadding her clothes into the hamper and thought that after a quick shower she'd climb into bed with me—but the water had kept running, there in the darkened bathroom, and I knew something was wrong.

Finally I stood up and undressed and went into the newly redecorated bathroom.

She was crouched in the shower, her back to the spray, shivering, rubbing a bath sponge over her back and bottom. She must have been doing that for most of the hour, because her back was raw and red, and in another scrub or two I wouldn't be able to touch her because her blood would push through the tiny abrasions of her skin at my call.

The noise I made in my chest was raw with animal aching, and I opened the shower door hard enough to crack the glass and turned the tap off so violently that the handle twisted off in my hand. She didn't protest at all as I scooped her into my arms dripping wet and wrapped her in a towel. All she did was shiver and turn her head into my chest without meeting my eyes.

I held her on my lap and dried her hair, then took her into the bedroom and slid one of my plain white T-shirts over her head. She had a drawer full of nightgowns that Green and I had both bought her, but the only thing she seemed to want to wear in our beds was our T-shirts.

"I'll kill him," I said softly when she was spooned against me under the quilt.

"It's nothing he did," she replied weakly. Her first words since I had found her in the shower.

The darkness closed over us, but I knew she was awake. There was the subtle scent of mustard flowers in the air, so Green was talking to her. Thank the Goddess—if anyone could help her, Green could.

And then, as if to make me a total liar and fool, Green's voice echoed in my head. *"She won't let me comfort her."* His voice was aggrieved.

"Well, fuck," I said back intelligently. *"If she won't talk to you, we're screwed."*

"According to Nicky, of all things that was not a problem."

"She said it was nothing he did." Even in my mind, my expression twisted. *"Of course, she was scrubbing her back raw."*

"I need to be there," he said, and I ached for him. We all hated to be gone from Green's hill, and Green was the rule rather than the exception.

"What have you found out?" I asked.

"The sylphs think it smells like death. It turned five of them into piles of dust, and the entire community lived in fear. Nobody saw its face. Nobody knows its name. Nobody has a fucking clue."

"Well, if you're looking for good news on the information front...." And I proceeded to brief him on Cory's little run-in with the toxic werecreature.

"Eventful night," Green thought musingly. Then I could hear the humor seep back into his voice. *"And she still managed to take care of Nicky. A bit frightening, our little Goddess, isn't she?"*

I looked down at her still form, almost positive she was simply lying still and spiritless and not sleeping at all. *"Yes,"* I agreed simply, and even that little bit of humor left Green's presence in my mind.

"I think," he said after some deliberation, *"that you need to pretend to sleep."*

My mind turned into a giant question mark.

"She needs to talk to someone, and if it's not you and it's not me, that leaves one person—and you don't admit he exists, and she won't go talk to him if she has to explain herself."

"Erplglack...." I truly had no answer to that. Green was right. Green was right, but I still wasn't going to admit.... It didn't matter. He was right. She needed to go to the garden, and I needed to swallow my pride and let her go.

"Good night, brother," Green saluted, and then the scent of mustard flowers was gone. I tightened my hold on Cory's midriff for a second, that clenching motion we all make before our bodies relax for the night, and then allowed my breathing to soften, to grow shallow, and my hand to grow limp and heavy on her hip. I worked so hard at pretending to sleep that by the time she finally slid out of bed, I was truly asleep.

I dreamed of Adrian.

I am four years old, and Adrian is swinging me up over his head in the silvered darkness of the garden. I am taller than human children, but even though this maneuver is awkward, I scream for it over and over again. Adrian is a vampire, and his muscles never tire, and he never complains. He simply laughs, flashing fang, and swings me higher and higher until I finally fly up toward the tops of the trees, and Adrian levitates up to catch me. We come down in a controlled drop, and I am shrieking with excitement.

"Again! Adrian, again!"

But Adrian is catching looks from my mother, who is flickering around with the other pixies and nymphs, visiting, gossiping, watching the children play in the mild gardens in the spring dark. He runs a hand through his virgin-lamb's-wool hair and shrugs.

"No, mate—your mum'll skin me alive, and even vampires have their limits."

I sigh. Any other sidhe, and Mom wouldn't care—but a redcap... well, there's a reason most redcaps are shaped like a pile of rocks. Adrian tousles my hair and gives my mom a questioning look. She sighs, and I can hear her voice drift across the garden. "Go ahead, Adrian—if anyone is sure not to drop him, it'll be you."

And suddenly Adrian's arms are wrapped around my middle so tight I almost can't breathe, but I don't care, because there's a big slice of dark between the silvered green of the lawn and my bare feet, and I can feel the wind through my toes. We are wheeling over the tree tops in what is probably a gentle glide around the garden but to me feels like a roller coaster and a parachute ride both at the same time. I am too stunned to even wave at my mother, but she sees my big eyes as I look at the tops of the trees and study the stream that runs without reason through the grove to pool in all of the important places in the gardens.

"Oh, wow...," I breathe. "You do this every night, Adrian? Take me with you.... I want to go flying every night forever."

"That would be lovely, mate," Adrian laughs in my ear, "but you'll grow up and find better things to do with your time."

"There's nothing better...," I sigh.

Adrian laughs again and swoops around the gardens again and again and again, until finally I fall asleep with the wind in my face and Adrian's gentle laughter in my ear.

It was a memory I was dreaming. It happens sometimes, especially for elves, because our lives are longer than mortals, and sometimes memories are less real than dreams. So in the way of dreams, I was suddenly...

...thirteen years old. I am rangy and strong and by no means fully grown, and I am on fire with perhaps the dumbest idea I've ever had in my life.

My mother had been reading human fairy tales to me. The night before, it was about the woman who had a taste of fairy fruit and made her husband go and fetch her another taste, and then the two of them got into a world of trouble. It was a metaphor for the sidhe's ability to addict mortals with a taste of their sex—my mother was very careful to spell that out. "No kidding, Mom," I'd replied with thirteen-year-old arrogance. "It's not like some stupid human is going to go climbing forty-foot walls for a lousy peach."

My mom had ruffled my hair. "I don't know, Bracken—we don't grow them here, but the peaches in this area are something special." She'd closed her eyes then and smiled. "Big as your fist, so sweet you could swear the Goddess herself had lived in the tree...." She came out of her reverie. "There are orchards not twenty miles away," she said after a moment, "but the earth changes up here, and we forget sometimes how close the most wonderful things can be."

She had looked so wistful, and I had been difficult lately—defiant, angry, insisting that I have my own room in the hill when Green was already expanding as fast as he possibly could. Keeping the hill temperate and fertile took a great deal of power, and putting more rooms in right now would tax Green to the point where it would be hard to keep us safe. I knew that, but it didn't stop me from whining incessantly. But tonight, I was going to make up for it.

"You're going to what?" Adrian's expression is alarmed and bemused.

"I'm going to drive to Ophir and pick peaches," I say again, as though Adrian is deaf. "Can you come with me?"

Today such a request would be no big deal—but when I was thirteen years old, Foresthill was a gas station and some cabins, and the road in was mostly dirt, slicing through the sides of the canyon like a razor-thin apple peel. The double bridge that stretches across the river now did not exist then. Instead, there was the terrifying drop down steep roads to the two short bridges at the bottom of the canyon—and after we had crawled our way back up the hill to Auburn, what is now an eight-lane highway connected to Route 49 was then a two-lane road nearly as dangerous as the dirt track that would lead us there. And our vehicle was certainly not Arturo's Cadillac.

"I don't know if the panel truck goes more than forty miles an hour!" Adrian exclaims. He is looking at me with alarm. "Bracken Brine Granite op Crocken, do you even know how to drive?"

Back then, when farm boys were helping their parents by age ten, everybody knew how to drive, but on the sidhe hill, it was a valid question. The panel truck (and in fact all vehicles any of us got into) had to be washed in salt water and heavily spelled, even to this day—although Green was careful to wax and buff his fleet of cars after the first salt water wash.

"Yes," I say proudly, "I most certainly do." Green had let me practice, but he had made a point of crafting a halter of triple-thick canvas and leather and insisting that I wear it. Where another sidhe could go through the window and heal in moments, again, my redcap abilities would make healing slow and painful, with the loss of a lot of my precious blood. But I've been driving the truck for a month, and I am reasonably sure that once I get it out of the gravel drive of Green's hill, the rest will be cake. So I am arrogant about this endeavor, but I want Adrian's help. Besides, Adrian is fun and exciting, and my hero worship has grown to intense proportions by the age of thirteen, and I want to prove that I am fun and exciting too.

"Please, Adrian?" I say, allowing some of my wistfulness to creep into my voice. "I really want to do this... and you're the only person who would understand." And this is true. The ratio of sidhe to lesser fey is always very low—all of the children I have grown up with are lesser fey, and by age thirteen, their biological imperatives are to mate and to fix things and to dust. There is no one my age at the hill who would understand rebellion and redemption, but I know that Adrian does.

Adrian's expression is pained. I have won already, and he knows it. He shakes his head. "You had better drive like the flaming wind, mate, because it's already ten o'clock and sunrise is at five. July? You have to pick bloody July to go hauling off into the hills for fairy fruit? Why not just make it Litha and sign my death warrant while you're at it!"

But I laugh, because I know that Adrian will never die, and Adrian has already fed from one of his werekitties (I watched him this night, to my delight and increasing discomfort—would he feed from me someday, I wondered, thrilled), *and we both hop into the truck and take off.*

It takes us four hours just to get to the orchard. It would have taken an experienced driver less time—but I have never driven outside of Green's hill, and when I realize the scope of the shattering drop to my side, my knuckles grow white on the steering wheel and my shoulders strain with tension. I could survive that drop, I keep telling myself. My parents made a lot of how it took hours instead of minutes for deep wounds to stop bleeding, but I would still survive. Adrian, being wise and loving me more than I could possibly imagine at the age of thirteen, is judiciously quiet about our creeping pace outlined by the shaky glare of the giant head lamps at the truck's front. He makes light conversation so the silence does not grow burdensome and allows me to drive us through the night with what feels like pure will.

When we arrive at the farm, things go much faster—we both move in what Cory calls hyperspeed but we used to call Goddess's grace. It would have taken two humans eight or nine hours to pick enough peaches to fill the back of the panel truck with neat little boxes. It takes Adrian and me two hours. The peach fuzz coats my body and itches, and even my muscles ache a little from the climbing and the stooping and the hauling. However, it is also beautiful, working like bees in the moonlight, talking softly over the sleeping silence of the scented orchard. And when we are done, I look proudly into the back of the truck and then at the graying sky. And my heart starts to pound in panic.

"Fuck," I say, the swear word coming crudely from my mouth for the first time in my life. I look at Adrian. "Holy Goddess, Adrian— we—you'll never get...." The full import of that gray sky stops up my throat. Adrian needs to be in dark. Absolute dark, or he will conflagrate spectacularly and die, and I will have killed him with my foolishness and my self-absorption.

But Adrian smiles easily. "Don't worry about it, mate. We've got a tarp, we've got boxes.... We'll make do."

And so we do. It is terrifically dangerous—and if any vampire I knew today wanted to attempt it, I would chew their ears off for even mentioning such a thing—but we are deep into plain-folk territory, and I have no glamour to hide my identity (that usually comes a bit after puberty, and I was a few years short), and even if we could convince some poor human to put Adrian up in their cellar, they would probably have me shot and mounted on their wall before the next sunset. We haul all of the boxes out of the truck in record time, and I cover Adrian in the tarp at the bottom of the truck. I balk at the next part. "You'll bruise, mate...," I say foolishly. The sky is already lighter, and the air feels like it has dropped from eighty degrees to sixty-five in the last fifteen minutes.

"I don't bruise, Bracken, and I don't breathe," he says briskly, smiling reassuringly from under the tarp. His skin is pale and he looks painfully young. "But I don't have much time, so stack away," he finishes and then disappears under the thick oilcloth, and I have no choice.

So stack I do. We'd picked enough peaches to fill the back of the panel truck, and I stack every last box on top of that helpless lump underneath the tarp. I have packed the first two layers when the actual light from the sun hits me, and my breath fails in my chest for a moment. Holy Goddess holy Goddess holy Goddess holy Goddess... and no fire. No conflagration. No flaming death for my best friend, and now I can breathe myself. Of course, now I have to drive back, and breathing becomes optional once more.

I'm surprised I don't hit puberty on the drive back, because it seems to take three years instead of three hours, and when I pull up the gravel to the small wooden building where the truck is kept, the sun is very bright. It is at least nine o'clock in the morning, and the wrongness of having a vampire—of having my *vampire—in the back of the truck in this much sunshine makes my hands shake with nausea and fear. Green is waiting for me, and the expression on his face is an indescribable mixture of worry, love, anger, and stark terror.*

I slide out of the truck, for once in my life afraid of Green, hoping he will come up with a punishment worse than the ones I have been giving myself on the tortuous drive home.

"Where is he?" Green's voice is tight with anxiety, but he is not advancing, not threatening with his considerable height, and for some reason his self-control is so much worse than his spitting anger would be.

"He's in the back of the truck," I say, trying very hard not to cry. "He's under the peach crates and the tarp. He should be fine if we get him into the garage." Green nods, and I go to open the wooden doors while Green parks the truck. I hear him inside giving orders to the sprites and know that the peaches will end up on our table for many days, and

even in the winter they show up in preserves. I can't eat them. Not even in the winter, when they bring sunshine and beauty with them in every taste. Now, more than sixty years later, I can't even eat a peach-flavored candy without remembering my own stupidity, my own relentless will, and what it almost cost me.

Green comes out of the garage and I can see the floodgates of his self-control shatter, and all of his fear for his beloved comes crashing on my thirteen-year-old head. He seizes me by a shoulder and hauls me close to face him, and I've been holding back tears for the last three hours and now they come flooding out too.

"Goddammit, Bracken Brine Granite op Crocken—do you have any idea what you've done, any idea at all? Adrian has been nothing but good to you in your life—he's loved you like a brother—and you repay him with this? You put his life in danger, for... for fruit, *for Christ's sake!" He is yelling, but it isn't loud enough. He is roaring, but he still loves me in spite of his anger, and I am still standing and I don't deserve to be. "By all that is holy, what in the fuck were you thinking?" And his stark pain, my own remorse, drive me to my knees before him.*

"I'm sorry...," I blubber. "He said it would be okay! I wanted peaches for Mom, because I've been such a total shit, and...." I'm sobbing, and I can't seem to catch my breath. "And... and... and... Adrian said it was okaaaaaaaay...."

And Green, blessed Green, can see now that I've punished myself more thoroughly than he could think to, and he's gathered me up into his arms as I sob on him like a mewling child instead of the man I thought I'd become. I carry on like this for quite a while, and when I've calmed at last, Green strokes my hair, which is starting to grow long like the adults' in our hill. "Okay, mate," he whispers, and his cheeks are wet too. "I understand—more perhaps than you think. But you've got to know.... Adrian, he'd do anything for us, Bracken. He'd kill or die for us. If you asked him to fetch the moon, he'd fly until he froze in the atmosphere and plummeted back down to earth and shattered in a million pieces, and his only regret would be that he didn't get the bloody goddamned moon like he promised—do you understand?"

I nod, safe in the shelter of my leader's arms, and sniffle. I hadn't understood last night, but right now, after living the sweating terror of the last few hours, I figure I know well enough.

"I bet you do." And now, only now, is Green's dry humor back in his voice. *"It's our job, mate, to make sure Adrian never has to make that choice. Right? You and me, the people here... it's our job to make sure Adrian never has to hurt himself for us, okay?"*

"Okay," I say in a shaky little voice that I can barely admit is my own. *"Okay, Green, I promise."*

And I kept that promise too, I thought, coming awake for just a moment. I kept that promise until Adrian blindsided us all into breaking it. But I'm not done dreaming yet, and now I'm...

...seven years older and standing in Adrian's doorway, listening to Hank Williams pleading to know why someone didn't love him. The song is playing on the curious vinyl disc spinning on the brown contraption Green has brought home. None of the other sidhe are impressed, but Green and Adrian and most of the vampires (who know what a record player is) have listened to disc after disc until the music, infectious and holding the promise of a great rolling thunder of sound, has called me into Adrian's room in the darkling.

"You like this one," I say, surprising Adrian as he lies on his back, head on his laced hands and booted feet crossed. The yellow light coming from the electric bulb by his bed makes him look slightly warmer, slightly more human. He is wearing jeans so snug I can measure the bulge at his crotch, just the way the "bad boys" do, with a white T-shirt holding snug across the hard and wiry muscles of his chest. He looks up, his autumn-sky blue eyes lighting when he sees me. I have been creeping down the stairs from the sidhe quarters to see Adrian since before I could walk. My mother swears that the first time they realized I was a redcap I had fallen down the staircase in an attempt to see Adrian one hectic evening, and they saw that my blood didn't stop immediately.

"Yeah, mate...," Adrian is saying. *"Hank Williams, Patti Page, Jerry Lee Lewis.... There's something great building here. I can hear it in my bones."*

"So...," I say, and swallow.

I have been sexually active since I was sixteen, and none of my people have spared a blink for it. I've enjoyed sidhe, lower fey, werecreatures, and vampires—for reasons I still don't understand, they seem to fall into my bed whether I'm paying attention or not. But Adrian—my mate, my friend, my brother—I don't understand his complete indifference to me. I know he loves me. For my people, attraction and affection means the sharing of flesh is a given. I have seen him and Green together, and I have seen him with women—even human women, which I do not understand—so I know it isn't because he isn't attracted to men, or that he is monogamous with Green. I can't seem to find the center of my hurt, find the reason for his rejection. I have told him, casually, that I've never bunked a mate before. I meant I've never made love to a friend before, and he is my best friend. Green told me (in bed, as he helped me nurse my broken heart) that Adrian thought I meant I'd never done a man. I haven't disabused him of this notion—I was that hurt, that I'm hoping pity will get me where I think love should have gotten me already.

Adrian is looking at me now, his blue-sky eyes suddenly sharp and soft with compassion. He swallows, one of the many human gestures he maintains that seems perfectly at home on his marble-pale, leanly muscled vampire's body.

"So...," he repeats as though he is making fun of me, but there is no sign of smile on his still face.

"So." I clear my throat, and using Hank Williams's words, ask, "When will you love me, Adrian?" Trying not to beg.

The expressions that cross Adrian's face then make perfect sense to me, the adult dreaming this moment, the man who knows what Adrian endured as a child, and the strength that he must have had to still love anyone—Green, me, Cory, anyone. To the young man I was, it only leaves me confused.

"I've always loved you, Bracken Brine," he says gently. "But I'm not wired like you, right? I grew up human...." His face twists in a way that takes my breath away even as I dream it. Pain. That expression was pure pain, and I had been too callow to know. "It takes me a while to wrap my brain around the idea that you're not the little nightmare who used to make me take him flying until my arms 'bout fell off," he finishes. But he isn't telling me no, and so I take another step into his room.

"Is your brain wrapped yet, Adrian?" I ask shortly, suddenly wanting him with a force that makes my mouth dry and my palms sweat.

I didn't know then that it was because I loved him. It is not the same way that I now love Cory, it is not the same way I have always loved Green, but it was love and it was powerful, and at this moment in my youth, it has me by the throat with fear and wanting in a way I had never known and have never known since.

In the dream, a grin crosses Adrian's features, a soft expression I have only seen on his face when he is looking at Green, but now it is aimed at me. If my mouth was dry before, it is the fucking Sahara now, and I'm embarrassingly hard under my tight jeans. My mother made them for me, just like Adrian's, to fit my more than human dimensions. But they are just as tight as the human jeans, and the head of my cock is suddenly poking up past the low-slung waistband. I am so filled with desire for this, for my friend, that I don't even think about shifting and hiding my want. Let him see, I think defiantly, painfully.

"I'm working on it, mate," he says, and he looks at me, and I can almost see him rearranging his sight—looking at me not as a child or as a friend, but taking in the shape of my body: long, muscular, and built with the sensuousness of my people. His gaze brushes my crotch, my body exposed for him, and it touches me almost physically. His look when his eyes reach my face is both arch and hungry. My face is beautiful to humans, I know. My parents and Green have frequently warned me as I've become more and more adventurous that I mustn't visit humans until my glamour kicks in, or humans will simply strip naked in front of me and offer themselves as sacrifices. As an adult I know that they were partially kidding—joking in hyperbole to make me aware of the frightening power of the sidhe. But in this moment, as beautiful as I know I am to humans, I am suddenly, achingly awaiting confirmation from Adrian that I am lovely to him. Adrian has lived with us for a mortal lifetime, at least—he won't be awed simply because I am sidhe, he will think I am truly beautiful. When I look at him, my breath catches in my throat with the possibilities of his beauty, and I want him to look at me in the same way.

He stands suddenly, and I realize that he is shorter than me now by several inches. He has always been larger than life, but now he is not only just slightly taller than the average human, he is also looking....

Scared. Adrian is afraid of something.

"You've grown up strong and lovely, mate," he says now, and his voice is creaky and tight. "But...." He looks away, makes a sudden vague gesture with his hands, runs them through his spiderweb hair. His features, which are pointed, with a sharp chin and a sharp nose and cheekbones that cast shadows on his cheeks, are now drawn tight almost to the point of his feeding face. "You people.... I am not your one and only, Bracken. If you move on to another girl or another bloke and... never visit my room again to play chess or listen to music with me or haul

me off on another goddamned quest for something stupid like moonlight for the lower-fey bathroom or something...." He looks up at me and I am amazed and devastated at the trickle of crimson that is running down the side of his nose. *"It would kill me, mate. It would downright destroy me. You've got to promise me that when you or I move on, we will still be brothers."*

I take a step inside his room, and I can hear my heart pounding in my throat as I reach behind me and close the door. Another step and I am there in front of him, and I reach over to his face and trace the trickle of a tear with my finger and bring it to my lips. I am a redcap—blood is my calling and my passion—and his tears are as sweet as nectar and honey. I reach out again, and this time I cup his slender, cool cheek in my large palm—and now I am his protector, and the world has flip-flopped on its axis.

In a skin-tingling rush, I understand what Green was trying to tell me when I brought his beloved home covered in a tarp and wooden crates of peaches. Suddenly I understand truly, in my core and body and soul, Green's frantic need to protect Adrian from himself. Suddenly I feel, with a pressure that makes my lungs expand tight in my chest, Adrian's desperate, painful, devouring need to be needed. My mentor, my brother, my hero, oh, Goddess, Adrian, you never knew how badly we needed you. You never understood how desperately you were loved.

"You couldn't get rid of me, brother," I say gently in my dream, and the relief shining from his eyes makes me want to wrap my arms around him and protect him from anything that might ever hurt him. Oh, Adrian, my brother, my lover, my hero—how could I leave you behind?

I awoke suddenly, just as, in the dream, our mouths met and tangled in a kiss of such sweetness that I have never been able to give it a name. I realized first that Adrian had left me behind instead—and second, that I heard his voice and Cory's coming down the granite staircase. Cory had gone to the garden for a visit and left the trapdoor open. I was suddenly filled with anger and fear, and a denial so sharp its bitterness canceled out the sweetness of the remembered kiss. *Adrian is dead,* I told myself. His voice was an illusion, forced on me by my memories and my grief. *Then who is Cory talking to?* I asked. And then I refused to answer.

The granite staircase to the top of Green's hill starts in the hallway from the main sitting room to the darkling. By a trick of sound, voices up in the garden seem to resound in Cory's room and Green's room and nowhere else in the vast house—or at least that's what I told myself. I was on the verge of charging up the staircase to get Cory out of the cold when I heard her voice, and I found myself arrested on the first step, waiting to see what had upset her so badly that she couldn't even talk to Green about it.

She laughed, a tired, gentle sound in the night. And then a question in that other voice, the one that couldn't possibly be. "No, it doesn't make me sad," she protests. "It's just that... you, Bracken, Green... it was like a big secret club, and I can't believe you all let me in." Her voice dropped. "It's an honor that I dream not of," she quoted, and I could see in my mind that little half smile that she usually gave when she used poetry, hers or someone else's.

A question. *My* question. And because it was mine, I actually heard his voice in my head. "So, luv, what really brings you up here tonight? Isn't it date night?"

"Oh jeez, Adrian, not you too. Does everybody know about date night?"

"Think of it like high school, luv. They all know about date night. They all know when you and Bracken are fighting. They all know when you and Green are making love. I'm pretty sure that by tomorrow, everyone will know you had to come up to the garden to talk to a ghost in the moonlight." The voice dropped with conspiracy and compassion. "But only you and I will know why."

"I miss you, beloved," she chided. "Isn't that a good enough reason?"

"No" came the honest answer. "I know you miss me, but you're here now because you don't want to talk to the people who are there for you in ways I can't be." I felt a moment of stark compassion. How hard to be forced to be an observer in the life you had once vibrantly participated in. *She's not talking to anybody.*

"Bracken and Green are too good for me," Cory all but whispered, and I wanted to rocket up the staircase and take her in my arms and make her take that back.

"Bullshit" was the adamant reply. Goddess bless... nobody. "That's the sort of crap you believed about yourself when I first met you. You remember that? It took me months to convince you I was serious. That's time—"

Her voice broke as she finished the sentence for him. "—that we could have had together and didn't." A deep, shuddery breath. "And that's a cruel truth, beloved."

"Not any more cruel than what you're doing to yourself now." Adri... the answer sounded softly, and until I had to silence my own breath, I didn't realize I was weeping. "Corinne Carol-Anne Kirkpatrick op Crocken Green, even a vampire's ghost must be gone by dawn. What is eating a hole in your heart? Was date night so bad? Was it so horrible to suffer his touch...?"

"No." She swallowed. Even down the staircase I could picture her face—the tight jaw, the determination not to cry. "It was great. It was fun, and when he touched me, it was...."

"Nice?"

"Wonderful," she corrected, and a horrible rock settled in my stomach.

"And that's bad?" I wanted to ask the question myself, I thought irritably, and be the bigger man about her binding to Nicky Kestrel.

"The touching felt good... and I... I...." Goddess. I could even hear her blush. "You know, A—that thing you're supposed to do when you're... doing the thing we were supposed to be doing."

"Where I come from we call that a climax." I found myself breathing through my nose and suppressed the laughter. If he couldn't be there in the garden, he certainly couldn't have that same inflection, that same sense of goddamned humor....

"That's funny, we Americans call it an orgasm," Cory retorted archly. "And yes, I had one. And it felt great. But it didn't feel right. You, Green, Bracken—I know what making love feels like. There's a sacredness... a holy dark, moving through your body, and everything, your skin, the sky, your lover's eyes, it's special and amazing and beautiful, and this was... it was sex words and nerve endings and... fucking." She spat the word, with venom and self-loathing, and again I was stunned still. Cory was a master at that word, and I was surprised to hear her mastered by it.

"It was lust!" Ad... the voice sounded older, compassionate, wiser than I remem... than it should have. How would I not know about that wisdom? Where was I when he grew wise? "Your problem, beloved, is that you've fallen in real true love with every lover you've had until this moment. If you'd been the average kid, you would have gotten your first bang in the back of a car at fifteen, and it would have taken you another ten years to figure out what real love feels like compared to the sheer joy of getting laid. You got laid. You liked it. That's not a sin, that's a blessing!"

And as wise as it was, and as much as I would have wished I had said the same thing, it only made her cry. "But... but... I forgot the goddamned condom, and I could have gotten pregnant for... for... *fucking.* I promised... myself, anyway, that if I was going to get knocked up it would be Green, and Bracken, and not Nicky. Not first. That's the least I can give them, you know?"

And I couldn't stand to hover at the foot of that staircase anymore. "I don't care!" I crashed up the stairs, bellowing at the top of my lungs. "I don't fucking care. A baby is a joy, and you don't get to crucify yourself because just once you acted like a twenty-year-old human girl instead of a two-hundred-year-old sidhe princess. For Goddess's sake—get pregnant, have a goddamned flock of birds, but don't hurt yourself for being human."

She looked up in surprise from her huddle on the granite bench Green had erected as Adrian's memorial. Pale ankles peered out from under my T-shirt, which went past her knees, and thin wrists were lost in a giant denim jacket I had worn twenty years ago. She was staring at the far end of the bench where... I would not see where. He had left us. He had left *me* behind, after all I had done not to do the same to him, and he was *not* sitting at the far end of that bench, a pale hand on our beloved's ankle, moonlight hair fluttering in the slight breeze that Green allowed to pass into this consecrated place.

In an effort not to see, I allowed myself to look around the grove. The trees here were flourishing—the rainfall had been unusually heavy this year, and Green's power didn't need to do much to make the erotic dance of trees lush and rich with leaves. I saw the figures of the three of them—Cory, Adrian, and Green—in the lovers' dance they'd done the night Cory's power had erupted, creating this place. The original Goddess's grove was a quiet little meeting of trees down in the garden, but after this place was created, everyone but Green, Cory, and me forgot about that one. A stray memory of the morning after the night the three of them had spent together crossed my mind—Cory looking at me and Arturo in panic, knowing that now we knew what she'd been doing with her two lovers, a very human fear of judgment for something that had been beautiful, but not human.

"You know how to make an entrance, beloved," Cory said into the sudden silence.

"Am I your beloved?" I asked tightly, meeting her eyes.

Her shock and hurt made me feel worse than I already did. "Of course you are," she whispered. "How could you even ask?"

"Because you're out here talking to nobody instead of in our room, talking to me!"

Her mouth opened, and I saw her eyes making pained contact with... with thin air. She must not have liked what she saw there, because her mouth thinned, and her eyes grew obstinate.

"You've been everything that is lovely to me in the last two days, Bracken Brine. Please don't screw it up now by being an ass. No..."— when I would have objected—"go on down the stairs. I'll be down in a minute, I promise." I was going to press it... I was going to insist, but her face softened for a moment, and she reached out, forcing me to move closer to her to take her hand. She pulled it to her mouth and kissed it, her lips soft and a trace of wetness chilling my palm. I put my palm to her cheek and felt the tears that I had heard break in her voice, and I could refuse her nothing.

"I won't be long," she promised, and I nodded and turned away before I could test my resolve and look for a reaction at the other end of the bench.

As I walked toward the open trapdoor, the other voice said, "He's still so angry at me." And the hurt in the whisper that couldn't be almost drove me to my knees.

Before I could stumble down the stairs, Cory replied softly, "We all were, beloved. I had you for a heartbeat, and my anger almost killed me. He had you since he was a baby—he's, like, existentially pissed off...."

The world quirked. "I know... I know... but I never miss him so much as when he's right there in front of me." It was the last thing I heard before I absolutely had to get the fuck out of Adrian's garden. I tripped on the way down. I *tripped*. I'm a sidhe—we have eyes in our feet and the Goddess moves with us—the sound of my knees hitting the floor at the foot of the stairs almost surprised me as much as the pain. But neither of them surprised me as much as Cory's sudden hand on my elbow as I crouched there, dazed and hurting in ways that had nothing to do with my smarting knees and palms.

She helped me to my feet silently, then crouched there on the floor and checked my knees for blood. There was a little, but not enough for my calling, and she kissed the scrapes gently as they healed under her lips. I put my hand down to help her up, but she stayed there for a moment, her hazel eyes gleaming in the light from the living room window.

"I only wish your heart healed this quickly," she said softly, and she took my hand when it started to shake. I had no words to answer her. She stood up and touched my face, and her hands shook as well. "He'll be there when you're ready," she promised. "No, no… don't answer. Just kiss me, beloved. Just kiss me, and we can heal each other…."

And I couldn't get enough of her… her taste, her mouth on mine, her hands on my skin. We moved to our room and fell to the bed, and I forgot my size and I forgot my strength and lost myself inside her—in her arms, in her body—forgetting even that tonight was date night and that tonight of all nights she was less wholly mine than most nights. I forgot everything but that she was my beloved and she would heal my heart if she could.

Afterward she lay quietly, passed her hands over my face, and didn't comment on my wet cheeks.

"I was right," she mumbled, obviously exhausted. "There is a holy dark, beloved, coursing through our bodies, bones, and blood." Poetry—she was so tired her poetry leaked through.

Her breathing evened, and she was well and truly sleeping. Before I knew it, so was I.

The Goddess, blight her, cursed me with one last dream. I never kept track of human years as they passed. Adrian and I were exclusive to each other for a short time (with the exception of Green, of course—always, always Adrian and Green—their love set the rhythm of the sun and moon). Adrian once told me it was nine years together all told, and it seemed like a big number for a short time. All I remember was…

…Elvis is asking me if I'm lonesome tonight from a jukebox that spills into the summer air. Adrian and I are checking out a bar in town because the werecreatures hang out there. Their population has been growing slowly with that of the vampires, and Adrian likes to make sure the lost ones that end up in his keeping feel found after all is said and done. We have fought often for the last few months. We don't fight like a bickering couple—we beat the hell out of each other and then laugh about whatever the hell we were thinking about before we do. But we are still fighting, and there is a restlessness in both of us that we won't voice.

A human girl comes out of the club, and I check my glamour twice—it kicked in shortly after Adrian and I came to be, and Green and the other sidhe have drilled me on it constantly ever since.

The girl looks at me, and I see that she is uncommonly pretty—blonde hair caught up in a ponytail, one of those full skirts, and a button-up shirt with round sleeves and a round collar. A little of my glamour drops, and she turns to me with an "Ooohhh...." Her expression is besotted, and I find that I don't mind so much when a pretty human girl looks at me like that. Adrian touches my shoulder and says, "Watch yourself, mate," and suddenly I'm about two seconds from planting my fist in his face. I turn to him with a snarl, and it's there in his eyes. The reason we've been fighting, the reason I've been pushing him to take me out on the town.

My world comes crashing down in a heartbeat—Oh, Goddess, I'm going to have to leave Adrian behind. The bleakness I feel at that moment is enough for me to turn away from the pretty human girl with all that promise of ripeness and beauty at my beck and call.

Suddenly Adrian smiles, part of his mouth quirking up, and I recognize the look—it's the look he gives me when he's daring me to catch him, the look he gives me when he's going to fly naked past a mortal to make a clean dive from the sky into Lake Clementine. It's the look he gives me when he dares me not to come. And he turns that smile up a watt, then turns it to the pretty human who is looking at both of us in awe, too naïve to recognize the look or the touch on the shoulder for what they are.

"'Ello, luv," he says, cranking up the British in his accent and the charm in his grin. I return his look, his smile, the glint in his eyes, and get back to the girl. She looks like she's about to melt into a puddle, and the game is on.

I get home the next evening and meet a pretty nymph coming out of Adrian's room. Adrian and I look at each other evenly for a minute, and then he cracks a grin. "Have a good one, mate?"

"Absolutely, brother," I return, at a loss for anything more profound.

"Good," he says with a challenge, "because the next one's mine."

"You wish!" I put as much bravado into my voice as I can and pray this moment won't lapse into awkwardness.

"So—swimming in Lake Clementine tonight? Lots of birds there." The thought is tempting, and I let it show on my face.

"I'm more in for a game of chess," I reply, *knowing that's what he* wants.

He smiles and sets up the chessboard on his bed.

I remembered the rest of the night in my dream. I beat him three games out of five.

CORY
Running

MY FEET made a rhythmic thud on the rubber track, and I tried with all my might to move like my body didn't hurt.

Bracken had forgotten himself the night before. He never forgot his strength, ever. He had taken my body with enough force to push himself inside of me cock first, and I had tried and tried and tried to wrap myself around him and to make it feel all better, but I couldn't. The results were sore thigh muscles and, well, soreness higher than that, and it was only one part of my misery as I tried my first run under a threatening gray sky.

My breath wheezed in my chest and my throat felt like broken glass, and I realized my feet were going faster than my healing body could manage. My breath labored even louder than the sound of The Killers cranking from my iPod—my Christmas gift from Nicky and Renny—and after three laps around the track, I grudgingly slowed to a walk. How embarrassing. I mean, three-quarters of a mile? There was a big woman out here—I mean really big, with a friendly smile—and I was pretty sure she had just lapped me at a brisk walk on her fifth lap. I gulped air like it was on sale and suddenly heard a *thud-thud* behind me. A girl about my age with dark glossy hair in a ponytail pulled up next to me and slowed to a walk too.

"It's too cold to be running anyway," she said on a disgustingly even breath, and I could tell she was trying to make me feel better. Bracken glared at me broodingly from across the track, thinking seriously about hauling me away to the gym shower and carrying me around the school for the rest of the day, and Renny and Nicky were reading on the bleachers next to him. Suddenly a pleasant face and a word of encouragement were the sweetest things life had to offer.

"That's...." (*wheeze*) "nice" (*wheeze*) "of" (*gasp*) "you." I was going to finish up with "to say," but she laughed and spared me the trouble.

"Here.... Keep moving, but slower," she advised and slowed her walking pace. "First day out on the track?"

I nodded, feeling like a total fool.

"Yeah, it's hard—that first lap, you think, 'I rock, I'm a god, I can do it'… and by that third? You're thinking, 'I suck, I'm a dork, I'm gonna die.' Been there. You just gotta keep coming out." She nodded enthusiastically, and her ponytail bobbed. Her face was a perfect oval, with a little piquant point of a chin and a turned-up nose. I remembered hating cheerleaders in high school for being so perky, but here, on this dismal track with the waving oak trees beckoning from over by the parking lot and the elephant-sized clouds scudding under the sky, I was thinking maybe cheerleaders were underrated heroes.

"I was sick this winter." *Oh, good, I can talk now—I'm not a total mutant.*

The girl nodded earnestly. "That'll do it. I had bronchitis last year—it took me weeks to build back up to where I was. What got you?"

A giant flying bird whom I was now married to, his giant sadistic bird leader who was now an idiot washing dishes in a hotel I made out of sex and desperation, gut-wrenching worry over Bracken—hence the hotel—sheer exhaustion, and a healthy dose of grief. "It was kind of a bunch of stuff," I said. We weren't really walking now—we were more meandering down the last stretch of the track. "I ended up in a coma for a week. When I came to, I had the body tone of overcooked asparagus."

The girl's eyes got really big. "Wow, that's serious sick," she breathed. "Are you sure you're supposed to even be out running?"

I turned to her in a panic. "Shhhhh…," I hushed, totally serious. "If Bracken hears you, he won't let me out of the freaking hill for a year!"

Pretty Ponytail looked quizzically the two hundred yards to where Bracken was watching me like a hawk. Elvish senses are sharper even than vampires', and he had indeed heard me say his name.

"That totally hot guy?" she asked. "I mean, my boyfriend is totally hot too, but this guy—he's, like, more beautiful than should be allowed by law. Is he your boyfriend?"

"Husband," I corrected, smiling slightly because, in spite of its accidental origins, Bracken's bonding with me was still a source of quiet pride.

"Where's your ring?" she asked, and I looked at my hand in surprise yet again. You'd think I'd just remember to ask Bracken for a hunk of metal for my finger, right?

"We haven't found one we liked." Dammit, it wasn't a lie... we just hadn't gone looking for one yet. "The ceremony was very private." *That,* at least was true—the ceremony had been the two of us in bed, screaming out each other's full names. Of course, we had shorted out every lightbulb for a two-block radius with the power of the binding, but only the other people in the apartment knew how it happened.

"But you're really married?" She was positively goggle-eyed. "I mean, you're both so young!"

"He's actually a lot older than me," I responded. Like sixty years or so.

"Well, he's totally hot. Why isn't he out here with you?"

"He works out in the morning." In the morning he went walking Green's hill, all bazillion acres of it. It took him about half an hour.

Ponytail nodded like this made total sense, and I thanked God for the weirdness of human men. I looked up at Bracken and the others, and Renny waved as we neared. I'd gone four laps—but I'd walked the last one. I looked uncertainly at my new friend, who seemed to know more about this whole exercise thing than I did.

"Yeah, a mile's good the first time," she said encouragingly. "Are you going to be out here again?"

"Monday through Thursday, same time same place," I returned easily. "I'm Cory, by the way."

"Well, you'll see me here!" She sounded excited about the possibility, and I almost looked around to see who she was talking to. "I'm Davis Stacia Kelly, but everybody calls me Davy."

I blinked a couple of times. "And you just tell people that?" I asked before I could stop myself. Even before I'd met Arturo and Adrian, I'd been guarded about my name. It was... it was a part of me, and I wasn't sure if I wanted the world to have free access to all parts of me.

"I know—my boyfriend keeps telling me that I shouldn't, because of identity theft or something, but all my credit cards are Daddy's, and he's got about a gazillion fail-safes on our money anyway."

I had to smile. She was very unselfconscious about Daddy's money. Where the people in my hometown used to irritate the hell out of me when they talked about their hot cars and vacationing in Europe and getting their ins to Princeton, Davy had a sort of innocence—she knew she had the money, but it apparently didn't make her better than anybody else.

"It's more of a privacy thing, I guess," I returned guardedly. "But it's good to meet you, Davy. See you tomorrow? Maybe I can actually go a whole mile by then."

"Oh, no," she returned seriously. "I mean, definitely, I'll see you tomorrow, but you're going to want to stick to what you're doing for at least a week! See you tomorrow!" And with that, she waved and trotted off to finish her run.

"Who was that?" Renny wanted to know.

"Someone who's not above sweating," I shot back. "Her name's Davy, if you want to run with us."

Renny measured Davy judiciously from across the track, as though assessing a threat. "If you teach her to knit, I'll rip out her lungs," she said after a moment.

I laughed. "Renny-cat, you're the only girlfriend wild enough to knit with me."

Renny made a sound something like a purr, and I gave Bracken a sweaty peck on the cheek. "I'm going to shower—meet you at Human Sexuality."

"Where six people who aren't remotely human are going to learn the basics of something most of them learned at the hands of a sexual god," Nicky said sourly.

"I'm human," I said defensively and watched Nicky's eyebrows rise. "Partly!" I added and danced away happy, forgetting for a moment that I was sore, afraid, and confused.

Half an hour later I was not so happy and the soreness in my unmentionables was back again, added to muscle stiffness from my pathetic little trot around the track. And the questionnaire in front of me was giving me fits.

The professor hadn't come in yet. We sat in one of the lecture halls that sometimes doubled as a theater in the psych building, and the TA—whom I suspected of being a sylph, she (?) had been so genderless—had passed out the questionnaires and told us that Professor Hallow would be in momentarily, then disappeared. It had all seemed mellow and groovy until I got a good look at the questionnaire.

Answer all questions honestly. Answers will be read out loud anonymously in class. If you don't want an answer read, the registrar's building is in the northwest corner of the campus. Feel free to drop.

Cute. Clever. And I was soooooooo *not* answering these questions honestly.

Question 1: How long have you been sexually active? Answer? About nine months.

Question 2: How many partners have you had in that time? And here's where it got tricky, because the answer was about four, almost five (if I counted a very sexy vampire who had gracefully bowed out so as not to make things difficult between Bracken and me), and even I knew that was too many lovers to have started so late in the game. I wrote down "three" hoping that only the ones I'd chosen for myself would count.

Question 3: Have you ever had multi-partner sex? Answer? Well, yes. But while it may have officially fit the bill as "multi-partner sex," emotionally it had felt more like "lovemaking cubed"—so that's what I put.

Question 4: Have you ever had sex when you didn't want to? Why? Well, because Nicky would die of neglect if I didn't, and it wasn't really either of our faults that we were stuck together like this and he was my friend and I didn't want him to die. I guess it wasn't really against my will, right? I just wrote "No."

Question 5: What's the most unusual place you've ever had sex? Oh, brother. In Green's garden, in full view of Green and every other member of his court? Right—like I was going to put that. Or how about in a nasty, skeezy warehouse that was transformed by my sexually induced power into a five-star hotel? I sighed and wrote "under the stars."

Question 6: Has sex ever been painful for you? Well, yeah—when your beloved is the size of some sort of gag gift from an adult toy store only much, much bigger and harder, and, well, superhumanly powered, and his heart is so broken you'd let him fuck you to a pulp just to ease the pain, it tends to inflict a few bruises. I wrote, "Love has always been more painful than sex." And liked it so much I underlined it twice before I moved on.

But there were thirty questions just like that, and for every answer I wrote down on paper there was another, less human answer in my heart. I glanced over at Mario and LaMark who were behind us and noted sourly that they seemed to be doing just fine. Of course Mario was still grieving for his one and only mate, and LaMark hadn't bonded with anyone yet. Green was still trying to figure out a way for the non-hetero Avians to bond in such a way that it would allow the Avians to live. They didn't have much to write.

But a glance at Renny, Nicky, and Bracken was another matter altogether. I wondered if I looked as uncomfortable as they did, and figured I must. Bracken caught my eye, and we exchanged a moment of profound unhappiness. Elves couldn't lie, I knew, not even on paper, and I wondered how he'd managed to dodge some of those trickier questions—like how long he'd been sexually active (over fifty years) or how many lovers he'd had (like he'd kept track!) or what kind of birth control he liked to use (mostly force of will).

"Green has a lot to answer for," he said grimly, and as much as I wanted to defend my other beloved, I stared at the mess of half-truths and creative thinking in front of me and had to agree.

The TA collected our questionnaires, and the professor came in—a tall, aesthetic-looking man who smiled politely at the TA and then stood at the podium and started talking about sexual mores and expectations in America.

"Most of our expectations are based on fiction and media, and not on reality. It's like there are two sex worlds out there—the fantasy we can never have, and the funny, odd, very physical human reality we're stuck with." There was some brief laughter, and he continued. "And that is why the questionnaire. It is easier for us to see how truly off base our expectations are when compared to the experiences of living, breathing people we can relate with on a human level."

It was about the fifth time he'd said the word human, and I got a sudden buzz on my nerve endings. I called up a little bit of power, and....

"Holy shit." I saw Bracken rubbing the bridge of his nose next to me. Renny and Nicky straightened in their chairs and leaned forward for a closer look, and Mario made a surprised hum in the back of his throat.

In reality, he wasn't aesthetic-looking at all—he was stunning, an elf god of about seven and a half feet, with pale white hair and blazing blue eyes. And he was leafing through our questionnaires with mild puzzlement on his face. He read the answers to a few out loud with no incident—"*When were you first sexually active?* 'Twelve—with the babysitter.'" (surprised laughter) "*Have you ever had multi-partner sex?* 'Only if my vibrator counts.'" (more laughter) "*What's the strangest place you've ever had sex?* 'A Volkswagen Beetle.'" (A lot of pained grimaces) And some more in the same vein. And then:

"Have you ever had multi-partner sex? Answer: 'Well, when... when my boyfriend was teaching me how to make love to my... mate, he kissed me the way he kissed me the first night we made love and then told me to kiss her that way....'" Then he squinted a little, looked up into the audience, and grimaced. "Short answer, yes," he interpreted, and I could see Nicky turning bright red out of the corner of my eye. As an Avian, Nicky could lie his ass off, and I'd figured he had—how did details about our night with Green manage to surface on his paper?

Without making a show of it, Professor Hallow moved Nicky's paper to the back of the stack. *"Has sex ever been painful for you?* Answer: 'Well, when your beloved's the size of a gag gift from an adult toy store...'" The class erupted into laughter and my jaw dropped open, but it didn't end there. The professor went on, and the laughter stopped. "'...only bigger, and harder, and superhumanly powered, and his heart is so broken you'd let him fuck you to a pulp just to ease the pain, it tends to inflict a few bruises.'" As the laughter died down and people gasped in sympathy, the professor added, as though driving a point home, "'I've always found that love hurts much more than sex.' And that's the truth, boys and girls, isn't it?" There were somber nods, and I tried very hard not to weep with pure mortification.

I turned to Bracken with stricken eyes. "I swear to God I didn't write that."

"You thought it," he said, with a twist to his mouth. "You should have told me."

"There are some things you shouldn't have to live with, Bracken Brine," I snapped, and then shut up because a tear had spilled over and I didn't want more to follow.

But the agony wasn't over yet. My paper obviously got thrust to the back of the pile, but the next one was Bracken's—as was made obvious by the answer to the question *What's your biggest fear during sex?*

"'I'm afraid of hurting my beloved, because she's tiny and fragile and she's been hurt so many times, and I am big and clumsy and stupid.'" And now the class wasn't laughing any more, and I wanted to die, and Bracken wanted to jump in the coffin with me.

"You're not clumsy and stupid," I said just loud enough for him to hear, not even daring to look at him.

"I hurt you," he said back, looking straight ahead.

"I let you," I said. He took my hand in his, and we sat there blindly through the rest of the class. More answers were read, including one from Renny—I was sure, because it expressed a concern that a lover was unwilling to turn "terminally furry" as a lack of commitment—that the prof managed to spin to something else, and then the homework assignment was given and the class filed out.

Bracken and I were on the verge of getting the fuck out of there before any more of our personal life could spill out on the floor like noodles from a box when the professor called out, "Green's children—a moment of your time?"

I closed my eyes and grimaced, but Bracken was the one who said "Fuck." Renny and Nicky both said "Son of a bitch!" and LaMark and Mario sighed.

Reluctantly and counting each breath, we filed back to our seats and sat, regarding our professor with extremely unfriendly eyes. Professor Hallow approached us, looking grim and apologetic at once. He was truly extraordinary to look at once you got past the glamour, but I wasn't dazzled. This sidhe had just hurt my beloved, and I was angry.

"Did you forget something?" I snapped. "Like the machete in our innards? Did you have some salt you wanted to sprinkle? A rack you forgot to put us on?"

"An apology to make?" he interrupted with a sad smile. "I'm so sorry, all of you. I put a compulsion on that questionnaire to answer honestly—it saves us all a lot of bullshit at the beginning of the class. What happens with the Goddess's children is that their first answer—the one they make with their hearts—looks to me to be clearly printed on the page. I had no way of knowing, until I got to a few specific words, that there were things you very much needed to keep private."

It was understandable, but my gaze was still extremely unfriendly. "Didn't Green tell you we were coming?"

A nod, a kindness I didn't deserve. "Yes, little Goddess, he did. But I have four sections of this class. I didn't know when to expect you, and it simply slipped my mind." He surveyed us all, from Mario all the way down to me. "That being said, I hope you don't mind if I intrude some more. I think you all need to talk to someone objective and understanding about the burdens in your hearts. That's why Green sent you to me, you know. He is usually the sounding board for his people, but Cor...." He struggled for a moment not to say the whole of my name—all of the elves did at first. "Cory... Lady Cory... you, Bracken, Dominic, and Erin—you're all suffering from terrible burdens. I could tell that from your answers, if not from the defensiveness in your postures, and Green knows that you're not in positions to talk to him as honestly as you might. I'd like to make appointments, if I may, with all of you. I understand you have a break between your classes?"

My face twitched, and I could have blessed Green and cursed him at the same time if he'd been there. My feelings must have been strong, because there was a sudden smell of mustard flowers and a gentle *"For me, beloved?"* in my head, and I nodded reluctantly.

"Fine," I said, feeling ungracious. "Fine. Whatever. What are your office hours?" He told us, and I shrugged. "I'll go first—tomorrow at noon, then, before I run. Bracken can see you while I'm running. Nicky and Renny the next day, Mario and LaMark the day after."

"You need to eat," Bracken said unexpectedly, and I shrugged.

"Before I run, after I run... whatever...."

"No, you need to eat. You can't just blow it off, Cory." His jaw set, and I remembered the words "tiny" and "fragile" from his answer. I took another deep breath, but before I could speak, the professor stepped in.

"I'll bring lunch—my sprites have a line on some excellent pizza." And I was so grateful to him for heading off an argument that had nothing to do with lunch that I looked up and smiled in honest gratitude.

"Thank you—that would be perfect," I said and was surprised when Hallow extended his hand. I was feeling more kindly toward him than I had been a minute ago, so I took it as though to shake hands and was surprised when he brought it to his lips instead.

"Any time, Lady Cory," he said seriously. I felt a sudden, soft buzzing in my body, and the only thing sexual about it was its location. Otherwise, it was like the stroke of a hand through my hair—pleasant and soothing, but not arousing at all.

I blinked, the soreness left over from the night before suddenly gone. "Thank you again," I said quietly, feeling better about things than I had in a while.

"Again, any time," he said, smiling kindly. "I'll see you both tomorrow." And our meeting tomorrow suddenly didn't seem so onerous.

And that was it. He turned to go, and we started filing out, but suddenly I had a thought. "Professor Hallow!" He turned toward me, and I continued, "Has there been anything hinky going on... you know, with… with the Goddess's children? There was something really awful here, about five days ago, and it was up in Auburn too… and Green said it attacked the sylphs in the bay area this fall. I was wondering if you knew anything."

The sidhe's brilliantly blue eyes sharpened—his whole posture sharpened—and I got a shiver of excitement. This was important to him. "Five days ago?" I nodded. A look of profound sorrow passed his ageless, flawless features. "I had a TA named Jon, a werecreature. Not one of Green's, but I was trying to get him to go up and talk to the vampires. We were… close." They'd been lovers. "Five nights ago, I felt him die." He shuddered. I knew the depth of Green's grief for his lovers, and any lingering resentment I'd held toward Hallow faded. Of course he'd forgotten we were coming to his class—he was just trying to make it through the day without shattering into powdered pain.

"I'm so very sorry," I said, wishing I could do something better than that. "I know…." My heart constricted and my voice trailed off. "We all know how you feel."

He smiled at us, brilliantly, sadly. "I know you do, Lady Cory. Any help I can give to find this… thing, I'll give you gladly…." His voice hitched. "But not today, if that's all right with you."

"Yeah. Yeah, that's fine," I said. He turned and exited gracefully, whereas the rest of us simply fled the room.

The six of us grouped together for comfort the rest of the day but had little to say to each other. It was like we were afraid if we opened our mouths, something else embarrassing and personal would spill out, so we had only a few words about everyday things and nothing about our upcoming meetings with Professor Hallow. However, when Green called that afternoon, I did let him know in my own special way that I didn't appreciate being blindsided like that.

"Better beg forgiveness, luv, than beat you over the head, drag you kicking and screaming, and have to play dirty pool with not just you but all six of you in order to get permission," he responded, and I had to laugh. All was suddenly forgiven—just hearing his voice on the phone made my knees melt a little and my lingering resentment evaporate. And he did have a point. If we were reluctant to talk to Green about something, then getting us to be counseled outside of the hill would be a struggle. With my forgiveness came a moment of easy silence, of wanting, of hearing him breathe on the other end of the phone and wishing I could feel his breath on my cheek. The moment grew so painful I knew I had to end it or fall apart. Since I already hurt, that's when I told him about Jon Chase and Hallow's recent loss.

"I didn't know," Green said softly. "Hallow's always been independent, which is fine, but I wish he'd come to me with this—or to one of you, for that matter. I'll call him tonight."

I'd tried to talk to Ellen Beth to see what she knew about Jon, but she had opted to drive herself to her classes. As soon as she got back to the hill, she had locked herself in the downstairs room with Chris—who, all reports said, was experiencing withdrawal symptoms that made heroin look like Diet Coke. Marcus had been in the process of bribing the sprites to clean up the sweat and vomit even as I'd talked to him, and the look he'd given me was grim. I relayed all this to Green. His own grim silence was enough to let me know that this problem was growing rapidly more pressing than our personal concerns, and we agreed to keep each other posted. Before I hung up, there was a sweetness in the air, the mild spicy smell of wildflowers, and Green's kiss on my mind, and for a moment I allowed myself to miss him so badly my chest felt squashed and my throat swollen. I felt the same thing from Green.

"Hurry home, beloved," I urged, and his silent pledge to do just that should have helped the weight on my chest, but it only made it heavier.

Bracken was out during dinner. The Avians were establishing a colony of sorts out in Camp Far West. The property was cheaper than in Foresthill and it offered open foothills, a lake, and plenty of hunting room for jackrabbits, field mice, and even fish. What it *didn't* offer was the suffocating sexual ripeness that the hill represented. Since their first sexual relation established their mating connection, one bad encounter on a powerful night, and they could be bound for life. Using Nicky as a cautionary tale, Bracken and the Avians we'd brought with us from the city this Christmas were building onto the four bedroom house Green had bought on some horse property out there, trying to give the independent Avians a little breathing room and some pride after getting caught up in the madness of a leader who was bent on leading them all to their death.

So it was a quiet night—a dinner where the banter was forced—and then I took a visit to the vampire's common room, where the copper smell of blood and the clean smell of bodies that didn't sweat was as comforting as the gossip about who was feeding from whom. Marcus asked me if I wanted to watch *Sin City* with him and Phillip (who were not only back on speaking terms this evening but bantering like they were going to be in each other's beds before the movie was over, along with Phillip's werepanther girl of the day), but I had homework to do and declined.

So only a little later, Renny, Nicky, and I were flopped on my bed doing homework and carefully avoiding any reference to the incredibly embarrassing personal revelations of the day. Or rather, they were doing homework and I was trying not to weep blood over my physics book. I had written out all of the problems, but when I tried to make the next step, my brain blocked up with math panic. I'd been rereading the chapter for an hour and it still wasn't making any sense. I was about two seconds from running to ask Arturo for help. I would have rather asked Grace, who knew math, but she and her daughter had established a tenuous truce, and they were working the store together. I figured if Arturo didn't know the answer, *he* could call Grace. If Phillip hadn't had such a hard-on for everyone everywhere, I would have asked him—but by now he, Marcus, and Tina were probably doing insane naked things, so that would get pretty damn awkward. As it was, I had nowhere to turn. Nicky might know, but that would mean addressing him personally; Renny had taken a poetry class instead of physics for just this reason, so I didn't even want to bring it up to her. Suddenly Bracken stuck his head into our room.

"What's wrong?" he asked.

I blinked, surprised to see him, and then tried to shrug it off. "Nothing." I thought I sounded perfectly normal, but Renny and Nicky looked at each other, gathered their stuff, and left the room just like that, leaving me with my mouth open and face-to-face with a stubborn Bracken.

"Well?" he asked again, his patience thinning as he stood in front of the bed looming down on me—like I wasn't short enough standing up.

"It's stupid!" I blurted. "It's just this stupid physics homework. I don't do math. I took college algebra and thought that would be fine, and now I've got this lab class and the equations just sort of swim around in front of my eyes like fish. I get the concepts, but when I look at the page all I see are numbers and letters, and they don't connect at all.... And how did you know, anyway?" I looked up at him, suddenly wondering when he'd gotten back. "Don't you have your own homework? It's physics— it's dumb and I can deal with it, and... I mean, I deal with weredogs in withdrawal and big scary birds and I do okay, so shouldn't I get to agonize over homework without making you crazy?" My voice cracked and I couldn't go on, and out of nowhere I started to cry. I couldn't say who was more surprised, Bracken or I.

I was in his arms in a heartbeat, and suddenly I felt myself giving in to the urge to just hunker down in his arms and have a good cry. My shoulders shook and my breath caught, and for just a few moments I was one big sob. The storm passed eventually, and I found that Bracken's arms around my shoulders were comforting and his chest under my cheek was the bedrock of the world, and even his smell made me feel better.

"You'll always make me crazy," he said into my hair. "You make me crazy fast asleep in the moonlight. You make me crazy when you're swearing so foully the flowers in the garden droop. You make me crazy when you're knitting a sweater I'm not supposed to know is for me." There was a pause, and he took a deep, shaky breath. "You make me crazy when you're missing Green and so am I, but you won't tell me because you think it will hurt me when it won't, because I miss him too and the two of you are still home to me." Another pause, and another shuddery breath. A quiet whisper. "You make me crazy when you forgive me for being angry, when I'm not even angry at you."

"I'm so...."

"Don't say it," he ordered. "You'll only make me crazy angry, because you don't have a thing to be sorry for, and I can help you with your physics, okay?"

I laughed, just enough to make myself hiccup. "Okay." We were quiet then, but neither one of us seemed inclined to move. After a moment I touched his cheek. "I love you, *due'alle*."

"I love you too, *due'ane*," he said, and still we just sat there quietly, listening to our hearts beating, remembering that we didn't always have to hurt each other to love each other.

"Do you think you'll like the sweater?" I asked tentatively. After all, it was almost done.

He laughed softly and kissed my cheek. "I think I'll wear it until you're sick of seeing it."

I sniffled a little. "You have no idea of the capacity of my ego," I said grandly. Now he laughed in earnest and hugged me tighter, and neither of us seemed to want to move, so we just stayed there, talking quietly about nothing.

We did eventually get to my physics, but not for a long time.

AT 1:38 in the morning, a psychic scream ripped through Green's hill, sending me tear-assing down the hallways to the staircase to the lower darkling and hurtling downward before I think Bracken had even touched the floorboards. I heard the shocked voices of people filtering in after me, but when I arrived at the safe room—the origin of the scream, and the place where Chris Williams had been withdrawing—Phillip, naked and wet, had just gotten there and was concentrating on working the dial lock for the room.

I stood there, vibrating on my toes to keep myself from urging him to hurry, because heaven knows that only makes people fumble what they're doing, while a crowd of Green's people filed in after me. There was a foreboding, pressing weight in my chest and a lingering, familiar stench in the air, and we could all hear, even through the enforced steel walls, Ellen Beth shrieking in distress. I turned to the people in the hall and called Arturo, Grace, and Marcus forward, then shooed everyone but Bracken back. (Marcus was also wet and naked—and here I was with my mental camera on stall.) To my surprise, Officer Max—wearing boxer shorts—waded through the crowd with Renny at his elbow and Nicky tagging along behind them.

"Max, this is going to be bad," I said urgently. "If you don't want to be ass-deep in Green's hill, now's the time to bail."

Max's mouth quirked. "I'm balls-deep already," he said, and Renny, naked as a sylph, actually blushed. I hadn't thought she could.

At last the tumbler clicked and the door swung open, and I felt Bracken's hand on my elbow along with a sudden pulling sensation. Then my mind was frozen, recoiling in horror, and there were black spots swimming in front of my eyes as I tried to make sense of what I saw.

Ellen Beth was alone in the room where she had once been with her beloved, and she was covered in blood and shrieking loud enough to shatter glass. I have seen blood in all forms. I have even seen bodies exploded by sound into a big greasy spot of blood and bone, but I had never seen anything like this off orange-black color, nor smelled any blood with the stench of garbage and vomit. There was another pull from my hand as I moved instinctively back, and I turned quizzically toward Bracken. My beloved was staring at the blood like a child would stare at a pretty, poisonous snake, murky eyes wide, lips slightly parted. I pushed at him to break the spell, but it was like pushing a boulder, and Arturo and I locked eyes around Bracken's body. Blood called to Bracken—any blood, even this grotesquerie—and he must not touch it.

"I've got him," Arturo barked, and without pausing he wrapped his arms around Bracken's middle and heaved. Bracken is a big sidhe, but Arturo is just as big and stronger in power, and Arturo picked him up easily and hauled him away without breaking a sweat. Beside me I heard Renny give a little mewl of distress, and I turned to Max, distraught. She had lost her beloved like this, I thought, sickened. So had I, but where Adrian's blood had been sweet and fine, and Mitch's blood had been human and real, this bitter burnt-orange crap was an abomination. I stepped hastily back from the blood that had pooled behind the door and turned toward Max.

"Get her out of here," I said softly, and Max nodded. Good—he would protect Renny where he wouldn't protect himself. That spoke well of them both. When Max hauled Renny into his arms and waded back through the crowd, Nicky faded into the background as well, and I turned toward the scene again and once again tried not to pass out.

I was still trying to breathe and to not smell the stench and to think all at the same time, and I realized that it would be a lot easier if the shrieking, which had carried on uncannily through our silent revulsion, would only stop.

"Ellen Beth!" I called, because she still hadn't stopped shrieking. "Ellen Beth!" But nothing was getting through. She was staring at the epicenter of the blood explosion through wide open eyes, dripping with the foulness that had once been her beloved, staring at the place where Chris had probably stood even as he'd died. My first impulse was to walk up to her and smack her to get her attention, but I didn't want anybody—especially little mortal me—touching that blood. I turned to Phillip, who was looking at the fouled blood like it was going to make him hurl. Good—at least I wouldn't have to bind and gag the vampires in order to keep them away from this crap.

Suddenly Grace stepped forward, and bless the mother in her, she knew how to handle a hysterical woman covered in slime. "Phillip," she barked, "go get a tarp or a raincoat or something, and gloves—you know where I keep the cleaning shit—and slickers for you and Marcus. And jeans and boots...." Phillip was raising his eyebrows like she was talking to a child.

"Dammit, Phillip!" I snapped. "This is fucking important. You listen to Grace, you do what she says—she's trying to keep you alive."

"Damn straight." Grace nodded, then continued, "Don't touch her, don't touch the floor. The two of you need to scoop her up, take her down to the garage, and hose her off. When she's completely clean, wrap her in another tarp, take her to the pool in the smaller Goddess grove, and dump her in. Leave her there until one of the sidhe comes out to heal her. Don't touch her skin. Don't touch her hair. Don't touch the water running off her body. Do you hear me?"

"Yeah, I got it!" He threw up his hands like this was no big deal, and I felt a stab of panic.

"Phillip, don't blow us off. Marcus saw this guy. You can smell that evil shit in the blood. Do you get us? We want you to fucking live!" My voice was getting shrill, but I couldn't help it—Ellen Beth was still screaming, her voice getting higher in octaves but not softer, and Arturo, who should be here to help me, was off locking Bracken in a blood-proof room or something, and it was me and Grace and this... horror, this abomination, and people needed to listen.

Phillip looked at me, finally with somber eyes. "I hear you, Lady Cory." He disappeared, moving in hyperspeed, and I was left staring helplessly at Ellen Beth, who was still hysterical.

"And that," said Grace with satisfaction, "is why we waited months for you to come back. Now do something really important and shut her up so we can think."

Bless her, I thought, *bless her bless her*.... I smiled grimly and turned to the shrieking that seemed to be escalating, if that was even possible.

"Ellen Beth!" I tried again. "Ellen Beth Williams!" There was a fade in her screeching, and I tried again. "Ellen Beth Shrick Williams, beloved of Chris Williams, werecreature by Jon Chase, child of...." Hell, like I knew her parents' names? "Of the Shricks, Ellen Beth Shrick Williams, listen to me." And she was, her eyes white like boiled eggs against the crap-orange nastiness of polluted blood that took up the rest of her face. Those eyes rolled toward me and she whimpered, and I had a moment to wonder if I had looked like that when I'd been covered with Adrian's blood before I blocked the thought out of my mind so I didn't come fucking unglued.

"Ellen Beth," I said after a moment of eerie—if thought-clearing—quiet, "we're going to wash you off. We're going to try to make you... clean... of whatever it is that infected your beloved. We're going to make you want to live. But you have to calm down. You have to let the vampires hose you off, and you have to let them put you in the Goddess's pool, and you have to let the sidhe touch you to heal you, or you might end up just like Chris, and that would really suck!" I was nodding as I spoke, and wonder of all wonders, she began to nod as well.

Arturo was still wrestling Bracken, and dammit, I needed to talk to a sidhe. "Grace—I need a healing sidhe. Any ideas? Someone who would know whether or not this would be a threat to themselves?"

Grace closed her eyes, thought, shook her head. "Ask Green," she said, and I wondered if I was actually that stupid.

"I'm such a dork," I muttered. *"Green."* And I didn't have to try for urgency or panic or even control—it was, oddly enough, all there.

"What are—God, Goddess and other...," he swore, because I let him see through my eyes. *"Don't touch it, beloved,"* he begged, and I gave a silent amen.

"It's got Bracken totally hypnotized, and Arturo is wrestling him to safety. I need someone who can gauge if she can be healed, or cleansed or whatever, but who won't put himself in danger."

"How about herself?" Green asked, and suddenly in my head was a vision of a tiny fey with features so delicate they were almost transparent and eyes the loveliest shade of violet—Sweet. Sweet was a sidhe, but she was smaller than most of her kind, and she tended to be promiscuous even for a species that specialized in sensual abandon. I hadn't known she was a healer—I guess you tended to underestimate a person when they were hitting on everyone you knew, including yourself. Green had needed to pull her aside when we'd gotten back at Christmas and carefully explain that infidelity on Bracken's or my part meant a painful, nasty death for Bracken in order to get her to stop trying to climb into Bracken's bed on the nights I spent with Green. But she was also kind and compassionate, and she had a pixie's humor, and she was one of ours. She was there by my side almost before I called for her, and just as she arrived, Marcus and Phillip—or so I assumed, because all I saw were bulky, fluttery black blurs—came hurtling down the wide hallway with its high ceiling.

"Ellen Beth," I called, holding my hand up to forestall the boys. They stopped in midair and hovered there, covered head to toe in gloves, jeans, boots, and even breath masks and goggles. Ellen Beth's eyes rolled wildly in their orange mask of tainted blood, and her breath came unevenly in pants, but I had her attention.

"Ellen Beth, they're going to cover you, move you, and hose you off, and then they're going to have you strip down and put you in… in a special pool of water. Do you see the woman next to me?" Ellen Beth's eyes darted to Sweet beside me, and she nodded jerkily. "She's going to…." I looked at Sweet, shrugged. The rule at Green's hill was sensual and consensual—no one ever violated it. "She's going to see if touching you is safe for her. If it is, she's going to lay hands on you, however you want her to, she will lay hands on you and make sure you're going to be okay. Do you understand?"

Ellen Beth nodded, and her lips moved. "Chr… Chris…." She shuddered.

I closed my eyes, swallowed. "I know, sweetheart, I know," I whispered. "We'll help you with that too, but it will never go away."

I nodded to Marcus and Phillip, who swept in and out, wrapping her up and whisking her out before my eyes could make sense of their motion. Sweet turned in the stillness afterward. "Don't worry," she said with a smile. "I'll tend to her."

"Tend to yourself too," I answered. "Only touch her if it's going to be safe for you. I mean it, Sweet. We don't want to lose you, either."

Those tiny features lit up suddenly with a warm, genuine smile. "Bless you, Cory—I'll be fine, but thank you so much for worrying." She turned and followed where the vampires had gone, her naked body even tinier and more vulnerable than Renny's had been when Max had hauled her out of the room.

There was a heavy silence, and as I looked after Sweet's retreating form I realized that the crowd at the entrance was waiting for me to say something—anything—to give them direction. Grace nodded at me, encouraging, and I turned toward the group.

"This blood is toxic, people," I said, sticking to the basics. "I want as few people in contact with it as possible. We're still trying to find what caused it, but until we do, and until we get this cleaned up, I don't want anyone near it. It's just not safe for you. Green is researching this… whatever this is. Any information you people have, any encounters or godawful smells or terrible sounds or anything that reminds you of this… abomination, you need to tell one of us about it. Arturo, Grace, Bracken,

Renny, Nicky—you know who you look to, and you know we look out for you. Keep your eyes open. But for now, go back to sleep, and thank the Goddess this hasn't touched us before."

There was a rumble of satisfaction, like they'd needed to hear the proclamation in order to retreat in good conscience, and Grace spoke up next to me. "Nicky—Nicky, you stay. We need you."

Nicky sorted himself out from the gathered, and I looked at Grace in surprise.

"How were you planning to clean this up?" she asked me bluntly. "Because, honey, I don't think there's enough bleach in Placer County."

Oh. "Power?" I asked, and we both nodded. "A shitload... a purge... and enough of it to vaporize the furniture and the electronics and melt it into the metal on the floor." It was extreme. It was frightening, because the last time I'd unleashed that much power to that sort of purpose, I'd almost melted the mountain I'd been standing on.

"I...." I looked at Grace and saw her shake her head. I couldn't say it—I couldn't say I was afraid my control wasn't good enough, because everybody in the damned hill had supersensitive hearing and they were now all tuned to *me,* and that much uncertainty could carry down the damn corridor and undermine everything Green had ever worked for.

"So I get to be a battery?" Nicky said, looking at the two of us and trying to guess what we weren't saying.

I pulled out enough to smile at him reassuringly. "After the other night, darlin', did you doubt it?" That got me a truly happy smile. I checked the corridor behind me and realized it was cold in here with all those people gone, since all I was wearing was one of Green's T-shirts. Bracken had fetched it for me before we'd gone to bed, and as we fell asleep we'd both breathed in Green's smell like it was a wood fire and hot chocolate on a snowy day.

I took a couple of steps back from the doorway, and Grace stood behind me. Then I held out my hand, and Nicky clasped it firmly. Purposefully I remembered sex with Nicky the other night, and it had been *good* sex, and all my nerve endings *had* lit up, and now that buzz of arousal built in my stomach, buzzed around, and filled my chest. I thought of Bracken, and how tender he'd been tonight, making up for the bruises from last night, and my chest grew tight. Then I thought of Green and that wild moment when he'd been in a bed full of naked, beautiful people, and I knew I had to let out the charge in my chest or it would stop my breath.

I held out my free hand, palm out, and saw the supercharged blue glow take it over. It too built and buzzed and fueled and became massive, and then, with a prayer to the Goddess, I thought about walls. I wanted it to expand—but only to the first layer of the metal wall in the darkling room. I didn't want it to melt any more than that. And when I had the dimensions of the room firmly fixed in my mind and knew what I had to do to make my power fit, I let it loose.

There was a clean melt, so hot and so intense that there weren't even any fumes left as the furniture and wood paneling and carpet and television and stereo all vaporized into light, and then the blood fought back.

My power surged against my hands, and I pushed harder. Then a zap of my own whirling light came charging toward my chest, and now I was pissed.

"Fuck you!" I screamed. I didn't know what was fighting me, but nobody did that with my own will—and my anger did the trick, because the bolt blew back into the room and we heard a sizzle. Suddenly the room was down to three metal walls, the inside of the door, and a slightly cooked ventilation shaft, all of which gleamed as though freshly cast and polished.

I stood and stared into the room for a moment, making sure it was clean and we were safe. Then my knees buckled, and Nicky's too, and we both sank gracelessly to the floor, leaning against each other shoulder to shoulder.

"Cocksucking motherfucking son of a whore's bitch," I swore with a shaking voice. "Fucking blood tried to zap me with my own power. This fucker's gotta go down, and hard…."

"Ah, the dulcet sounds of my beloved," Green said in my head, surprising a smile from me as I flopped limply against Nicky. *"I especially liked the part where you imagined me in bed to fuel your power surge."*

I blushed. *"It worked. I'm glad you were with me, beloved."* And I swallowed against tired tears. I wanted him *here,* with all of us, and me in particular.

"I'm packing as we speak," he replied grimly. *"But I don't know when I can get a flight out."*

"Of Marin County?"

"Of Houston. I got here an hour ago."

More weak tears. *"I'm sorry, beloved. I'm sorry we need you right now."*

"Shhhh.... Never be sorry for that. Now let Grace tend you, right?"

I nodded, but as Grace came to scoop me up I said, "Get Nicky first—put him in my bed with Brack, okay?"

"Oh yay," Nicky said weakly. "Puppy pile."

I felt Nicky's weight move, and my side became cold with his absence. I added, "And Green's on his way."

"I don't know why," Grace said, taking pains to make sure I didn't flop against the hardwood of the floor as she scooped Nicky up. "You did just fine on your own."

I giggled weakly because I thought she was being facetious, and suddenly Arturo was there picking me up off the chill floor. "I don't see what's so funny, Corinne Carol-Anne," he grumbled softly. "She's right—you're doing very well."

"But I want Green!" I realized I was whining, and Arturo knew it too, because he laughed.

"Well, far be it from me to get between the two of you when you want each other."

"How's Bracken?" I asked, too tired for another blush. The stairwell was moving by me at a sedate pace, and I knew Arturo was taking his time so we could talk.

"Unconscious. Damned blood call was not letting him go tonight."

"It was the... toxin, the poison... whatever was wrong with Chris's blood, it dicked with Bracken's mind but good," I said. I had felt weaker before—after using power, or when I'd been really sick—but the men in Green's hill liked carrying me around, and I was pretty grateful for it right now. I leaned my head against Arturo's chest and sighed. "Bracken's going to be so pissed about this."

Arturo grunted. "It's in Bracken's nature to be fierce about many things."

"Arturo, that was almost poetry...," I said, surprised and pleased with the description.

"I learn from the best, Corinne Carol-Anne," he replied enigmatically, and then we were in my room and I was getting tucked in between Bracken and Nicky. Even exhausted, the two of them had rolled away from each other, leaving a clear space for me on the gargantuan sidhe-sized king-sized bed. Arturo tucked the covers up around my chin and I cuddled up to Bracken's too still form. Nicky spooned up behind me and the lights went off, and I was out.

An hour later the sound of Renny's screaming shot me bolt upright in bed, but before I could scramble out from around the boys, Max came through my door with a sobbing Renny in his arms.

"She needs you," he said, and Bracken grunted and shifted over some more, which made me happy because it meant his sleep was natural now and not Arturo-induced.

"Everybody hop in," I grumbled, trying to focus in the dark. Max laid Renny between Nicky and me and was going to leave the room, when I said, "You too, Officer Max, if you want. There's plenty of room." Because there had been something lonely and lost about that retreating back in the plain white boxers.

"Bracken won't kill me in my sleep, will he?" he asked, but he was climbing from the foot of the bed to fit himself between Nicky and Renny, and I was surprised to see that his homophobia had receded to the extent that he didn't even bat an eyelash when Nicky turned in to him blindly, searching for human comfort.

"Not without warning," I yawned and settled down again, this time with Bracken at my back and my arms around a shivering Renny.

"It was bad for her," Max said, fitting his arms around mine and meeting my eyes over Renny. "To see someone else die the way Mitch did."

"And Adrian," I surprised myself by saying tightly. "It didn't do a lot for me to see it either."

"You're handling it better," he stated.

"Adrian's blood was better," I told him. "Vampires go out the way they've lived. Adrian's blood… it was almost cleansing. Sweet and good and life affirming, even as he died again." Max's eyes grew thoughtful, even in the dark.

"And Renny didn't kill a hundred people with her grief," I added harshly after a moment. "Or suck the life out of the men she loved when it still threatened to kill her. I can't let my grief or my love or my passion hurt the people around me any more than necessary."

Max was a mortal human, and he had previously regarded me with both desire and contempt. What I saw on his face now was much gentler, and much more important. "Go to sleep, Lady Cory," he said, and I grimaced.

"Not you too…," I yawned. It was three in the morning—our alarm went off at six.

"Yes. Me too. Now hush, or you'll wake my beloved."

I smiled as I fell asleep, because I knew Renny was really truly in love with Max. To hear this stoic cop, who once upon a time didn't seem to have any poetry at all in his soul, use that word, gave me hope that there would be a happy ever after.

GREEN
Funky Man

HOUSTON WAS chilly and grim in January, Green thought dismally as he hauled his suitcase and duffel bag from the hotel to the rental car. Not that Foresthill didn't have its share of snow, but... but not on Green's temperate hill, anyway. The flat, cast-iron colored sky of Houston was uninterrupted by any mountains but the man-made kind, and the effect was, to a sidhe who had spent the last hundred and fifty years in the Sierra Foothills, oddly claustrophobic.

Green wanted home so badly he could taste it in his throat like an old lover.

There was a wild-eyed homeless man crouched at the corner of the hotel, scenting the wind like a hound. His skin was crusted with grime, and hair of an indeterminate color lay twisted into dreadlocks close about his scalp, visibly crawling with vermin. The look he gave Green was the look of a dog who had been beaten so badly he didn't know whom to turn to in search of food.

"That's him...," the man half sang to himself, looking at Green longingly from eyes so brown they made mahogany look gray. "That's the fine and mighty lord, gonna turn, gonna turn, gonna turn away the funky man...."

Green stopped short. Looked at the man. Blinked. Blinked again. Dropped his duffel and came closer, trying hard not to gag at the smell.

"Hello, brother," he said cautiously, looking at his fellow sidhe. He hunkered down, not close enough to intimidate, but close enough to look, stunned and appalled, past the filth and grime of living from the tainted, buried earth of the city. "You've been alone a long time."

Those brown eyes glistened silver, true silver, and Green caught his breath as a drop of molten metal rolled down the filthy face, since only a true sidhe could weep silver when moved.

"Funky man's no one's brother," he choked. "Funky man got left behind, funky man's got no more mind. No one sees the funky man, no one wants to. No one can."

"I see you, Funky Man," Green said gently, his mind racing. Sidhe were strong. They were brilliant. And those who were mad were quietly mad, alone in the woods or the hills where no one could call their madness anything but the behavior of a fox or a bear or a rabbit. Sidhe didn't just... break, like cheap plastic toys, to become a part of the human wreckage that littered the cities.

"You see me...," Funky Man whispered. "You see me, you turn away. But I had to try, fine lord, just to see you... just to hear the voice of a man who was my brother. Hollow man came and sucked me empty, brother sidhe... and funky man's been so alone...." Now more tears, not the silver kind, but the plain brine of flesh and blood, came spilling over Funky Man's face, washing away thin curls of grime. In the relatively clear spaces, Green could see that the man's skin wasn't dark brown, or chocolate colored as he'd first believed, but a gold-toned violet so deep that it only took a little dust, a little grime, to act as the glamour that his lost brother could apparently no longer conjure.

"The hollow man?" Green ventured, not wanting to upset Funky Man any more than necessary.

"Pretty...," Funky mumbled, "so pretty.... Pretty human boy, love them human boys and girls... they used to be my whole wide world, but hollow man done sucked me dry... didn't give me a goddamned why... all funky's left to do is cry...."

The hollow man. Green shivered. He hadn't had any news at all of their enemy, this creature who tainted blood and addicted werecreatures and killed sylphs and smelled like fermenting flesh. But Funky Man, whoever he once had been, had known this threat up close and personal, and had only partly survived.

And besides, Green thought wretchedly, looking longingly at his duffel and the rental car he'd bribed a puzzled mechanic to douse in salt water and herbs before he'd driven away. Besides. He couldn't just leave this lost brother, this wretched desolate Funky Man, who had hunched out in the cold waiting for the sound of a fellow sidhe's voice and the dismissal of his eyes. But oh, Goddess... Goddess....

"I want to go home, Funky Man," Green said miserably, feeling plain salt tears start in his own eyes. "I have a beloved, and family, and lovers who need me, who are under attack even now."

Funky Man made a miserable keening sound in his throat. Before he could break into sobs, Green threw a reluctant arm over his shoulder and felt the sigh that rippled through the man's body at simple animal contact.

"I want to go home, brother," Green said, feeling wretched. "But I want to take you with me, okay?"

And Funky Man lurched against Green's shoulder, sobbing in earnest now. "Oh please, my brother, please… don't leave me in the cold anymore…."

"No," Green said, being careful not to let his plaited hair brush against Funky Man's lice-ridden head. "But how about a bath first, right?"

"Right… right… all is right…," Funky Man chanted, and Green was grateful that it was three thirty in the morning, with no prying eyes to see as he grabbed his duffel with one hand and hauled Funky with the other back into the hotel and up the two floors to his room, which was, after all, paid up for another four days.

It took two tubs of hot, hot water and half of the generous amount of the homemade shampoo in Green's duffel. Midway through, he summoned a couple of sprites—they seemed to rotate to travel with him, for which he was ever grateful—and had them fetch scissors, a clean brush, clean comb, and a box of RID lice shampoo from a local pharmacy. He spent the second batch of water cutting Funky Man's hair, then treating his scalp for the lice—which had, on the sidhe's rich blood, grown bloated, fat, and even slower than these vermin usually moved. Funky Man wept quietly through the ministrations, looking at his long, clean, pitifully thin limbs mournfully, petting his severed dreadlocks with doleful fingers and then dutifully allowing Green to wrap them in a plastic bag along with his rank clothes for disposal.

"I was beautiful," he wept. "I was sidhe, and I was so pretty. So, so pretty."

"You are still pretty, brother," Green said kindly, rubbing a now clean, gold-violet back soothingly with a bath sponge. "You are still pretty—but we need to fatten you up and make you strong, and you will feel well again."

Funky Man nodded, happily it seemed, and rested his head on his arm as Green finished with one last wash of all cracks, crevices, and hidden parts. There were scars on the sidhe's body, when the sidhe never scarred—scars from scrapes, from cuts, scars around his anus, where, heaven knows, he had probably been violated on the streets. Adrian had possessed those scars too, Green thought, and in spite of a hundred and fifty years of healing, and Cory's magnificent healing effort in the garden one magic-filled summer night, they had never left his marble-white skin.

"Good touch, lord of leaves, good touch, lord of shadows...," Funky sang, and Green made an effort to pull himself back to the present, making sure to put just a little bit of power in his touch, a little bit of healing, not enough to startle. But that didn't stop him from remembering Adrian.

Adrian had been beautiful and broken too, Green mused, but in spite of the similarities of the situation, and the actions of bathing and healing a filthy, damaged victim, the similarities ended there. Where Funky Man had been despondent, Adrian had been full of rage. Green had let Adrian take out the rage on his own quick-healing body, and then had taught him what real love could be. He wasn't sure if Funky Man was strong enough for that kind of healing, not now, not yet. Green bundled Funky Man into a towel, rubbing the thin limbs—still straight, still with the possibility for strength—until the violet-gold skin pinkened and glowed with health and a remembered vitality. He thought that, even more important than the weakness, or the skin color or even the species, was the most vital fact of all.

Green had loved Adrian dearly, even from that first glower of those furious sky-spangled eyes. Just as Adrian had loved Cory with one touch on her palm, and she had loved them both in spite of all her efforts to the contrary, Green had loved Adrian as his beloved from the very start.

Funky Man was a brother, and they might even share their flesh together, but Green wasn't sure, here in this lonely, quiet hotel room in the middle of the night, if he had room for one more heartbreak of a beloved in his sore and battered soul.

After Funky Man was dry, Green sent the sprites for food. They returned, exhausted and only at half their usual glow, with what appeared to be Grace's leftover vegetable lasagna, and Green almost wept with gratitude. He cupped his hands and bade the seven sprites to gather there, and then he bent his head, close enough to see the tiny details of their other-than-human faces. Legend said that the sprites were made when the Goddess and the other took the forms of birds and rodents and bats and flying bugs, and often their piquant faces took on those very characteristics. Softly, with gratitude and love, Green breathed a little power onto his tiny gathered brethren, and they glowed brightly again as they collapsed on each other in an instant, satisfyingly spelled sleep. "Good job, my little ones," he whispered and placed them carefully in the top of his duffel bag.

When he and Funky had finished off the lasagna—Funky ate voraciously, but had room in his stomach for very little in order to be full—Green wrapped Funky Man tightly in a brown-and-green quilt that Grace had made him just for travel to help him remember home. Together they lay, Funky Man's thin, shivering body balled up into a tight wad of self-defense. Green gathered him into his arms, soothing and singing, until Funky Man's shivering subsided and he began his own humming in his throat. As miserable as Green was to be alone and away from home, he had to smile. Good—brother could still sing.

The darkness of the hotel weighed on them both for a moment, and then Funky Man spoke, his voice still moving up and down to the tune Green had started.

"Green man has a beloved. Beautiful, is she? Tell me 'bout beloved, green man, won't you please tell me?"

Green's throat caught. Ah, Goddess, to talk about Cory. He'd been locked in business meetings with humans since he'd left the sylphs. Although he was familiar with the people who dealt with franchise holders, he'd scrupulously kept his distance from them—he'd never mentioned his personal life, he never shared lunches with them. As far as most of them thought, he still lived in England and was as gay as an Easter parade. And sometimes, he thought, according to their standards, so he was.

"She's not beautiful to humans," Green said roughly. "But she smiles, and the world grows brighter. She has a mouth like a sewer rat—unless she's using it on you, and then it's like an angel, or unless she's speaking from her heart, and then it's like the thunder of a thousand waterfalls. She's human, but in one month she managed to love me and our beloved, and when he died she survived the loss. Barely, but she survived. She even grew stronger. Her heart's too big for just one beloved—especially one who has to spend so much of his time with his people—so I share her with another, except it never feels as though we are sharing because she gives us everything with every breath. And she doesn't see it. Good men love her, fine sidhe, beautiful vampires, heartbreaking shape-changers—and she doesn't let us down." It came pouring out of him, praise for Cory, frustration that he couldn't be home for her, and Funky Man lay still in Green's arms and listened.

"Funky man likes humans," he said after a quiet moment when Green's heart was too full to speak. "Humans love funky man like sidhe never could."

Green grimaced there in the dark. "We can be a cruel species," he said harshly.

"Not you, green man," Funky reassured, yawning, and Green wondered how hard it must be to sleep on the streets, how many years of exhaustion had haunted the battered Funky Man. "You're all that is good. Be here in the morning, green man?" And the pleading note in his voice hurt to hear. "Don't be no dream of funky man?"

"I'll be here," Green reassured, and with that, Funky Man faded into a sweet, deep sleep.

Green couldn't claim the same. His mind drifted to Cory, and although he was weak from helping her earlier, and it got harder and harder to move in and out of her mind, he visited her bed, where she lay snuggled with…. He had to smile. With everyone, it seemed. Even Max had climbed in, and Nicky had spooned him as naturally as if he'd been Green himself. Scary night, Green thought sadly. It had been a scary night, an awful sight for all of them. For Bracken and Cory and Renny, it had been a night of cruel memories resurrected in the most brutal of ways. He would call in the morning, he thought, kissing her brow with the unsubstantial presence that he was. He would call her and disappoint her, and she would hear about Funky Man and say "Of course you have to stay, beloved."

And he would miss her even more.

CORY
Aversions

THE ALARM went off at six, and I was the only one who moved. I started off by shoving at Bracken until he groaned, "Wha'th'fu?" and I said, "School." And then I shoved him into the wall so I could crawl out between Renny's overgrown-tabby-sized body and his own oak tree-sized one.

Renny surfaced from under the covers—she had ended up with the comforter drawn completely over her head, while the rest of us had our heads lined up on the pillows like children—and said, "School? Are you fucking kidding me?"

"It's Tuesday—we haven't even had these classes yet!" I urged, heading toward the bathroom. "If we don't go today, they're going to drop us."

"Aw, crap," she said at the same time Nicky muttered, "Oh Jesus, Cory." Then I heard a thump and a "Shit!" and figured he'd forgotten that he was on the end of the bed and had fallen off.

I turned around at the bathroom and saw Nicky crawling up from the floor to go use his own shower and Renny moving quietly out of bed so as not to disturb Max, and I smiled. "Bracken?" I said.

"Ugghhh...."

"Do you realize that the only people left in that bed right now are you and Max? And that one of you is naked?"

There were two more thumps and an "Oh... oh... ewww.... Ickkkkk!" and an "Oh, Jesus, shit, Cory, did you have to bring that up?" and suddenly the two men were standing up and facing each other with eyes that were completely awake but brains that were obviously catching up.

Renny turned around at the bedroom door, saying, "Which one of you big strong men just squealed like a little girl?"

"I think that would be the bisexual one," I said, raising amused eyebrows in my beloved's direction.

"Oh, crap," Max said, blinking with disbelief at Bracken's naked body. "Don't you have to put a red flag on that thing if it's not in the garage?"

"Be careful, little man," Bracken answered with grim amusement, "or it will reach out and touch you."

"You win. You're obviously the, uhm, bigger man." And with that, Max flashed an ironic grin at me and turned to follow Renny out the door, leaving me laughing softly and shaking my head.

"Feel better?" I asked Bracken as he moved in for his morning hug.

"About what?" he asked complacently, and I laughed some more and raised to my toes so I could wrap my arms around his neck and pull him down for a kiss.

"About the amount of testosterone in your ego," I replied after a touch of his warm lips on mine. I was only partly facetious now, and Bracken's expression grew dark.

"What happened after Phillip opened the door?" he asked seriously.

"You looked at the blood and disappeared," I answered in kind. I did him the courtesy of not hiding how worried I had been. "The blood was... contaminated. Poisoned. Obscene. I can't explain it any better. You know what real blood looks like—and this wasn't it."

"Where did the blood come from?" Bracken asked, and I had to blink twice.

"You don't remember *anything*? No, no, obviously not...." I shook my head, started over again. And found it was harder to say than it had been to see. I swallowed, took a breath, swallowed again, and said, "He'd exploded. Chris Williams—there was no bone shrapnel, no...." I'd seen them when a vampire had exploded on me, when Green had killed the men who had killed Adrian.... "No sticky bits. It was just blood...."

Bracken closed his eyes. "Ah, Goddess...," he moaned. His arms came around me, crushing me against him like he could protect me even from the memory, and I knew suddenly that I'd been waiting for Bracken or Green so that I could fall gently apart about this. I'd been strong last night. I'd led our people. This morning I got to tremble like Jell-O in an earthquake.

"But it was bad blood. It wasn't clean or powerful. It wasn't even... human or were or anything anymore." Now I was cold, and only Bracken could warm me.

"I'm sorry. I wasn't there for you. I'm so sorry...."

"It's not your fault, beloved. It wasn't anyone's...." I sniffled, and I knew I had to pull myself together. We had to leave, and I had to check on

Ellen Beth, and I just couldn't do this. Not right now. "The blood fought back," I said after a vulnerable moment, and I was pissed off enough about this to pull my spine up and stop shaking. "Nicky was there, and Green was in my head, but it put up a hell of a fight—whatever the fuck it was, it tried to zap me back."

"The *blood?*"

"Whatever was in it," I amended. "But it pissed me off."

Bracken smiled a small smile, and I knew that he was having his own reaction. We all remembered, we all had dreamed about it, we all woke up with the cold sweats. Arturo, Renny, and I got to remember Mitch watching Renny change to cat form with a puzzled expression, then a sudden, panicked look of discomfort, then pain—then his body, like red paint in a centrifuge, simply becoming gore. And so many more of us, Bracken included, remembered Adrian's defiant smile as he swooped out of the sky to grab the silver net that he thought was threatening us, but was really a trap for him. And we remembered his body fragmenting like a popped water balloon, and the fine spray of blood that had covered us all.

"Well, I'm rather pissed off about getting sucked into it so badly that I don't even remember it," Bracken said after a moment. We both swallowed, sort of a tandem vow to be pissed off instead of devastated, and then I grabbed his hand and hauled him into the shower. We didn't make love, but we did touch an awful lot, and Bracken whispered lazy suggestions in my ear about what we could spend our days doing if I wasn't so hell-bent on going to school.

"I was all for quitting," I reminded him wistfully as he toweled my hair dry. "Green insisted we keep slogging away."

Bracken grunted. That was the one argument he had no retort for, and we both knew it. Conversation stumbled then, both of us thinking about Green and how badly we missed him, I guessed, and we fell into the morning routine we'd begun to establish in December when we'd become roommates as well as lovers.

Of course, my routine was a lot simpler now—a year ago, before I'd met Adrian, I would have spent twenty minutes glopping on mascara, packing on white powder, and penciling my eyes black, then another ten carefully arranging my spiky goth silver earrings and making sure none were missing.

Today I had a delicate row of yellow-gold hoops in a sweet little line up each ear. The sprites had put them in as I'd slept on Christmas

Eve, and it had been a true surprise and a splendid gift. They never got infected, never caught on anything, and never needed to be taken out. I liked the look—it was a compromise between the insecure bitch I had been when I'd met Adrian, the pathetic mess who didn't wear any jewelry at all that I'd become after Adrian died, and the stronger, wiser person I'd become in the last year.

The makeup, however, was still a project under construction. I had lightened up on the makeup after I moved to Green's hill, and for the last month or so, Bracken and I had been waging a silent war over whether or not I should wear any at all. I bought it, Bracken threw it away, and the sprites (who liked me best) rescued only the stuff they liked from the trash and often added colors of their own. I was particularly fond of an earthy mauve eye shadow that was spangled with gold. Bracken would see me put the makeup on, grunt "You don't need to wear that crap," and then throw away only what he didn't like. Through the last few weeks we had arrived at a couple of mutually satisfactory makeup schematics. The mauve eye shadow stayed, the black lipstick—left over from my goth days and applied when I was in a snit with Bracken—was worn once and never seen again.

Bracken went to the kitchen to get breakfast and then back to our rooms to get ready. I had just finished shoving my running shoes and sweats in a plastic bag and then shoving the bag into the backpack with my knitting and water bottles (oh, yeah—and my schoolbooks) when Arturo came through the door without knocking.

"Cory, Green's on the phone for you," he said abruptly, and I blinked, the simple motion covering up a well of disappointment.

"Won't we see him today?" I asked, but I guess I already knew the answer to that.

"He's found... a brother. A sidhe—who's met our enemy," Arturo replied, and he looked so distressed that I found I wanted to comfort him, instead of being comforted myself.

"That's good?"

"He's been... on the street. Green says he has... scars. And... lice. And... gray in his hair."

Oh, Goddess, no wonder Arturo was shaken, I thought, a bit horrified myself. "And he didn't have a leader? A hill of his own?" No brothers to care for him? No sisters to share flesh with? No Green to make it all better?

"No one." Arturo swallowed. "Green wants to bring him home, but we're working out how. A simple saltwater wash on a rental isn't going to do it with this guy...."

"The Cadillac," I said abruptly. Of course—the Caddy was Arturo's favorite car. It had been herb and salt washed and spelled and blessed and driven so many times by elves and sidhe that the lower fey actually slept in it when they felt the urge. The lower fey were like canaries in the magic coal mine—what was bad for the higher fey usually got to them first.

Arturo's eyes widened. "Of course. Who's going to drive it?"

I sighed and rubbed my forehead. I needed to get on the phone with Green.

"He's talking to Grace right now," Arturo reassured gently, and I gave him a weak smile.

"Okay. How's he sound?" I asked tentatively, already sort of knowing the answer.

"Weak," Arturo replied baldly. "Frustrated. Missing you. Missing home. Before, he's only been gone a week at most. This is his longest trip away from the hill."

I swallowed. Oh, my beloved—so far away from our touch.

Our touch.

"Go get Nicky," I said abruptly. "Get Nicky, tell him to pack, tell him Renny and I will take notes for him at school. And..." (*think think think think*) "...get Leah, if she's game." Leah had a revolving pantheon of shape-changers and sidhe in her bed—sleeping with our leader should be no big deal. "If not, find another shape-changer who is. If you can find a sidhe who won't get sick in the travel, find one." Instinctively I looked toward my wall for a window, but my room was toward the middle of the hill—the wraparound bay window affected the living room and all the bedrooms across the hall, and although there was a skylight that seemed to come and go at odd times when I was sleeping in, it didn't appear in the corner now. "The sun's not up yet, right? We've got about half an hour." Arturo nodded that I was right, and I went on, thinking as I spoke. "When I get the phone from Grace, have her find a vampire who wouldn't mind sleeping in the Caddy's trunk and have him jump in right now. We want one of everybody, but especially Nicky—he's tied to me, I'm on the hill...." I swallowed, feeling sad and hopeful and helpless, even as I planned my ass off. "Green needs his people, Arturo. Let's get them to him."

Arturo nodded, a slow smile making the silver caps on his teeth flash. "I can drive, Corinne Carol-Anne, if you like."

A part of me leaped at the idea, but I found myself shaking my head—and blushing furiously. "Uhm... Green's going to need people who... who can touch him," I said lamely, not becoming uncomfortable with the idea of sending lovers to sustain my lover until actually having to put it into words.

Arturo's copper lightning-colored eyes widened, and he looked vaguely embarrassed. "I should have thought of that," he said sheepishly, and I put my hand on his arm and then launched myself into the full hug.

"We all miss him," I said softly. "If I wasn't next in the power chain... if the hill didn't need me... I'd be over on the next flight and I'd walk home to be with him." I smiled a little as I felt the comfort of Arturo's completely platonic and unconditionally accepting arms around me. "And Bracken would be with me."

I felt Arturo nod as his chin brushed my hair. "And you would have magnificent adventures in the wilderness," he said lightly, "and I would still be left behind."

"With your vampire queen," I said, and felt a stillness. Oh, no.... "Give her and Chloe some time," I suggested. "Grace loves you—you know that...."

"Speaking of...," he replied brusquely, obviously not wanting to discuss the matter. "You need to go get the phone."

A minute later I was taking the phone from Grace and pointing her toward Arturo, making kissing faces at her and glaring. Then Green spoke, and I didn't have time or brain cells or heart muscles left for anybody else because he sounded sad and tired and *Oh, Goddess!* I missed him so badly I had to sit down in the middle of the room and rest my head against the couch.

"How you holding up, luv?" he asked gently.

"As well as you are," I told him with some sincere irony.

"Oh, no. I expect much better than that from you, Corinne Carol-Anne." And finally there was his humor, the faint irony that made him Green. "So—have you tested the limits of the bed?"

I had to laugh. I had dreamed of a field of mustard flowers and lupines last night—he must have been checking up on me. "Sleeps five. We could probably fit another werekitty at the foot, but Bracken might kick her off in his sleep." I giggled. "You should have heard him squeal like a little girl when he realized he was in bed with Officer Max. Absolutely priceless."

We both shared a laugh before sobering in the same breath. "I'm sending you a care package," I said brightly into the strained silence.

"Cookies and letters?" Again, that try for humor.

"I know you've been sending the sprites for food, so cookies are the last thing you need!" Grace had been making a fresh batch of cookies every night and placing them on the table. She told me that in the mornings about half of them would be gone. The thought of Green filching cookies like a depressed little kid made me want to laugh and cry at the same time.

"I've been good—last night it was the vegetable lasagna. Funky Man thought it was the best thing he'd ever had."

Funky Man. "Is that our brother?" I asked, wondering at the name.

"Yes—I don't know who he was before he met this 'Hollow Man,' but he's become Funky Man now." Green's voice was soft and distressed, and I wondered how hard it must be to see a fellow, in a race known for its pride and power, pulled so low that even humans wouldn't look at him.

"What's he doing now?" I asked, genuinely curious.

"He's huddled in a corner wearing a terry cloth robe, eating Grace's cookies and watching *House of Mouse* on cable. I don't know when I've seen anybody so happy." And now his voice was warm with affection, and with the satisfaction of seeing someone he cared for contented and well.

"Well, then, of course you have to stay." Green's breath caught for some reason, but I was on the verge of losing it completely so I just kept on talking. "Your care package is coming in the Cadillac," I choked out. "You need to let them take care of you, beloved, so you can bring our brother back to us and be well and strong."

"You're very good at this whole 'leader' thing, you know," he said, and I could tell his voice was choking up too.

"I learn from the best," I managed, and then I fell apart. "Green, I've got to go. Nicky's here—I'll give the phone to him, and he can take directions, okay?"

"Beloved...," he said, helpless to stop the flood of tears, and we both knew it.

"I love you, you're the sun and the moon and the stars, and I know you love me too.... Here's Nicky."

And with that I thrust the phone up at Nicky. Bracken, who had heard most of the conversation, came up behind me, and as soon as Nicky had the phone, he scooped me up in his arms to let me come unglued if I needed it. I tried really hard not to need it. I struggled out of Bracken's arms, trying to hold myself together, but I had a feeling that the damage had been done. I was tired, I was depressed because Green wasn't coming home, and I had started out the day crying. It was going to be one of those days where it sucked to be a girl, because—I could feel it in my throat—any dumb-assed thing was going to set me off into tears again, but I was damned if I was going to go that way without a struggle.

"I've got to check on Ellen Beth," I managed, wiping away my carefully applied makeup with a few swipes of my hand. "Bracken, could you get my backpack?" He nodded, giving me the space I needed to pull myself together. Nicky had written down directions and said his good-byes to Green—private good-byes, like mine had been, because he loved Green too—and was just cradling the phone. "Nicky, can you come with me?"

Nicky nodded, and we went walking through the great house toward the sidhe levels—they were the ones graced with two stories of wraparound windows and a staircase that brought them straight to the garage and from there outside, so they could walk their land and stay strong.

"I'm sorry to pull you out of class, Nick," I said after my (swear to God) last sniffle. "He needs one of us—he needs a connection to the hill, and beloved hands on his skin, and all the things we give him—and the hill needs my power...." I trailed off, knowing I was putting this so badly I would probably offend him for life.

"No problem at all, Lady Cory," he said, ignoring all the possible offenses—a character trait that made me love him. I mean... I guess I really did love him, didn't I? The thought dropped in on me like an anvil from heaven as I prepared to send him away. It was not as much, or the same, as I loved Green and Bracken, but... he'd been inside my body... he was my friend.... "I mean," he was saying, "I guess it's my calling in life, right? I make a great battery."

I stopped in my tracks and whirled to face him, suddenly realizing how my own struggles with our binding and Nicky's own bad fortune had affected him, when I had been too blind to see. "You are more than a battery," I said fiercely, looking him dead on in his especially round, bird-shaped light brown eyes.

Nicky suddenly looked very wise. "C'mon, Cory," he said gently. "We both know I'll never be your beloved. I'll never be Green's beloved. I'm an obligation. It's just good to have something to give back, that's all."

And I was on the verge of tears all over again, fuck everything and its little dog too. "You're my *friend!*" I said angrily. "Do you have any idea how important that is?"

He was still looking at me, condescension in the angle of his head, in his eyes, and I could tell he didn't.

"Nicky—do you remember when you used to call me, back in the city?" I said on a note of desperation. "Green would call me every sunset, because that's when we missed Adrian the most, and we'd talk for an hour, and then he'd have to go. And then you'd call, about an hour later—and you weren't my lover, and you didn't want anything from me, and there was no pain between us... and we just *talked.* We just *talked* about anything— music and classes and stupid television shows and action-adventure movies...." I shook my head. "I *treasured* your phone calls, you stupid dork. They came to mean something to me because you *weren't* my lover, and you still wanted to be around me, and you've seen enough of Cory the Superbitch to know that this is a big fucking deal...." The angle of his head had changed, and I could tell he was listening, and that impassioned me more. "And besides! This thing you're doing with Green—you're taking my love to him in your body. You realize that we both have to love you for you to do that, right? It may not be the kind of love you dreamed about as a little kid, but you're nourishing both of us... and that's an important thing! You know that, right? That you're important to us?" I was already weak with tears and, goddammit, nothing could stop them. "You couldn't be who you are to Green and me if you were only a human battery," I said on another sniffle, and suddenly it was Nicky holding me and not Bracken. His body was slight and mortal and small, but he loved me, and he loved my beloved. Everything I'd told him was true, and I gave back his hug with sincerity and even with the sexual attraction that had bloomed to life the other night, and he returned in kind. Then his mouth was covering mine, and it wasn't a passionate kiss—it was a kiss of friends who happened to be lovers, and it was just right.

He broke away for a moment, and we held the hug. "Thank you, Cory," he said softly. "Don't worry. I'll take care of him for us, okay?"

"Okay, Nicky," I replied. "I love you. Maybe not the way you want, but it's still love."

"It's more than I could ask for," he said kindly. He kissed me again and turned around to trot down the hall. I watched his slender form walk away and couldn't help worrying about how sad it was that Nicky hadn't thought to ask for someone to love him the way I loved Green or Bracken. Doesn't everybody deserve a beloved? But time was pressing and I could ask him that when he got back. For now, right now, Nicky would be okay. And hey, for the moment anyway, the tears were pushed away.

Sweet's door was still locked, and indeterminate sounds of either grief or lovemaking were coming through it, so I had to table Ellen Beth's plight for a while. I said good-bye to Nicky, Leah, and Willow (a tall, well, willowy sidhe with pale green skin, silver-brown hair, and willow-bark silver eyes), cautioning them to switch drivers often, let Ellis (who was safe in the trunk of the Caddy already) drive at night, and stop if they needed to. I kissed Nicky good-bye again, on the mouth, with tongue, and made sure they all had Arturo's numbers and mine in their cell phones, then shooed them on their way so I could herd us students out the door as well.

As I put my black peacoat on over my green hooded sweatshirt and gathered the others to me, I told Arturo to call me on my cell phone at school if anything came up. Officer Max came into the living room as we were getting ready to leave and put his hands on Renny's shoulders, pulling her back against him.

"I'll drive too," he offered. "In case you and Bracken need to leave."

I was going to tell him that wasn't necessary—but judging by the way Renny was rubbing against him, I figured that she needed more comfort than Bracken or I could give her, and that to Renny, it was probably vital. "Thank you," I said softly, looking at Renny's misery. "That's really awesome of you, Max."

"Any time, Lady Cory," he returned, his mouth quirking up.

At that moment Bracken came in, hauling my backpack and his, and looking at me with narrowed eyes. I wasn't sure what he was mad about until he set my pack down with a thump and a raised eyebrow and said, "Go ahead. Lift it up. I dare you."

Between the knitting, the running gear, the four bottles of water, the three textbooks, and the binder, it must have weighed around thirty-five pounds. I hauled it up with an "oomph" and was throwing it around my back to catch the other strap when Bracken launched into a monologue of profanity that heated even my cheeks and plucked the pack out of my hands. Swinging it up over his own shoulder—the one not carrying his own pack— he finished up with a snort and a "Damned stubborn woman."

"Thank you," I said sheepishly. He snorted again, and finally we all managed to get out the door.

The day was a blur of note-taking and knitting during lectures to stay awake—the latter earned me a couple of dirty looks from professors, but I've discovered I listen better when I knit, so screw 'em. At nearly twelve thirty, I left Bracken in the library—with my backpack, at his surly insistence—and walked to the psych building where Professor Hallow's office was situated. As I trotted dutifully through the chill sunshine and plentiful shadows, I realized that I'd been dreading this little conversation all day.

Hallow was waiting for me, the promised pizza sitting on his desk still in a box, and I had to laugh.

"You didn't really need to feed me," I said, a little embarrassed, as I sat down.

"I did if I wanted to live," Hallow retorted lightly. Then, seriously, "You look like hell, Corinne.... Lady Cory. Bad night?"

I grimaced. This was, sadly, probably going to hurt him more than it hurt me. The story of the night came pouring out, and I was right. By the time I had finished up with Green's new friend and his postponed trip home, Hallow was pale, and lines of grief had begun to pull at the corners of his mouth and eyes.

"I'm so sorry," I said at last. "I know that was hard to hear. That's how Jon went out, isn't it?"

Hallow shook his head. "I don't know, actually. I just... I felt him die in my heart. You know how that feels?"

Yes. Adrian had marked me twice before he died, and once as his soul left his body. Any mark like that, like the one between Bracken and me, or between Nicky and me—well, when the person who shared that mark is gone, it leaves a big gaping hole in... everything. Your heart. Your soul. Reality at large. "Yes," I said after a moment. "Yes, I know. I'm really sorry you had to go through that. Is there anything we can do?"

Hallow dragged a hand over his face, lost in his own pain, I guess. There was a moment of silence, and I was comfortable with that, with letting him grieve. Suddenly he focused his sharp cerulean eyes on me. "Very neatly done, Lady Cory," he said after a moment. "You slid right out of your role as patient and right into the role of Lady Protector."

I flushed. "I was just doing what...." I trailed off, uncomfortable with how that sentence was going to end.

"Doing what?" he asked flatly.

"I was just trying to help," I finished with dignity. "I know what your pain feels like. I didn't want you to feel alone."

"You can't feel alone as part of Green's collective," Hallow told me, his eyes growing kind, and I smiled.

"No. That's what's wonderful about it," I agreed, relieved.

"But you have a unique position in the collective, don't you?" he asked, and I almost groaned. I glanced at the wall clock and saw that it was a few minutes shy of the time for Bracken to start on his way over.

"Well, I'm neither fish nor fowl, am I?" I asked back. "I just do what anybody there does—I use the Goddess's gifts to help the Goddess's people, right? You know, we're almost out of time...."

"We've got a few minutes yet. You haven't even eaten any pizza!"

"I'm not hungry."

"I'll tell Bracken," he said with a smile, and I snatched a piece of pizza from the box and took a bite. It was Mountain Mike's—and he'd ordered it with meat. My chewing slowed and I savored for a moment. While my mouth was still full, he looked at me curiously and asked, "How old are you, Cory?"

I blinked and swallowed. "Twenty," I said through half a mouthful.

"Wow—you're still a child, even to humans."

"Yeah," I swallowed the rest. "I'm practically a fetus. Can I go now?"

"So how did it feel to be commanding Green's hill last night?" Shit. I guess not. I set the pizza down on his desk, suddenly not hungry in the least, and he continued. "Something horrible happens, and everybody turns to you and voilà! You've got the answers, and you hope they're right but you don't know. Your ou'e'hm is a thousand miles away—how do you feel about that?"

I looked at him blankly, then looked at the clock. Gratefully, I stood and started to back away. "You know, I've got to hurry if I'm going to make it onto the track!" I said brightly, moving toward the door.

"I can freeze the doorknob shut until Bracken gets here and knocks it down," Hallow replied sweetly. "It's a legitimate question, Cory. How did you feel about taking over Green's hill last night?"

I needed to be out of Hallow's room before Bracken showed up, I thought, trying to ignore the cold sweat that was making my hands clammy. He'd bitch about me eating, I'd have to go running on a full stomach, everything would fall to hell.

"Can I just go?"

"Answer the question—it's not hard." He sounded all kind and paternal, and it pissed me off enough to give him the truth.

"Fucking inadequate. Are you happy now?"

"Not yet. One more question before you go." Because I had my hand on the door handle even though it was locked in place.

"Fine," I said, knowing my eyebrows were drawn together and my expression was totally hostile. "Can I leave then?"

"Absolutely," he promised. "But here's the thing: Green trusts you. Adrian trusted you—he gave his people to you. Hell, even Arturo looks to you. Bracken has literally put his life in the beating of your heart. Why feel inadequate? Why not feel confident?"

I felt tears threaten—it seemed to be a day for them—and I swallowed fiercely. "Because I don't know what they see in me," I whispered at last. "I never have. And I have to get the fuck out of here right the hell now." And like magic the door handle turned in my hand and I was gone, trotting blindly down the hallway and hoping to meet Bracken in the quad so I could get my running gear from him and go straight to the track.

I had just cleared the psych building, and could see the student union off to my left and the library beyond that, when I heard a voice calling my name—my unmarried name. I was already so entrenched in being Cory Op Crocken Green that I didn't know the idiot shouting "Cory Kirkpatrick!" was actually talking to me until a meaty hand descended on my shoulder and I was swung around to face the star offensive tackle of my high school football team.

"Cory Kirkpatrick! I knew that was you! Jeez—you get deaf since high school?"

"Chuck Granger," I said, feeling dumb. He'd put on a little bit of weight or lost some muscle, and his complexion had cleared, but he had the same broad features and bland blue eyes that a lot of girls had thought were handsome in high school. His mother and mine were both in the same gardening club, I remembered vaguely. I'd been unaware that he knew my name, much less that he would be able to recognize me across a college campus and then mortally embarrass me by shouting my name in front of two hundred loitering students who were eating in the space outside Kinko's and the pub/cafeteria. A kid in flip-flops and cargo shorts—maybe even the same kid I'd seen in the administration building—was staring at us curiously, as though interested in the kind of girl who would make a guy like Granger hunt me down in the middle of a crowd.

"Cory, dude, you didn't even hear me! I didn't know you even made it into college!"

Suddenly I remembered why I had hated high school—and the human race in general—before I grew up, got laid, and found out the world was a larger place than the Chuck Grangers in it. "I had a 3.8 in high school, Chuck—I don't know why that's such a surprise," I said coldly. He looked blank and then offered a great courtesy laugh in exchange.

"Hey—you got all cleaned up, Cory. I hardly recognized you across the quad there. How come you didn't hear me calling you?"

There was a sort of leer on his face now. He was standing uncomfortably close, and abruptly I remembered something else about Chuck Granger: he was a frequent entrée when the vampires partied at Lake Clementine for food—and although the vamps rolled his mind to help him forget, his free will was still his, and he always (*Always!* Marcus had said with disgust), *always* wanted to be fed upon, ravished, sated by male vampires. This alone wouldn't be a bad thing, certainly not from Adrian's vampires, but when there were no vampires present, he was a self-proclaimed ladies' man and the county's most frequent user of the word "faggot." It was hard for the vampires to respect their dinner when it didn't even recognize the truth of its own humanity.

"I'm married now," I said, swallowing past this new info processing through my brain. "It's not my name anymore."

"Shit—I didn't know you were married! My mom didn't tell me!"

I took a step back and Chuck followed. I looked behind me, hoping Bracken had emerged from the library so I could get away from this guy. "My mom doesn't know yet," I said unwillingly, and to my horror, Chuck bent his head conspiratorially.

"Well, I can keep a secret, Cory—right?" He winked like we were friends, and my stomach started to churn.

"Right," I agreed, backing up another step.

"I mean, like, if you could score for me, I could keep a secret for a long, long time." He smiled suggestively, and I stopped backing up so suddenly he almost knocked me on my ass. Abruptly, this totally shit day had jumped into Alice's surreal toilet.

"You want me to score?" I couldn't keep the horror out of my voice. "As in drugs?"

"Well, yeah. Everyone knew you partied in high school—I mean, marriage doesn't stop the good times from rolling, right?" He was practically drooling in his eagerness for a new connection, and I could only be thankful that it wasn't me he wanted, because then I *would* be sick.

"Yeah, I partied," I said, because yes, I'd been at parties. "But I never did drugs. I wouldn't know where to find drugs if they were grown in my own backyard."

"Oh, come on, Cory. You had the hair, the earrings—I bet you've even got a tattoo. We all knew you were a good lay—just share a little of the party juice, that's all."

I was a good lay? Well, I was, but nobody from high school would know! He was getting closer, and his sweaty, hammy hand was on my arm, and he smelled like cheeseburgers and beer, and I had *baaad* memories about the smell of beer—and it wasn't like I'd been all chipper and enthusiastic about life before this asshole accosted me.

"I'm not sure whether to be flattered or nauseated," I said. Bracken had (yes, at last!) emerged from behind Douglas Hall, but he hadn't seen me yet. I was hoping he could just kind of blithely sweep me away before I had to fry this asshole to his last teeny-tiny testicle pube. "But I think I'll settle on horrified," I finished. "Chuck, I never did drugs in high school. I never did guys in high school. And I'm really hoping you'll just apologize and back away and this won't get awkward or anything, okay?"

Chuck's face hardened, and the lines at his mouth became saturnine and bitter and prematurely old, and he grabbed my arm hard enough to leave bruises. "Dammit, Cory, don't hold out on me—I just want some fucking crank, that's all. You're acting all high and mighty and pure, when no one who looked like you did in high school could be a fucking virgin, and all you goth punks got high. Everyone knows it, so just give me the name of your connection and it will all be copasetic, right?"

My mad came on, and I know I started to glow like a fucking lighthouse, but not to mortals—not to Chuck. And that was when I smelled it. It was faint, like a garbage truck on the next block, but it was there. "Chuck, you're jonesing right now, but it's not for crank—and if you don't let go of me, my great big husband is going to rip off your arm and beat you with it, okay?"

And like that, Bracken was right there at my elbow, and Chuck was so surprised that he not only let go of me but finally (praise Jesus!) took a step back and out of my face. He turned pale, and suddenly his hands were shaking. I risked a look at Bracken and noted that his eyes were burning—literally, a golden ember color shot from his irises—and that he'd dropped his glamour to the extent that any mortal who was paying attention could see his curved, pointed ears.

"Glamour, Brack," I whispered urgently.

"Fuck glamour," he said back in a growl. "Who is this asshole, and why shouldn't I kill him?" But I noticed that his ears returned to normal and his eyes stopped glowing like a laser.

"He's some jerk from high school who thought I could score him drugs," I said wearily. Chuck was backing away quickly, like Bracken was something out of his worst nightmare. "He's jonesing on the Hollow Man too… but he was an asshole before that."

"I'm sorry…," Chuck stammered, and Bracken was suddenly in his face, holding his throat with one large, graceful hand.

"You're pathetic," Bracken said, anger burning through his voice and probably through his skin as well. "But you're nowhere near sorry enough. If you talk to her again—if you fucking look at her or think of her or imagine her or wonder about her or delude yourself that you're worth the ground she spits on, I'll break you in half and let you live. If you touch her again, I'll break you in half and call your heart through your chest one drop of blood at a fucking time." Bracken released him, and Chuck sat down abruptly. Then he scrambled to his feet in the other direction, screaming the one thing he had left in his arsenal as he went.

"My mom'll be thrilled to hear about your wedding, Cory Kirkpatrick!" he jeered, and then he was running away from Bracken like a pig running away from a wild bronco.

Bracken looked at me, his chest pumping hard with anger, and he reached down and seized my hands.

"Did he hurt you?" he asked roughly, and Goddess help me, I lied.

"No." I tried to smile with my lie, but I don't think I did a good job. "But the look on his face when you grabbed him by the throat was priceless." I stood on my tiptoes and kissed him, a reassuring kiss that quickly turned fierce as Brack tangled his hands in my hair and checked my body over. He noticed the bruises when I winced, and stepped away from me to look at my arm and got angry all over again.

"You lied," he said, rubbing my arm gently.

"Baby, you're late for Hallow—we've got to go...."

"I'm early for Hallow," he replied, puzzled. "Why are you out so early?"

"He let me go." Not a lie, exactly.

"Did you eat?" Instant concern.

"I had a bite." Jeez, I was getting good at this. "But I'm okay, right?"

"Are you?" he asked, suddenly so serious, knowing me so well that I couldn't prevaricate or split hairs.

"He smelled like Hollow Man, Bracken," I said after a moment. "And he shouted my maiden name across the campus. And my meeting with Hallow was... hard. And I need to go. I need to run. Please, baby... just let me run?"

Bracken held my hands to his lips, kissed them softly. "You need to run from me?" Hurt.

I shook my head, and the first honest smile since I'd gone into Hallow's office stretched my cheeks. "I could never run from you. You'd run and find me and take me home and make love to me until I came to my senses. No, beloved... I need to run from myself."

Bracken nodded—Goddess, he was so damned wise sometimes, it was spooky how much he was like Green. "I'd find her too." He bent down and kissed my brow solemnly.

"I look forward to that." I broke away and reached for my pack, which was over his shoulder. He reached for his pocket instead and pulled out the plastic bag that had my running gear in it. I grinned at him. "Come get me on the track, okay? We can walk to our next class...." Then I turned and trotted away, running from myself before I'd even gotten my Nikes on.

BRACKEN
Attractions

I WATCHED her disappear past the library, blending seamlessly into the other young humans wearing sweatshirts and jeans and jaunty little ponytails, and felt completely helpless.

Running from me?

No. Running from myself.

The complete truth. Why would she need to run from herself? Didn't she know she was perfect?

Sourly I looked in the direction that the detestable asshole had run. Of course she wouldn't know—she'd been dealing with people like *him* all her life. I hated this world. Relentlessly I shoved my glamour over my features, but that didn't stop my scowl from scaring people out of my path as I trudged to Hallow's office. Good. I liked being scary.

But when I shoved my way through into the book-crowded room with the ugly green tile, Hallow appeared unimpressed.

"Bad day?" he asked mildly, and I grunted and sat down, wincing as I heard the padded chair beneath me creak under my weight.

"Bad night. And any day here with humans is a bad day." I was starting to get angry all over again when I caught sight of the piece of pizza in the trash can—the one with a single bite taken out of it. My eyes flew to Hallow's, and a pained look crossed his features. I opened the box that was on the desk and practically snarled.

"Did she tell you she'd eaten?" Hallow asked gently, and I did snarl then with pure frustration.

"Worse. She told me she'd 'had a bite.'" I seethed.

"My—she is getting very good at being just like us, isn't she?"

I growled—no words, just a grumbling, menacing purr that shook the windows and made Hallow blink slowly in surprise. The meeting went downhill from there.

Twenty-five minutes later, I was striding to the track, Max and Renny practically trotting to keep up with me. Renny was chattering about human conventions or some shit like that, and I would have ignored her completely but Max risked death and put his hand on my arm.

I swung around to crush him like a bug, but Officer Max had learned a lot from Green in the last year. He took a step back, then stood his ground with his hands lowered and waited until he had my complete attention.

"I know you're worried, Bracken," he said gently after a moment, during which I reminded myself that Cory would be very mad if I killed her friend. "But storming onto the track and dragging her off is just going to embarrass her and piss her off. At least wait until she's done with her run, and then ask her if you can get her something to eat, okay?"

"It's not like she lied to you...," Renny said unhappily, and I swung away from them both.

Of course she hadn't lied to me, with the exception of telling me she wasn't hurt—which was a lie she tried to make truth so automatically it leaped off her lips before she even thought about it. She had just split hairs, led me on so I wouldn't fuss, and protected me from her own shortcomings like she was worried I wouldn't love her if I had to help her in any way, shape, or form. I had one real job on Green's hill, and that was to keep her safe—and if I wasn't becoming enthralled and putting her in danger from magic ass-kicking blood, then she was prevaricating her way out of taking good care of herself. Didn't she see what she meant to us? Didn't she understand that something as small as skipping lunch was a prelude to grabbing death with both hands?

I was getting ready to do just what Max told me not to do—storm onto the track to confront her—when I saw her running. I stopped, just stopped, to watch her. She would never be graceful, I thought—her legs were too short, and even underweight she had flaring hips that were good for walking with purpose, but not for running—but she moved with energy and a simple human joy of exertion. Her stride had evened out from yesterday, and her breathing wasn't quite as labored. The human girl with the glossy brown hair ran next to her, and again it appeared as though her mouth hadn't stopped moving once, but Cory was nodding at her and smiling, and looking relaxed and absorbed in what the other girl was saying. When she'd left me, her shoulders had been hunched, her mouth had been tense, and her eyes had been drawn together at the brow.

I sighed, easing the tension in my back, and turned toward the bleachers. Our backpacks hit the steps with a loud thump, and Max and

Renny visibly relaxed as they saw me sit and stare at Cory making her way around the track, her sneakers pounding out a crisp thudding that I could hear even though they were on the far side from me.

Renny plopped down next to me and leaned against my shoulder. "She doesn't know how important she is." Her voice, always quiet, almost faded away in the wind.

"She knows how important she is to *me*," I replied, my eyes never leaving Cory.

"Not really," Renny corrected. "But she's learning. Give her time to learn."

"Some asshole from high school was..." My whole body snarled. "...hitting her up for drugs when I saw her in the quad. If we were at home, I could have killed him."

Renny patted my shoulder. "If we were at home, I would have helped you. But the human world has always been... unkind... to Cory, to people like her. It's going to take more than a year in our world, even more than a year with Green—and definitely more than two months of fabulous sex with you, O Mighty Man-God—to get past the rest of that crap, okay?"

Max sighed. "On behalf of all stupid humans, I'd like to apologize?"

And Renny surprised us both by turning to him and snapping, "You don't have to stay human, and you know it." And with that she left my side and scampered off toward the track, preparing to run with the other girls in her jeans and sneakers.

"Fuck." Max stared after her unhappily. I was so grateful not to be the only clueless bastard I knew that I didn't even mind when he sat a companionable distance from me.

"Absofuckinglutely," I agreed, and we just sat for a moment, watching the women we loved run.

It was pleasant and lulling to listen to the wind and the thud of their feet on the track and feel the chill sunshine on our faces. There is a goldness to sunshine in winter, a thick preciousness that makes you long for it even as it chills you. For a moment, I got to forget that we were surrounded by freeways and just minutes away from a seething sewer of drugs and prostitution, and that I had to go in with Cory to her physics class next—the only course she had every day—and watch her stare at the professor with bewildered desperation because, of all the things she did with ease, physics was just not on the list.

"We don't have rings," I said abruptly into the silence.

"Hm?" Max just looked at me.

"It's a human convention, isn't it? Wedding rings?"

Max nodded. "Yes. It's not as effective as... as binding yourself to mortality or... or turning furry, but it's all we've got." He sighed.

"She wants to bite you, doesn't she," I stated, suddenly feeling some empathy for Max when I hadn't thought myself capable of it.

"Yeah. Most of me wants to do it," he admitted after a moment.

"What part of you doesn't?" I was suddenly curious. If I had been human, I thought mournfully, I would have taken any way out of the human world I could possibly find.

"The part of me that went to Bible school and sang 'Glory Hallelujah' and meant every word of it." Max sounded sad.

"You can still worship God." I actually turned to him, absurdly touched by his faith. Cory was right. He was a good man—he was just badly schooled. "The Goddess will just want a little respect, that's all."

Max smiled, a smile so sad it could only be human. "Thanks, Bracken," he said sincerely. "That's good to know. Shit...." Something on the field had caught his attention, and he was already up and running before I could turn and see that both Cory and Renny had stumbled, and Renny had actually gone to her knees.

I didn't think, I *moved*, blurring past Max and arriving at Cory's side before her ass hit the ground, and holy shit, she looked like she was going to throw up, and I knew she didn't have anything in her stomach to lose.

Renny was clutching her ears and keening when Max arrived. He gathered her up close and tried to shelter her head with his body, and Cory was biting her lips and trying to keep control. "It's him," she whispered fiercely. "It's him.... I don't know where, but he's nearby. He's... pulling at me somehow...."

"Make him stop calling your name!" Renny whined. "He's shouting your name, and it hurts!"

"Are they okay?" I looked up at the girl—Davy, wasn't that her name?—and then at Max, who grimaced at me and shrugged.

"PMS," Cory said, with quicker wits under siege than I had on any given day. "I guess our cycles are in sync, because I've got really bad cramps."

I looked at her and blinked. PMS? Cramps? From what?

Renny pulled herself together enough to say, "Yeah, it's my first day—I don't know what I was thinking....," before murmuring urgently to Max, who turned and started toward the bleachers.

Davy wasn't buying it. "At the same time like that? Really?"

Cory swallowed hard, and I wondered how much time she was going to spend vomiting to pay for her self-control now. "We've been rooming together for seven months. It happens."

"But I thought you were married...."

"She is," I said shortly. "We're all in the same...."

"Boarding house," Cory supplied gamely. "But Davy, I've got to go...." I was moving toward our packs already, and the girl was trotting to keep up with me.

"I know—I just want to make sure you're okay...." She cast a sideways look at me, disapproval in the lines at her mouth. "Jeez, you were there awfully fast, uhm...."

"Bracken," I supplied.

"Yeah.... Do you ever let her out of your sight?"

"When I do, she doesn't eat," I said darkly and had the grim satisfaction of watching Cory cringe.

Suddenly Davy's expression lightened, and she stepped in front of me and gave Cory a pat on the arm. "Okay, I'm convinced, you're in good hands," she said brightly. "Isn't it nice to have someone who will kill or die for you, right there at your beck and call?"

Cory suddenly looked very old and very tired. "It's a terrifying responsibility," she said seriously, resting her head against my chest. "Never take it for granted." I picked up my speed and left Davy just looking at the two of us thoughtfully, her usual smile nowhere to be seen.

We got the hell out of there, Max moving surprisingly fast while carrying Renny. I had everyone's packs on my back as well as Cory in my arms, and we made good time heading through the quad toward the riverside parking lot until Cory stopped me urgently in front of a trash can to lose stomach acid—because there was nothing else for her to vomit. When she was done, Renny said, "It's over. Please... let's just sit...."

And so we found a tree and sat, backs to the tree, women on our laps, and caught our breath.

"It was calling your name?" I asked after the shivering had stopped. I fished out two water bottles for the girls. Cory drank and spat, then drank gratefully. Renny sipped delicately, still more cat than girl when faced with crisis.

"It was calling Cory's name," Renny said seriously. "Cory Kirkpatrick op Crocken Green."

"I felt a pull," Cory admitted, nodding, "but it wasn't strong. It was like… like when Green is willing me to sleep, but usually I can't resist that. This I could turn away from if I wanted to. Of course the stench didn't shore up my will any, but it didn't make me all jumping in my pants to answer the call…."

"It knows your name," I said darkly. All the precautions we had taken, and still it was her name that would do us in.

"Not all of it," Renny assessed. "It knows her maiden name and her married name, though."

"Thank you, Chuck Granger," Cory snorted with complete disgust. "What a total waste of skin." Her body shivered again, and I tried to gather her in.

"I will kill him," I said sincerely, feeling so good about the thought that I almost forgot I had been furious with her only half an hour ago.

"That's not necessary," she said gently, and suddenly she was touching my face like she was trying to comfort me instead of the other way around.

"Well, I have to do something!" I burst out. "I can't *hear* this thing, I can't *smell* it—and if I can see it, it must be doing a spectacular job of hiding from me, because I'm as blind as Max whenever it's around. How am I supposed to protect you when I can't even see what's after you? How am I supposed to take care of you when you won't even be honest about whether you're taking care of yourself?"

There was silence then, a grim, uncomfortable silence, and I felt horrible because it wasn't like the women hadn't been scared enough as it was. Then Cory spoke up unexpectedly, her voice lighter than it had been. "Bracken?" There was a note of teasing that I couldn't understand.

"Yes." I couldn't look at her for a moment, I was so angry and worried at once.

"You know what would be really awesome right now?" Again, those gentle fingers on my face.

I looked at her, and even my ears were wary. "What?"

"Chicken soup. A really big cup of chicken soup. With some of that cornbread they have at the Roundhouse." She smiled weakly up at me, and I could tell that now, of all times, she was trying to apologize.

"Chicken soup?" I asked blankly. I had no response for this. No response for the apology, no response for the request. Did all human women baffle their human men, or was it just my sorceress losing her great, clumsy sidhe?

"Yeah. My stomach just wasn't up for pizza today. Would you baby me a little and get me some chicken soup?"

It really was an apology, I thought, seeing the uncertainty on her tired face and her remarkable green-shadowed brown eyes trying hard to meet my own gaze. I'd heard worse. I kissed her forehead, touched my cheek to hers, and nodded. "Chicken soup?"

"A large," she insisted.

"One for me too!" Renny piped up, and I actually smiled over my shoulder at her.

"Anything for you, Max?" I offered, and the smile the man gave me made me glad I had.

"Chili," he said. "There's something addictive about college-campus chili."

I set Cory down gently, propping our backpacks around her, and she smiled up at me as I did so. "Thank you, beloved," she said formally, and I swallowed.

"You're always welcome." I trotted off happily to do her bidding.

It was gratifying to watch her eat when I returned, and see color come back to her cheeks and her posture become straighter. The smile she gave me when she was done was hale and hearty—the brilliant smile she used without guile or purpose that made all men, including myself, besotted and stupid with love for her.

"The smile was a bit much," I grumbled as I sat on the cold wet grass next to her.

"What smile?" She looked blank, and finally, finally all my anger slipped away as if it had never been.

"What are 'PMS' and 'cramps'?" I asked, because I'd been wondering.

Her eyes grew impossibly large in her pinched face, and her mouth opened and closed. Renny broke into a peal of giggles, and Max smiled evilly.

"That's my cue to take Renny to her next class," he said with a certain satisfaction. "May the Goddess show you mercy, my brother." Then he stood up and pulled Renny to her feet, and with his arm wrapped around her tiny body, they walked into the green of the quad and were gone.

We sat in the cold winter sunshine for another minute, and then Cory stood stiffly and offered her hand to me. "I'd pull you over in a heartbeat," I said and stood up myself, ducking to keep from hitting my head on the branches of the pine tree we had been sitting under. Our bottoms were both damp from sitting on the ground in the winter. I swung our packs on my back, then moved toward her with purpose.

"I can walk!" she protested.

"I know you can." I scooped her up, ignoring her little squeal of protest. "I can carry you." I took two steps out and turned toward the big new engineering building where her physics lecture was held. "Now what is PMS, and why would you and Renny get cramps?"

I almost dropped her when she explained it to me. "All human women do this?" I asked, horrified. "*You* don't!"

"They do when they're healthy and functioning right," she explained patiently. And then, so quietly I almost couldn't hear her, "And I *did.*"

I stopped abruptly. "When did you last?"

"Early May," she replied softly. Right before she and Adrian had gotten together. Before her life had changed and her heart had been broken and the world had come apart at the seams. "Sudden weight drops or gains, stress, low or high body fat—they get in the way of the whole thing working right," she tried to explain, but my silence became hot. Then, quickly because she could read my mood better than anybody, she finished, "Please don't get angry all over again, beloved. That's why I started running, because just feeding me wasn't doing it. I figured that if I build muscle and appetite, maybe I'll start putting on weight and you won't have to worry so much, okay?"

I closed my eyes tight and nodded, because I believed her, and her sudden push to exercise made much more sense. She wasn't just doing it for her own health, she was doing it for my—for our—peace of mind. Okay. That was the Cory I knew.

"Besides," she went on gamely, "I'd much rather hear about your talk with Professor Hallow."

I blew out a breath in frustration, and suddenly the whole conversation came spilling out of me like the anger I couldn't spill at

her because that wasn't where it belonged. "What's there to talk about?"
I asked grumpily. "It was all stupid questions—Are you worried about
Cory? Well, duh! Has he seen you? You're all skin and hips! Is it hard to
love Adrian's lover? Well, that's the freaking easy part. The worst part
is that she's just like Adrian and where's *that* going to get me? And do I
think Adrian would be okay with us? And why the fuck should I care, the
bugger's *dead,* and if he didn't love us enough to hold on to you then I
deserve you now, don't I? And how do I feel about Green? Well, shit—
how can you not love Green? Do I give a fuck if he's your lover too?
What does he take me for, some stupid pissant human who doesn't know
the goddamned difference between a lover and a car? I mean, *Jeeeeesus,*
how stupid can one elf get? He knows better than that shit, and why he
thinks I wouldn't miss Green when he's been the sun in my sky for most
of my life is beyond me. What a fucking moron," I finished on a huff as I
sat on the dirty beige tile floor of the physics classroom, and Cory made
a suspicious sound against my chest.

"What?" I asked, but she just shook her head, her eyes bright with
what looked like laughter, and I couldn't for the life of me figure out
what was funny. "No, seriously, what?"

"Nothing," she said, her voice not quite cracking. "It's just good to
know that Hallow had better luck with you than with me, that's all."

"Hallow?" Mario asked, plopping in the seat next to me. Mario and
LaMark didn't have the same break we did on Tuesdays—in fact, this
was the only class besides Hallow's that Cory shared with the two Avians.
LaMark took the desk on the other side, and I stayed on the floor—those
little human-sized desks just didn't do it for me, and I couldn't hold
Cory if I was sitting in one. "How was Hallow, by the way? I mean…."
Mario grimaced. "I may be an Avian, but I'm, like, Mexican. We don't
do therapy—we leave that for you white people, right?"

"Apparently the whiter you are, the better you do," Cory quipped
gamely, giving me another one of those bright-eyed glances.

"Bracken?" Mario replied, his voice teasing. "Man, that boy don't
need therapy. Give him a tree to beat up, and he's just fine—he's all
emotions, all on the surface, aren't you, Brack?"

I thought about my outburst to Cory and flushed. "The sidhe think
repression is a silly human thing," I said with dignity, and Cory touched
my shoulder in such a way that for a moment it felt like just the two of us
in a room full of bored students.

"It is, sweetie," she said softly. "But leave us our little quirks, okay?"

"You people have too many quirks," I replied gently, and then the professor came in and we all dutifully took out our notebooks and began to copy what he put on the board.

Cory fell asleep about halfway through, her head leaning heavily against my shoulder until her hand fell into my lap and her notebook slid to the floor. I took her notebook, filled with cramped notes in her bizarre and tiny handwriting, and filled in the rest of the lecture, clarifying what the professor left out, drawing diagrams that would help her understand all the things he assumed she knew but that she obviously didn't, and generally doing the man's job for him. He was a tall, angular man with a scant nest of gray hair and a beige plaid shirt tucked into a pair of khakis that were pulled over his rounded stomach, and he kept casting dirty looks at me as I wrote.

"You should wake her up," he said at one point, interrupting his own sentence. "She needs to hear this."

"I'm taking notes," I replied mildly, wondering if the man was blind to the fact that I could squash him like a ripe plum under my (ugh!) shoe.

He bent down, putting his face offensively close to Cory's, and said, "Hello... young lady... you need to...." He trailed off, because I lowered my face between them and glared at the man.

"She's sick," I said abruptly. "She's sick, and she needs to sleep, and my notes will do," I growled. Something must have frightened the man, because he backed away quickly and nervously resumed his lecture from across the room. I heard LaMark whisper "Glamour, Brack," and for the second time that day I repaired my disguise in the human world.

Finally—finally!—class ended, and as I shifted both packs on my back, pulled Cory into my arms, and began to stand, she started to wake up. "I can walk," she muttered groggily. I ignored her.

"What's the deal?" LaMark asked. We stood, waiting for the rest of the class to filter out the door. The professor was packing up his notes and looking at me uneasily. I shot him a glare, then turned my attention to LaMark and said quietly, "The Hollow Man was at the track today. I didn't see him, but he was calling Cory's name—he pretty much took Renny out too."

"How?" Mario asked seriously. "Because in the middle of class the two of us heard this sound like fingernails on a chalkboard that almost made us black out...."

"That's how," I replied. It was the end of the day, and we were the last to leave. The feel of a hand on my shoulder in the deserted hallway surprised me. I spun around, surprising Mario, who didn't know where I was going, and confronted a human male in a hooded sweatshirt with cargo shorts and what Cory called flip-flops. I looked at his face and had a momentary impression of "older than he looks" before I had to squeeze my eyes shut against a dizziness that made me stumble. Mario put a hand on one shoulder, LaMark on the other, and that steadied me enough to say "I'm sorry? Did you need something?"

"Yeah, man…." I couldn't see the color of his eyes, I thought. He should be pretty, enormously pretty—attractive enough to pull at me, although I hadn't been drawn to a man since I'd licked Cory's blood from a vampire's fangs when he'd blooded her in front of me—but… this was not a good, clean attraction. It was… strong, and steamy, and too sweet—repellent—like a lover who had stayed too long in rank sheets…. "I thought it was really great, the way you got into Prof Dann's face like that. I mean, he was being a total prick…."

As he spoke, Mario and LaMark both groaned, moving their hands from my shoulder and covering their ears in pain. I was still lost in the hollows that were his eyes, mesmerized, besotted, bespelled by what wasn't there to see. And then Cory made a horrible retching sound in my arms, and I found I *could* focus on something else besides the boy in front of me as she struggled so hard that I dropped her. She fell to her knees, one hand on the ground, one hand out in front of her glowing with power.

"Christ, it's him!" she shouted, and another wave of dizziness washed over me, but this time I fought it—because there she was, crouched on the floor between me and our enemy, and I was damned if I'd let her fight this battle alone.

Mario and LaMark were suddenly not there, big predatory birds in their places, screeching at full volume to drown out the sound of Hollow Man's voice, and I saw a glow in his eyes and had enough presence of mind to shout, "*Shield!*"

The glow in Cory's hands extended, attenuated, and burned brighter, like electric Plexiglas between us and our enemy, who stood glaring at us through the crackle of her power. He held his hand out to me—and suddenly I, who was a redcap, and who could call blood at will, felt my own blood respond to someone else's calling. I retaliated by throwing my own hand out in front of me, and the moment I felt his call recede, I had the satisfaction of seeing surprise on his face as I called blood on my own.

"Nah, nah…," called the Hollow Man, one hand still out for my blood but the other now clutching his chest and wiping at the blood starting from his eyes. His voice was… small, I thought with a distant part of my brain, and sounded as though it wasn't coming through his throat. But there was no time to puzzle out why. "Remember what my blood does to your people."

"Cory, how good is that shield?" I shouted over the sound of powers colliding, and in response she held her free hand behind her. I slapped my free hand into hers, there was a surge in the sound of crackling, and she responded, "It's fucking invincible." Just to be sure, I spat, watching with satisfaction as my spittle sizzled on the wall of luminous blue in front of me.

"Your blood will never touch us," I told him grimly and then screamed with exertion and joy, because my power is a joy, and there was an explosion from the Hollow Man's chest that landed with a splash, a thump, and a sizzle on Cory's shield.

"Eww!" Cory made a face as the Hollow Man's burnt-orange heart thudded against the shield an arm's length from her face and burst. Then she screamed in anger as the blood began to spark and flare amber against her shield, the two elements dancing in a fight for space and dominance. "Oh, that's the fucking end!" she hollered, and the shield glowed brighter blue, then green, then white—and when it turned white, I felt my own strength tapped. Suddenly Mario and LaMark were human, one on each shoulder bearing me up, and Cory hadn't stopped swearing, but that was okay because we were winning, dammit, she was winning, and the Hollow Man was glaring at us with unconcealed evil. The terrible hole in his chest dripped orange viscera, a stark testament to the obscenity of his existence.

And then the last crackle faded and it was over, Cory's strength intact and the blood destroyed, cooked, cauterized so cleanly off her shield that there wasn't even vapor to testify to its existence.

"Stay away from our people," Cory ordered grimly, and I could feel her body readying for yet another charge. She was building power to fire, I thought with surprise. All of that, as exhausted as she was, and she was getting ready to wipe this fucker out of existence. But she needed time after her battle with the poisoned blood, time to ready herself, time to charge, time to make sure we were safe as she fired.

"Someday, you will be alone...." The Hollow Man spoke, but it was not the young student's voice anymore. It wasn't a sepulchral wail, but it had a grating timbre to it that worked its way up the soles of our feet and felt like sandpaper in our joints. Cory's charging became more purposeful. "Someday, you will be alone, and I will be there...." As she drew in a breath and pulled back her shoulder to throw, he was gone— destroyed body, grotesque blood, hellish (and still small) voice, and all. He had burst into smoke so thin and acrid that only Cory's shield protected us, and not even the belated ball of power she threw at the place where Hollow Man had been could destroy it.

I fell to my knees behind her, our hands still linked, and Mario and LaMark with me. Together we knelt panting on the floor of the empty hall, surveying the blackened space on the far wall of cinderblock where her last burst of power had crashed at less than full strength.

"Fuck," Cory whispered. "I must be slipping—that wall should be toast."

"You were still charging," I said, although she knew that. She expected too much from herself.

"Nice work with the whole blood thing," she said, still kneeling on the floor in front of me, her hand wrapped around her back to clench mine. "I've never seen you work as a weapon before."

"Definitely glad you're on our side," LaMark said from my left, and I grunted a thanks.

"So...," I said, letting go of Cory's hand and standing with an effort, "did anybody get a look at the bastard's face?"

"Yeah," Mario said. "He was an average college white boy, even when his chest exploded and he got all *Exorcist* on us. You were looking right at him."

"More than average," LaMark said regretfully, confirming my initial impression of uncommonly pretty.

"I couldn't see him. He was... like his name—hollow, no substance. His eyes led nowhere," I said, bending down to shoulder the packs, which had slid off my shoulders when Cory had struggled out of my arms.

"Well, that makes sense," LaMark surmised. "The vampires can smell him, the weres can hear him, the fey can see him for what he is...."

I cringed. The vampires could smell him, and Cory had been face-to-face with him. The sound was unmistakable, and now I knew why she had kept her face turned away and stayed on her knees while we spoke. So much for chicken soup.

"Goddess!" I swore and dropped the packs with a thump. I was mortally tired of hauling the fucking things around, anyway. I reached down and yanked her backward, away from the mess that had spattered at her knees, then pulled out the last bottle of water, ripped off part of my T-shirt from under my sweater with a jerk, and began to clean her up.

"Do you have any idea how tired I am of barfing?" she asked wearily. "Probably almost as tired as you are of cleaning me up."

"The smell is that bad?" LaMark asked. Unbidden, he had run to the nearest drinking fountain and filled up one of the empty bottles that had rolled from her pack. She took it and drank gratefully.

"The smell is that bad," Cory affirmed, nodding and trying to stand up. She wobbled for a moment and then, looking purposeful, put her hand against the wall. I sighed and went to pick up the packs again, but to my surprise I found the two Avians had beaten me to it.

"Even you are looking tired, O Mighty Warrior," Mario said. "Although I think it would serve her right if we dumped the knitting out of Cory's pack, because it's hellaciously heavy."

Cory, who had been trying desperately to stand still and focus her eyes, suddenly snapped a glare at Mario. "I can still singe your tail feathers, bird boy," she threatened. "That sweater will be finished by the time my shift's over tonight, and if you want to live, you'll leave it where it is!"

"We're not working tonight," I said firmly, scooping her up. On days like this, I was so used to her weight in my arms that I felt naked without her.

I watched her sort through several retorts to that—the first, of course, was that she was fine and could work. The second would have been that Grace needed us. But then her eyes fastened on my face, and her hand came out to pull my shaggy bangs out of my eyes, and she smiled tiredly. "Of course. You're right. Grace can find others to work— I'll finish the sweater at home."

Mario had just said I looked tired. Obviously, the only way to get her to take care of herself was to let her take care of me.

"He knows who we are now," Cory assessed, still trying to reason things out in my arms. "Thank you, Chuck Granger. But we hurt him, I think. Maybe, while we try to find a way to fight him, we'll be safe...."

"As long as we stay together," I muttered.

"Oh good," she said brightly. "Couples counseling—Hallow will love that!"

"If it doesn't drive him nutsy-cuckoo," Mario said with a laugh.

"Serve him right if it does," I grumbled, and together we emerged into the thin late sunlight where Max and Renny were waiting, wondering what had kept us.

NICKY
The Rules of the Road

"I LOVE you, Nicky. Maybe not the way you dreamed as a little kid, but it's still love."

The words haunted me. *She* haunted me. Every day, I lived with her, I talked to her, I even made plans to touch her, to hold her, to be inside of her, and it was still like living with a dream. And every time I saw the way Bracken looked at her, or the way Green smiled at her only, or heard the timbre of their voices when they said "beloved," it became obvious, so painfully obvious, that I might be fucking fabulous as a friend, but that I was not even in the running as a lover. How could I measure up to the two of them? How could anybody?

And it wasn't like she led me on. She treated me with respect and friendship, but she was very careful not to touch me, even casually, so that I would maybe, just for a moment, hope that she could love me. Not even hope. There were times when I knew she wouldn't have minded a hug, or a kiss, or even, when she and Bracken were fighting and Green was with someone else, a spare bed. But she wouldn't come to me—she wouldn't ask to come to me—because that would be too much like using me, and that love she was talking about was real, although it made me bitter sometimes, and you don't use a friend.

So her words haunted me, and that sweet kiss we had shared, and her obvious distress that I wouldn't know she valued me, and the way she loved Bracken enough to call him names and fight with him but she won't even let herself hold my hand.

And I missed Green too, so much that I couldn't breathe. Less than two months ago, I'd been as homophobic as the next redneck. How could I reconcile the Montana farm boy with the sex-happy maniac in Green's bed, when I couldn't get Cory to look at me as a man at all?

It was all roiling around in my head as I drove the sky blue Cadillac. Leah was singing loudly to Sheryl Crow on the radio while Willow slept on our luggage in the back, and suddenly Leah stopped singing and looked at me.

"What the hell has got your panties in a knot?"

I blinked and looked away from the glory that was I-5. "Not a blessed thing," I said sourly and returned my gaze to the road, but Leah hadn't finished with me yet. She was a very pretty girl, with long black hair and eyelashes so thick and dark that her brown eyes didn't need any makeup, but I was a bird and she was a werepuma, and that steady, unblinking gaze was really unnerving. Suddenly she nodded, as though figuring something out.

"You're horny," she said abruptly and then started humming to the music again.

Well, I was. Green was gone, date night felt like years ago—yes, I was horny. "So what?"

"Nobody on Green's hill goes horny," she stated. "It's the one thing we don't have to worry about, which is good because the whole rest of our lives are pretty fucking complicated. You're horny, and you're complicating things, and it's making me crazy. Willow and I will fuck your brains out at the hotel. 'Kay, Willow?"

"Wonderful," Willow purred from the back, and I almost swerved off the road. I hadn't known she could talk. "Can I lick his phallus? Humans taste so good down there... even werecreatures. Can I lick you too, Leah? Soooo good...." And dreaming about multihuman orgies, Willow fell back asleep, I guess, because we didn't hear from her for a while.

"I can't do that," I said evenly, trying to ignore the hard-on I got just from thinking about it. *Would Ellis join in too?* a part of me wondered, and I mentally cursed myself for adding that thought. I loved making love to Cory, but playing with Green's body had made me appreciate men too, and on the whole, my cock was hard in my pants and I had a good six hundred miles to go before we rested and I could jack myself off to relieve the pressure.

"Of course you can," Leah frowned. "It's not like Cory and Bracken, where somebody will turn into mushy goo, right?"

"No—nobody will turn into goo," I said aridly. Leave it to Leah to take something as painful as Cory's binding with Bracken and make it that breezy and simple.

"Then why can't you get laid?" She wasn't blinking again, and I found myself thinking about it for the first time.

"My people are monogamous," I said after a moment. "We're raised to believe you get a mate, and you do your best to make it work, and if you can't, you still make it work because your mate has to like you enough to fuck you once a moon or you die."

"I get that," Leah said, nodding her head earnestly at me from across the seat. "But this is different. Your mates can't be monogamous. They don't *want* to be monogamous—and that's no slam on you, Nicky, and certainly no slam on them. I mean, Adrian brought Cory home last summer, and we knew—the whole freaking hill knew—that she'd be, like, our lighthouse, you know? Brilliant, beaming in hope and strength—and that Adrian and Green would be drawn to her like really big, beautiful moths. Some of us even guessed that Bracken loved her too. Loving Cory, loving Green—that's just a sign of your good taste, really. And believe me, I've slept with practically everybody at the hill *but* Cory. I can tell you something about taste, good and bad."

"Bracken?" I asked, curious. He was so beautiful—too beautiful to have been celibate for any length of time.

"One night, I got Bracken *and* Adrian," she said dreamily. "It was like being cooked on the rocks of passion, if you can buy that corny-assed metaphor...." She giggled at her own pun, and I smiled a little too. What could I say? I'd been raised with the same porn as every other American boy. I just had to keep telling myself that it wasn't for me.

"Did they do that a lot?" I asked, perversely curious. In a way, I was already sharing Cory with Bracken and Adrian. I was just wondering if they'd made a habit of it, that was all.

"Mmm...," Leah sighed, then opened her eyes and looked sideways at me. "No, they either competed for women or banged each other silly. It was sort of as a favor to me, I guess."

"How do you mean?" What I really wanted to ask was if they were as passionate together as Bracken and Cory or Cory and Green, but I thought that a yes to that question would have been more than I could stand.

Leah sighed and shook back that amazing black hair. "Do you have any brothers or sisters, Nicky?"

I shook my head. "No. I think Mom and Dad wanted more, but...." I shrugged.

"I had a little brother," Leah said, and my heart stopped at the word "had." "Mikey—he hated it when I called him that, but I was six years older, and I just had to rub it in."

"What happened?" I asked into the sudden sadness.

"Leukemia," she said quietly. "When he was ten. Mom and dad left me at home at night to go to grief counseling, and I stayed home and got high."

"I'm sorry," I said sincerely.

"Oh, don't be—I laid half the county that year." Leah laughed. "Mom and Dad came home early one night and caught me pulling a train with the basketball team. I'd taken half a bottle of valium and a fifth of whiskey. By the time they got home, I was passed out and being banged in my own barf."

"Oh God, that's awful!" I said, horrified. Poor Leah—all that grief, nowhere to go but down. Great, another pun.

"Yeah—they took me to the hospital and got my stomach pumped. While I was there, Dad brought my suitcase to the hospital room and told me that he and Mom weren't prepared to deal with an incorrigible daughter. He cut me a check for five thousand dollars and said I was on my own."

And now I was too shocked to have anything to say at all.

"By the time Adrian saved me, I was one hit away from being a total crack whore."

"Adrian saved you?" It was an odd choice of words.

"Haven't you heard about Adrian's 'saved'?" Leah asked, legitimately curious. "Half the werecats and three-quarters of the vampires are people Adrian saved. You see, the thing with Adrian was, he didn't care how far down you'd been—he just saw how high you could go. I mean, we had one conversation. One. He made love to me—not fucked, not banged, not drilled. Made love. Swear to the Goddess, it was my first time ever. And then he asked me the first time I got high. I told him it was after my brother's funeral, and suddenly, for the first time since Mikey died, I found I could cry on someone, you know? And then he said—I'll never forget this—he said, 'The drugs are killing you, luv. You're too good a person to go out that way.' And then I really did cry, because my body was screaming for a hit even as he said it, and he didn't mention the sex, and he didn't give a damn how many people I'd banged, he just cared that I was killing myself. That's when he gave me the choice, vampire or werecreature. At first I didn't believe him, but he bared his fangs and grew his feeding face—although he didn't feed from me, because my blood was too screwed up—and I believed."

So he really did save them, I thought, suddenly feeling gratitude for Adrian, my rival, Cory's first beloved. In that moment, I understood why his death could send the entire hill into a tailspin of grief. Before, I had only blamed him for leaving the people he loved. Now I knew more of him.

"Why a werepuma?" I asked, and Leah smiled. Even from the other side of the car I could see that smile—and, another revelation, I knew with everything in me what Adrian had first seen in Leah, because if she had smiled at him like that even strung out and stoned, he had to have known what was inside.

Leah's smile faded after a moment, and as she finished her story, I heard the grief that it had taken drug addiction and the loss of her humanity to expose. "After Mikey's first round of chemo, all his hair fell out and he was getting teased at school. One day I went to walk him home, and these kids were all around him yelling names, and I just lost it… started beating the snot out of the little bastards, you know? So Mikey started calling me Wildcat after that. When Adrian gave me the choice, it was the only thing I wanted to be."

"It was a good choice," I said quietly. I was glad she was talking to me. As sad as her story was, it was good to connect with another human being. It seemed sometimes that my whole world was wrapped up with Green and Cory. It was a hard sphere to travel in. As much as Green loved us all, he was a god—a real living breathing picture of beauty whose every touch felt like the hand of grace. As much as Cory thought she was just a town kid whose life had taken a left turn, there was something bright and shining about her—something that drew men and man-gods around her like roses drew baby's breath. For all the tragedy in Leah's life, she was real and earthy and true. Cory dazzled me. Leah just made me happy to listen. Besides, I sighed, gazing ahead at the dreary gray sky and the long straight shot of I-5 through rock and cow country, the stretch of country from Bakersfield to Pasadena was as boring as watching The Weather Channel without a picture.

"It works for me." She grimaced. "Of course, I had a little trouble making relationships work in the first few months."

"What was the trouble?" I asked, genuinely curious. I'd always been other than human. What did it take to adapt?

"I kept trying to have them." She laughed, but it wasn't a happy sound.

"I don't understand." But I thought I did.

"I didn't get the total 'no shame' thing, you know? I thought, 'no drugs, no sex unless it means something'—you know, whole new me. The trouble was, I didn't even like sex. Once I was having it sober, it was pretty meaningless unless I was in cat form, and there weren't that many straight pumas out there who wanted a piece of this pussy, if you know what I mean."

I rolled my eyes. Puns—she was good at them. "So...."

"So... that's where Adrian and Bracken came in. After our night together—and a couple with Green—I sort of realized that I didn't *love* love any of them, not the way... hell, name an actual couple at Green's hill, and you know what I mean. But I cared about them, and they cared for me, and *damn*... the things they could make my body want. Anyway, I figured out that unless it was the right person, it could just be pleasure, and that as long as it really *was* pleasure, it just wasn't bad."

I nodded. I understood the theory, I thought, feeling like a virgin, but did not yet have the practice. "Why not Adrian and Green?" I asked.

Leah snorted, and suddenly I felt her hand on my thigh and realized that she had moved over on the Caddy's big bench seat. I breathed deep and smelled cat in heat and cinnamon perfume, and I almost saw spots as all the blood in my big head went flooding to the smaller one.

"You know why," she breathed softly, seriously. "You've been with Green and Cory. What did it feel like?"

I closed my eyes against the memory, opened them again, and autopiloted through the gray flatness of central California. "I felt like a pagan trespassing on holy land," I said thickly.

"Yeah," Leah breathed. Her hand traveled up my thigh, found my hard-on, gave it a gentle squeeze. I sucked in a breath.

"I don't know if I can...," I said, but my voice was high and squeaky, and I was betting that I could in about thirty seconds flat, if my cock was bare and her dark lips were wrapped around it.

"You have to, Nicky," Leah said seriously, still touching my thigh. "You keep looking to Cory like she will look back at you the same way one day. She won't. She's our leader, the queen of our hill, and the Goddess custom made her for the job. And she *loves* you—but not like she loves Bracken. Not like she loves Green. And you should be glad of that—because I've seen how intense she gets with either one of her beloveds. She would scorch you and cut you, and you wouldn't know which wound to tend to first."

I felt tears start at my eyes, and not from the pain in my crotch, either. "But I will always love her...," I said, feeling like a total pussy. And not either of the kinds Leah had been referring to.

"Of course you will, Nicky." Leah was leaning her head on my shoulder, and her fingernails were tracing my zipper with deliberate provocation. And so help me, I wanted her. Goddess, I wanted *anyone* who wanted me without reservation or remorse. "But has she ever led you on? Has she ever, once ever, let you believe that you could be what Green is to her? What Bracken is? What Adrian was?"

"I love you, Nicky. Maybe not the love you dreamed of as a kid, but it's love just the same."

"No," I said, and this time a real tear fell, trickling down my cheek, splashing on her hand as she fondled my cock through my jeans. "She wouldn't want to hurt me by lying."

"No, she wouldn't," Leah agreed, leaning in to lick a teardrop as it pooled in the corner of my mouth. "She's a good person. She wouldn't want you pining away for her, and she wouldn't want you sacrificing any chance at all of finding the right person—or even a person for right now—because of a misguided sense of monogamy that even Cory can't hold to."

"I would feel... unfaithful...." But her clever fingers had undone my fly, and my zipper with it, and my cock was there, covered by silk boxers that Green had bought me for Christmas.

"Then tonight, before we break at the hotel, call her up and ask her," Leah said throatily, and I whimpered as her fingernail scraped at the ridge of my hypersensitive head through the cooling silk. "But right now, pull over in that dirt turnout so I can take care of your little problem before you wreck the Cadillac and kill us all."

I didn't argue that the only person who'd be in real danger in a car crash was Ellis, and that was if the trunk popped open. I didn't argue that technically oral sex was still sex. I didn't even protest that maybe I should call Cory *right now.* Because Leah was right. Everything I was to Cory, everything I needed for myself, everything I learned from Green, all of it would be made better if my body, at least, was sated and pleased before I looked to them for my happiness. And Goddess, I wanted Leah's lips on my cock almost as much as I wanted Cory to love me.

I veered off the road in a cloud of dust, bumping enough to wake Willow and make Ellis's body thump in the back as we peeled into the turnout. As the car fishtailed to a stop and I fixed the brake with my foot, Leah pulled my jeans to my hips and engulfed my prick with her mouth—and suddenly I was coming, coming so hard I saw stars behind my eyes and groaned with lost innocence and lost dreams and with the simple animal pleasure of lust and promise of love that had replaced them.

Leah laughed, swallowing, wiping my come off the corner of her mouth with a red-tipped finger, then sat up, kissing me on the mouth. I tasted myself on her lips.

"Call Cory tonight," she whispered as I reached for her breast through the tightly buttoned red silk shirt she was wearing. "But live for the moment and fuck me right now...."

"Oh good," I heard from the back seat as Willow woke up. "A rest stop. I haven't tasted sex in at least eight hours...." She giggled giddily and did something to the front seat that rolled it flat and almost even with the back. Her hands came over my shoulders, pulling me into her lap. Her silver-green breasts were bare and pointed with brown, and I needed to taste that elven flesh, to feel it between my lips and teeth. I turned awkwardly, and as I did so, Leah stripped my pants down to my ankles and pulled off my shoes. In the time it took me to suckle on Willow, feel her nipple explode into my mouth and her hands clench in my hair, my body was exposed, cooling in the open air. Then I wasn't cold anymore. I was covered and hot with lips and with soft hands and I was lost, found, disappearing, becoming... becoming sex and flesh and dreams.

CORY
A Little Taste of Family

"WHAT IN the blue fuck happened to you two?" Grace asked as Bracken crashed gracelessly through the front door into the living room. I had felt his strength flag as he'd carried me up the stairs, but I'd stopped protesting that I could walk since the parking structure at school when he'd barked that my very bitching was making him tired.

"Shitty day," I mumbled against his chest, holding my hand there to reassure myself that his heart was beating in his body and we were still alive.

"Yeah... a few rude professors, a lost notebook—just a run-of-the-mill crap day," LaMark muttered with his trademark sarcasm.

"Hey—I flunked a pretest!" Mario protested ingenuously as he moved down the hallway to drop our packs in our room.

Bracken flopped into the white brocade couch, which groaned under our combined weights, and grunted, "Don't forget a little 'session' with Hallow." I wasn't sure if he was being sarcastic or sincere, and that alone made me giggle.

"Yeah, yeah...," Grace muttered, and I could hear her eyes rolling as she made kitchen sounds behind us. "So if I feed you, will somebody be able to give me a straight answer?"

"Grace, how come you always manage to feed us?" I asked, suddenly curious. "I mean... you've got a billion and six things to do. I love your cooking, but can't somebody else do it?"

"I like cooking," Grace protested mildly. "Besides, all I really do is prepare big portions of meat to cook. The nymphs and sprites take care of all the veggies and pasta—they know my recipes. I only actually make plates for my own children, little Goddess," she said gently. She must have worked in hyperspeed, because she moved forward with a plate of roast beef and potatoes for me and veggie lasagna for Bracken, and we had practically just walked through the door. "Bracken, my darling, you're going to have to put her down if she's going to eat this."

Bracken opened one eye and said, "Not if all she's going to have is a bite."

I wiggled out of his lap and scowled at him. "I apologized already! How long are you going to make me pay for that?"

He sat up completely and actually graced me with a bitter smile. "As long as it keeps making you eat," he said smugly, and I took the plate from Grace gratefully and stuck my tongue out at him. He waggled his eyebrows at me, I rolled my eyes, and we declared a truce and started shoveling food in our mouths.

"Thank you, Grace," I said through a full mouth, then swallowed. "And thank you doubly for fixing my plate." Because she'd said that she really only waited on her own children, and that made me one of her own. It wasn't a small thing.

"My pleasure." She winked kindly at me. She handed a plate to LaMark, then one to Mario, and they took a spot on the dark green couch across from us. Then she sat down on a stuffed chair across from us and put her elbows on her knees. "Now, before I call someone to take your places at the store tonight, tell me what happened."

"Hollow Man," we all said together through full mouths. Bracken set some sort of speed record for chewing so he could say "You eat, I'll talk." And then he launched into a pithy explanation of the day's attacks.

When he'd finished talking, I was still sawing away at roast beef. Grace looked at me and said, "Well, do you have anything to add?"

I took a bite and chewed thoughtfully before answering. "He left out the waste of skin and water that shouted my maiden name across the quad," I said with a shrug. "That's one of the reasons Hollow Man could pull such a whammy on us at the track—he knew part of my name. It gave him enough strength to knock me and Renny off guard. Hey— where *is* Renny?" Because she and Max had left in Max's Mustang right as we'd left. They should have been here by now.

"She called to say she was staying with Max," Grace said, and we raised meaningful eyebrows at each other. We'd been prophesying for some time that the two of them would have to weather a huge storm if they were going to make it together, and based on what Renny had been trying not to say in front of Davy today, I'd put money down that the storm had arrived. "Who shouted your name?" Grace asked, jerking me back to the big bad guy.

"Some jerkoff I knew from high school." I frowned at Grace. Grace mostly fed from the weres, but she kept a maternal eye on our people so she might know. "You've heard the guys talk about Chuck Granger?"

Grace thought about it, nodded. "Yeah—they hate him. Apparently his blood's pretty tasty, but...."

"But he's an ignorant redneck who uses the word 'faggot' like we use the word 'brother,'" Phillip said nastily, coming out from the hallway. "Why?"

"Because he smells like Hollow Man," I said grimly, and Phillip whistled.

"That's bad," he said thoughtfully.

"Yeah—really is. So, how often was Chuck dinner?"

Phillip shrugged. "We all take turns snacking on him... the men, I mean. He's just so sad. He waits for us. He doesn't know who we are, or what we do, but... but he'll stay out at the lake late into the night, and past the season when it's warm, because he remembers that he likes to party with us, and I think...." Phillip shrugged.

"The only time he gets to express his sexuality is with the vampires," I finished, feeling like Hallow, and Phillip nodded.

"He probably has some sort of residual memory of being... I don't know. Happy and free, I guess," he said. "Like I said—just sad."

"I'd feel worse for him if he hadn't just given part of my name out to the Hollow Man," I said, and Phillip's eyes widened. The vampires and shape-shifters were very cognizant of the whole "name is power" thing, at least on our hill.

"Well, that's a recipe for disaster," Phillip prophesied grimly, and I nodded.

"I'm sure there's a way we can fight it," I said, looking regretfully at my last piece of roast beef. "I mean—it wasn't that strong, really. If I was ready for it, I could fight it, no problem." I popped the roast beef in my mouth, and the room grew quiet for a moment. I finished chewing, swallowed, and added, "But we need to find some way to make us safe from his ability to... to level us at one blow. Hey... actually...."

"What?" Grace asked, taking our plates from us. She gestured to the kitchen to ask if I wanted more, but I shook my head no. I was still hungry from using all that power and then puking up, but now I was so damn tired I didn't think I could chew. She nodded and disappeared for a minute.

"I need to take more vampire blood tonight," I said, nodding decisively. Then I spoiled that by yawning. "The vampires I've blooded with didn't go down nearly as hard as those I haven't yet. We can think of some way to drown out his voice for the weres, but for now we have a way to protect the vampires, and we have to use it." I yawned again and opened my eyes wider to try to stop doing that.

"Nap first," Bracken said grimly behind me. I would have fought him, truly and honestly, but his head had tilted back to the couch and his eyes were half-closed, and suddenly I didn't think I could make it off the couch.

"For just a minute," I conceded. I blinked sleepily at Phillip. "I'll be up around... what time is it now?"

"'Bout 6:00—sun set at 5:28," he answered promptly.

"I'll be up around...."

"You'll be up when you're ready," Grace said briskly. Then she was taking off my shoes and swinging me around so I was lying with my head in Bracken's lap, and taking off Bracken's shoes as well before pulling out the recliner so he could stretch out. I fell asleep so quickly I didn't remember if I came up with a timeline or a plan or not.

I'm not sure how long I had been asleep, but when I woke the room was empty of everyone but me and Bracken. I yawned groggily and realized that what had awakened me was a small, compact body climbing up my middle and making itself comfortable between my butt and the back of the couch. I blinked my eyes open, and it occurred to me that I knew this little person.

"Graeme?" I asked uncertainly.

"Yeah. You're the pretty girl who said the F-word. My mommy didn't want me to play with you, but Grace-who-we're-not-supposed-to-call-Grandma said that you'd guard us with your life, and that Arturo would too, and that my mom should either get over her prejudices or go back home."

Ouch. "So you get to play with me after all?" I asked, still partly asleep.

"Yes, and you look fun—you made the whole store glow the last time I saw you. Can you do it again?"

As if! "I'm sorry. I already made my school glow today, and it's kind of exhausting. Maybe we could do something else." Inspiration. "Do you like movies?"

The little face with its dark red hair and brown freckles lit up with its own glow, looming above me from the perch on my hip. "We've been staying in a hotel this week since Mama came down to see Grace. I miss my TV. My daddy says we have every Disney video known to man."

"Good—so does Green. How about we let you pick one out, okay? Hey—don't you have a brother?" I sat up carefully so I didn't squash the little person or dump him on his ass, and made my way to the video cabinet and the folding wooden panel that hid the seventy-inch plasma television that Green kept in the front room. The sidhe room had no such convenience, but Green, Bracken, Arturo, and a few others of the sidhe adored television, movies, and music with a passion that few humans I'd seen could match.

"My brother's outside with Arturo. Gavin wanted to see the pretty gardens in the moonlight, but I've got a cold and my mama told me to stay in here so I couldn't. Arturo told me to stay in this room and to not be loud and wake you up." He thought for a moment, realized that maybe he hadn't followed *this* order to a T, and finished with, "I wasn't loud, was I?"

I had to laugh. "Nope. Not loud at all. Here—you pick out a DVD, and I'll go get something to eat. You hungry?"

"Do you have pie?"

"Grace always has pie," I reassured him, because I could smell caramel apple pie from the counter as I spoke. In a few moments, I was sitting on the couch with another plate of dinner, sandwiched between a slowly awakening Bracken and an excited Graeme and watching *The Incredibles.* Bracken hadn't seen the movie yet, and I had to caution Graeme that he wouldn't get another helping of pie if he didn't stop telling Brack what came next. Then Gavin came in and promptly flopped down in front of the television—damp jacket, shoes, and all. I got him to take everything off so we could put it in the kitchen by bribing him with apple pie, and we all—Arturo included—settled down for the rest of the movie. It was sort of fun.

Kids laugh at all the good places in a movie, and remind you that you can laugh out loud, and they make oohing and ahhing sounds and little bits of commentary when things are exciting, and they know all about the DVD extras, so we got to watch the extra short films that went with it and listen to the *professional* commentary too. When everything was done, Gavin turned toward me with a face so much like his grandma Grace's it made my heart constrict and said, "So your superpower makes rooms glow, Cory—does it do anything else?" I had to elbow Bracken as he snickered.

"I bet it's a shield!" Graeme said excitedly. "Like Violet's in the movie—can you turn invisible too?"

"No," Bracken said beside me, "but she can turn it into a weapon, like Gazerbeam could."

"So she could carve things into the bad guys! Do they bleed?" Graeme, the more bloodthirsty of the two, wanted to know.

"Bracken's the one who makes them bleed," I said with a sweet smile at my *due'alle*.

Bracken grinned at me wickedly, and I rolled my eyes. "No," he said, "it's like when Luke Skywalker's hand gets cut off by the light saber. It both cuts and burns."

Both boys made oohing sounds, their eyes wide.

"She can also throw fireballs," Arturo added, enjoying the play of truth and story, and the boys looked at me with new respect in their eyes. "She's taken down entire buildings."

"And built them up again!" Brack added enthusiastically. I glared at him, because the story of how I made that particular building was so *not* suitable for children.

"Do you have a superpower, Arturo?" Gavin asked.

"Superstrength," I said pertly, and Arturo looked totally surprised. "He could probably lift up this couch with all of us on it, if he could balance it right. And he has superspeed too."

"I can also turn into a tree, if I want," Arturo said with dignity twinkling from his copper-lightning eyes.

"Wow! Awesome! Can you make people bleed like Bracken?" Gavin liked the tree thing, but blood was always more exciting.

"No—that's Bracken's specialty," Arturo answered back gravely, winking at us over the boy's heads.

"How does Bracken do that?" They both wanted to know.

I smiled ghoulishly. "He can sing to the blood," I whispered. "He can hold his hand out to the bad guys and call their heart through their bodies until it explodes out their chests and their blood goes everywhere!"

"Ooohhhhh!" Two sets of shining eyes turned toward Bracken, and I was surprised to see him flush. "Really—can you really do that, Bracken?"

"Sure!" I said blithely. "He did it to a bad guy just today."

"Did the bad guy die?" This from Gavin, who was looking concerned.

"Unfortunately, no," I replied, meaning it sincerely. "But his blood was poisoned—that was pretty exciting."

"How did you avoid the poisoned blood?" Gavin wanted to know.

"Cory's shield." Bracken laid a hand on the small of my back as he said it, and I could tell he was enjoying himself. I'd wondered if he would like children, but he was a natural. "We worked like a team—like *The Incredibles*. It's more fun that way."

"Have you ever gotten hurt?" they asked, and suddenly the game wasn't fun anymore.

"Yes," I said after a moment, when Bracken and I locked eyes. "People get hurt when they're defending the people they love. It can be really dangerous."

"But you're okay?" And their concern was touching.

"Yeah, sure. But that's because Green was here to heal me," I said.

"Who's Green?" they asked, and a wave of longing swamped over me, and I could feel it emanating from Bracken too, and even from Arturo, across the room.

"Green's the leader of this hill," I said simply. *Green's my lover, my beloved, our rock, our root, our sky*, I wanted to say, but I managed to choke all that back. "He can heal people. Bracken here heals most wounds on his own, if they're not too deep, but sometimes his power works on him too and then he needs Green to stop the bleeding. If I'm hurt, I always need Green's help." I looked at Arturo for approval, and when he nodded, I rolled up my right pant leg. "See here? This burn would have crippled me, if Green hadn't helped." I pulled my shirt down from my shoulder, which looked like a grenade had exploded through it. "This would have killed me. I can only be a superhero if I've got superheroes with me. You guys—you don't have superheroes with you, so you need to keep yourselves safe, okay?"

Two sober pairs of eyes regarded me brightly, and I mustered up a smile. "Hey, you guys decide—do you want to watch another movie, or do you want to play a game? I'm pretty sure the sprites can pull up Monopoly or something. You hash it out, okay? I'm going to go get my knitting."

I was on my way back from my room, wondering why kids were so much easier to deal with than full-grown humans, when the phone rang. It was Nicky.

"Hey!" I said happily, "How's the trip?"

"Great," he said. "Uhm... really great."

Something in his tone made the back of my neck ripple. "How are you all getting along?"

"Great. Mmm... I mean, *really, really* great!"

"Okay, Nicky," I snapped. "Spill it. What's going on? And if you tell me everything's great again, I'll reach through the telephone line and strangle you."

"Uhm... sex," he said at last. "We're having sex. We're having sex in the car when it's stopped. We're having sex in the car when it's going. We stopped here at a hotel to have sex for a few hours before we go again. And I'm not sure if I'm cheating or not, or if this is going to bother you... but I'm really enjoying the whole rest of it."

I was so surprised I dropped my bag of knitting on my foot. "Really?" I asked. "You, Leah, Willow, Ellis... you're all...."

"Having sex," he said happily.

"Uhm. Okay." I thought about it for a minute. A part of me was jealous, but I squashed that part ruthlessly. Nicky deserved to be happy and free, and if this was making him happy, well, that was good. I thought about the times before Bracken, when I'd grabbed Nicky's hand when we were in a crowd and hadn't worried about what he'd think or about leading him on, or the times I'd hugged him or kissed his cheek. Anything that led us back to that point, I thought wistfully, would have to be a good thing.

"Really?" he asked, and I smiled. It was a little bit watery, but it was still a smile.

"Yeah, really," I said through a rough throat. "Seriously, Nicky—I want you to be happy. If this makes you happy, even if it only makes you happy for now, then you go for it. Have all the sex you want. Have more. Bring it to Green—it will make him strong, and you will both be happy and strong when you come back to me, okay?"

"Okay." And his throat sounded rough too.

"But you'll both come back to me, right?" I asked and hated the plaintive note in my voice. I was glad for him, I reminded myself. With all my heart I was glad.

"You're my north," Nicky said thickly. "You'll always be my north. And you know you don't have to worry about Green. He'll always come back to you, Cory. I don't think he wants to live another two thousand years if you're not with him for your lifetime."

I nodded. I knew that. "I love you Nicky," I said without qualification. "Go get laid."

He laughed a little and rang off, and I was left feeling lost until I sat next to Bracken and joined Arturo and the kids in watching *Shrek 2*. Bracken had seen this one before, and it delighted me to hear him laugh at his favorite parts—for some reason he really liked that damn cat with Antonio Banderas's voice. But as I sat down, he felt a stiffness in my shoulders and leaned over to ask "What's wrong?" in my ear.

I almost said "Nothing," but I was still feeling bad about that afternoon, so I shrugged. "I'll tell you later—it's not big." But then the phone rang again, and it was Green, and I forgot to tell Bracken after all, which was unfortunate because it might have at least warned him about what was to come later.

Green sounded alone and sad, and it hurt me to talk to him, but I sat in the kitchen and talked quietly and knit, rehashing the day's events. He was exhausted from the usual round of meetings and from caring for Funky Man, and there was a silence on the phone as he recalled the terrified trust the shattered sidhe had placed in him.

"But I did meet an old friend," he said after a moment. His voice brightened, and so did I.

"A good one?" I asked hopefully.

"About to be even better, I think." The suggestion in his voice was unmistakable, and I was so happy he wouldn't be alone for the night that I laughed with a full heart for the first time since he rang. "So tell me, how was your day?" he asked, and it was easier to speak.

I told him almost everything, from the attack by Hollow Man to the fight with Bracken to Nicky's sudden new life. I glossed over the meeting with Hallow and gave him the barest details about the meeting with Chuck Granger, but that was more because they seemed unimportant next to the other stuff. He wanted to know why I hadn't called on him for power with Hollow Man, and I said kindly, "You're busy healing, beloved. Bracken and I dealt. We're exhausted, but we dealt. You need to be strong so you can come home to us."

"I hate this," he said darkly. Although I said a private amen, for his ears I replied, "We need you to be strong when you get here, because we're going to be falling apart. Don't worry, Green, we haven't stopped needing you. *I* haven't stopped needing you."

The fight with Bracken amused him—more than I think he let on—and when I asked him why he thought it was so funny, he replied, "Because I expected you two to dance the moment you got together. I'm just enjoying the show, that's all."

I snorted. "Well, then you're going to love this." And I told him about Nicky. Green was delighted.

"Really? The whole Cadillac is a traveling orgy? Next to meeting Eric, that's probably the best news I've heard all day."

I blinked. I guessed between the hurricanes and the oil industry and caring for Funky Man, on Green's end, at least, it really was. "Since it's traveling your way, I'm glad you think so," I said warmly, but my beloved knew me too well to let it go.

"You're hurt," he said gently.

"I'm a stupid human," I said with a sniff. "It's good. I mean, most of me knows that it's a good thing... but...."

"But he was ours, and now we have to share him with the world?" Green was always wise.

"I'll get over it," I said with dignity. "I'm not dumb. What we were doing—date night with me, whenever you were free and *not* with me with you—Nicky deserves more. You can't just dole out love like cookies.... It's sort of the opposite of cookies. Too many cookies make you sick. Not enough love does the same thing. If we'd have kept on, Nicky's heart would have gotten sick. Maybe this way we can have each other, and Nicky can stay well."

"But he was yours, and now you have to share him with the world," Green repeated.

"Yeah," I sighed, honesty forced on me at last. "He was ours, and now we have to share him with the world."

"Goddess, I love you," he said, so fervently that the tears I'd held at bay actually flooded over.

"I love you too," I choked. "When Nicky gets there, you'd better play and play and play, do you hear me?"

"I'm way ahead of you, beloved," he said with some heat. "And then I'll come home to you."

We rung off shortly after that, and when I cradled the phone, I looked up and saw that Grace and Chloe had come quietly in through the front door and were finishing the movie with the boys. The credits rolled, the last little mutant donkey flew off into the sunset, and Chloe called briskly to the boys to get their things, it was time to go.

"Can we stay here, Mama?" Graeme wanted to know. "Cory and Bracken have superpowers—maybe if we stay we can see them use them!"

I flushed brightly, not having realized that even the best kid is a complete rat fink when he's told a good story.

"They do not have superpowers," Chloe snapped impatiently. "Superpowers are for television and not real life. Now let's go."

"But, Mama…," Gavin protested. "Cory made the store glow that one night. And Bracken can make a bad guy's heart jump out of his chest! And Arturo has superstrength."

"And Grace can fly," Chloe said impatiently. "Gavin, where's your coat?"

"It's right here," I said from the darkened kitchen. "And Grace really can fly." I don't know what made me add it. Honestly, I don't. But it irritated me that a woman who had just discovered her dead mother—looking no older than herself, showing her fangs, and everything—should completely dismiss the whole "superpowers" idea.

"I don't want to hear it from you," Chloe snapped, and her face flushed with real anger. "You're the one who filled their head with this crap. I should have known better than to leave my kids with a foul-mouthed teenybopper and her hunk-of-the-month."

"It's not crap," Grace said evenly from behind her daughter. Her expression was a terrible mixture of hurt, dismay, and gentleness. "It's the truth, all of it—although I have the feeling they were telling the boys just to make them laugh. And Cory has been responsible for every creature under this hill since she came back from the city in December, and Bracken has been killing himself to help her. They deserve your respect, Chloe."

"Right, Mom. You keep lecturing me about respect, when you're the one who left your family to have a party with a bunch of pretty young men," Chloe snapped nastily, and now *my* temper flashed.

"You have no idea what your mother gave up for you," I hissed, taking a step forward and letting my anger blaze out of my eyes. "She hurt every day, knowing that you and your sister would never know that she'd been with you your entire lives. When you walked into the store last week, her heart broke, because she was thrilled to see you and at the same time terrified that you'd be exactly the same judgmental bitch you're acting like right now."

"My mother *died* when I was a little kid!" Chloe raged. "And I learned to live with that. Do you have any idea what kind of grief that is?"

"You're goddamned right I do!" I raged back. "The difference is that you act like grief gives you some special pass here in your mother's home, with her people. You don't seem to realize that to be at this hill, that kind of grief is practically a membership requirement—and your mom's one of the charter members."

"Yeah—who'd you lose that makes you such an expert?" Chloe asked nastily, and I saw the anguish on Grace's face and couldn't go on.

"None of your freaking business," I said quietly, subsiding and taking a step backward. "Graeme, Gavin, it was nice to see you—I really enjoyed our night together. Bracken, I'm going down to share blood with the vampires. Do you want to come?" He'd stood up when the argument had started, as surprised and helpless as Arturo, I think, and unable to put himself between the three of us for fear of hurting the wrong woman. Now he blurred—just to spite Chloe—and scooped me and my knitting bag up in hyperspeed, blurring us across the hall and down the stairs to the darkling common room before I could even register Chloe's expression.

When we got to the foot of the stairs, before turning right into the darkling hall, he slowed to normal speed and chuckled quietly. When I asked him why, he replied, "The last thing I heard was Graeme saying 'Wow—he has superspeed too!'" I laughed a little and leaned my head on his arm.

"Green said hi," I said quietly.

"Did you tell him hi for me?" he asked, but we both knew he didn't need to.

"Of course."

"You talked for a long time."

"I was complaining about you," I kidded, and he leaned over and kissed the top of my head.

"Yeah, I'm an asshole, I know."

I turned toward him, and suddenly the whole afternoon, the argument, the prevarication, his smoldering anger and my defensiveness, it all melted away. "You're perfect," I said and pulled him down for a fervent kiss. "You're everything I needed and didn't know I needed. You're everything I couldn't survive without, and I never knew, even when I was dying without you. You, me, Adrian, Green—we would have found a way. You said you would have died rather than compete with Adrian when he was still here, but it wouldn't have happened like that. We would have found a way, the four of us, because there can't be a me without a Green, and there can't be a me without a you."

Bracken's eyes, always the color of a still pond in shadow, glimmered brightly. "Dammit, Cory...," he said thickly, "you can't just hit me with something like that. You have to give me a card or something, or we have to be in bed. I don't know what to do with romance when we're standing in a hallway about to go work."

I smiled and knew my own eyes were bright too. "Just tell me you love me, asshole, and we can get a move on."

"I love you, asshole," he said smartly, and I laughed as he lifted me up and kissed me, and then we just held and held and held. We were interrupted by Phillip, clearing his throat down the hall in front of the common room.

"You know, we all fall asleep around dawn," he informed us—the sarcastic bastard—and Bracken reluctantly set me down.

"Yeah, yeah," I grumbled. "Work, work, work."

But the truth was, I enjoyed blooding the vampires. I hadn't, at first—at first I'd been totally icked out by the idea of tasting a stranger's blood, and vice versa, but then it turned out that I had an interesting ability. We weren't sure if it was because I was a human marked by a vampire or because I was a sorceress marked by a vampire, but either way, I could *taste* the thing that had most dominated the daylight life of the vampire whose blood I was sharing.

And they could taste me.

I had tasted Adrian's blood one night, one unforgettable night when we were making furious, healing love in Green's gardens by moonlight, but I hadn't known about the ability then. I had been covered in Adrian's blood tears as he relived the most awful, scarring moment of a short life, and when I tasted them, all I could taste was copper and salt.

It wasn't until I started blooding the other vampires that I realized this meant that Adrian's daylight life had been totally marked by tears and blood.

But Marcus had tasted like dry-erase marker and coffee, and I had looked at him and said, "You loved being a teacher, didn't you?" He had wept at my feet, a joyous, cathartic weeping that validated everything

Marcus had loved about his life. Phillip had tasted like snow and hot chocolate, and that made me happy, because he still loved snow skiing, although the hot chocolate was a thing of the past. Bryn had tasted like wildflowers in the spring, Chet had tasted like a teriyaki burger smothered in mushrooms and like wet dog at the lake, and Ellis had tasted like pizza, milk shakes, and the fuzzy sweater of the first girl he'd ever felt up. It was a lovely moment for all of us, to know and be known for the thing that made you the most you. Dying, resurrecting, feeding on blood and sex and passion, these were frightening things—identity-defying, terrifying changes. It was a joy greater than words could say for the vampires to know that the thing, the taste, of what had made them the person they were still coursed through their veins.

And then they tasted me, and as our ritual, something special to their being the only known vampires with a human queen, I guess, they told me what I tasted like.

The answer always made them weep blood, and it was always the same.

Unless they visited me in my room, as Ellis had the week before, blooding the vampires was an informal affair. I sat, sometimes with Green, sometimes with Bracken, on their common room couch—the vampires favored black leather, which kind of icked out the elves, but they dealt—and knitted and visited until one of the vampires approached me. The ones I knew best simply sat next to me and waited for a pause in the conversation, but the shier or more reluctant vampires knelt before me on one knee and formally requested a sharing of blood.

Today, the first one to approach was a tiny wraithlike girl with flyaway blonde hair who had been about sixteen when she'd died. She was one of Adrian's first saved, except he had saved her from a life of forced prostitution in mining camps. She'd been dying of tuberculosis at the time, and he had saved her from that as well. Her name was Lila, and although she'd been dead for over a hundred years, she had never quite lost her fear of humans. She approached me formally, wearing a loose white dress with a hand-knit shrug over the sleeves, and bent to one knee.

I put my knitting down and smiled at her. It was hard to remember that she'd been born before the beginning of the Civil War.

"I'd like to request a blooding, Queen of Night," she said softly, and I nodded.

"Of course, Lila—it would be an honor." Because it would be. It was not lost on me that she had waited so long; after so many years with Adrian as a leader, acknowledging me must have been like changing from breathing air to breathing water. Or not breathing at all.

She took my hand in her own tiny dry one, and it was like being touched by an empty vinyl glove. Then, because I had no fangs, she punctured her own wrist as she held my hand, and I drew it to my mouth to taste the slow blood welling from her cool skin.

I blinked. "Rabbit stew and applesauce," I said after a moment. Then, more thoughtfully, "Poppies... thousands of them. The smell of...." Not a lover, but a girl she'd loved. "The smell of your little sister's hair," I finished quietly.

Lila's face was small and pointed like a diamond, and the skin stretched tightly over it, stark white with black eyes in frightening contrast. A single splash of scarlet slid down the side of her nose. She nodded, somberly. "Heather died the year before I did," she said simply. She didn't explain how she knew the taste of rabbit stew.

Instead, she drew my wrist to her mouth, and with a tiny, rabbity sort of nip of her own, she punctured my wrist with one fang and sipped. Her eyes closed on their own, her whole body shuddered convulsively, her throat made a sound like a toddler singing to himself—and suddenly she wrapped both arms around her knees, making that low, sad, cry-singing sound into the cradle of her body. "Oh Goddess... Goddess.... They all said it, but I didn't believe...," she keened, and I stroked her hair awkwardly and looked around the room. Marcus and Phillip were there in a flash, arms wrapped protectively around the tiny, eternally old child, and together they pulled her out the door from the darkling common to their shared rooms.

There was a respectful quiet then that was interrupted by an irreverent female voice saying, "What did she do to that kid, Mom?"

I looked up from where Lila and the boys had disappeared and saw Grace at the hallway entrance, Chloe in tow. Arturo stood behind them, one hand on Grace's waist, and she had covered that hand with her own. At Chloe's interruption of the sad, terrible tableau, Grace looked sharply at her daughter and hissed, "You stay there and shut up, Chloe. There's something I think you need to see."

And then to my complete surprise and total mortification, Grace flashed across the room and sank to one knee in front of me.

"No...," I said, feeling helpless, but Grace overrode me, speaking loudly and formally into the now silent room.

"I ask to share blood with you, Lady Cory—beloved of Adrian, Lord of Night, beloved of Green, Lord of Day."

"You don't have to do this," I all but begged. Grace and I had never blooded. My respect for her—my love for her as my surrogate mom— had never questioned her loyalty, had never worried about weakness. It would be like wondering if the sun would rise the next day. Grace would be there for me, for Green, for the hill, because she loved us and would not think to do otherwise. What need was there for a blooding ritual meant to instill loyalty and bonding when we were family in the best sense of the word?

"I really do, my queen," she said gently and took my unblooded hand in hers, then pulled her own wrist to her mouth and bit.

She held out the slow-bleeding skin, and I took it toward my lips, feeling like a little kid who's been given her first beer. This was Grace... I couldn't subjugate Grace... but I was her leader and she was offering me fealty, and I guess I had to. Trying not to let my hands shake, I touched her wrist with my mouth and pulled, then closed my eyes to get the flavors just right.

"Cinnamon sugar cookies...," I said on a choked breath. "Sipping Diet Coke while knitting in a room with a big window... lake water in your mouth while watching your children play... the smell of your babies' skin... the taste of little girls' perfume... the sound of their laughter... the mints your husband used after he'd had a beer and still wanted to kiss you... sharing the first chocolate-chip cookie out of the oven with your daughters...." There was more, but I couldn't go on. Goddess, God, child of love, how could she have lived, missing them all so much?

Grace looked up at me from eyes washed with crimson, so much blood running down her face from tears that it puddled on her jeans, leaving big splotchy stains where it fell. With hands that shook even worse than mine, she pulled my wrist to her mouth and took a solid, clean bite, then sucked once, twice, hard and purposefully. Then she tilted her head back and let out a cry of anguish, and I knew the sound—it was a louder version of Lila's keening, a softer version of the scream that Marcus had given. It was the sound made by every vampire I'd blooded except Adrian and Andres, who had both been above me in the hierarchy.

It was the sound of someone who had wanted to live, and who had died because living had not been an option.

"Sunshine," she cried. "Glory, Goddess, and hallelujah, my queen, you taste like sunshine." And, sobbing, she leaned her head against me, and I wrapped my arms around her and let her weep longingly into my lap. Eventually the sobbing stilled, and another vampire—a young man who had been found dying from a car crash next to his dead beloved—stepped hesitantly forward to take her place. Arturo waited at Grace's elbow to help her up, and she went easily into his arms, bonelessly, as trusting as a sleepy kitten. I met his eyes miserably. A week ago I had called half the kiss because I saw Grace cry, and now I was the one who had made her cry.

But Arturo's look was kind. "This was good," he said quietly. "Chloe needed to see it, to see you be... you. To see her mother's world. Don't ever apologize for being the leader your people need, Corinne Carol-Anne."

I almost lost it, broke down completely, because for once I was so glad to hear my entire first name. "Promise me something, Arturo?" I asked plaintively as he half carried, half walked Grace toward the doorway where a frightened, wretched Chloe was waiting for her. He turned. "Promise me you'll never call me Lady Cory?"

He smiled, flashing silver-capped teeth. "You of all people should know that lying does not come easily to my people," he said over his shoulder. Then they were gone, and I was left face-to-face with the burden of being Lady Cory, Queen of the Vampires, until I'd blooded a few more of my people. Being royalty sucked large.

Glen stepped forward hesitantly and knelt at my feet. He'd been a sharply handsome young man with dark blond hair, and all that he had lost from his actual life was gazing at me from burning eyes. "Will I really taste sunshine?" he asked. They all wondered if it was real until it happened to them—which is pretty much how us mortals looked at death, I thought.

"That's what I'm told," I said back and accepted his offered wrist. But when I tasted his blood, I blushed. It tasted like me. Well, it tasted like me when... when Bracken or Green had been buried between my thighs and then came up to kiss me, and I was a glaze on their faces and a tang on their tongues. I was silent for a moment, mortified that I would have to explain what it was he missed, until I actually thought about it.

Glen would get to taste *that* as often as he wanted, here at Green's hill. Shape-changers, other vampires, even elves would give him any taste he wanted for free—he would have no cause to miss the taste of a woman. I swallowed then, and took another taste, and realized....

That taste of me on my lovers' lips was really just *me*... and because it was from an intense place, it was me squared. What he missed wasn't the taste of a woman during lovemaking, it was the taste of a particular woman. He missed this woman with the same intensity that I missed the taste of Adrian.

My eyes misted. I'd held it together through Grace, but this moment, on top of that one, undid me. I spoke into a breathless silence, because usually I would announce the taste of the vampire almost immediately, and I had been silent for some time. "What was her name?" I asked quietly, and he bowed his head over my proffered hand.

"Amber," he told me. "Her name was Amber."

"She's still in your blood," I said, and I hoped it would help. I didn't even wince as he reopened the wound at my wrist.

He breathed deeply, a reflexive movement only since vampires didn't breathe, and sighed. "You really do," he said, and he looked at me with happy tears in his eyes. "You taste like sunshine. And Amber." Then he stood and kissed my cheek and faded into the crowd of vampires like paper into a stack. I sagged against Bracken, feeling wrung out and limp already. Suddenly Phillip and Marcus stepped forward from the crowd.

"That's enough," Phillip said roughly, meeting Bracken's eyes. "That's enough. Our queen serves us well, and she can blood more of us on another day."

I half expected protest—but Bracken had swung me up into his arms already, and Marcus had parted the crowd, and what greeted me instead was a respectful silence, a quiet bowing, the parting in a small sea of people as my beloved bore me away.

"Whereto, my lady?" he asked, his voice teasing as we cleared the doorway, but I wasn't in the mood.

"Don't." I used to go for months at a time without tears, really I did. But the day had been emotion-fraught and I was exhausted, and it felt like I'd been fighting them all day, and I was more weary of the fight than I would have been of the actual tears. "Don't. Not you. Never you, Bracken. Please? You have to promise me...."

"Wait… sh… sh… sh…." He cradled me against him now, stopping at the end of the hallway where hopefully no one could hear us. "What am I promising?"

"I'll never be 'Lady Cory' to you…," I wailed, and the look in his eyes only confirmed my worst pain.

"Corinne Carol-Anne Kirkpatrick op Crocken Green," he said, and my full name falling from his lips like heavy gold garnered my complete attention. "You know very well that the only person at the hill who will never be obliged to bow to you is Green."

Damn Bracken. Damn all elves. Damn the powerful sidhe and their compulsion for the truth. Damn it all.

But, as though sensing I wouldn't make it without some sort of reassurance that I would never have to command him, he smiled—a rarity enough for Bracken, who wore his grimness like most people wore shoes. "But that doesn't mean you don't get to bow to me in bed, right?"

Okay. Damn everything else, but bless my beloved after all.

"Right," I sniffled. "But first I'm going to finish your damn sweater, okay?" I'd stitched most of it together during the movie and had been working the neck on circular needles as I'd sat with the vampires. Just two more inches and a few woven ends, and I'd be good to go.

And finish it I did, in the quiet of our bedroom, sitting in one of the two overstuffed chairs Green had furnished it with when I hadn't been looking. Bracken sat next to me, working on homework.

"Whatcha doing?" I asked, after thirty minutes of blessed silence during which my nerves magically realigned like little loops of yarn into a peaceful fabric. I was in the process of binding off, and pleased that I could talk and finish at the same time.

"Physics," he said shortly.

I groaned. "Goddess. I'm going to have to do mine in a minute."

"Whose work do you think I'm doing?" He looked at me as though I were stupid, and I almost dropped one of my last stitches.

"You can't do that—he'll know my handwriting!" There were actually many more reasons why he couldn't do my homework for me, but I was still young enough for the first thing out of my mouth to be "We'll get caught."

Bracken grunted "Hardly" and tilted the paper so I could see. Instead of Bracken's flowing old-school numbers and cursive letters, I could see a compressed diagram filled with my small neat figures.

I was too impressed with his forgery to come up with a good reply for that, so I swore for a couple of minutes while I finished the neck and wove in the yarn, complaining the whole time. "Dammit, Brack—how am I supposed to learn the damn subject if you do it for me?" I asked finally, standing up with the sweater in front of me. *It's a good thing I used chunky yarn,* I thought irritably, because it was huge—on me it went past my knees. If I'd used sport-weight yarn, it would have taken me a year.

"How are you supposed to learn the subject if the professor is a stupid asshole who can't explain things worth shit?" he retorted, his eyes narrowed in mutiny. "You don't need to know physics to learn business or politics or law or psychology. *Those* are the things you *need* to study, and you don't need to stay up until two in the morning when you're already exhausted from fighting off bad guys and leading your people. Whether you like it or not, you *are* our Lady Cory, and you need to learn to do what other leaders do and delegate! Hey—is it finished?"

The question, asked with a tone of wonder and delight, completely threw me off track. "Yeah...," I said diffidently. "Do you like it?"

His eyes widened, and a shy smile quirked at the corners of his mouth. The argument, I guessed, was over. I thought he had won—at least for the moment—but we were both gazing at the sweater in appreciation, and he didn't notice enough to gloat. I smoothed the fabric under my hands and glanced up at him to see if he really did like it.

"It's great," he said simply. "Let me try it on."

The yarn was an acrylic/wool blend, so I didn't have to worry about blocking, and I practically danced as Bracken shucked his shirt to his pale sculpted torso and then slid my sweater over his broad shoulders and tightened, elongated abdomen. It was a little snug in the chest, so it stretched with him, and it fell down past his belt line, his narrow waist and hips lost a little in the swing. *There aren't patterns out there for a sidhe physique,* I thought fretfully, and some of the stitches were irregular even under the bumpy yarn.

"It looks homemade," I said, trying not to be depressed. Bracken didn't notice.

"It's good. It's very good," he said sincerely, moving to the bathroom to look at it in front of the mirror. He ran his hands down the textured fabric, and his smooth forehead wrinkled. "I can... I can feel you... in the strands.

The wool… it carries you with it. Sweat and oils, and… and thoughts, almost." He turned. "What a magical thing humans do. I never would have guessed something so simple had magic in it."

I smiled at him, a smile so wide it stretched my cheeks and made my eyes squint, and so heartfelt I could barely hold his gaze. "You like it," I said, really knowing the meaning of the word "delight." I'd felt this way when I'd given Green his scarf, but then, Green was Green—anything I did for him filled him with joy and wonder. Bracken was different—much more difficult to please, much less inclined to accept and enjoy. And my smile seemed to move something in him. He looked away, almost bashful, like a schoolkid getting a cookie from a sweetheart, then held out his arms for me. I burrowed in, loving him so much my heart hammered against my ribs and my lungs couldn't fill.

"You will knit one for Green?" he asked hopefully, his voice rumbling against my ear.

"Oh, yes," I said, my face mushed pleasantly between that spot where pectorals and sternum meet. The yarn sat patiently in a huge ziplock bag under the bed, and I had already picked out the pattern.

"Good," he said happily, his skin moving restively under the sweater. "That's good," he repeated, and, physics forgotten, we had another of those long quiet hugs that I had enjoyed even when Adrian had been alive and we'd just been friends, but that I cherished now.

Eventually we got ready for bed, and I was just dropping off to sleep when his chest rumbled sleepily next to my ear. "So…."

"Uhm?"

"When you blooded that one vampire… Glen?"

"Uhm-hm?"

"What exactly did you think you tasted, when you first had his blood?"

I laughed sleepily. Trust Bracken to notice the complete mortification and the terrible blush. "Tell you what, beloved. If we don't get into a snit and no bad guys show up tomorrow, I'll give you a demonstration tomorrow night, okay?"

He chuckled, also sleepily. "That's a deal."

And that's all it took. The phone call from Nicky, topped with one thought of arousal—just enough to set a tired tingle through our bodies—and the gateway was opened.

GREEN
Sex Cubed and Healed Twilight

THE FRANCHISE meeting broke up, and Green suppressed a yawn. He'd started acquiring gas stations about twenty years before, when the mini-marts began to spawn on every corner and Adrian noted that many of the were and vampire recruits seemed to live at such places. The business aspect of running something so very utilitarian and so very profit based had always been the most onerous part of Green's job as leader of his hill. He looked forward to his bi-yearly trips to Texas like a hyperactive nine-year-old looked forward to a three-hour car trip to visit a dying aunt.

"Green—so good to see you!" Green looked up from the papers he was shoving into his canvas briefcase, and the first genuine smile of the day crossed his features. Eric Reynolds had been a sixteen-year-old runaway panhandling in the streets of Houston when Green had first met him. Reynolds was actually one of the wealthier names in the area, but Eric's personality and sexual proclivities had been an uncomfortable fit with the excessive conventionality that came with wealth, privilege, and a father convinced that real men killed animals for sport and by no means ever felt up other men for pleasure. Eric had been dying then, of starvation and disease, but Green had cleaned him up and healed him—much the same way he had cleaned Funky Man and healed Adrian—and then, because he could only heal symptoms but never the root of a terminal disease, Green had given him Adrian's choice. Vampire or werecreature—which would he choose to be? Eric had chosen werecoyote, but after a couple of years and some serious growing up, he had not, in the end, chosen Green's hill.

Instead, he had taken the education Green had offered and the stake money as well (long since paid back), and had established himself in the oil business, working long and hard until his father had been in the uncomfortable position of being bought out by his estranged son. Eric had offered to relent on one condition—he wanted back at the family table for holidays, companions included. Eric's father might have been a son of a bitch, but his mother was a gentle woman, devoted to her children and devastated by her son's exile. Eric also had two younger sisters whom he missed dearly. Father Reynolds had no choice, and the last time Green had spoken to his young protégé (now in his mid-thirties but looking much younger thanks to his werecreature status), he had just walked his youngest sister down the aisle, by her request. Eric was a living reminder that sometimes the human world did have its vital attractions.

"Eric—Goddess, it's good to see you. I'd almost forgotten there was a reason I didn't hate this town."

Eric grinned, the expression suiting his fine-boned little-boy face, and ran a hand through expensively cut sandy blond hair before he sobered. "I was so sorry to hear about Adrian," he said after a moment. "How's Bracken taking it?"

Green grimaced. Eric had played with both of them when he'd lived with Green—of course he'd know how truly devastated Brack would be.

"He still hasn't forgiven our love for up and dying on us. And to be truthful, it took a hell of a lot for me to forgive him too, the stupid bugger. If it hadn't been for Cory, I don't know if either one of us would have made it through this year."

"Cory? Have I met him?"

Green laughed the kind of bittersweet laugh that made his eyes close tightly before he could take a breath and answer. "That, my friend, is a very, very long story."

Eric smiled unabashedly, the grin carving deep, charming dimples in his cheeks. "Great. As it happens, I'm done for the day."

"Dinner, then?" Green asked, cheered at the thought of not having to go back to his hotel room with only Funky Man for company. He'd set the two of them up in a suite in anticipation of Nicky's arrival, and had left the meetings twice to check on his lost brother. Both times had found Funky Man sleeping in front of the television, and both times he'd been so happy to see Green that he'd alternately hugged him like an overgrown child and petted his hair in awe and woe for his own lost beauty. Green was sure his brother would improve with time and care, but for the moment a little sane company was a welcome relief.

"Absolutely. My treat," Eric agreed, and Green stood as they readied to leave the posh and grim office building.

"My thanks. I do have to return to the suite by eight to make a phone call, though," Green warned, "and to check on somebody."

Eric looked sideways at his old leader from speculative eyes. "Does this mean my plans to stay in your room are premature? Because right now, I'm so single it hurts."

Green laughed—a great, booming, relieving laugh. "No, my friend, I'd say your plans to stay in my room are exactly what I need. And believe me, I'm the last thing from single anyone could claim."

Again Eric nodded, and he clapped a hand on Green's shoulder, which was about even with his own head. "Good, my brother, because I would have been terribly disappointed."

Dinner was at a small Italian place with good wine and better pasta and, Green had to admit, fabulous company. Eric was completely enthralled by Green's description of Cory—her long, uncertain courtship with Adrian, her brief, brutal courtship with Bracken, and Green's own guileless assumption from the moment he saw her that she would someday be his as well.

"It figures," Eric said good-naturedly as they polished off a bottle of wine and moved on to a deep-fried ice-cream confection. "In fact, I should have known."

Green raised his eyebrows. "What an odd thing to say. I must tell you, the whole situation surprised the hell out of me."

Eric narrowly missed snorting wine out his nose. "I don't see how. The three of you.... I mean, I know you and Bracken were never a thing, but... but you and Bracken were both so bound up in Adrian that whoever he brought home to love, well, you'd be bound up with him or her too."

Green blinked thoughtfully. "I never thought of it like that. And Cory—well, you can be certain that when Adrian brought her home, she was prepared for him to be her one and only forever and ever."

Eric sighed. "Poor baby—how is she adjusting to life on the hill?"

Green thought very carefully before a smile bloomed at the corners of his finely sculpted mouth. "She's... adjusting," he said sincerely. She and Bracken would learn to mesh. She and Nicky would find balance. She would learn to stand without him and take strength from him when he was there. "I have a special faith in my beloved."

"You have faith in us all, leader," Eric said softly. "That's why we try not to let you down. You 'bout done?" And with that, he covered

Green's hand as it replaced the check with his card, and Green gazed into those little-boy-blue eyes with a burning emerald of his own.

"Not even close—you?"

Eric swallowed, as though his throat had gone dry suddenly. "I've got all night."

FUNKY MAN was delighted to meet Eric, a new person who knew Green and, as he said frequently, "a pretty human boy." Eric, true to all of Green's children, was both kind and gracious to a person so damaged that even his name was in ruins.

"What are you watching?" Eric asked, eyeing the Disney cartoon with amusement.

"*Kim Possible*," Funky replied with a full mouth. Green had brought him takeout lasagna from the restaurant. "She's a pretty human girl, like sidhe, but not real."

Green raised his eyes and took a better look at the cartoon. He and Eric flanked his guest, slouching on the generously sized couch, and although not a look was exchanged and no skin was touched, there was a growing, palpable, delicious tension between the two men that Green enjoyed savoring enough to stretch out the length of an easy, excruciating half hour. "Not bad, Funky Man," he said after the episode was over. "You about have her pegged. We're going to retire, then—all good with you?"

Funky Man looked at Green slyly from faded gold-violet spangled eyes. "Retire, Green Man? Is that what we call it these days?"

Green laughed, clasped his brother's hand in his own. "You may call it whatever you like, Funky Man, and you may have it if you wish."

Funky shook his head. "Not yet, Green Man. Still too broken inside."

Green kissed the dusky violet skin, released the thin hand, and ran a caress down the shorn scalp. "You'll heal, my brother. You'll heal."

Eric's expression as he pulled Green into the bedroom was somber and kind. "If he heals, it's because he had the luck to find you."

"More like the Goddess's will," Green said thoughtfully. Then the door shut behind him and he turned, grasped Eric by the shoulders, and threw him back against the wall, mating his mouth with Eric's into a hard, hungry kiss, and the subject was tabled for the moment.

Eric didn't need healing, like so many of Green's lovers. He didn't need mating and tenderness like the sylphs. Unlike Cory, he wasn't human and would heal any bruises almost instantly. Eric was hard bodied and starving for flesh, and he gave as good as he got. Sex was sweaty, pounding, and muscular, exulting in the physical, in the joy of fucking, and after Eric had thrust again and again and finally shuddered and spent himself into Green's moist flesh, the two of them collapsed, laughing, facedown against the creaky, inadequate hotel bed.

"Oh, Goddess," Green groaned good-naturedly. "I miss my bed back at home."

"I'd bet that's not all you miss," Eric replied, playfully biting at a flawless, pale, green-tinted shoulder.

Green looked peacefully at his friend from sated, sideways eyes. "You'd be right. You're fascinated by her, aren't you? You haven't even met her."

Eric's head was pillowed on his arms, and it made the act of looking away awkward. Green, recognizing discomfort in a human lover, moved his body, covering Eric's side, keeping his sweated skin from cooling in the aftermath.

"Eric?"

"I had to leave, you know," Eric said, his voice muffled by his arms. "I had to leave. I would have fallen in love with one of you—Adrian, Bracken, you—it was coming, like a glacier, or an earthquake or a tidal wave, and I had to leave because I knew... somehow, I knew that the person one of you chose to love would be the focus, the lens through which all of your loves would pass, and that she'd have the strength to take that love and reshape the world. And I knew it wasn't going to be me."

Green knew, without a doubt, that there would be tears stinging the skin of Eric's arms. He answered the revelation, which was not the surprise he might have once thought it to be, in the only way he knew how.

He kissed the sweat from a tanned shoulder, from his spine, down toward a pale buttock, which he bit just hard enough to gain a startled, surprised yelp. Then back down to a thigh—humanly furred—then to the back of a knee, a tender Achilles tendon, and back up, making tender, needy love to his old protégé, to his friend.

When the time at last came to thrust his own body into Eric's, his lover was sobbing for him, pleading and begging for possession, and Green was aching, bursting with the need to possess, with the need to come.

And with the first shock and slide of one flesh into another, from nearly two thousand miles away, he felt Cory awaken.

And with her awakening, he was plunged into a sexual kaleidoscope, down his connection through his binding to Nicky—who was penetrating, being penetrated, tasting, being tasted, all at a moment in a tangle of limbs and nerve endings and orifices that even Green would have had trouble sorting out. Then he was inside Nicky, feeling all that Nicky felt, giving Nicky his own experiences, and in a frantic burst to be himself, he instead followed Nicky's connection to Cory.

Cory had been shouting in her sleep, and her throat was raw, the demands now issuing from it surprising Green because she so rarely demanded anything in bed, content to match with passion and be led in experience. But now she was shouting, and a puzzled, frantic Bracken was pounding into her, suckling on her (no mean feat for a body so much larger than Cory's), and his clever hands were exploring, invading along the sweat-slickened, come-wetted cleft of her bottom. Then, even as her shouting stopped, he was inside her and she was exploding, hurtling through space with the force of a supernova, her power unleashed, out of control, following Green back through Nicky, who shouted and spilled Avian-filtered power and seed onto all those with him, and then back to Green, who spent himself in release and then held his breath, feeling her titanic surge of power fill him, push at his skin, and threaten to explode out his eyeballs and through his very pores.

He exhaled, seeing wisps of light escape his lips to tangle through the darkened room, settling on the bed—which to his surprise shifted almost immediately to a solid, darkened-oak version of the one he had at home—and pulled away almost frantically from Eric, who had climaxed so hard in the blaze of magic that he had collapsed on the bed and was now barely inching his way toward consciousness.

As Green sat back on his heels, there was a timid knock on the door. Then it opened, and Funky Man was in the doorway, sounding lost and frightened in the complete dark.

"Green Man, all the lights went out.... Is it all good, Green Man?"

And still the power buzzed along his skin like electric millipedes, walking, scurrying, crawling, and raising gooseflesh at every step.

"Come here, brother," he said hoarsely, and Funky moved obediently forward. His eyes in the dark were limpid dark-purple pools of heartbreaking trust.

Green fumbled for Funky Man's hands in the dark and felt Eric shift and moan in repletion beside him, and all of this, even the touch of the dry, shriveled skin with his own, was secondary to the power spilling through his veins, along his capillaries, thundering in his chest. *Goddess, he groaned inside his head, how does she stand it all?*

"You're glowing like the moon, Green Man," Funky whispered, and Green summoned a light-lit smile.

"And you'll glow too, brother," he replied and covered Funky Man's mouth in a gentle, sexless kiss.

Magic made a tremendous booming whoosh in his ears as it flooded out of his body and into his brother's, churning like a waterfall, spinning like light in a dark-matter blender. Furiously the magic poured from Green to Funky Man, filling his lungs with clean, disease-free air, cleansing his skin of pain, of scars, of the memory of scars, filling his muscles with blood and fat and tissue, shoring up his bones to the sturdiness of trees. His hair, which had been a gentle violet stubble, sprouted, grew, cascaded to his shoulders, to his waist, past his hips, spangled with gold and silver and gleaming like the night. Funky Man made a groan, a scream of surprise and ecstasy and the pain of healing, the sound itself swallowed by Green's mouth as he continued to spill healing born of the thunder of sex and the tenderness of love and friendship and of all the things that bound Cory to Green through the grace of their other lovers.

Finally the flood diminished to a river, and the river to a stream, and the stream to a trickle of power that drifted from Green's mouth into the room in general, circling the lights and giving a soft ambient glow to the three surprised men sitting, kneeling, lying stunned about the bed.

"Funky Man?" Green asked hesitantly, looking at his brother's profoundly beautiful healed body in the soft light. "Are you all right?"

"Green?" The voice was no longer quavering, or wandering, or lost. "Your name is Green." Wonder. Stark wonder. "And my name…," he said, and he looked up at Green with a beautiful, whole, healthy face lit with pleasure and amazement. "My name is Twilight."

"Goddess," breathed Eric from his side. "Goddess.... Green, what did you do?"

"Not me—it was my beloved. Look at you, Twilight," he whispered as Eric fell back asleep, depleted from his share in the power exchange. "You're whole."

They sat, frozen in aftermath, so fixed on the loveliness of a once-ruined brother that when the phone by the newly made bed rang shrilly, they both jumped.

"That," said Green practically, "would be Bracken. And his first words are going to be 'What in the fuck was that?'" He stretched over the bed to pick up the phone.

"What in the blue fuck was that?" Bracken snapped at the other end of the line.

"I was close," Green muttered to himself. Then, "How is she?"

Bracken grunted. "Asleep. She was asleep for most of it—even when she was... well, screaming for me to...." Green could actually hear Bracken's blush over the phone. Bracken, who had probably had every gender and humanoid species under the sun, in every position possible and a few that technically weren't, was blushing. "She doesn't usually make demands," he finished uncomfortably. "At least not with me."

"Nor with me either," Green said gently. "They were Nicky's demands...."

"Nicky's?"

"She didn't tell you? Nicky, the rest of the care package in the car, lots of sex? Any of that ring a bell?"

"It's been a bitch of a day," Bracken snapped shortly. "We didn't get to her conversation with Nicky."

"Unfortunate."

Bracken snorted. "So, we're fast asleep, suddenly she starts making these really...." Again, that audible blush.

"Erotic?"

"Pornographic. Pornographic demands—and she's making them at the top of her lungs, and, well, I'm doing my best, but I'm only one sidhe, and then she's suddenly awake and really surprised, and I smelled you—you were there with us—and then it was a big fucking wash of light and I practically came out my toes and when it was over, she said, 'Well, that was weird.' And then she fell asleep."

"'Well, that was weird?'"

"She was too goddamned tired for poetry. What in the blue fuck happened?"

Green sighed, scrubbed his face with his hand. "Nicky was having a... rather crowded encounter, I was... visiting a friend, and Cory was, apparently, accosted in her sleep through her connection with Nicky. From Nicky to Cory, from me to Nicky—suddenly she wasn't just having sex in her dreams, she was having everybody's sex in her dreams. And because she does what she does during sex...."

"Power...," Bracken breathed. "But Green—where did it go? It was a fucking huge charge. I could feel it. If it was all of us together, where did all that power go?"

"Into me," Green said simply. And then, with a hand stroking Twilight's lovely purple hair, he added, "And from me, into Funky Man—who's been healed. Completely. Even his scars are gone, Bracken. His hair grew back, he put on flesh—it's like his body had never been ravaged by power in the first place."

"Even his scars?" Bracken asked, his voice laced with pain. "Green... Adrian's scars didn't... did they?"

Green breathed deeply. "No. No, brother, they didn't. Because it was just Cory healing him, I think. That's not where her power lies. But this was Cory's power, through me. I'm good at healing—with a few exceptions."

"My heart is not your problem, leader," Bracken said lowly, "and it's not the issue here. This was huge. It was huge, and it was exhausting, and like I said, she had a bitch of a day. Is this going to happen again?"

That was an excellent question. "She learned to control it before, with practice. I think the more experience Nicky gets, the more he'll learn to close off that connection and she'll learn to block it as she feels it coming on. In the meantime...." Nicky would be there the morning after next, the afternoon at the latest. How much sex could he get in, considering that they would be on the road part of the time? "In the meantime, we'll just have to ask our little land yacht of love to keep their activities in check unless you two have some warning...."

"I think it only happens when she's asleep," Bracken interrupted thoughtfully. "If Nicky's new... lifestyle... started this afternoon, then it didn't hit Cory at all until now. I think I can handle it if we're together...."

"Well, given that Hollow Man is still out there, you don't have much choice, do you?"

Another grunt. Bracken could convey more in that one sound than many men could in a college thesis. "Not really."

"Anyway, we'll just make sure they call you before they make any more stops."

"Yeah, that's a phone call I want to get in the middle of class."

Green found himself laughing. Bracken as a student—he wished he could be there, could be home, to see the transition. Abruptly he sobered. "I want to be home," he said softly. "This is the longest I've been away from home since 1912." He had gone to Washington, DC, actually, lost and determined to legitimize his land deed by smooth talking, theft, and glamour, because otherwise the government had claimed that his land was open to public development.

"We want you home," Bracken said softly. "If Funky Man is healed... if he remembers his name, can't you leave without him?"

Green blinked and looked at the newly reborn Twilight, who was holding his hand up to the softly glowing ambience left over from the power surge, flexing his strong fingers and touching where his scars used to be. "By the time I could book the flight, the Cadillac would be here," he sighed. "And after what just happened, I think we need to let Nicky get some more experience in so he can control his part of our little house of power. No—it was a good plan, and we'll stick to it. You won't have to shoulder that alone much longer."

Another grunt, this one with humor. "Good. A couple of nights like this would kill me."

"You'd go out with a smile."

"Amen."

And with that they rang off, leaving Green alone in the room with Twilight's quiet wonder and Eric's sated snoring.

CORY
Around

THE CAMPUS track was starting to feel like an old friend, and Davy's chatty, supportive presence wasn't uncomfortable either.

Renny ran beside me, lost in the pain of her own heart. She'd broken up with Max the same night Green and Nicky had invaded my dreams, and her hard-won humanity, so tenuous after Mitch died, was gradually leaching away again. I made her come to school by telling her that she needed to keep Nicky up-to-date, but this week she'd started wearing those loose-fitting wool-sack dresses again, which was a bad sign. She had a high metabolism, but it was still colder here than in San Francisco, and she was just setting herself up to shed her humanity and start running wild as a giant hundred-pound tabby cat again. I'd forced her to wear sweats today, ostensibly to keep me company on the track, and since she'd developed a quiet, almost pathological jealousy of Davy, it had worked.

Davy was oblivious to all of this. She seemed to find me almost irresistible as a friend, and Renny was simply a part of the whole package. I didn't understand the attraction—hell, considering my problems relating to my native species, it baffled me completely—but I did appreciate the company. Today, like most days, she was talking about her boyfriend, Kyle, her glossy ponytail bobbing jauntily behind her and the fierce, bright wind whipping her purple scarf. She had a number of these scarves—I'd asked her about them, and she said her mother crocheted them by the dozens. When I asked her why she always wore them, she'd blushed charmingly and said, with a happy, brazen edge, "Hickeys. Kyle loves to chew on my neck, and they hide the hickeys." I'd found myself blushing too, which, considering my own love life, was pretty silly, but true nonetheless, and we'd giggled and jogged in silence for a while.

Today I got to hear more about Kyle's job woes. Kyle had been out of work since June, but he still slept days because he liked night work. I'd never gotten a bead on exactly what it was Kyle did for a living, but that could be because until this week I'd spent most of my time on the track wheezing like a broken accordion. Today I was simply breathing hard, and I looked to the stands to show Bracken that I was getting better. Bracken was so relieved that I'd actually started looking him in the eye after that really embarrassing night of channeling all of Nicky's sex demands into our own bed that he actually waved and smiled. We'd gone to our session with Hallow together today, and it just goes to show you how warped our life was that this was the least uncomfortable subject for us to bring up.

"So...," Hallow said after the whole thing just spilled out of us, "did you enjoy it when you woke up?"

"I didn't mind it the whole time," Bracken had replied grumpily. "She's the one who seems to forget that sensual and consensual is the rule."

They had both turned to me, waiting for my answer. I'd been red from my toenails up. "I came, didn't I?" I asked hostilely. "And if Green hadn't been there in my head, I might have blown off the top of the goddamned hill, so maybe my sexual preferences aren't the problem here."

"And if Nicky hadn't been there in your head, you wouldn't have needed Green," Hallow had said reasonably. "So maybe we need to focus on whether these are your desires or his, so you can figure out a way to block him when he's in your head."

"We've already figured that out. All I need is a little warning," I replied, and even I knew I was being surly.

"But what about you, Cory?" Hallow asked patiently. "There's a difference between doing something in your dreams and being possessed to do something against your will. Bracken needs to know what it is you do and do not want."

I'd scowled into the teeth of his indulgent smile and tried for some dignity. "Bracken has access to many of the most erotic moments of my sexual history in sculpture," I'd said distinctly. "If he needs to know about a particular act, he can always use the garden as a reference."

Bracken blinked, thought for a moment, and a truly lascivious grin split his features. "I'll take that as a yes, then," he'd said brightly. "That's excellent."

I'd scowled at him even more furiously and told him to shut up, but he'd been so happy to realize that what we'd done together hadn't been all Nicky's little orgy that he'd completely ignored me and had spoken openly with Hallow about the night Green, Adrian, and I had created the erotic garden while I slumped in my chair and wished I was a hamster or something.

So now, seeing his smile and his relaxed wave, I thought that maybe my mortification had been worth his happiness. Then Renny spoke up from my side.

"I miss Green," she all but growled, and I knew that it wasn't just Green she missed, it was a person in her bed.

"So do I," I said. "But that's not going to help you, and you know it."

"Who's Green?" Davy asked from my other side, but before I could answer she went on in that careless, prattling way she had that I enjoyed but that drove Renny bonkers. "Because Kyle says his old boss was taken over by a guy named Green, and I could never figure out if Green was his first name or his last name—although, you have to admit, it's a little strange as a first name, but it's common as a last name. I mean, it's your name, isn't it?"

"Kind of," I answered numbly, trying to sort out what she'd just said, because between this, and Kyle's love of hickeys, and the way he only slept during the day, and even Davy's odd attachment to me as a friend, a nasty suspicion was beginning to form in the pit of my stomach. "Who was Kyle's old boss?"

"Some guy named Crispin, but I could never figure out if that was a first name or a last name either.... Are you okay?"

Because Renny and I had actually tripped in tandem and gone down, and I could feel my knee smarting on the all-weather and hoped it wasn't bad enough for Bracken to make it bleed more.

"We're fine," I said quietly, putting my hand out to steady Renny's arm.

Renny looked at me directly for the first time in days and stated the obvious: "She doesn't know, does she?"

I shook my head. All those guileless hints, all those blithe references to Kyle's work habits, to his love for chewing on her neck—all of it— she couldn't have just dropped that information off like clothes at a secondhand store if she'd realized her boyfriend was a vampire.

"I've got to go," Renny said, popping up like her knee didn't hurt. Knowing how fast werecreatures healed, it probably didn't, I thought sourly, but that didn't keep me from making a plea.

"Renny… no, you've got a class…."

"Consider it cut," she growled, and I could hear the change in her voice already, as we both flashed to those horrible, horrible moments in our lives when the world had exploded in crimson.

"Renny, you don't even have your cell phone," I pleaded, because when we'd lived in San Francisco, we'd started looping her cell phone around her neck so when she changed back from werecat I could come bail her out. But she was already loping down the track in a graceful, catlike trot, and Bracken and I looked at each other helplessly across the field.

"Where's she going?" Davy wanted to know. I looked at Davy, not wanting to see if Renny actually waited until she was out of sight to morph into a kitty, and wondered what I was going to do with her now.

"She's going to see a Goddess about a cat," I said obliquely. "Hey—can I see your scarf?" I was acting on a hunch, based on Davy's odd attraction to me as a friend, and since we'd been about to start our cool-down lap anyway, it wasn't as awkward as it would have been if we'd been running.

"That's nice," I said, running the textured fabric through my hands. It really was nice—Davy's mom didn't just go back and forth in rows, she did pretty stitch patterns and shells and post stitches and things, and it was truly an original work. But while my mouth was making the compliment, my mind was kicking itself in the ass. It was worse than I had thought. I looked over to Bracken, who had been watching me carefully since Renny and I had both tripped, and saw his grimace. Yes. This complicated things a bit, because instead of just glamourized vampire bites, which were what I'd expected to see, I also saw an unmistakable glow, this one in sort of a dark fluorescent green. It was bright enough for someone with power to see even from across the track and the football field. It was also the same glow I saw on my own neck every day, except hers was in one layer instead of three.

Davy wasn't just Kyle's lover—he'd marked her.

A vampire mark wasn't something you could take back or rescind or even apologize for. Adrian hadn't truly meant to mark me the three times he'd done so—he had loved me. His soul left his body, and it was drawn to me guilelessly, passionately, and when it blew through mine, his mark had stayed, binding me to him even tighter. If he'd marked me one more time, my mortality would have been tied to his. Bracken, I knew, still harbored a wound, a small hurt, that Adrian had never marked him, even though their relationship had been very different than ours.

We were too far away from Bracken for me to hear him speak, but I had no problem reading his lips. Shitfire indeed.

"You know," I said conversationally after giving Davy back her scarf, "Green runs all sorts of businesses. I bet he could give Kyle a job if he needs it."

"Now, who is he, exactly?" Davy asked.

"He's my boss," I said truthfully. "Other than that, it gets complicated. I'll give you a card for the store where we work. If your boyfriend wants, he can come over and see Grace—she runs the shop. Even if Brack and I aren't there, she can give him an, uhm, interview, and a place if he wants one."

"I don't see why he wouldn't want a job!" Davy said, so innocent she made my stomach ache. "I mean, I think his finances are getting pretty desperate."

We were rounding the track to the bleachers now, and I moved up the steps to where Bracken sat. We sent speaking looks to each other as I rifled my backpack for my wallet. I pulled out the little card, bloodred with silver writing—Grace's little joke—and rolled down the terry cloth band that hid the puncture marks on my wrist, then casually brushed Bracken's hand. He called, just a little, and a single drop of blood welled up. I brushed the edge of the card on the blood, humming "Somebody Told Me" by The Killers as I did so, and nonchalantly handed the card to Davy, making sure the sweat from my fingers left a print.

"Give this to Kyle," I said, willing with my power that she not lose the card or forget it. "We're working tonight and Thursday, and probably Saturday too, if he wants to talk to me directly."

"Awesome!" Davy tucked the card in the pocket of her sweatshirt, then beamed up at me with such sweetness that I wanted to weep. "Kyle will be thrilled!" With that and a little wave, she disappeared down the bleachers to finish her run (she did three miles to my one), and I plopped next to Bracken and leaned my head wearily on his shoulder.

"She doesn't know, does she?" he asked, knowing the answer.

"Not a clue," I told him sadly. "But at least it explains why she wanted to be my friend."

Bracken looked at me, puzzled. "The mark wouldn't do that. I think she just likes you."

A secret ache in my heart went away. "That's nice to know."

"Where's Renny?" Another question he knew the answer to.

"By now? On the bike trail, killing birds."

"Shit and damn," he swore. "I wish she'd give Max a little more time."

I thought for a moment. "They will find a way," I said with surety. "Max has changed too much... hell, *Renny* has changed too much for them to give up on each other without more of a fight."

"You haven't changed at all," he said, looking at me thoughtfully.

"I don't wear black lipstick anymore."

A smile ghosted across his grim mouth. "But you still fight... well, everything." He moved his hand to the back of my neck. Almost absentmindedly he started pulling strands from my ponytail, fingering them smooth.

I scowled up at him. "What do you mean?"

"Hallow," he said softly. "You refuse to talk to him—which is too bad, because you've got some weight pressing you down. It would make your chest lighter if you just talked."

I felt my scowl deepen just so my face wouldn't crumple. "I do okay." I resisted the urge to pull away from that comforting hand.

"'Doing okay' is what was killing you before Christmas. You know that, don't you?"

I cringed. I'd refused to let Green heal me—I had been afraid I would suck him dry, and the pain of denying him was so great it had hurt us both. "I don't want to hurt people with my own crap, okay?" Goddess, I was dumb, I thought belatedly. You didn't tell the elf, the multipowerful sidhe who'd just given up an eternity of sensual pleasures with, well, whomever he cared to be with in order to live a scant lifetime with you, that you'd rather hurt yourself than hurt him. It was a grave freaking insult, that's what it was, but Bracken took it better than I expected.

"You hurt me by withholding it," he said softly. "I hurt when you hurt. We haven't made love, not really, since the night Green got in your head, and now Davy's a vampire's lover and Renny's falling apart and you're pulling further away from me. We need each other, Cory. Not even in the romantic way—in the physical way of needing to feed emotionally from our own bodies. You pull away from me to help me, you kill me with kindness."

Fucking swell. One more thing to press against my lungs. Fine. "You want me to talk? Fucking groovy. I'll talk. You want to know what I'm feeling right now? What the weight is on my chest?" I pulled away from him abruptly, leaning on my elbows and glowering at the track where the world's most innocent dinner trotted blithely around, unaware of the heartache she'd inflicted. He waited expectantly, but I couldn't speak right away. Instead I sat and watched her, hurting for her and for the naivety that was so charming and would be gone so soon. The silence stretched until I could feel the cold from the metal bench seep through my sweats, and finally I could no longer hold on to the pressure on my chest, the one that had started small when Green had left but had grown progressively harder to bear.

"I'm feeling overwhelmed," I said after a moment, the words hurting even as they passed through my throat. "I was supposed to hold the goddamned fort, not rally the fucking troops to fight the bad guys. Green left, and it sucked, but I thought I could hold it all together. And then Hollow Man attacked, and Grace's past burst in on us, and we had exploding people in the basement, and Renny broke up with Max, and Nicky decided to go all free love on me, and Green got delayed with maybe the saddest freaking sidhe of all freaking time, and I'm failing my stupid physics class, and now after all my resolve to try to relate to my own goddamned native species, it turns out that the one friend I've made is in mortal danger because she's not quite mortal after all. The only thing I've managed in the last two and a half weeks is my fucking yarn."

I wasn't crying, I thought proudly. I was whining like a baby girl, but I wasn't crying. I used to be so tough, until this winter when I'd cried more than in my entire life previously—but not today. Today I wasn't crying.

Then Bracken leaned over my back, put his chin on my shoulder, and wrapped his arm around my waist. "Now was that so hard?" he asked, doing a fair imitation of Hallow.

"Yes," I growled, and he breathed a little laugh into my ear. It made my stomach clench and my nipples tingle, just that little breath next to my ear.

"Was it worth it? Do you feel better?" His large warm hand came up to the small of my back, and I suddenly doubted my ability to stand.

"It was worth it," I said carefully, truthfully. I suddenly felt stronger, more able than I had since I'd watched Green's yellow hair disappear into the drab airport. "Are you sure I haven't changed?"

"Since I had to force you to say it, I'd say only a little." He laughed again and moved his other hand to my thigh, making me shudder.

"Enough to love?" I asked plaintively, another weight pressing down where the first one had left off.

"I'd love you if you didn't change," he whispered. "I love you now that you have changed. Any way, I'd love you, *due'ane*," he finished, and that did nothing to stop the sudden wanting. We'd had no heart for more than perfunctory lovemaking since the night my brain had exploded with other people's sex, and now I was aching fiercely to have him inside of me.

"I love you too, *due'alle*," I choked. And then, unnecessarily, because the must flooding my panties would be as clear to him as baking cookies to a human, I said through a mouth dry as crumbs, "I want you."

"If you don't shower, we've got forty-five minutes before physics," he whispered against my ear, and I actually gasped with desire.

"Where...."

"That little room... where we changed...," he muttered brokenly, and then I was up, trotting down the bleachers, knowing he'd be right behind me with our packs.

The room was thankfully empty, and Bracken froze the knob with power even as he closed the door behind us. I went to strip off my sweatshirt, but Bracken came behind me and seized the hem, pulling it over my head before I could even gasp. His hands came to the band of my sweatpants, and all of a sudden I was naked, without even time to be cold in the chill little room because his mouth was devouring mine, his massy body covering my small one, his hands everywhere, burning and kneading and touching. Before I even knew that he was naked too, he'd whirled us both around so I was pressed up against the wall and literally sat me upon his body, sliding, stretching, pushing into me where I was swollen and bursting with the need to have him.

With his hands on my hips, he moved me up and down over his shaft, dragging, stretching, pounding inside of me, and I pressed my hands against the painted cinderblock and made broken sounds of pleasure into my arm, his body essential to mine. I shivered from my toes up, my eyes exploding in stars, my orgasm ripping a groan from me that I could feel down to my womb. Then he was there, coming, coming, flooding my body with his seed, clutching my breasts from behind me and groaning into my ear while I shuddered again, and one more time, in aftershocks and pleasure and love.

When it was over, we stood embracing, panting in the chill barren room. The smell of sex filled it, heating it with the fury and the power that was us.

Our shaking hands eventually stilled, and he helped me back into my clothes, using my panties to clean me off before throwing them in the little trash can in the corner. I flashed to the last time we'd used this room, and a smile quirked my lips even as I collapsed on the Naugahyde couch.

"I think we just justified the existence of panties, Bracken."

He laughed a little too, and came to hold me in his lap. "I think we also proved someone's theory of spontaneous combustion," he laughed and I chuckled a little more. There was quiet as we took advantage of the last ten minutes before we had to get moving, but Bracken, being Bracken, was not content to let the silence stay.

"Don't ever be embarrassed in front of me," he said seriously, and instead of cringing, or even replying, I leaned against him and closed my eyes. Maybe I needed to hear this. "Don't ever be mortified because of sex. Don't be embarrassed because you're uncertain, or afraid, or overwhelmed. You work very hard to be a leader, but you get upset if your *due 'alle* is forced to kneel to you. You refuse to show me weakness, or lean on me for support, but you get angry if I go to Hallow or Green to see what's going on inside your head. Don't you see, Cory? I'm your release valve. I'm the lover who can be your equal, who can be…. I'm the most human lover you will have."

I looked at him, his alien beauty, his ferocious size, his overlarge eyes, and the irony was almost funny. Except he was right. My relationship with Bracken was the closest thing I would ever know to a human mating—hadn't the other night proved exactly that?

"Give me time, Bracken Brine," I said softly. "I'm the most human Goddess's child you will ever know. I'm bound to three different men, and it's all about finding a balance with the three of you, okay?"

"Okay," he said, stroking my hair back from my face. "Okay. Just remember I'm on your side of the teeter-totter, yes?"

I smiled, suddenly a little misty when dumping my crap all over his lawn hadn't done it. "Hey, that's almost poetry. That's awesome."

"I learn from the best," he said, kissing my forehead and then shouldering our packs to lead the way to class.

"You're the second person to say that to me…," I murmured. "What the hell does it mean?"

But he only laughed and took my hand as we walked through the blue and brown shadows of the campus.

When we sat down in physics class, I was surprised that Bracken handed me my knitting instead of my physics folder. This was, unequivocally, the one class I didn't knit in. I made a sound of protest in my throat, but he just looked at me levelly from those brackish eyes and said, "You knit and think. I'll take notes." I opened my mouth a few times and blinked, but he closed my backpack calmly and sat with my notebook on his lap.

"I mean it, Cory," he said, and the tone of his voice was the kind I only argued with during a knock-down, drag-out, which I was so not prepared to have right now.

"The professor will have kittens," I said, stunned, even as my fingers found their way across the knitting and my heartbeat slowed down as the wool/silk blend absorbed all my stress.

"Good," my beloved replied serenely. "We can take one home. You need a pet, and the sprites need something to do." And that was that. When Mario and LaMark sat down near us, they raised their eyebrows, then took in Bracken's bland expression and shrugged. The professor's eyes bulged out, but Bracken just smacked him with that level gaze, and the man paled a little and went back to his lecture. More vectors, I thought miserably—but the yarn beckoned, Bracken would explain it to me much more clearly than this banana would, and I had other things on my mind.

That night he wore my sweater to work.

I glowed for the first two hours as we waited on customers and stocked shelves, and then Davy walked in with a medium-sized, thick-chested vampire who looked extraordinarily pissed off. My glow sort of faded after that.

"Davy—nice to see you," I said sincerely. Part of my motivation behind issuing the invitation for Kyle to become part of our kiss was to keep Davy safe.

"I'm glad you're here," she said, and although her smile was genuine, her eyes flashed unhappily to the man beside her. "I've been trying to tell Kyle that you're for real, but he seems to think you wouldn't give him a job if he was the last guy on earth."

I pulled a reassuring smile from somewhere around my toes. "Don't worry. Here—you look around, and Kyle and I will go in back and interview, okay?"

I looked up casually at Kyle and tried to order him with my eyes to comply. He gave a hard nod, his chiseled chin looking like it might shatter with tension, and I turned back to Davy, who was glancing around the store curiously. "Hey—you've got a pretty big yarn section. Do you think I could look at that? My mom wants to make me another scarf."

"No problem." I turned around to call for Bracken and found that he was right behind me and in the process of raising his hands to my shoulders so he didn't startle me silly, which he did anyway. I muffled a shriek, and our eyes met—and there wasn't any amusement at all in either of us, but I kept my voice light anyway. "Beloved, how about you show Davy the new shipment we got in today, and I'll go talk to Kyle. Okay?"

"Are you sure?" he growled, and his eyes flickered to Kyle, who was now looking both awed and uneasy. He obviously saw through Brack's glamour and was wondering if it was a trap.

"Grace is back there," I said easily. "She can help with the interview."

Bracken nodded and exchanged a long hard look with the vampire behind me, then moved off with Davy so smoothly that she didn't even cast any anxious looks over her shoulder.

"C'mon in back," I said tersely, moving from behind the register and gesturing for Renny to take over. Renny had been waiting by the car in cat form after class, and she'd been so contrite about running off that I'd told her she could make it up to me by helping at the store. There was a delivery truck and inventory to count, and the whole little mall itself was having a big post-Christmas promotion, so it was busy enough to justify her help.

Kyle followed me through the store and we both crowded into the miniscule office, where Grace was already doing paperwork.

"Cory, couldn't it wai—Good grief. Who the fuck are you?"

Kyle actually looked relieved at the rudeness of the greeting, as though making nice to keep Davy happy had put him under a great deal of strain.

"I'm a guy hoping this isn't a fucking ambush, is who I am," he growled back, then turned to glare at me. "What in the hell is this about, anyway?" And he pulled out my card, which, to the three of us, was glowing with power, practically singing with the compulsion for Kyle to come and speak to me.

I swallowed. "You're in danger," I said baldly. "You're in danger. There is a big bad motherfucker out there, and he's leveling vampires, and you're all alone. Davy said you're 'looking for a place'—is that true?"

"Well, yeah—but not with you!" He looked incredulous and baffled, as though he couldn't believe we were actually having this conversation. Maybe the compulsion I'd put on that card was stronger than I'd planned.

"Why the hell not?" Grace asked, clearly affronted on my behalf.

"He's one of Crispin's," I said gruffly.

"Oh." Abruptly, Grace sat down on a counter still littered with paperwork. "I didn't know any of them survived."

"Only those of us who didn't go to fight that night," Kyle replied, looking embarrassed.

"Why not?" I asked, studying him. His eyes were brown—deep, plain brown—and he tried to bespell me for a minute, I think just to see if he could. He quit trying, then looked away. "So why didn't you go?" I asked again, and he shrugged.

"Sezan... he was crazy. A certifiable lunatic. And... he did something to Crispin. I mean, Crispin wasn't the most compassionate guy in the first place, but... but by the end there, his brain was mush and crap and not much else. I...." And now he looked me in the eye, and his own expression was filled with a deep shame. "I was there when they brought your friend to Crispin." He jerked his chin in the direction of the front, and I realized he was talking about Renny. Renny had been kidnapped the morning before Adrian had been killed, as an incentive to make us all go confront Sezan, Crispin, and the other vampires. "She was... she could hardly speak to human beings, she was so damaged inside. We'd killed her beloved as nothing more than an experiment, to see if it would work, and now we were using her as bait, and... and it wasn't fair. I looked at her and thought, if we had to destroy someone that fragile to get what we wanted... maybe we were on the wrong side. The sun set that night, Crispin gave the call from Sezan's van, and everybody flew out. Except I veered off at the last minute and went back and got my stuff, and... and I've been on my own ever since."

He swallowed, a reflexive action, and for all his burly toughness, I saw what this admission had cost him.

"Join us," I said bluntly.

"No." And still, that vulnerability. "I'm a deserter and a traitor, but your people.... I kept wondering when Crispin's people were going to come after me... and then, a month later, I met a werecoyote who told me you killed them. I don't know how you did it, but your people...." He looked at me directly now. "What kinds of monsters can completely eradicate an entire kiss?"

I felt myself pale and wondered if my knees would buckle, and I knew Grace had put out a hand to catch me if I fell. I waved her away, but when I spoke, it was from a raw throat.

"You love Davy, don't you?" I asked, holding on to my thready voice. "You marked her—that takes a commitment that humans can't even dream of."

He met my gaze, and I could tell he was wondering if I was threatening him, and I thought wretchedly that I was doing this all wrong.

"Yeah, I love her."

"And if something happened to her... if she came riding to your rescue and trying to help you and she disappeared into a rain of blood before your eyes—what would you do?"

And his expression became fierce, his jaw started to extend, and his eyes started to whirl redly in a true hunting face. "I'd murder the world," he growled.

I nodded and felt my own face and throat tense so badly I hoped I could still speak. "Of course you would. You say that and you believe you'd really murder the world, but you know what, tough guy? That's only because you're pretty sure you can't really do it." I was wearing a hooded sweatshirt, and I reached up and pulled the front of it down on the left, and I could tell by the way he stepped back that the full depth of the three marks glowing from my neck had hit him. "I got this third one when your boss blew up my beloved and he blew through me. And then my other beloved held me while I tried to murder the world. And let me tell you, it was a lot easier to do than it has been to live with, so you think long and hard about what you want for yourself and what you want for Davy before you think that's the solution to protecting your lover, okay?"

"You… all by yourself… you did that?" He hadn't heard a word I said, I thought miserably. He was still back at the part where I had killed his entire kiss.

"There wasn't a force on earth that could have stopped me," I told him evenly.

"Is there now?" he asked, backing up a step.

"Absolutely." I nodded. The first tear rolled down my nose, and I ignored it. "It's called regret."

Kyle nodded helplessly. "And you want me to join you?" I winced at the horror in his voice.

"It doesn't have to be me," I conceded and wiped futilely at the tears falling freely now. "Andres—he's in San Francisco—he could keep you safe. You could live here and blood with Andres—that's not a problem.…"

"Crispin would have killed me before he let me sit on someone else's territory," Kyle snapped.

"Well, Crispin's dead and I've already told you I don't take lives lightly," I snapped back. "Don't you get it, asshole? This isn't about what I did last summer, and it's not about your friends. It's about you, and it's about Davy. You are naked, and alone, and…. Kyle, this thing out there, it did a flyby—just a flyby, mind you, no actual contact—and every vampire for a five-mile radius who hadn't blooded with me keeled over for a good half hour."

"You blood them?" he asked, and it was like everything I said, he was back three steps trying to catch up.

"Yes, I blood them. Adrian gave them to me—how can I run his kiss without blooding them?"

Kyle looked blindly to Grace, such utter incomprehension written over his broad features that I couldn't even fathom what he didn't understand. "Did Adrian blood you all?"

Grace nodded. "Of course he did. How else could he run his kiss?"

Kyle shivered. "You people—that's… it's…. Crispin told us it was… sacred. Holy. Like marriage. He only blooded us if we'd done something to really please him."

I blinked. "It is," I said honestly. "It is sacred, and it is holy, and... and like any good marriage, it's protection. Kyle—the vampires I blooded got queasy, but they didn't collapse. Being tied to me, or even being tied to a leader, it keeps you safe. The Hollow Man—he sucked the power out of a full-blooded sidhe, you understand that?"

"How is that possible?" he asked, and he apparently tabled the other part for later so he could deal with it on his own terms.

"I don't know, but Green found him. He was so ravaged, he couldn't even remember his name. He had scars, Kyle... scars and lice from living on the street. Do you know how hard it is for the Goddess's shining ones to become so stripped...."

"Goddess...." He blinked, and then his eyes sharpened. *"Had* scars? Did you kill him?"

And now I blinked. "No, we healed him," I said, feeling lost and muddled and like I couldn't in a million years make contact.

Kyle sat down on the office chair Grace had left vacant. He sat so abruptly, the wheels skidded backward until the back hit the counter, but he didn't even notice. "You healed him? How is that possible?"

I blew out a breath and mopped up the last of my tears. "I wield a great deal of power under... certain circumstances," I told him. "I've only committed mass murder once. The rest of the time, we try to do something constructive with it. Okay?"

"You healed him?"

"Green healed him. I was the battery."

Kyle nodded, then shook his head. "You people are a real mindfuck, do you know that? I'm so lost. You killed my entire kiss, and now you want to take me under your wing like a giant mama bird?"

"I killed the people who murdered my beloved," I told him in a stony little voice. "Don't forget that, Sir Vampire. Don't forget what you'd do yourself to protect your loved one. The Hollow Man has seen us together, Kyle. He knocked Renny and me down when we were on the track with Davy. I don't know how clearly he sees mortals—all he saw was three girls with brown ponytails, running. When I saw she had a vampire mark, I almost hyperventilated—if he can't really see who we are, what's going to keep him from attacking her instead of me? She's defenseless, Kyle! Like a kitten. Whatever you decide, you need to remember that you can't watch her all the time, and I can. That you're limited by the night, and I'm not. And that I love Davy too."

Kyle scrubbed his face with his hands, then ran a hand through his sandy brown hair while he was shaking his head.

"I don't even know your goddamned name," he said after a moment.

"Cory," I said, surprised.

"That's not all your name," he muttered, then held up a hand when I opened my mouth to reply. "No. Don't tell me. Or don't tell me why you can't tell me. I just need to know what to call you in my head, when I think about your offer."

I grimaced at Grace, and she raised amused eyebrows at me. I wasn't going to say it, so she did. "Lady Cory," she said softly. "She's our lady, our queen, *ou'e'eir* to our Lord Green, *due'ane* to Bracken, *ou'e'ane* to Nicky."

My face flushed, harshly and deeply, and I looked away. "Lady Cory will do fine," I said through a gravelly throat, shaking my head and resisting the unqueenly urge to hiss "Jeez, Grace..." under my breath.

Kyle nodded. "Lady Cory, Vampire Queen, and Elf Lover— gotcha." And then he sighed. "I'll think about it, my lady. It's a good offer—I know I'm stupid, and about three steps behind what's going on in the world, but even I can recognize you're making this offer from a good heart. I just don't know if it's enough."

I nodded and looked away. Then I was struck by a sudden thought. "Look, Kyle—don't just talk to me, okay?" I started searching the counter for a stack of business cards that Grace and I kept handy, and I found the two I wanted and handed them to the handsome, beleaguered vampire in front of me. "Here—this one is Andres's card. He'll be waiting for your call. This one's for a hotel reservation in San Francisco—there are darkling rooms and everything." I swallowed and felt embarrassment flood me. "Take Davy. It's a real ritzy place—she'll like it. You can talk to Andres while you're there."

Kyle looked at the two cards, surprised. "Thank you, I guess," he said with half a smile.

"Just...," I sighed. "Just consider us, please? If not me, Andres." I ran my own hand through my hair, forgetting that it was longer now and in a ponytail. The elastic band sproinged off and hit the back wall, but none of us noticed. "It's a big scary world out there when you're alone in it. Believe me, it was bad enough when I was just a gas station clerk—I can't imagine what it's like to be alone when you know the monsters are real."

Kyle nodded and turned around, shouldering his way through the small doorway and leaving Grace and me alone in the little room. Grace slipped a cool arm around my shoulders, and I leaned into her gratefully.

"Does Green know?" she asked softly.

"Know what?"

"That you're still carrying that weight from the night Adrian died."

I looked away and shrugged, hearing his voice in my head even as I thought about it. "*Of course I know, beloved.*" His voice in my mind was stronger, *closer,* than it had been since he left. Green was coming home to me. The knowledge filled me, gave me back the strength and heart that had been sucked right out of me when Kyle had walked away, and when I answered Grace, his presence was shining out of my smile.

"Of course he knows," I replied happily. "Green knows everything."

Grace leaned in for a hug, and I leaned back into her cool, rigidly vampiric body, which somehow felt warm and maternal to me because she was Grace. "He's on his way home, isn't he?"

I nodded. "I need to go tell Bracken. He'll be thrilled to get rid of me for a day or two."

"Doubt it" was the prompt reply. Then, "What can we do about Kyle?"

I shivered. "Not a blessed thing. It really is his decision. Maybe we can ask some of the sprites to babysit Davy, though." I bit my lip, thinking. "I'm really worried about her, Grace. Me, Renny, Davy... he could be after me or Renny and get her by mistake...." I shuddered. All that innocence... it was too awful for words.

Grace nodded. "I hear you—but you're going to have to get Green or Bracken to talk to the sprites."

"They like me," I said hopefully and then ventured up front to see Davy off.

BRACKEN
And Around

SHE WOULD have been okay then, but only a few minutes after the job interview with the glowering vampire, her worst nonsupernatural nightmare walked through the door.

First the vampire came out and ignored me, searching for his perky human. The girl—as charming as the children Cory and I had entertained—started chattering excitedly about yarn, and her lover was trapped there in the craft store when Cory came out of the back room glowing brightly.

"How'd it go?" I asked, curious. It was vampire business—even Adrian hadn't let me in on vampire business.

Suddenly her glow dimmed, and she flutter-touched my back to comfort herself. "It really sucked," she said softly. "But I gave him Andres's card, and maybe he'll turn to Andres. I'd like to find some way to protect Davy, but it will have to be subtle—he won't like it if he thinks he can't do it himself." Then she smiled again shyly, brightly. "But Green is coming home. He's getting close—probably tomorrow morning, I think."

That brightened me up too. The perky human came up and smiled at us so guilelessly I was sure her vampire had convinced her that all was well.

"Thanks, Cory." She was gushing. "Kyle's more optimistic than he's been in weeks—and I'm sure my mom will like the yarn...." She held up her purchase bag, emblazoned with the same wreath Cory had tattooed on her back and that I had around my wrist and up my arm. "This was really awesome of you."

Cory gave a passable imitation of a real smile. "Any time," she responded automatically.

"I'll see you on the track tomorrow, right?"

Cory hesitated. "Maybe not, actually. We've got... family... coming home from a trip tomorrow. We may need to be here."

Davy looked disappointed. "Oh… well, I'll run without you, then…."

Cory and Kyle exchanged looks cautiously, and he nodded and touched Davy's shoulder with reverent fingers. "Actually, babe, how about you wait until Cory's there to go with you, okay?"

Davy looked fondly at her lover, and his eyes glowed, but only faintly because she loved him and he knew it and didn't want to hurt her fragile mortal mind. "Okay," she murmured happily. Then she gave Cory a quick hug, which surprised us both, and took his hand and led him out of the store with hardly another word.

Cory sighed. "I hate this," she said softly.

"He loves her," I said, because it was true and I didn't want her to worry about this thing with everything else she had on her mind.

"You and I both know that's not always enough, beloved," she said, taking my hand in hers and kissing it. Then she moved to take the register from Renny, who was looking peaked and trapped and who probably needed to change into a kitty cat and curl up in the stockroom for a nap.

I went back to stocking shelves around the unexpected crowds of humans, but then I felt, rather than saw, her flare of panic. It seemed to zing the whole store, filling it with tension, and when I looked toward the door I could see why.

I had met Cory's mother twice before. Both times she had struck me as having both the best and worst of what humanity has to offer. In appearance she was smallish, although taller than her daughter, and slightly built. One of those vital, stringy, active women who seem to grow tougher as they age. She wore her hair in two graying braids wrapped around her head, probably for much the same reason Cory had worn hers short for so long—it was convenient and easy—and she dressed in jeans and T-shirts or sweatshirts. Again, much like Cory. She loved her daughter—a thing Cory did not (in typical human fashion) seem to be sure of—but it was a tense, uneasy kind of love, like the love of your own image in a warped mirror. That odd human thing of not liking everything your child showed you about yourself seemed to slip between her love for her child and her good intentions more often than was comfortable for any of us. If she warned Cory against getting fat one more time, I was truly going to lose my temper with the woman.

But what came out of her mouth as she rushed toward her daughter was more alarming and potentially more hurtful than that.

"You're married?" she practically screeched across the store, and the shining flush that Cory had worn since she'd told me Green was on his way disappeared, leaving her cheeks the color of old linen.

"Oh, shit," she replied, her eyes big in panic.

"Well, are you?" And Mrs. Kirkpatrick was upon her, face-to-face across the register, and I didn't even have time to put my box down and come to Cory's rescue before the scrap was on.

"Who told you that?" Cory asked, although we both knew it could only be that dickhead's mother, because he had threatened, and this was the only weapon he'd had.

"Justine Granger." Cory didn't look surprised. "She said her son saw you selling drugs with some guy on campus you claimed to be your husband."

Now Cory was infuriated. "She said *what?* Her fuckheaded son almost ripped my arm off trying to score, and he told her *I* was selling? And you believed them—without even asking me?"

Her anger must have pushed past her mother's fury, because now it was Mrs. Kirkpatrick stepping back in surprise. "Well, Cory... I mean... we know you did in high school...."

"The *fuck* I did," Cory shot back, totally oblivious to the stares she was attracting. Her cheeks went an uneven crimson. In this moment she was the angry, hostile child that Adrian had been courting, and I was shamed by my words earlier in the day. She had changed—she had become a better person than this, and I had not seen it. "I wasn't stoned, mother, I was pissed off, and I'm getting there again now, so you had better just back the truck off of this topic because I'm at work and you're in the wrong, okay?"

I was standing helplessly, again, at Cory's side by now, and Renny, who had heard the beginnings of the argument, came up to take Cory's place at the register. Cory looked at Renny's drawn, anxious face, and an extraordinary thing happened. She took a deep breath, and right there in her mother's presence, she became Lady Cory, Corinne Carol-Anne Kirkpatrick op Crocken Green, the woman I'd become accustomed to having at my side.

"I'm sorry, Renny," she said, and her face paled from its first blotchy flush of anger, leaving two spots of color on her cheekbones. "You go back and take your break, sweetie. I'll be fine."

"Are you sure?" But Renny looked tired and sad, and even I wished her a nice nap in a knot of tawny fur.

"Yeah. I'm sure. I'm all done shouting—you go sleep." Renny turned and, with a few anxious backward glances, retreated to the stockroom, shedding her sweatshirt even as she left. "So, Mom," Cory said on an even, controlled breath, "why did you come by?"

Mrs. Kirkpatrick flushed. "Are you married?"

Cory nodded. "Yes. Yes, I got married before Christmas."

And then came the hurt that was the root of all the anger. "Why didn't you tell us? You didn't invite anybody...."

"It was a... uhm... a very private ceremony," Cory said, blushing, and I put my hand on her shoulder in support. Private indeed, I thought unhappily. Humans did big ceremonies—pretty dresses, flowers, sunshine, and poetry. For that matter, elves usually did too. Cory had been married against her will and without her knowledge—not just once, but twice, and both times in my bed—when, as much as I knew she loved me, I had not been her first choice. Of course, by the time Christmas had rolled around, I had become a necessity to her by both heart and will, and so I could live with everything that came before. But still....

"Private!" her mother was saying. "It was so private I don't even know who you're married to!"

A totally adult expression crossed Cory's face—so adult, so ageless, that if I didn't know any better, I'd say it was elvish. "Well, Mom," she said with a cunning smile, "who do you think I'm married to?"

Mrs. Kirkpatrick's gaze flickered from my possessive hand on Cory's shoulder to her guarded adult face, but Cory wasn't stupid, and her mother wasn't either. "I saw you on Christmas," she hissed, as though I couldn't hear her. "I saw the way Mr. Green looked at you. I saw the way that Nicky kid flirted. Don't act like it's a given. I know you loved Adrian this summer—how can you recover this quickly? Marriage is forever, Cory."

Again, that elvish flicker of the lips. "Mother, you're not telling me anything I don't know," she murmured. "Bracken and Green are still mourning Adrian too—we always will. Can't you be happy that I'm married to a man who loves me unselfishly? And if you want to believe that I'm married to all three of them, well, that certainly makes me look like something special, doesn't it?"

It was as though she were born to equivocate like elves, I thought with grudging admiration. As much as it had irritated me when she used this same tactic with me, I don't think I could have walked such a fine line, and I've been living with God's limitation on the Goddess's get for my nearly eighty years on the planet.

Mrs. Kirkpatrick swallowed, and I could tell Cory had won. Not even someone as tough and as pragmatic as Ellen Kirkpatrick could tell her daughter to her face that she wasn't that special, and admitting that her daughter could possibly be married to three men was quite out of the realm of human possibility. "I don't see a ring," she said at last with dignity, and finally—finally!—I had something to contribute.

"They're on order," I told her quickly, saving Cory the pain of having to equivocate again.

The look my beloved gave me was well worth the time and effort I'd put into choosing the rings and asking the fey goldsmiths in Colfax to make them. (Faerie metalworkers are a sour, bitchy sort of elf—not pleasant to work with at all.)

"Really?" Cory asked, and there was nothing in her voice but vulnerable, beleaguered woman, thrilled at seeing one good moment in a whole host of bad ones.

"Really," I told her and bent to her ear. "All four of them."

A charmed smile blossomed across her face, making her humanly plain features so lovely that every one of Green's people in the store actually turned to smile at her as she aimed that smile at me. Then she aimed that smile at her mother, her eyes bright and clear. "I'm going to have a wedding ring," she proclaimed proudly.

"Well, are you going to have a ceremony to go with it?" her mother shot back, and it hurt to watch that smile fade.

"Mom… we've already…," she began at the same time I said, "We can if you would like."

Cory's eyes met mine. "Can we?"

Why not, I thought. We could have a ceremony that would satisfy Cory's family but that would leave those of us who were the Goddess's children under no illusions as to whom she was bound to, and in what ways. "Sure," I said, swallowing. Suddenly I felt the weight of making her happy resting on my shoulders, and it had never felt so burdensome.

"We can have it in the Goddess grove. We'll have to talk to Green, of course... and Nicky...."

"Why Green and Nicky?" Christ, was that woman sharp.

"It's Green's garden too, mother," Cory said acidly. Then she spoke to me with that soft, wanting, charmed and thrilled woman's voice, and I thought that I'd dance on cold steel to get her to keep talking to me like that. "We could... when, do you think...."

"After finals," I said hopefully. Surely Hollow Man would be dead and neutralized by then. Surely we would be safe enough this summer, and Cory could have some desperate peace and some time to celebrate her relationships instead of fret about how to make them work.

"Summer in the grove...." She smiled a misty, wistful smile. "It's everything I wouldn't have known how to plan, really...." Suddenly she looked up, realizing that a small line had formed behind her mother. "Mom, give me a second," she ordered. "I'm working here."

And surprisingly enough, her mother did move, and Cory proceeded to do her job, sparing a smile and a brief comment on purchases as she did so. An older woman came up, and Cory recognized not only the customer, but her purchase.

"You decided to get more?" she asked, fondling the same sort of yarn that had gone into my sweater.

"Well, my first project came out so wonderfully—my husband actually wears it!"

Cory cast a shy, sideways glance at me. "So does mine," she said, infused with quiet pride.

Her mother left shortly after that, with a sniff and a promise— or a threat!—to be in touch shortly to ask about wedding plans. The rush eased, the store closed, and as I came up behind her, my beloved surprised me by leaning her full weight against me.

"Is everything done?" she asked. I checked with the two vampires who had come in after hours to help stock and count, and they nodded. Renny came padding out of the stockroom, a neatly tied bundle of clothes in her mouth, and Cory rubbed her tawny ears for a moment, still leaning on me. "What day is it?" she asked suddenly, as Renny bumped her hand for more stroking.

I blinked, checked the calendar at the register, and said, "The eleventh... why...." Then suddenly remembering human conventions, I asked with a bit of panic, "The fourteenth is Valentine's Day, isn't it?" I was supposed to do something on this day, but I was fuzzy on the details. Didn't it demand some sort of grand romantic gesture?

That got me a tired chuckle. "Yeah. Don't worry, Bracken—you just gave me the best Valentine's Day gift ever. You can forget about it forever, actually. You're covered." And still she leaned against me, taking as many moments as she dared, I guess, to shore up her courage. Then, "Beloved, would you mind taking a walk in the Goddess grove with me tonight?"

I sucked in my breath, unsure how to answer, but she saved me by saying, "Don't worry, I don't think he'll be there." And suddenly I was equal parts shame and relief.

"I'd be happy to," I said, wrapping my arms around her more securely and squeezing as tightly as I dared.

Her body relaxed another fraction, then tightened again, and she said out of nowhere, "Green's coming home, people. He'll be here by morning. Let's go home."

Everyone in the store heard her, and a quiet cheer went out. I could see her smile, even though I couldn't see her face. With a little sigh, she turned into my chest and whispered, "The rings are a wonderful gift, Bracken. I can't thank you enough."

"You haven't seen them yet," I mumbled, embarrassed.

She tilted her head up, and I saw her tired, happy, distant eyes. "You thought of them. For me, I know. You guys wear studs in your ears sometimes, but mostly you don't do jewelry." She stood on tiptoe, and I bent down so she could kiss my cheek. "It's a lovely thought. I can't wait to see them. Thank you."

Then, without looking at me, she moved away, hand on Renny's head, and I couldn't shake the feeling that there was something I had missed about the conversation, something I should know about but didn't.

The feeling didn't leave me as she took my hand and walked me up to the garden. It had started raining as we'd left work—that hard, insistent rain that comes this time of year in Northern California and promises not to stop for at least two weeks. It was an unfortunate rain—in the valley it would flood plains and threaten levies, and there were always places like Rio Linda and the Delta that would have to evacuate families; places where sandbag brigades would become a common duty for volunteer firemen.

Up here in the foothills, it meant that the mornings would not be nearly so chilly—gloves, hats, and scarves often littered the SUV when we piled out after traveling from the foothills to the valley—and in the areas surrounding Green's hill, snow was common enough to be a nuisance instead of a delight. Of course, with the lack of cold would come prematurely melting snow, swollen streams, flash flooding, and land the consistency of a Florida swamp. Even on Green's hill, where weather could be controlled by magic, water saturation was a simple fact of physics.

Tonight the rain in the Goddess grove was mitigated by the power that had made the grove, that was still inside Cory's fragile mortal body, and that Green wielded through her. It fell down in a gentle mist, and although it was by no means warm, it was certainly not a deterrent to the two female bodies, naked and pale and gleaming in the wet and the ever-present ambience that came from the grove itself.

Cory made a little hum in her throat when she saw them, and then, recognizing the women as Ellen Beth and Sweet, made another sound, this one more like sympathy and dismay, and seized my hand to haul me away from the loveliness that would always be two women making love. (Of course I stopped to watch. I am sidhe, and there is nothing to apologize for in appreciating beauty.)

To my surprise, instead of just retreating to our bedroom, Cory kept hauling at my hand, and we ended up on the grounds below the hill, Green's gardens. This time of year they were all crocuses and pinks and daffodils—these were flowers that bloomed in the lower parts of the foothills in winter, and they made sense here, where it was warmer than the surrounding areas, but still winter. There was still light streaming out from the three levels of windows that wrapped around the house, and the garden itself was alive with the tinier fey and the occasional vampire. It occurred to me that Green's hill really never slept.

When we found the grove of lime trees that made up the original part of the gardens, Cory actually stopped and took a breath and turned around to grin at me, a little embarrassed by what we had seen on the crown of the hill.

"I forget sometimes," she said, shaking her head.

"Forget what?"

"That making love in public places is not just for me and the men in my life," she said, exhaling on a laugh.

"We've never...," I started and then remembered our first time, in a skeezy warehouse in front of forty vampires, and I think even I flushed.

Cory laughed softly and sat abruptly in front of a tree, leaning against it, ignoring the sopping grass and the continuous mist coming down from the sky. She was in such an odd mood that for once I skipped the lecture about her health. "I don't think Green and I have ever...." She shrugged. "But then, we made the Goddess grove, so I guess that counts as public."

"Nicky?" I asked carefully. She had never given me details about date night, or how it had ended in such a way that it would destroy so much of her joy.

"Under the stars," she said, trying for casual. She failed, looking away from me. "It felt really good," she admitted. "I didn't know it could feel that good with someone who didn't make the earth move just by breathing."

I sat next to her and took her hand. "I am a sidhe, remember? I do understand about lust and pleasure."

"Yeah," she conceded. "But you gave it all up for me."

"It wasn't a hardship," I told her truthfully. It hadn't been. Being with her and only her was so simple and lovely I didn't know how to put it into words. And she was so complicated that practically every act of lovemaking was like seducing someone new.

"I can't do...." She turned her head, looked me in the eyes. "I don't understand how the human heart can be so complicated. Ellen Beth and Sweet... I get that. After Adrian died, Green and I would have just dissolved into one big howl of pain if he hadn't been inside me to fill some of that void. It almost doesn't have anything to do with love, although I love Green so terribly.... I don't understand how I can love the two of you so very terribly that...." Her voice trailed off. "My heart can do it so easily, but my brain can't explain it. I can't explain how just sitting in this garden with you makes me feel whole, but at the same time, if Green wasn't going to be here tomorrow, I'd fragment in a million pieces. I can't explain why I'm jealous of Nicky and all his lovers because I can't be there for him. I... I mean, we've been living this for nearly two months, and my heart can do it just fine, but my brain can't find the words to make sense of it."

"Does it have to?" I asked. "I mean, Cory, you're a smart woman, but you can't do physics to save your life. Your brain doesn't do that. Maybe what we need from you—and I know it terrifies you that anybody needs anything from you at all—maybe we just need you to think with your heart, the way you always do. Maybe it just doesn't need words. Balance isn't symmetry to the heart, Cory."

"Is that like some sort of freakin' elvish proverb?" she asked bitterly.

"Yes, as a matter of fact. But why are you thinking about this tonight? It's cold and it's wet, and before I nag you about getting inside and taking off your clothes, I'd like to know why we're here."

A noncommittal shrug, and still those distant eyes bored into the gray and misty night. "Kyle and Davy, I guess," she admitted after a moment. "It was like talking to a brick wall, but...."

And now it made sense. "It used to be just you and your vampire against the world, didn't it?" I asked gently.

"And the world was just as simple as Kyle thought it was," she finished softly.

We had been holding hands, but now I took her fingers to my lips and kissed. "The world was never that simple, beloved." I wasn't telling her anything she didn't know.

"No." She turned and gave me a misty smile. "But it was nice when I thought it was." Suddenly she stood up, all brusqueness. "What is simple is that we're freezing our asses off. I'm sorry—let's go inside."

"You're freezing your ass off," I corrected. "And there's not enough of it as it is."

She stuck her tongue out at me. In retaliation, I blurred, moving in hyperspeed, and swept her up in my arms, enjoying her breathless shriek as I fast-forwarded up the stairs and through the house. Her door banged behind me, and I made sure it was locked. If Green really was arriving sometime soon, I wanted these last moments private, me and her. I could share her, I could love our leader, but she was melancholy and sad and I wanted to be the one to take that away.

We made love, and she was right there with me in the present—no distant eyes, no thoughts about Adrian, no introspection, just me and our bodies and the things we felt for only each other on the surface of our skin. We fell asleep entangled, smooth limbs, tandem breathing, her wild, rusty hair tickling my nose.

In the dark of the morning, when the night things had retired and before gray broke the horizon, an electricity, a sweet scent of wildflowers, a warmth permeated the hill. I felt it and practically melted into the mattress in sheer relief, able to relax fully for the first time in nearly three weeks. I barely felt her suppressed hush as she extricated herself from my body (I feel like all elbows and knees sometimes when we are together) and slid out of bed. I heard a rustle as she put on the T-shirt we'd filched from Green's dresser, and felt her hand on my cheek followed by a sweet kiss, but I was truly asleep before she'd even closed the door to our room.

CORY
My Love Lies Waiting Silently for Me

I CLOSED the door behind me and waited in the hall, listening. When I didn't hear any voices from Green's room, I tried the handle—it was only locked when he was "with" somebody. The handle gave and I peered inside, almost afraid he wouldn't be there.

He was sitting in front of his dresser, a big light-oak affair with no mirrors, probably thanks to so many years with Adrian. The sprites were brushing his hair with little tiny combs, so many of them buzzing around his head that he looked like a weary angel, halo and all. His head was tilted back and his eyes were closed, and I slipped silently behind him, picking up a big wooden brush as I did so. The sprites cleared a path, and I took up the task myself, resisting the urge to hold the gold satin strands to my nose and inhale, just to smell him, real and in person, for the first time in weeks.

Green felt the difference in tension, though, and tried to turn toward me. I cupped the back of his head, saying, "Hold still, beloved. Let me tend to you."

"I've been tended to long enough," he said roughly. "Put the brush down, Corinne Carol-Anne, and let me hold you."

The brush fell out of my hands and thumped softly on the white area rug. Suddenly I was in his arms, and he was warm and vital and real and *Green*, and I needed his touch so much my hands were shaking with it. I ran them through his hair, mussing it, and his hands trembled their way through mine, pushing it back from my face. When my fingers found his curved and pointed ears, he made a sound like a cat does when you scratch the base of its tail. Then his mouth was on mine, and I almost wept. *Oh, my beloved, I've needed you so bad…. Tasting you is like taking a breath after holding it for the last three weeks.*

Our touch was fevered as we pushed under clothes and around buttons, and the sense that we were trying not to hurry, that we *must not hurry*, was only made worse when we were naked and bare against each other, tentative about touch and so hungry for it we almost forced our hands and thighs and arms past a barrier of wait. When we did touch, the meeting of nerve endings was magnetic—two forces belonging to each other, kept apart for so long that their meeting was nearly violent, truly inseparable.

We fell into bed in a tight tangle of limbs, and we might have simply rolled around like seals, but I needed to taste him.

I moved down his body, although his hands gripped my hair begging me to stay up with him, and wrapped my lips around his member, taking him as deep into my mouth as I could. I moved my head and tongue, once, twice, and then he rolled over, pulling himself from my mouth and slithering down my body like a tight ball gown being shed. I was eye level with his chest, reaching out to play with pebbled nipples the color of sun-gilt sand, when his cock caught in the crease between my thigh and hip and his breath caught in his throat. I knew that sound.

He buried his head in my shoulder then, his back bowing with the position and the effort not to... but he shifted and the friction rubbed him, and he was groaning into my throat and spurting against my stomach and hip and thigh, grinding into me again and again until he was done.

Our breathing took forever to still. Mine because I was not finished with the act we had begun; his, I think, because he was trying to master his embarrassment. He confirmed this guess when he said rawly, his voice sinking into its most obscure cockney British accents, "Bleedin' Christ, I haven't done that in more'n a thousand fookin' years."

I stroked his hair, holding him to my scarce breasts, trying for comfort and assurance, but in truth I was overawed by what it could mean. Green stirred, moving from me, and for once he was the one not meeting my eyes. I couldn't bear it.

"Don't...," I begged.

"I'm getting a washcloth," he said shortly. Even Green had a macho pride to wound.

I sat up in bed, looking curiously at the milky and clear fluids merging on my hip, running my finger through it just to feel it glide on my skin. In a fit of whimsy I used it to write "Green loves Cory" on my stomach, using the little heart like a kid carving names into a tree, and I grew so absorbed in the task that I didn't notice the water had stopped running in Green's bathroom until his shadow fell over me. I smiled up at him shyly, only to be devastated by the complete mortification on his face.

"Don't," I said again. "Don't—"

"I'm sorr—"

"Don't." I found myself perilously near tears, when I'd avoided them all day. "You think this is a failure, I know you do. Green, God of Sweet Desire, except with the one person he loves best. You don't know what this really is...."

"What is it?" he asked simply, sitting down next to me on the bed, his hair, glorious sunshine hair, shading his face from me like a curtain.

I ran my fingers through his seed, now growing cold and sticky on my skin. "This... this is the difference between sex and love," I said, my voice clogging in my throat. "This... is trust in love in a way I've never known. This is... this is what Bracken expects from me, but I haven't been able to give him until now, because you gave it to me first. This is every word I can't say but I feel in my heart to define how we love each other, and how it's different from how we've loved anybody else." My tears were falling freely now, and I figured I would return trust for trust and turned my distorted face to Green, who had shaken back his hair to see me clearly. "This is why I couldn't have survived another day without you, unless you had asked me to, and then I could do anything."

He moved my hand from my side and cleaned me carefully, setting the washcloth on his end table when he was done, then seized my hand in his own.

"When did you get to be so wise?" he asked me, his voice lighter, as he kissed my fingers.

"It was the first time you kissed me, after Adrian brought me home," I told him, sniffling a little.

"No... no...." He closed his eyes, took the finger I'd been using to write on myself and sucked it into his mouth, and my thighs clenched, reminding me that we'd started something that hadn't been finished. "That first night on the couch... when you asked me if Adrian and I were lovers, and I was so afraid that the answer I had for you would scare you out of his bed for sure."

"I don't remember," I said a little muzzily, because he had bent to my breast and started to tease my nipple with his tongue.

He lifted his head and gave me a brief kiss on the mouth. "I told you the truth. You said 'Good, because it sucks to be alone.'"

"And it sucks to be without you," I said, enjoying his shyest smile from close-up.

"And it sucks to be away from you," he finished. Then he began a long odyssey of kisses and caresses to the juncture of my thighs, where he tasted me, squared, for what was almost ever, and when he returned and I kissed him and tasted me too, we finished what we had started.

WE USUALLY talk in bed, but he had driven for hours to get home to me and was too exhausted for talk. When I heard the soft rap on our door just barely after a chill gray showed me the canyon beyond Green's window, I hurried out of bed and into his T-shirt to answer it before he woke.

It was Bracken, who smiled at me and kissed my forehead in greeting, and I leaned into him in return. "I know he needs his sleep," Bracken said softly, "so I won't be long. Nicky wants to go to school to check up on his classes and talk to Hallow"—I just bet!—"but I don't know if we want him to go if we're not there." What he wasn't saying was that Renny would be no help at all, and we certainly didn't want her to be there without us.

I nodded and blinked, trying to wake up. "Call Officer Max," I said through a yawn, and then, when Bracken's eyebrows rose, "You can't go without me. It's not happening. Renny can't go without us, and Nicky, LaMark, and Mario can't go alone. Max is still one of us, and he keeps his head with this shit—you saw him when Renny and I were knocked out. Today's his day off." I sighed, still leaning into him, enjoying his warmth in the dawn chill. "Besides," I said smugly, "it wouldn't hurt Renny to be reminded that he's still one of us, and that *we* can have a little patience with the man before we cut him off completely."

Bracken made a strangled laugh and bent to kiss me. "I told you that you're a very smart woman. I forgot to mention devious."

"It's a perk," I said grandly through another yawn.

In reply, Bracken seized my shoulders and turned me around, giving me a little shove back into Green's bedroom, where I crawled into bed next to my other beloved and slept soundly for another four hours.

Green disappeared at one point and returned with cold hands and a cold nose, towel-dried hair, and feet that were slightly damp because he had washed them after walking his land barefoot in the cold. Bracken did the same thing at least three times a week, so I was prepared for him. I rolled over, taking his chilled hands between my breasts and letting him bury his face in my neck. Of course this turned into lovemaking again, and by the time we were truly ready to get out of bed to shower and eat, it was almost noon.

There was corn chowder simmering on the stove and sandwiches in the refrigerator, and I made Green sit on the couch while I got us a tray. Most elves and weres are outdoors sorts—even in the rain—so the living room was empty of everybody except Renny, who was snoozing in front of the large bay window in the corner by the fireplace. (Enough of the fey had been born of or inside of trees that as soon as other means of heat had become available, Green had bricked over all the fireplaces and converted to natural gas.) We ate in a companionable silence for a while before I swallowed the last of my sandwich and cleared our dishes, then went to lean against my beloved simply because I could, and grilled him for information because neither of us was in a position to simply doze on the couch.

"So where's Twilight?" I asked—I was very curious to see our newly healed brother, after all.

"Sleeping with either Willow or Leah in their room," Green replied, a smile in his voice. "As soon as he was healed, all of his reservations about touching and being touched sort of went out the window."

"Lucky him," I said dryly. "So—did you all enjoy yourselves when the care package got there?" My voice was both coy and understanding, and Green's chuckle let me know he understood.

"Very much so," he said softly. "But nothing could compare to coming home to you."

"Ooooh... good answer."

"Truth." He nuzzled my hair, and I tried to keep my resolve to take care of some business before we just sat and cuddled. Before I could ask any more questions, though, he said gently, "You're tired and still too thin. I thought you were running to gain weight."

"I've gained stamina," I said optimistically. "I can run a mile without blowing like a busted air vent. That's got to be good."

"It is," he agreed. "I'm just.... Goddess, beloved—in a million years, I never thought we'd ask so much of you."

"Hey...." I took his hand, which was resting on my chest, and kissed it. "You know, nobody ever really expected much of me before you. I mean… I'm important here, for whatever reason. I'm important to good people. I'll do what I can not to let them down."

"Impossible for you to let us down," he said, and I turned to look at him. His eyes were half-closed, his arms were clutching me convulsively, and I heard Bracken's voice in my head. *You of all people should know that the only person in this hill who will never have to bow to you is Green.*

Green didn't need a queen right now. He needed a lover and, at the moment, a nap mate. I yawned and snuggled deeper into his arms. "Right back at you, beloved," I mumbled. I'd given us the day off to celebrate Green's homecoming. A couch nap at two in the afternoon was a celebration indeed.

Bracken apparently had the same idea, because about the time I was stretching on the couch and trying to sneak out from under Green's protective arm (I had to potty), he came wandering out of our room, blinking hard to make himself wake up. I slithered the rest of the way across the couch and met him in the entryway.

"How is he?" he asked quietly, ruffling my hair.

"Really tired—but he seems to be in a good mood." I was shifting from foot to foot, and Brack laughed at me.

"Go," he said. "I'm just going to get a snack."

When I got back, Bracken was sitting at one end of the couch, eating soup and crackers and talking with a full mouth, and Green was listening with his complete attention.

"He called your blood…," Green said in response.

"Yeah." Bracken nodded and swallowed. "But it wasn't very strong. I don't think he expected me to be a full-blooded sidhe or a redcap."

"He called your blood?" I asked, surprised. Bracken hadn't told me this after our last encounter with Hollow Man.

Bracken shifted in his seat and looked uncomfortable. "Well, yeah—it's why I used my call against him."

"You didn't tell me?" My voice rose. So did Green's eyebrows, and I tried to get a handle on my emotions.

"You were busy!" he understated. "And afterward you were yakking up a lung. Honestly, Cory, it's not that big of a deal…."

"The hell it isn't!" I spat, and a part of my brain realized that it was too late—after cruising on the lovely plateau of a relative peace with Bracken and then seeing Green again, my emotional railcar had performed a stomach-drop off a steep mountain and was now careening downhill sans brakes. Every detail of that day came staggering back to me—the way Bracken had protected me and fretted over me and carried me back and forth across the whole damned campus.... Dammit, couldn't he have told me he was in mortal danger too?

"It means you're vulnerable to him in ways that I'm not!" I replied, knowing that it was not the whole of my heart and I might never get the whole of my heart out, and it left me struggling for words. "It... it means that... that... dragging you to school every day when you hate it so much could get you killed, and that you carried me around campus when you were hurt—and that all your song and dance about me telling you stuff is just bullshit and you don't trust me enough to tell me that your stupid worthless precious fucking important life is in danger, you fuckheaded asshole."

The men I loved more than life itself were both looking at me with big eyes and open mouths. Green recovered first.

"Bracken, I'm going to excuse myself from this, as entertaining as I think it might be. Cory, when it's over, uhm, I'll be in my room. Twilight is coming in around three to talk—you may want to be there."

He stood up while Bracken and I glared at each other, kissed the top of my head tenderly and cupped my cheek. I looked at him with unhappy eyes and said, "I'm sorry. I didn't mean to—"

"I know you didn't," he said. "I think you've had a crash coming for a long time, beloved. I'm just glad Bracken's the one who got in your way, and not me."

"You're on the list," I muttered darkly.

He nodded. "I know it. You've been very rational about it all, but it can't change the fact that I left you when you needed me. Just don't be afraid to call me a fuckheaded bastard when you feel it, okay, beloved?"

I nodded. He kissed me again, this time on the mouth, and it almost but not quite melted my anger. Then he was gone, and I was staring at Bracken with unutterable hurt in my eyes.

"Why didn't you tell me?" I asked.

He shrugged. "Honestly, it didn't seem that important."

"I'll quit school. I'll beg Green. He won't say no to me, not if it's your life on the line. We can just stay here for a while and...."

Bracken stood up, and now he was well and truly pissed. "And hide? Don't do me any fucking favors, Cory. I've never run away from a fight. And don't ask Green for anything for me that you wouldn't ask for yourself, you got that?"

"Well then, don't hide things from me. My God, Bracken—all that shit you had to say about me keeping things to myself, don't you think I'd like to know that not only can this asshole hypnotize you with his blood but call *your* blood to him? I mean, if we know what he can do, we can stop him or protect you. Goddess, you don't know what he can do. You… you zoned out… you didn't see Ellen Beth wearing Chris's blood like a second skin…."

"Which is one reason I didn't tell you!" His voice crescendoed to a pitch that had Renny merrowring and jumping up from her spot by the window.

"Which is the biggest reason you *should* have told me!" I countered, and my voice rose to a shriek as well.

"Why, so you can throw yourself in front of me like you couldn't do for Adrian?" he shouted, and his porcelain face was mottled with the flush of blood at the surface.

"So I can *protect* you!" I hollered back, and I wouldn't, *couldn't* let the reference to Adrian rattle me. Goddess, Bracken was still so angry at him—and his next words confirmed that this fight had almost more to do with that anger than it had to do with me.

"The fuck you will!" He strode up to me and grabbed me by the shoulders, all the better to glare at me from his hellish height and try to intimidate me with his (truly) glowing eyes. "I told you before, Corinne Carol-Anne, that the one person in this entire hill who will never have to bow to you is Green. That means he's the only person on the hill who doesn't have the privilege and the goddamned fucking joy of throwing himself into traffic to protect you. Now I'll give you as good as I get when it comes to sharing my heart, beloved, but the sooner you understand that your life comes before mine on or off the hill, the better off we'll both be." And with that he hauled me up against him and crushed my mouth to his brutally, so brutally that I tasted a little blood from my lips, and then he thrust his tongue inside, tasting me and tasting me and tasting me, before he let go of my arms and strode from the room, leaving me limp and sinking to the carpet before he could even slam the door to the porch.

Blurring impossibly from his room, Green caught me before I hit the ground.

GREEN
The Sweet and the Bitter

"GODDESS," GREEN said into her hair as she tried to control her little hiccups of hurt. "I haven't heard a row that gorgeous since Bracken and Adrian were a couple."

"I didn't know they were ever an actual couple." She sounded surprised. She was leaning her head against his chest in the way she had that always pleased him. Everything else about her might be prickly and independent, but that head against his chest had always betrayed a sweet and absolute trust. "I just sort of thought they... I don't know... made love because they were so close it was inevitable, you know?"

"Oh, they did," he agreed, thinking sadly of how much she did not know, and how much of Bracken she needed to know before she understood him. Green himself was as open about his love as he had ever been—but it was hard, so hard, to suffer so many losses to an open heart. Bracken's heart had always been grimmer, angrier, more apt to argue with boundaries than Green's. Bracken, Green had always thought with admiration, would have killed Oberon before allowing himself to be enslaved for more than a hundred years as Green had.

Of course, Adrian had said once, when he and Bracken were *almost* exclusive to each other, "But if you were just like Bracken, beloved, I wouldn't need you like I need blood in my veins, now would I?" And now, as Green kissed Cory lightly on the lips, healing the small cut Bracken had inflicted, he knew the truth of this. Bracken would call to her blood, because that was his very nature. Green would heal her heart, because that was his.

"They did become lovers because of that," Green said, snapping out of his reverie. Goddess, eighteen hundred years of living and he had never been as immersed in the past as Adrian's death had made him! "But for a decade, almost, they were exclusive...."

"With a notable exception," Cory said, touching the lips that had just healed hers.

He grinned. "Did you ever doubt it?"

She looked at him soberly from her position against his chest, as though seeing something inside her beloved she had not thought of before. "Not once," she mused. "So they fought?"

Green set her down on his bed and lay next to her—just to talk, to touch, and to hold. It was what they had been doing on the couch—reconnecting. "Ferociously, especially toward the end. I swear, they broke more furniture in those two months than has been broken in the hill before or since."

"Why did they break up?"

Green smiled a little, a sad smile. "I think that would be obvious, luv. They broke up because neither one of them was you."

"I wasn't even born yet!" she protested, flushing, but he was very serious.

"They had been waiting for a woman like you since Bracken came of age, Corinne Carol-Anne. I'm not exaggerating. They made love to each other because that is what our people do. They fell *in* love with *you*, because that is who you are to them. Never forget that."

A small smile quirked at her lips. "Thank you, beloved. I wouldn't dream of it. What I don't understand is why they fought. I mean…." She wrinkled her forehead and stroked his hair back from his brow, taking a long, purring moment to stroke the curve of his pointed ear. "If they were ready to stop being a couple, they weren't bound by anything, Green—not even convention. All that bound them was habit…."

A memory flashed in front of Green's eyes: a deadly sun two hours over the horizon, the old panel truck safely in the dark of the old shed, and Bracken—much shorter, heartbreakingly young, and so devastated by his own mistake that Green could hardly have punished him more. "That…." He sighed, laid his head against her breast just to hear her heart beat, then shifted them so she was lying on him. "That," he resumed, "was my fault, I think. Yes, I'm pretty sure the reason they had to fight for freedom instead of simply ceasing to be together dated back to a very, very young Bracken and a damn fool quest for some peaches."

He told her the story then. Some of it he'd gathered from Bracken's frantic mother and father as they'd realized their son was gone from the hill with his favorite playmate, and some he'd gotten from an unrepentant

Adrian the next evening. It had been one of the few times that Green and Adrian had ever fought.

"His happiness is not more important than your life! Goddess blight *it, you fuckhead—you could have died!" Adrian had touched Green's hand then, woven slender fingers in with Green's elongated ones, and frowned prettily, autumn-sky eyes bright, and, as was often the case with Adrian, unexpectedly compassionate.*

"His happiness is just like yours, Green," he said calmly. "It's the only reason to walk the planet at all."

"Goddess," Cory said through a clogged throat and bright eyes. "That's so like him. Hell, it's so like both of them." She flashed a sudden, unclouded grin at him. "Bracken had rings made, you know—for the four of us. Bless him, he can be such a cranky asshole sometimes, but so good with the grand romantic gesture, you know?"

"Like peaches for his mother," Green nodded.

"Like peaches for his mother," she agreed. "So you made him promise to never leave Adrian behind—and he was ready to be nonexclusive, and Adrian wasn't, and… Bracken being Bracken, he had to fight with something if he wasn't going to get his way."

"I have no idea how they resolved the issue," Green said thoughtfully. "One day they were either beating the hell out of each other or inseparable. The next day, they were competing with each other for girls when they weren't shagging each other silly. Mostly competing for girls, though."

"They didn't compete for me!" she protested, laughing. "I think Adrian took Bracken by the station to scope me out one night, and Bracken looked at me through a window, and his expression got… well…." Her voice fell. "I didn't know it at the time, but it was his hurt look—when he gets all stoic and stone-faced, but he's bleeding inside…." She trailed off. "Jesus, I'm an idiot. I never put it together before…."

"At first sight, beloved. Just like Adrian. But Bracken would never reach for what his brother loved."

"And unlike you and Adrian…."

"The two of them never did share well."

She put her hand over her eyes. "So he just backed away. Goddess, he must be so pissed at Adrian. He just hands me over to his brother without a qualm, and then Adrian goes and dies. All that effort not to leave him behind…."

"And Adrian leaves him instead," Green finished. "Yes—you and I were mad at Adrian, but Bracken... oh, Goddess, his fury must be tearing him apart."

"Well, it's not doing any of us much good, is it?" she snapped, and Green nodded.

"A thing you must tell him the next time you can talk civilly. And in the meantime...." His hand had been stroking her upper arm. Now it shifted, and he stroked her little breast through her sweatshirt, feeling the nipple pop deliciously under his fingers. She arched, gasped, and he kissed her lightly on the lips. "In the meantime, we've got another half hour, and Bracken's loss is my gain," he said softly, and she took his face in her hands and kissed him back.

They were just getting dressed again, with a lot of touching and giggling, when there was a tentative knock on the door.

"Just a minute, brother," Green called, buttoning his fly and tugging his sweatshirt down. Cory straightened her T-shirt and ran a hand through her disastrous hair, and Green turned and laughed at her.

"Well, there's not a flipping mirror in here!" she protested. He just laughed more, moving toward his dresser to pick up the abandoned brush.

"Come in, Twilight," Green called again. Then he pushed Cory to the chair and sat her down, starting the brush through her hair even as Twilight entered.

"It's getting long," she was saying as the door opened. "I need to cut it."

"Please don't," he requested, and she flushed. Then she looked up at the doorway and gasped.

"Goddess," she breathed. "Green...." Then she remembered herself. "I'm sorry, Twilight. It's just... Green didn't warn me—you're so beautiful."

And he was. His skin was a deep and dusky purple, and his hair, silver-and-gold spangled, twilit violet. His features were classical sidhe, with the wide-set eyes and triangular face—but his eyes, which looked darkest brown, were sheened silver. His mouth, like Green's, was sensual and full, but unlike Green's, it had a serious turn, without the ever-present hint of laughter. He was the least human sidhe Cory had ever seen, and she was obviously delighted.

"Stop drooling, beloved," Green chided, enjoying her reaction very much.

"No, no, Green Man—you let her drool. Pretty human girls haven't drooled over me in a very long time."

There was a time when she would have protested being either pretty or human, but as it was, she simply grinned up at him and then winced as Green pulled her hair back into its habitual ponytail. He put a hand on her shoulder, telling her he was done, and she stood up and gave him a peck on the cheek. "Just for you, I won't cut it," she said sweetly, then hopped onto the just-made bed and crossed her legs under her. "Sit down!" she urged, pointing to the chair she'd just left. Green sat beside her on the bed, and Twilight did just as she asked, but instead of straddling the chair as Bracken or Arturo would have, he sat squarely in it and bowed his head slightly.

"Thank you for the invitation," he said formally.

"It's our pleasure," Green told him gently. "I wanted Cory to be here because she's been on the front lines with this thing, and I thought she should hear some of your story."

"There's not much to tell. You know that, Green. I know very little about what it was that attacked me and… and stripped me down to what you saw."

"Well, what is it you do know?" Cory asked, leaning forward. Her eyes were avid and kind at the same time. "We know that the sight of him makes the elves dizzy, the stench of him makes the vampires sick, and the sound of him makes the werecreatures scream in pain—but humans hardly notice he's there. It seems like he must be one of the Goddess's get, but he makes all of us sick, so I don't see how he could be."

Twilight nodded. "When I first knew him, he was human. Or— much like you, little Goddess—he looked and behaved so much like a human that nobody ever thought to look beyond."

"You knew him?" she asked delicately, hazel eyes shrewd.

"I loved him," Twilight said simply. "I've always had a fondness for humans. This one…." He grimaced, his handsome, lovely face looking for a moment like the wretched, starved creature Green had found huddling outside the hotel. "I cannot remember his name—I'm sorry. I think… I think he stripped it from me, when he stripped me of power, and… and I think after that, it was never really his again."

Cory leaned forward and took Twilight's hand in her own. "Don't worry about it, brother. You're whole and well—everything else is icing, right?"

"She really is yours, isn't she?"

"She's every inch her own," Green replied, but he touched her back under her shirt, where she'd marked herself just for him.

"So…," Cory said, losing a fight against a blush, "we don't know his name, and it wouldn't matter anyway… but how did he go from being your lover to being our enemy?"

"He had power," Twilight said bluntly. "Not a lot—not nearly what you can channel, little Goddess—but he had a modest amount of his own. It wasn't awakened until we came together, and then it was small things. Doors slamming all over the house when we fought, windows or vases cracking when we were making love, petty things, really."

"Destructive things," Cory said meditatively. "He did destructive things unconsciously…." She frowned, concerned. "Was he destructive in other ways?"

Twilight nodded. "Self-destructive. When we met, he was often drunk, and angry when he was drunk, but when that faded over time, I thought it was only the anger from abuse that caused it. Most beings, when treated fairly and well, will respond by treating others fairly and well."

Cory nodded. "It seems to work here." She turned her head and looked at Green. "So far," she said thoughtfully, "he sounds like one of Adrian's saved. Hell, he actually sounds like me."

"Except for the destructive part, beloved," Green reminded her. "In fact, although you tried very hard to look the part, mindless destruction is as far from who you are as this Hollow Man is."

"Yes, but I *was* angry," she pondered. Then, to Twilight, "So he was human, with some power. Then what happened?"

Twilight frowned, a supremely unhappy look that said he did not like speaking ill of an old lover. Cory looked on in sympathy and waited quietly for him to speak. "He was more than angry. He was resentful. The longer our association, the more resentful he became of the things that I had and he did not. He wanted the physical beauty… he wanted the power. But… you must understand. He was raised by his mother, and she died when he was just a boy. So much of his wanting, his endless needing, came from this feeling that he had been denied things—love, acceptance, power in his life—and that death was what had denied him these things. So he craved love and attention—he was an endless well for them. I could pour these things into him measured by gallons of tears, and still he would be empty. But the thing he most resented me having, that he did not, was my immortality."

Cory looked surprised, and Green laughed quietly to himself. She was convinced that she would grow old and wither and die, and she had made her peace with it even before age reared its head. But Green knew better. He'd suspected since he'd first seen her that she was destined for greater things than a humble death, defeated by time.

"He wanted to live forever?"

"Like all the things he thought he was owed, he craved it. But I did not know how much." There was a heartbreaking sigh, and the violet-skinned sidhe shook his head, his hair in all its glory rippling down his back like a river of night. "I am usually very... loyal, to my human lovers. Their lives are so short... begging your pardon, Lady Cory."

"No worries," she said.

"I don't mind age," Twilight continued. "In fact, it fascinates me. I tend to love my companions—"

"Till dust and beyond," Cory finished softly. "We understand, Twilight. It's okay."

Twilight nodded, swallowing hard. "But... but this one... I couldn't. He needed, and the more I gave the more he needed. It got so that when I looked at him, all I saw was a starry vortex of want. His personality, the nobility I had seen in him at the beginning, it all seemed to disappear— even his humanity was fading. I tried to break it off, and he grew angry beyond reason. He seemed to feel I was, once again, trying to deprive him of what was rightfully his... as though if I stayed with him, he would become immortal. He stormed away, leaving cracks in the walls of my home." He paused for a moment in thought. "I lived alone, on a small hill of my own. I remember I was repairing my house when he returned the next morning. He'd been to see the vampires...."

As though shouldering a huge burden, he sighed and continued. "Your vampires are...." He smiled. "I've met Ellis. He is young and impetuous and still... good. Your vampires are healthy. They are kind. The vampires in Texas.... Texas is a hard land. It is vast and frightening, and all of the reasons vampires become vampires in the first place, Texas threatens. They would not care if they were ruining a life, or creating a serial killer, or… making a monster. He was fey—he had enough fey in him to evidence power. What he became when the vampires turned him was… monstrous. I couldn't see him anymore—that figurative whirlpool I had seen was now real. I had a couple of werecreatures living in a cottage on my hill. As soon as he greeted me, they turned and started to howl, mrowl, and scream with pain. And where before he had just been needy, now he was mad. He was ranting about how I had turned everyone against him. Even the vampires detested him and how he was a monster—because he had turned, but here he was, awake in the day. I was afraid, I was terrified, but… but I had brought him into our world, the world of the Goddess, and I tried to calm him down."

"Oh, no," Cory said.

"Oh yes, little Goddess." Twilight nodded his head very seriously. "I went to embrace him, and he seized me instead. Like the vampires, he has the Goddess's strength. He bore me to the ground, sank his teeth into my neck, and fed and fed and fed… and if he had just taken blood, I could have lain there, broken, and recovered eventually. But he was fey—he took blood and took power, and my hill dried up around my body as he took and took and took. It was as though all of that need had been unleashed upon the world, only worse… much, much, a thousand times worse."

There was silence, and Green watched Cory's mind working on what she'd just been told. "What about the weres?" she asked after a moment. "On your hill… did he…."

"He infected them," Twilight said flatly. "When I came to consciousness eventually, their cottage was the first place I went for help. But he'd bitten them, fed from them, and… you know the nature of the werecreature… they often become two-natured because there is something the human world will not give them. They become the thing they love because of need. This monster, he is literally a hollow man—need is the thing that drives him, a craving for things he can never have because you have to be able to give something of yourself in order to get them. His need is addictive. The werecreatures on my hill were decimated—they lived, but they had been fed from…."

Twilight clenched his eyes in pain. "I spent many years on the streets after I finally wandered broken from my home, all true memory of what I had been broken and drained. I often slept in drug houses where people clenched their veins with pain and shook and groaned and pissed themselves with the effects of drugs and with withdrawals and all of the human pain that houses like that hold. My were-cottage...." And for the first time in his recitation, tears actually started rolling across the lovely purple cheeks. "It had been a happy place. My werecreatures were gentle people, often abused in their human lives. Their cottage was beautiful, and full of sunshine and gentle lovemaking and kind and easy humanity. I have no idea how long I lay there, senseless and bleeding, after Hollow Man was done with me, but when I had crawled to the were-cottage, it had become like the drug houses, only worse. He had spread his need to them through his bite... spread it and intensified it and made it awful and addictive and toxic. When I got there, one of them had already exploded with need, his blood putrefied beyond recognition. The others were screaming in pain. Goddess help me, there was nothing I could do but lie on the floor keening as their bodies lost composition around me...." And now Twilight well and truly lost his composure, burying his face in his hands, his shoulders shaking with sobs.

Cory made a low grunt in her throat. Her hand clenched around Green's, and he looked at her in concern as her face tightened, her cheekbones seeming ready to slice out of her skin. Moving so quickly he swore she was moving with Goddess speed, she wrapped her arms around their lost brother's shoulders and rocked him against her. "I'm sorry, Twilight," she said softly, her throat rough. "We've lived through that here. Please... don't live it again, not for us...." But the wound was too deep, and Green moved from the bed and began rubbing Twilight's shoulders, his touch strong and increasingly sensual until his eyes met Cory's over the shaking body, and she swallowed and nodded.

Leaning over and giving Green a kiss on the cheek, she said, "Let me know when you're free, beloved. Grace is having a formal dinner downstairs at seven."

Green nodded, and a weary smile quirked at his mouth. "You may want to go make up with Bracken, luv. I can't promise I'll be free tonight."

She swallowed again and gave the brightest smile she could manage. "Groovy. Makeup sex and coming-home sex in the same day. This job has its perks." She made him laugh before she bobbed shakily out the door, leaving him to the work he did best.

CORY
Conversations and Bouncing Balls

THERE WAS a strange werecreature waiting outside Green's room as I emerged. I was starting to be able to spot them—there is a supernatural grace about a were-animal, and true to my vampire sympathies, I could almost smell the animal they spent their alternate lives as.

"Hello," I said, startled. Then, as I remembered conversations with Green, "You must be Eric."

"And you must be Cory," he said, looking just as startled.

"Uhm…. Green's going to be busy for a bit. Twilight's in there. He… it was hard," I said awkwardly and could have kicked myself for the double entendre.

A wicked smile crossed his pleasantly freckled features, and suddenly I didn't feel so awkward. "If it wasn't, I'm sure it is now," he said with raised eyebrows, and I laughed.

"Have you eaten yet? I know you all got in late, but Grace left food."

Eric grinned again, only this time it was all excited little boy. "I was actually hoping for sweets—cookies, pie…."

"Probably both," I agreed, and suddenly that sounded much more attractive than going out to find Bracken, who was probably brooding through the gardens on the hill. "Let's go see!"

We found, in fact, several cream pies—chocolate, coconut, and Green's favorite, banana. Eric and I both eyeballed the chocolate. I cut a large slice for each of us, and we sat down across the table from each other and started chatting like old friends. Eric was full of stories of Adrian, Bracken, and even Green from twenty years ago.

"So, does Bracken still wear his mullet when he glamours up for the humans?" he wanted to know through a mouthful of chocolate pie.

I'd worn a smile through his description of Adrian and Bracken competing over a prom queen, using concert tickets and tricked out Mustangs, and I felt it fade. "He… well, first I…." I sighed. "He wears his hair short now," I said after a moment. "He cut it because… because he's freakin' Bracken and he's mortal, and it's some sort of symbol and now I can't get him to grow it out again."

Eric looked at me kindly. "Goddess bless you for just taking him on," he said after a moment. Then he added a little shyly, "You know, of course, half the hill heard you two this morning."

I flushed. "Half the hill hears most of our arguments," I said, shaking my head. Then I grinned a little. "Adrian told me that this place was like high school—without all the petty popularity crap. Adrian's right about most things."

Eric looked at me strangely. "You say that like...."

I swallowed again. It had been such a pleasant conversation. "He wanders the gardens a lot," I said, purposely not using the "g" word. "I don't know how often—he sort of threatened me by saying that if I started going out there too much he'd stop showing up. But... but when Green or I start missing him too terribly... he's there."

Eric nodded sagely, as though I hadn't just told him there was a ghost in our consecrated grove, and asked the obvious question. "What about Brack?"

I looked away. "He won't see him," I said, looking mournfully at my pie, which suddenly didn't seem as tasty as it had. "He... he looks around him or through him or over him, and... he's still so pissed off, Eric. Green sent us all to... to this preternatural counselor...."

"Hallow? He's a good man. Green had me go talk to him when I was thinking about leaving the hill."

"Yeah... and Bracken will go off on just about any subject—bitches about me and about Green and all the stuff he sort of opens up about anyway... but not about Adrian." Suddenly this stranger was reaching for my hand across the table.

"You're perfect for them, you know," he said after a moment. "I partly came to meet you, to make sure you would be... I don't know... worthy of these people. I love them, all three of them—even Adrian, although the son of a bitch went and died on us. For you, Bracken will get over being pissed off."

I looked up at him and smiled, suddenly feeling hungry again. "I'll just piss him off all on my own," I said, stuffing my mouth with a forkful of heaven. We laughed for a minute, and suddenly the conversation went back to being casual, between two new acquaintances again. Renny padded up to the table, eyed the chocolate pie, and licked her whiskers, so I cut her a large piece (Grace cooked for beings that had high metabolisms—there were, like, ten of each kind of pie in the massive refrigerator) and put it on the table. She leaped into the chair next to me and started lapping contentedly at the whipped cream, a happy rumbling starting from her chest, making the moment even more companionable and peaceful. It would have stayed that way, except Chloe stalked in, looking less than pleased to see me.

"Where's my mother?" she asked without preamble. "I need to talk to her."

Eric and I exchanged disbelieving looks, and Renny's purr turned into a growl. "Your mom is dead, Chloe," I said shortly. "She doesn't get her soul back until sunset—you've got, like, two hours."

Chloe shook her head in annoyance. "I don't want her to come out and play or anything—I just need to talk to her. And having that animal at the table is so beyond disgusting."

I felt my own growl starting in my chest. "Did you hear that, Renny?" I asked. "She thinks you're disgusting." And with that, Renny morphed into a tiny woman with unfriendly brown eyes and whipped cream on her cheeks.

Chloe was aghast but, sadly enough, not speechless. "Oh my God—she's naked!"

"Picky bitch, aren't you?" Renny growled and then turned back into a cat, lapping at the chocolate with fierce satisfaction.

"Your mother's not asleep, Chloe," I said into the shocked silence. "Just like Renny's not really a house cat. Your mother's dead. She doesn't breathe, she doesn't dream, she doesn't twitch. Her soul is with the Goddess right now, because God denied the vampires daylight—and if you want a more in-depth history lesson, you'll have to ask Green, because that story is just too painful."

Chloe looked at me, her mouth opening and closing, and I scraped my plate of the last of the pie and stood up.

"Are the boys outside?" I asked.

"Stay away from them," she snapped automatically.

"You want me to stay away from them, stop bringing them to my home," I replied evenly. "Your mother's room is way, way down the hall—the hall takes a left, a right, a right, and a left into the hill, so that sunshine doesn't even accidentally get into the darkling—and your mom's is the first door to the left. It's got a quilt on the front—you'll recognize it. If you get lost and wander into the room with the yellow door right across from it, I'll rip your hands off. Anyone in the hill will tell you I mean that."

Chloe simply stood, all five feet ten inches of her, and glowered at me. I returned her glare and then called cheerfully, "Hey, Eric—want to meet Grace's grandchildren? I bet they've never seen a werecoyote turn before."

Eric stood up smoothly and followed me out, Renny padding at our heels. As soon as the door was shut behind us and we were headed down the stairs toward the two childish voices raised out on the lawn, he let out a low whistle. "Wow. That was some serious hostility."

I sighed. "Yeah. We try to be nice to her because, I mean, she's Grace's daughter... but we can't always hide how much she pisses us off."

Eric grinned. "I meant *her*, Cory. She's definitely got it in for you."

Now I grimaced. "She's jealous," I said after a moment. "She's probably jealous of the whole hill, everybody her mom has mothered since she left her family. I'm just... I don't know. Of an age. Grace and I are pretty close, and I'm young, and Chloe just sees me and... wishes she was me, I guess."

The boys were playing tag on the front lawn, the one that everyone saw as they drove in, and I waved at them now. They grinned and swarmed up to me, wanting hugs and my complete attention for a few moments. I introduced them to Eric and Renny, who both obligingly changed, but only once. I'd kind of forgotten about the little-kids-seeing-naked-adults part, so to get over that awkwardness (and Gavin and Graeme's terrible excitement about the naked people), I asked them if they wanted to help me with my superpowers. I had something I wanted to try.

Both times we had confronted the Hollow Man I had needed to shield—not just from him, but from his blood and the vapor his blood produced when it was destroyed. I wanted to try a power shield that was... well, complete. Complete and mobile. A bubble of safety, so to speak. I had both boys stand separately on the lawn, concentrated a little, and called my power.

It was scrumptiously easy. I worked on emotional fuel, and at the moment I was up to my eyeballs in love, sex, and anger. The two bubbles of magic that appeared around the boys glowed iridescently, and their mouths made little "O"s of excitement. Graeme, the more adventurous one, noticed that his feet were now about three inches off the ground, and he gave an experimental bounce. His bubble bounced with him, about a foot into the air, and the acrobatics began.

The kids began to bounce against the walls of the bubbles, and the bubbles of magic began to fly. At first I controlled their flight paths in an effort to keep them from bouncing into Green's precious flower beds, but once they realized I was directing their bouncing, they begged me to help them fly, so I did. Using my power and my whimsy, I bounced them in the air, I juggled them, I whirled them gently together and then against each other. The littles heard their laughter, and suddenly we were knee-deep in a giggling horde of sprites, nixies, brownies, and such who used their combined mass of rainbow hands to bop the power balloons in the air like beach balls. Eric and I just sat and watched the boys giggle themselves breathless, tumbling about on a cushion of air. They were in the middle of a series of complicated aerobatics when Chloe came out, looking pale and angry, and made a little shriek of alarm.

"Stop that!" she commanded. "Stop that before you drop them!"

The littles all gave a unanimous whimper and dissolved into the landscape as fast as their little legs and little powers could carry them, and I concentrated on making sure the power bubbles bounced gently around on the whisper-soft lawn without jostling the boys too much now that the littles weren't there as a cushion. I spared Chloe a glance, then turned my eyes back to the boys and continued. "Chloe, if anything strong enough to crack through Green's power flies through this hill to break my concentration, we will all have a lot more to worry about than a six-foot drop onto grass as soft as a feather mattress."

"How can you be so sure?" she demanded. "You're like sixteen— what gives you the right to say my children are safe in your psycho world?"

"Hard experience," I said softly. "You do not want to know the things I've done with my power even when I've been weak. I'm not weak now."

Eric made a noise next to me and said softly, "Over there, in the Goddess grove."

I nodded. "Yeah. I see him." Bracken had been watching me since I'd come out and started to play with the children. I could feel his regard, his perplexed and unhappy concentration, and although I wasn't quite ready to talk to him, he was starting to break down my anger and reserve.

"Did you find your mother, Chloe?" I asked, avoiding the topic.

"Yes," she said shortly. "And you don't need to be so smug about being right."

I grunted, and even though I could probably throw the boys around in their shields for hours, I suddenly felt very tired. "If you have to work tonight, that means the boys will be staying here, right?"

Chloe made an unhappy noise—yes, but she didn't like it. Too damn bad.

"Hey, guys!" I called, setting the bubbles on the ground delicately. Graeme and Gavin took a couple of wobbly steps on solid ground and then fell on the grass, giggling. I called again and they made their unsteady ways toward me, falling into my arms and laughing for all they were worth. I hugged them and agreed with everything they said—*Yes, I saw you do that flip, that was amazing. No, I wouldn't have let you fall, you know that. Yes, if I'm not tired, we can do this again*—and then, when I had their complete attention, I told them, "Hey, guys, we're going to have a full banquet tonight down in the big hall. You want to join us?"

"Yeah!"

"Oh, wow! A full banquet? Like in Robin Hood movies and everything?"

I nodded. "Exactly like that."

"Can we sit with you, Cory?" Graeme wanted to know, and I had to shake my head.

"No," I said regretfully. "I wish you could... but you know those Robin Hood movies?" They nodded. "I'm sort of up at the head table. We've got important stuff to talk about tonight, and they kind of need me and your grandmother. But Renny here will sit with you—right, Renny?" Renny looked at me in surprise from her golden cat's eyes and then nodded. "And you'll get to meet Nicky, and Mario, and LaMark. They can shape-shift into birds." I dropped my voice conspiratorially. "And they can shape-shift with their clothes on!"

"Cool...," Gavin said, wide-eyed. He had been the most shocked when Renny appeared naked in front of him.

"Anyway, I'm going to have Renny and Eric take you guys inside to get dressed. We all get dressed up a little, and you," I swiped a hand over Graeme's grimy hands and ruffled Gavin's tousled hair, "are not dressed up yet. Don't worry—all we need is clean jeans and T-shirts, and a little less garden. Okay?"

The boys' faces fell. "We don't have any extra clothes," Gavin said disconsolately.

"I'm sure we can scrounge you up something. Renny, the lower fey quarters should have something for them." Nymphs, dryads, smaller trolls—there were myriad creatures that didn't grow much bigger than two small boys. "But you're going to have to change before you go there." Although it hadn't happened yet, there was a deep-seated fear among the lower fey that one of the werecreatures would forget who it was while in animal form and accidentally eat a brownie, nixie, or sprite because it thought the smaller creature was a bird. Like I said, it hadn't happened yet—although Renny had gotten rough when playing before, especially when mourning Mitch—but when you were smaller than five inches tall, you had the right to be a little paranoid. Renny nodded obediently and looked expectantly toward the boys.

"You can watch television in the living room while she gets changed," I said. "You remember where the DVDs are?" They nodded and followed Renny in, and then I turned to Chloe.

"Were there two big dogs with your mom?" I asked. Steph and Joe were the young couple that Grace was feeding from presently. As dogs, Stephanie was like a big calico Newfoundland, and Joe was a golden retriever. As humans, Steph was a tall, round woman and Joe was a thin, awkward man—they neither matched nor complemented each other physically—but they could finish each other's sentences, and you could scent their complete belonging together across the hill.

Werecreatures who were doubling as dinner sometimes slept watch over their vampires—partially to guard them, partially because it was a quiet place, and partially to keep the vampire from waking up too hungry, because a hungry vampire wasn't just a bad thing, it was a force of nature. Grace was fond of saying that Steph and Joe were her two favorite flavors, and they enjoyed the compliment.

"Yes," Chloe confirmed, surprised that I would know this.

"Good," I said. "They'll probably want to sit with the boys too. It will be a good table, and the boys will have fun."

Eric looked at me and darted his eyes toward Bracken. "Are you going to take care of that?" he asked delicately, and I scrubbed my face with my hand.

"Well, yeah!" I answered back in frustration. "I just… I just wish he'd forgive him, that's all. That would make it just a little bit easier on all of us, you know?"

Eric nodded somberly. "I know." Then he gave me an unexpected hug. "You are so good here," he said through a tight throat. He took a step back and smiled, then turned toward Chloe.

"You know, I was here when your mother first got here," he said conversationally.

"What were you, like two?" Chloe asked ungraciously.

"More like sixteen. Your mom used to sit out at night, until almost dawn. I was… well, pretty fucked up at the time. I'd come out here and sit at her feet, and then I'd start to worry that she wouldn't go in on time. That's when Adrian would come out and feed from me and offer me to Grace, and then we'd all go inside together. Sometimes Adrian couldn't make it, for one reason or another, and then it would be just me and your mom. And eventually, she'd start calling me inside all on her own. She hurt so bad back then—it was like she needed a fucked-up teenager to mother, or she wouldn't have survived. I bet you're bringing all that back to her all over again. How easy are you making it on her?" There was a pause, while Chloe opened and closed her mouth looking for something to say, and Eric tossed me a wave. "See you inside, Cory. I'm going to make sure the boys don't fill up on pie."

Chloe just stood there, searching for words, a reply, anything at all. I wasn't going to make it easy on her.

"I've got things to do before dinner," I said shortly. "And I understand you have to work. You can see yourself out."

I turned around and was almost to the smaller Goddess grove when Chloe suddenly asked, "Who is Adrian?"

I turned halfway. "You wouldn't understand if I told you," I said after a moment. "He used to live in the room with the yellow door." And then I turned back to where Bracken was waiting.

BRACKEN
"Other Foot" Issues

WE MADE up, of course. Well, more accurately, we made love fast and furiously behind the bole of the giant lime tree in the smaller Goddess grove—it wasn't like I gave my *due'ane* a chance to argue with me, after all.

But the difference between making up and having sex haunted me as I lay with my head on her stomach, scenting lightly at the juncture of her thighs. She smelled like Green, and like me, and like Corinne Carol-Anne Kirkpatrick op Crocken Green—like home. I would not jeopardize that smell, that taste, or that texture for all of the hard quickies in the garden that I planned to have in the years to come.

But it was a good moment, and I have a history of walking all over good moments with my king-sized feet, and I didn't want to screw that up either.

"Say it," she commanded, combing her fingers through my hair. I'd had it cut again, right before Green got back. She had bitched about that too.

"Say what?" I protested.

"I can hear it rattling around in your head, Bracken," she said mildly. So mildly that it suddenly felt like saying what I was thinking was not an intrusion into the moment, but an extension of it.

I turned to look at her. Her T-shirt was rucked up to right below her breasts, and her bra was poking out the neck of the T-shirt, and her sweatshirt was under her bare hips. Her jeans were pooled with her shoes, and one of her socks was about a foot above her head. Her eyes peered brightly at me from under lazy, hooded eyelids.

"Are we good?" I asked, the question rougher on my throat than I had expected. Her lips quirked, and I knew she was about to deliberately misunderstand me. "I mean, are we made up? Have we forgiven each other?"

And now her eyes grew overbright, and I could have kicked myself all over again, except I knew she had forced this conversation for the same reason I had thought about it—neither of us wanted this or any other argument hanging over our heads. Her hand came to touch my cheek, and then she struggled to sit up. I let her.

"I'll always forgive you, Bracken Brine," she said. Then she stood and started hunting for clothes, shaking her underwear out of her jeans and free of grass before shimmying into it. "It's just that...." She paused, and her tears overflowed, and she hid this by brisk motions of putting on her jeans and fastening her bra and hunting for her other sock.

It was painful to watch.

"It's just what?" I reached above her head to retrieve the sock from the lime tree. I handed it to her and then pulled up my own jeans and did the fly.

She sat down and put her shoes and socks on, dashing tears off her cheeks as she did so. Then she looked up at me with swollen eyes and an expression of such tender pain that I had to swallow past a lump in my own throat. "I can forgive you as often as I need to, Bracken," she said after a moment, "but we keep having the same argument again and again and again, and we will keep having it until you forgive yourself—and him. I'll forgive you every goddamned time, but it will never be 'all good' between us until you forgive Adrian."

My breath caught in my throat, and the backlash, the denial of what she had just said, was so great that what came out of my mouth next was damn near unforgivable. "Funny you should mention that," I snapped, "because I could have sworn that what set you off in the first place was being pissed at Green."

Her face went shock white, and her eyes narrowed darkly in the paleness. "You're goddamned right I'm mad at Green," she breathed, seemingly pulled upright to standing by her words alone. "But when I'm ready to yell at Green, you can bet your ass I will be yelling at *Green* and not you, Bracken Brine. I may be young and stupid, but I think I can tell the two of you apart."

Goddess.

I took a step backward, awed by her anger—and my shame—and lowered my eyes. "I'm sorry," I said. "That was wrong of me."

She took a deep breath of her own and reached out, brushing my hand to get my attention. "Right backatcha."

"You don't pull your punches, do you, beloved?" I said gruffly and was rewarded by the slightest quirk of her lips.

"Right backatcha," she repeated, dusting off her bottom and taking another step away. "I've got to go get ready for banquet." She turned away toward the house.

"Cory, wait...." I felt helpless and bereft, even as she turned back. "Can I come with you?" Goddess, that sounded weak and silly. Then she smiled, a whole complete smile, and her face lit up and she extended her hand.

"I was hoping you would." She leaned her head against my shoulder (well, my upper arm) as we walked up to the house.

The silence was sweet but not meant to last, and eventually, as we showered and got ready for dinner, she filled me in on what Twilight had said about our enemy. I found myself appalled and sickened, especially when she suggested that she might have something in common with the abomination that had done so much harm.

"You're nothing like him!" I insisted. I was trying not to be angry, but I was still throwing her clothes on the bed with undue force.

She grunted with exasperation, and without comment started pulling on what I had picked out. "I didn't say I was about to start corrupting people's blood and blowing up were-animals," she retorted. "I just said... I guess if I had been angrier, and"—she glanced at me sideways, her face softening—"less inclined to love, then I could have been just as vile."

"Never," I said darkly. I didn't know how she could see such awfulness in herself when Green and Adrian and I had only ever seen the light.

She smiled at me, straightening her clothes, and it was that same soft smile she'd given me over her shoulder. "I love you forever, you know that?" she told me, then shook her head and took stock of herself in the bathroom mirror. "You have good taste," she said quietly, looking at the full cotton skirt and sweater that I'd pulled out for her. The skirt was cream colored, but the sweater was a rich forest green. She claimed to have no knowledge of how either garment had ended up in her closet, and I believed her—Green was very good at giving gifts. Now her fingers moved restlessly to her hair—I'd had the sprites curl it and pin parts of it up so that much of it fell down in little ringlets around her face and neck. It looked romantic and soft and things she didn't see herself as, but it was also stunning and lovely, and I could tell she liked it.

"I could say the same," I teased, and she gratified me with a laugh and leaned back into the circle of my arms, dropping her hands from her hair to rest them on my wrists.

There was a comfortable silence, one that grew weighty as something grew in her mind.

"What are you thinking?" I asked.

"Green told me about the thing with Adrian and the peaches," she said softly, and I groaned. She turned and kissed me on the cheek. "No, it was sweet. Sweet and chivalric and all sorts of things I can't help but admire—for both of you, actually. No, what I wanted to know was...."

She frowned and looked up at me, biting her lip.

"What?" I asked, still trying to overcome my embarrassment.

"What was it like to have Green so mad at you?"

I swallowed hard. "Horrible. But still not as bad as what I was feeling toward myself. Why?"

She looked down again and chewed on her lower lip. "No reason," she demurred, but it wasn't very reassuring, and my eyes grew wide and my heart thudded in my chest.

"Goddess, beloved—what have you done?"

"Nothing! I've just got this idea... but we'll discuss it at dinner." She smiled gamely.

A knock at the door saved her from more of my questions, but I was left looking forward to the banquet—which I usually enjoyed—with a slick, scaly knot of dread coiling in my stomach and ready to strike.

The knock on the door was Nicky. I realized that I must have missed him just a little when Cory threw her arms around him and kissed him soundly and passionately on the mouth and my jealousy didn't even peek out from under its complacent basket.

"Nicky, Goddess—I've missed you!" she said breathlessly when the kiss was done, and Nicky stepped back, touching his mouth with wonder and smiling just a little.

"I should leave more often," he said, his voice dazed, and she laughed.

"Since I know you can't be gone more than a month, you just go on ahead and do that!" she replied. Her voice was arch and friendly, and I could tell it wasn't quite the reply Nicky was hoping for. What did he think—that he'd go out and get laid and she'd sit here pining away with jealousy?

"Well, it doesn't have to be just every month…," he said nervously, casting a sideways glance at me.

She had her back to me, so I couldn't see her expression, but I wanted to kick him. It wasn't jealousy—not anymore. I'd overheard enough that night in the garden for me to know that Nicky was not a threat to her love for me. Her enjoyment of his touch didn't change that, and his explosion of sex in her head had been so uncomfortable for both of us that even I had to recognize I needed to work with him. His venturing out with new lovers proved he was trying to find a balance, just like we were. But his timing sucked, and whether it was because he was young and callow, or simply terribly self-involved, I suddenly wished my beloved had more than one man who knew when to speak and when to keep his mouth shut.

"No, it doesn't," she responded after a pause and an unhappy glance over at me. I nodded encouragement and she smiled back, and the moment lightened. "But we'll talk about that another time, okay." It wasn't a question, and I realized that the mask she wore in front of everyone but Green and me, the one that said she was in charge of any given situation, had gotten more opaque and detailed in the last three weeks as well. I was one of the privileged two allowed to see behind that mask, and it was troubling to watch her put it on so easily.

They walked arm in arm on the way down to the banquet, with a lot of awkward pauses when Nicky tried to talk about his new lovers. Cory, being Cory, could lighten the tension a little—*So, does Ellis have more or less finesse as a lover than as a vampire?* she asked archly, and Nicky's reply was an enthusiastic *More!*—and a step and a sentence at a time, the awkward moment, awkward *relationship*, seemed to even itself out as we neared the banquet hall. We were about halfway down the staircase when Cory disengaged herself from Nicky and pulled back so that I could take her arm, and I appreciated the gesture.

She beamed up at Green, who sat at the head of the table with Twilight and Grace and Arturo, and there must have been some level of reserve to her smile, because his gaze sharpened. As she moved in to kiss his cheek, he said quietly, "What have you been thinking, beloved?"

"Later," she replied. "Let's not spoil dinner."

"You'd better not spoil dessert either," Grace snapped, not letting the pseudoprivacy of the moment bother her.

Cory smiled winningly. "Are the boys here?" she asked, and Grace's soft smile was answer enough.

"They haven't stopped talking about you and the garden," she said softly. "Thanks, Cory. Being out of school, away from home—it's been a tough couple of weeks for them."

Cory nodded, and suddenly she was all excited young woman. "It was *awesome*. Green, you should have seen it—I had these big glowing shields around them, and they were bouncing in them...." She chatted on, and I nodded in the right places. She was right. Her display of power in the garden had been wonderful—controlled, lovely, fun. It was power the way Green used power in his gardens—practice and pleasure and happiness—and it was one of the things that had made me determined to possess her. I had needed to make her mine, to make her forgive me, when she came searching for me afterward. How could you not want all of that joy and magic in your arms, if it came willingly?

Now she snagged Green's hand and brought him over to the shape-changer table, where Nicky was sitting in a seat Renny had reserved for him, and we got there in time to hear Renny introduce Eric, who was dressed nicely in a sport coat and slacks. Of course Eric had always been a good dresser, even when he was wearing regulation teen angst, but even Renny herself was dressed nicely in a fancy embroidered pair of jeans and a sweater I knew she'd filched from Cory's closet. She spent her time sending Officer Max carefully neutral looks that didn't hide the fact that she was hungry for the sight of his face, and vice versa. Cory and I exchanged bland glances and ignored the byplay as Cory introduced Green to Grace's grandsons.

"We've heard about you!" Graeme said, and Gavin nodded enthusiastically.

"Everybody missed you when you were gone. You're the reason Cory can be a superhero."

Cory laughed and looked abashed. "Green's really the strongest superhero here," she said softly. "He made all those gardens and this house, and he keeps us all safe." A flush was rising to her cheeks, and Green caught my eyes, both of us laughing. She was embarrassed, and it was charming.

Green bent down to the boys and grinned. "I'll tell you a secret, my lads—Cory is really the best superhero here at the hill. She just doesn't know it yet."

"He called us 'lads.'" Gavin ooohhhed. "Are you from far away?"

Green blinked. He never noticed when his voice and his accent moved into the measures of his birthplace, and the sound of his North Country and his cockney and even his Lake District sounded so natural to the rest of us that I don't think anybody had ever mentioned it to him. "I was once," he replied, bemused, "but now I'm from here, right?"

Both boys nodded. "Right," they said in unison, and Green laughed and tousled their recently combed hair, then nodded to the rest of the table. He put a hand on Eric's shoulder and bent down to ask him something, and Eric nodded and gave me a warm smile that I returned. Then Grace called to us from across the room, which meant that dinner was about to be served, and we all went back to our seats.

Dinner was, of course, excellent. Grace and her well-trained crew didn't miss a step, and although I couldn't name half the stuff on my plate (and the only thing Cory could name was "beef"), it went down easy. But none of my enjoyment of the food could stop the feeling of apprehension that Cory was turning something around in her clever head, and that when it spun out, it would be both surprising and terrifying.

Per tradition, when dessert was over, people came up and spoke to Green, Arturo, Grace, and now Cory about whatever was on their minds. Since Adrian's death, the shape-changers had sort of adopted Grace as their own—which made sense, since Cory didn't feed from any of them and Grace did—but Cory, Grace, and Arturo had all been on the hill to consult, and there were few demands on them tonight. Tonight, most of the audiences were with Green.

There was a cadre of the sidhe who ran businesses who were under pressure from a developer stationed back East to sell the land their businesses were on. Green listened attentively to their situation and nodded decisively. "Right," he said after a moment. "That's tricky, but I think I've got a contact who happens to be right here who can make this go away." He looked over to Eric and signaled our old playmate over.

"Look who's the big business hotshot," I chided as he approached, and he grinned and shook my hand.

"Look who's all married and pussy-whipped now," he shot back, and I could feel my face burn while Cory burst out laughing next to me, spraying her water all over the table.

"That'll be the day!" she gasped. "Boy, Eric, did you get the wrong impression about the two of us."

He bent down and kissed her cheek. "No, little Goddess, I'd say I got just the right one." He straightened toward Green. "What can I do for you, leader?"

Green outlined the situation, and Eric nodded. "I can take care of it in the short term," he agreed. "But Green, this guy—Orland, right?— he's bad news. We can put him off for a bit, but one of these days he's going to be a threat to be dealt with."

Green frowned. "Goddess's get?" he asked.

"Not that I've heard," Eric replied thoughtfully, "but I'm pretty sure he knows about us. He only seems to put pressure on businesses like ours, where the ownership has something to hide."

Green nodded. "I'll listen for the name," he said after a moment. "But for now, if you could take care of it in the short term, we have more immediate concerns."

"Can you gimme hallelujah," I said, and the table laughed. Eric declined an offer to sit with us—I thought he was hoping to further his acquaintance with Nicky, myself—but promised me we'd talk later, and the next group rep came up for an audience with Green.

The banquet hall was clearing out, and Green was looking very relieved as what appeared to be the last of the fey who needed his counsel bowed gratefully and backed away. (It was a cave troll looking for some help digging out a new cave near the Avians' property at Camp Far West. His own cave had been taken over by developers, and the property out by Sheraton was pitted with old mineshafts that would make up a cave troll's dream home.) With eyes sharpened by intimate knowledge and intuition, he turned to Cory and said, "Now, beloved, I'd love to know what has been eating at you while we've been eating our dinner."

Cory gave that game smile again, but was let off the hook when Ellen Beth, hand in hand with Sweet, approached our table in the now half-empty hall.

She looked… well, I'm sure she looked as we all had looked last summer—dazed, devastated, too tired, too thin, too worn, and too full of her own grief to care about the welfare of anyone else. But Green had come out of his haze to lead, I had emerged to remember that I loved Cory, and Cory had pulled her heart out of her misery in order to save her own life and then save us all. But Ellen Beth was a long way from all of that. Green's hand on her cheek looked like infinite compassion, and as I remembered, felt like boundless tenderness.

"Hello, little sister," he said softly. "You must be Ellen Beth."

She nodded quietly. "You must be Green. Sweet keeps telling me you'll make everything all right."

Green grimaced and looked reproachfully at the tiny sidhe, who, instead of looking abashed, gave Green a sweet and sly smile. "Sweet exaggerates, little sister. But I will do what I can."

Ellen Beth nodded. "Please, Lord Green. The emptiness… it's destroying me…."

Green nodded. "Of course, Ellen Beth. But maybe there's something you can do for us first, yes? So no one has to suffer as you have?"

She nodded. "Whatever I can do, Lord Green."

Green looked over at Cory. "Beloved—do you have any questions?"

Cory nodded and stood up so Ellen Beth didn't have to move. "Ellen Beth, do you remember me?"

The shadow of the young woman Cory had brought home nearly a month ago nodded. "You kept me alive," she acknowledged. "You told me you'd help me want to live." That last was faintly accusatory.

"You will, Ellen Beth," Cory said softly, "but it will take time. And for you, I think it will take Green." Green put his hand on her shoulder, and she felt for it, squeezed, and then returned her concentration to the matter at hand. "Honey, I need you to remember for me—you told me that Jon Case was dead, right?"

The young woman nodded, her thin brown hair waving at her shoulders.

"Could you tell me what he looked like?"

Ellen Beth blinked. It was such a simple request. "He was really cute," she said, half laughing, like it surprised her to remember. "In his early thirties. He was going back to school for his teaching degree. He had…

I don't know... hair like a surfer—brown and gold, right? Dimples at the cheeks. He looked young until you noticed the lines at his eyes."

"What did he wear?" Cory asked. Suddenly I knew where she was going with this, but I couldn't even guess what it could mean.

"Casual, I guess." That wispy smile, surprised at itself, crossed her lips. "SoCal—big shorts, sweatshirts.... If it wasn't so cold, he would have been wearing Hawaiian shirts and tank tops, I guess."

Cory nodded. "Thanks, sweetie, I think that's all. Oh, wait... one more thing."

Ellen Beth looked at her expectantly, any resistance or spirit erased from her body by grief. I thought of Cory, making the decision to go to school in San Francisco in order to reassure all of us at home that she was okay. It occurred to me, not for the first time, that Cory's strength was as important to her as her raw force of will.

"I need to know where he lived," Cory asked gently, and Ellen Beth nodded.

"I have his address in my purse. It's in my...." She looked at Sweet, flushed. "Our... Sweet's room."

Cory nodded. "Tomorrow will be fine," she said with compassion. Then she leaned forward and whispered in Ellen Beth's ear, something so low that even I couldn't hear it, but I could tell from Green's expression that he heard and approved.

He bent forward and kissed Ellen Beth's forehead, then looked at Sweet. "I'll see you both later tonight, if you wish," he said softly, and Sweet nodded, looking relieved. I knew from watching Green that healing a heart so sodden with grief was exhausting—Sweet obviously needed a little backup. "Give me a few hours, right? A little after midnight, then."

The women nodded, and Sweet led Ellen Beth out of the banquet room. Green turned back to Cory. "What?"

Cory smiled a little and raised her eyebrows. "He's not bound to anything, Green—not even his own body."

Green cocked his head and nodded, awaiting more explanation, and our little Goddess didn't disappoint.

She sighed and gathered her words. "Okay—see, the thing is— when he attacked us, he was using Jon Case's body." She glanced at me. "Bracken wouldn't remember, because the bad guy... fogs up sidhe vision with his evil, I guess. But what Ellen Beth just described to me was the same guy whose heart Brack ripped out a week ago. If you want to make sure, ask Mario and LaMark over here for a description."

"We believe you," Green said, nodding, and across from us Twilight nodded.

"It makes sense," Twilight said.

"And what he does to us…. Green, didn't you say the sylphs were, well, piles of dust after he was through with them?" Green nodded, and she went on. "Well, what he does to the werecreatures is similar. He… unmakes them. The force of the Goddess that holds their bodies together, he takes that. It's sort of a crossover. He wanted to be a vampire—but he had sidhe power, so he's a power vampire as well. It's what he did to Twilight… it's what happened to Chris Williams. Hell, it's what happened to Chuck Granger—except it's not his body that's unraveling, it's his personality. It was easy with Chuck, because even he's blind to what holds him together, but… well, you get the picture."

We nodded—it all made sense.

"It's his need," Twilight said softly. "His hunger, his want—he has no morality, no sense of self, no sense of… allegiance to any idea or person or group. He's not human, not sidhe, not even a proper vampire. He's not attached to anything, and he has enough power that this… lack of attachment… has become his…." The lovely, sad sidhe struggled for words.

"It's his power," Arturo said bluntly. "His power is to unmake things." Everyone who'd stayed conscious during Hollow Man's attacks looked at each other, remembering the thing that I couldn't. "He's very good at it."

"He is," Cory agreed roughly. "And once he's unbound a soul from a body, I think he can use the body as his own."

"Do you think his own body still exists?" Grace asked thoughtfully.

Cory shrugged, nodded, looked at Twilight for confirmation. He nodded too. "I think it must," Twilight said softly. "He's not immortal, not the way sidhe are. He's too self-involved, I think, to be able to release his hold on his own body."

"And he had somewhere to go," Cory added, looking at me, and now it was my turn.

"That's true. We destroyed Jon Case's body—it was over and done with. But he said he'd be back. I think he must have a place… a lair. Someplace to put his body and return to it when he needs it."

Cory blinked and turned to Twilight. "Brother, how long ago did he unmake you?"

It was Twilight's turn to blink. "I don't know, pretty human girl," he said after a moment. "My time on the streets—one big blur. And time runs differently as a sidhe... one lover to the next, you know?"

Cory grimaced and chewed on her lip. "Well, I'd place a bet that he's achieved what he wanted to—that he doesn't age or anything. But since he seems so... unattached, I guess... it would be a shame to risk his body when he can invade someone else's."

There was a grim silence at the table. This was a formidable enemy indeed. Then Cory cocked her head for a moment, as though something had just occurred to her. "I bet he's in his own body when he attacks us at night," she said thoughtfully. "Like when we were at the store that time. I bet he uses another body in the day."

"What makes you say that?" I asked.

She shrugged. "A guess, really. I don't know. It's just... I'd think he'd just be more comfortable in his own body at night—especially as a vamp." She laughed, self-conscious for the first time since she'd begun the discussion. "Maybe it's just a silly human thing."

Green smiled kindly. "I doubt it," he said softly. "Your instincts on these things are usually pretty accurate. I would imagine the question now is what can we do about him? If he rarely attacks us in a body that's his own, how do we destroy him?"

Cory sucked in a breath, as though shoring up her courage, and said, "Well, I have an idea...." And suddenly Grace looked at her in horror.

"Don't say it!" she said bluntly, and we all looked at her in surprise. "Don't say it, Cory!" Grace demanded, ignoring the rest of us. "You can't. I know what you're thinking, and nobody at the table will let you do it—and it's just better off unsaid."

Cory blinked and gave Grace a gentle little smile. "Don't worry, Grace, we're just tossing ideas out here. It's not like I'm going to raid Ellen Beth's purse and track down the address, then rush over there and give it a try. I just had an idea and thought I'd run it by people, that's all."

Grace, rock solid Grace, who dealt with her obnoxious, bitchy daughter with calm and, well, grace, suddenly stood up and started wiping down the table, the expression on her face furious and frustrated and terrified. "Well, I'm not even going to listen to it," she said angrily. "And when Green and Bracken tie you to the fucking bed to keep you from trying it, I'm holding the goddamned ropes." And with that she turned around and stalked away, leaving the rest of us blinking after her, completely stunned.

Cory looked at Arturo and made shooing motions, and Arturo looked torn. "I really want to hear your idea, Corinne Carol-Anne...," he said in a pained voice. "Anything that could piss her off that much has got to be entertaining, at the very least."

"I'm sure it's a laugh riot," Green said, his voice flinty, and Cory cringed. "I think we should all hear it before Arturo goes and makes sure Grace is okay."

Cory blew out a breath. "It's just an idea, people. I mean, think about it. This guy... he's sort of like an anti-me, right? He's a human with power who's gone all wrong, you know? He craves immortality. I know it's not the answer. He unmakes people, unbinds them. I just spent a significant amount of power helping to bind us all to Green. And every night I go to the vampire quarters and blood more of our people and bind them to me even tighter. I was just thinking that... if I blooded this guy... he'd be bound to us. He'd be assailable, right?"

"Jesus," Arturo breathed. He looked at Green, who was flushing from his throat up, and then at me—and I don't know what my face looked like, but between the two of us, he sat up hurriedly and said, "I'm going to go calm Grace down." And with that, he grabbed Twilight's arm. For a relative newcomer, Twilight must have had a sense of things here at the hill, because he practically leaped out of his chair, and then it was just the three of us and Green's terrible anger.

"No," he said flatly. "No."

"It's just an id...."

"NO!" he thundered, and she winced, not exactly surprised—I thought because (although she was careful not to talk about things like this) she had seen Green angry before. "*You will not put yourself at risk like this for just an idea!*"

She gasped, and her eyes grew bright. Then she took a deep cleansing breath and stood her ground. "I don't think I would be," she said softly. And then, stronger because Green's eyes, usually tranquil and warm, had actually started to throw off sparks—not just an expression in our species—she added, "Green, listen—"

"I will not let you—"

"Just listen to me!" she all but shouted. She almost risked a look at me but decided against it—which was probably a good thing, because I was starting to catch Green's anger, and I'm often angry and knew she would see it flushing on my throat and blazing in my eyes. How dare she?

"Both of you, just listen!" she said, softer now—but it didn't matter, because everyone still in the banquet hall (mostly at the shape-shifter table) was now riveted to the unforeseen drama at the head table, and in this hill, nobody would walk away to give us even the illusion of privacy.

"Green, Bracken's life depends on mine. I know that...," she said softly, tears trembling at her voice.

"So does—"

"Shhh... shhh...." She moved forward, to the space of lovers instead of combatants, and held her hand to his lips. "Don't say it, beloved. Don't say it. I know... in my heart I know, and I refuse to believe it's true because you must live forever. You must. I can't live at all unless I believe that, okay? So don't say it... but I know. Our existence, as precarious as it is, relies on all three of us, okay? For better or worse, we're bound together so tightly, by so many strings of love, that if one of us dies, the rest of us... we're doomed." Now tears broke in her voice and my anger faded, but Green's anger was still there, unreasonable, panicked, sparking from his eyes and making his breath quick in his chest. "So do you think for a minute that I would risk my life—that I would risk *our* lives—on something that *might* work? On an idea? Green, beloved, it was an idea. It's a possibility. It needs to be thought about, because if something as simple as a vampire blooding could keep this guy from killing any more of us, it should be considered. Isn't that what you've always taught me? That whatever we need to do to protect our people should be considered?"

"Not you," he said rawly. "Risking you is no longer an option." His voice rose again, and she stepped back, away from his anger and pain and unreasoning panic. "*By the Goddess, Corinne Carol-Anne, I will have your word on this!*"

She closed her eyes and fought for control. "I... I don't know how to fight with you, Green. It's not something we do. You need... I've...."

She choked on a sob and her face crumpled, and I sighed and put my face in my hands. Dammit. Goddess fuck it all. Couldn't one of us comfort her tonight? "I've got an anniversary to honor…," she choked out, and then she turned from both of us and fled up the stairs.

"Aww, fuck," Green groaned, and even though I blurred to get in front of him, he had taken two steps in her direction before he ran into me with enough force to almost knock me on my ass.

"Goddess, Green… leader… no. Give her space. Between you and me today, I think she's had enough of freaked-out elves, you know?"

"Right," he said, dazed. "Right. Of course." But his body was still straining against mine to follow her. From behind me I heard someone running up the stairs. At the last second, Green looked away, and I knew without looking that Nicky had gone outside to hopefully do what the two of us could not.

The tension sighed from him in a rush, and he sank to his chair with a helpless little sound in his throat. I joined him, my hand solidly on his shoulder. It occurred to me, distantly, how much we all seemed to need from Green, and how rarely he seemed to need something from us, and the honor of being allowed to comfort him was suddenly terrifying.

"What did she mean by that?" he asked after a moment. "About having an anniversary?"

I shook my head. "I got nothin'. I know last night she was wondering what the date was."

Green nodded. "Did you have any idea what she was plan—"

"Not a clue," I broke in vehemently.

"Why would she—how could she even think—why would she even dream about putting herself in danger like that?" He was completely amazed, and if I hadn't spent the last three weeks sharing most waking and all sleeping moments with her, I might have been too.

"Green…," I said hesitantly. "Leader, she's just trying… I mean, can't you see that she's just trying to be you?"

He recoiled like I'd slapped him. Hard. "I never asked her to do that," he protested, shocked.

"I know you didn't," I replied as gently as I knew how. "None of us did. You just… you had to have been here for the last three weeks and watched her try so hard to… to get a handle on things. To be our leader because you left her in charge."

"I left all of you in charge!" He was beginning to sound a little angry, and I couldn't blame him.

"I know it," I said bleakly. "She was just best suited for the job, that's all."

He sighed again, scrubbing his hand over his face. "I think what disturbs me the most is this... assumption... that she and this Hollow Man are related somehow. That they share a kinship beyond the obvious, you know?"

I nodded, remembered her run-in with Chuck Granger, and had an answer, but not one he'd like hearing. "That detestable asshole...," I began, "the one she ran into at school...." I shivered, not even wanting to put it into words. "Humans are stupid, Green. That fucker thought she was trash, and he's not even worth the ground she spits on. She grew up with that. I mean... I didn't really understand until her mother came crashing into the store wanting to know how she's screwed up her life now, but people—humans—they've undervalued Cory practically since she drew in her first breath. That's why she thinks she has to prove something to us. That's why she thinks she has more in common with Hollow Man than we can ever see. She's been told it exists."

Green shuddered, and for a moment I thought he might actually be ill, physically ill, at the table. But he was our leader, and he was all that was compassion and strength, and he swallowed hard and nodded. "I forget sometimes," he said, his voice distant, "how brutal the human world is. I mean, we can be cold...." He looked me in the eyes, and we both nodded. We'd both been touched by sidhe frost on our hearts. "Bitterly cold, but humans... brutal. Emotionally brutal. Physically brutal...." He shook his head, came back to the present, looked me in the eyes. "But we can't allow her to pay the price for the brutality of her species, brother." He closed his eyes again, and now he was seeing something I could just tell I'd never seen. "I... I could not survive if another beloved had to do that."

He wasn't talking about Adrian, and I wanted to ask, but I found my tongue had bound itself to the roof of my mouth. What came out when it had unstuck itself was both wise and awkward. "I forget, leader, how many years you've lived."

A ghost of a smile touched Green's lips. "I do too—when I'm holding her." Ah, Goddess. Then he shook himself, and the Green we all loved was sitting by me, when a broken, confused man had been in his place. "Brother, it's times like this when I wish we could drink ourselves blind."

I laughed a little, but my humor was not as strong as my leader's. "Leader, it's times like this when I wish I could still offer flesh as comfort," I said formally.

Green inclined his head. "And it would be formidable comfort, indeed," he said with a profound gratitude and a wink. Then he rose from his chair and said, "But I've waited long enough, and now, I think, I should go apologize to our beloved." And he headed for the stairs. He put his foot on the first step and turned to me. "Is there… anything you'd like me to tell him… while I'm out there?" he asked delicately.

I closed my eyes and shook my head. "No." But my voice was weaker than it had been on this issue. "Not yet."

"Fair enough," he agreed. "Peace, brother. I'll have her back to you before midnight."

With that he was gone, leaving me alone at the table, sincerely wishing the same thing he just had. Some nights it really would be helpful to be human and able to drink myself blind.

NICKY
Giving Up and Looking Up

I'D GONE thundering up the goddamned granite stairs like some sort of idiot on a white charger when I heard another voice echoing from the crown of the hill.

I was so surprised that I instantly turned into a bird.

I flew into the Goddess's grove in a swish of silent feathers and perched in the branches of one of the biggest oak trees, looking down in shock at the two figures sitting close on Adrian's marble memorial bench.

The one who wasn't the love of my life was nearly transparent, and the memory of moon-white hair fluttered under her careful fingers.

"You're so upset, luv…. I don't know how to comfort you…," Adrian was saying. (It must have been Adrian—was there any other ghost with white hair who would be comforting Cory in this place?) He sounded distraught, and I was a little surprised. Weren't ghosts supposed to be either angry or at peace? Stupid question. I shook my head, bird style, fluffing the feathers at my neck.

"It's okay," Cory sniffled. "I mean… he's been furious with all of us at one time or another. He only gets this mad at people he loves, right?" A breath of air was forced from her. "Either that or people he's about to kill."

"Well, I think you're going to live." Adrian had the same dry humor Green did, I thought in shock. I don't know why this surprised me. I guess… I guess I had expected a saint. Saint Adrian, patron of lost souls, converter of the damned to the saved, Goddess-style.

"Hope so," Cory replied, her voice growing sharp and spirited. "Thanks to Bracken, I'm starting to like makeup sex."

Adrian's ghost laughed outright, and the feathers down my back stood to attention. He sounded like bells. His laugh was followed by a sweet and comfortable silence, which Adrian broke by saying, "So, luv… happy anniversary?"

Cory nodded. "Yeah…." She had been huddled on the bench—her eyes focused on the transparent hands resting on her own warm human ones, I thought. Now she looked at Adrian's face, and I could see the honest, bittersweet smile on her tearstained face. "Here's to the day I finally looked up."

"I'm so glad you did," he said quietly—almost too quiet for even my bird senses to register.

"Are you sure, Adrian?" she asked, her voice low. "I mean, I put you through hell... and then.... I mean, you might still be... well, here, if I hadn't been on that hill."

"You know what love is—right, luv? It's when you're more afraid of losing love than losing life...."

She laughed, and it was a bittersweet sound. "I said those exact words to Bracken about two months ago."

"And how is fuckhead, then?" Adrian asked, and I was so surprised at the epithet that I almost screeched. Cory wasn't surprised at all. She laughed, and again the sound was bittersweet. I wondered, there in the night filled with the smell of prey and the feel of wind, when I'd last heard her make a truly happy sound, without words to back it up.

"He's...." She sighed. "He's picking fights with me that he needs to be having with you, A," she said after a moment. "But he's also being truly wonderful, and... so wise. I mean, he was probably always wise, but... we don't always see it, because he's got such stiff competition, you know?"

"I wasn't wise tonight," Green said softly from the trapdoor, and I fluttered my feathers in surprise. It was a good thing all of the players in this little drama had better things to think about than me, I thought miserably. I didn't want to be here, I so didn't want to be here—but here I was, and I found it impossible to look away. Adrian was beautiful, I thought in awe, with that new sensibility I'd developed since I'd spent nights in Green's arms. He had pointed features, cheekbones so prominent they were almost elven, wide-spaced eyes, and a pointed, poignant vulnerability to his translucent expressions. He was beautiful, and wry, and human. And he'd given his life (or undeath) to save the two people I now loved best in the world. How did I compete against that, how *could* I compete against that, when all I ever wanted was to live, to live and to love and to know that the people I loved with all my heart loved me back?

"Impossible for you not to be wise, beloved," Cory said back. I saw her hand reach instinctively for Adrian's, and Adrian reach back, and when their hands touched... nothing. A wave of pain so intense I could almost hear it rolled off of woman and ghost powerfully enough to almost knock me off my perch in the sky.

"I hate to interrupt your anniversary," Green said, striving for lightness, "but I can't for the life of me think what it could be the anniversary of."

Cory laughed, the bittersweet sound that was starting to make me cringe. I could suddenly see why elves hated deception of any kind. That laugh alone was a lie, an attempt to deflect us all from whatever she was really feeling. Would the Goddess strike an elf with nausea and cramps for a laugh like that?

"The end of my blindness and the beginning of my stupidity," she said harshly, and a translucent hand reached ineffectually to stroke her face. I realized that although I couldn't see her face from this angle, I could see her beloved's eyes. They were the most amazing shade of blue—so blue they were the only real color in the moonlight, and I could see them from my perch in a tree overhead.

"The beginning of your awakening, Corinne Carol-Anne," Adrian's ghost said softly. "That's nothing to be ashamed of."

"I'd worked at your gas station for a year and a half, Green," she said in a harsh whisper. "A year and a half, right? And one night I look up and Arturo touches my hand, and holy shit, there's this whole world out there I never imagined. And the next week I look up, and there's Adrian. And he's beautiful, and he seems to think I'm pretty interesting, but… I didn't believe him. I mean… how could I be that interesting? It had to be a scam, right?"

"Oh, my loves…," Green said. "A—how could you let her do this to herself?"

"I can't seem to stop her, beloved," Adrian said, and there was an edge of exasperation, of humor, to his voice that would have made me break cover if I were in human form. But birds can't really laugh, not even in surprise, so I was safe.

"So he's got to court me, right?" Cory said, right over them. "He's got to court me, and badger me, and every night I go home and dream of him and wonder about him, and suddenly every thought, every wish I've ever had about love and sex and wanting is centered on him, but… but I looked up in February, right? So a year ago, I looked up and saw him. But Green, I was too scared to reach for him until nearly May. And I didn't know…."

"None of us knew…," Green soothed, but she was distraught, and I couldn't blame her. The news of her fight with Bracken had spread like wildfire, and we'd all seen her fight with Green, and now here she was—lost, lost in a past that would forgive her, had forgiven her, if only she would let it.

"But I'm mortal. Of all of us, shouldn't I have known? Shouldn't I have guessed that there's not enough time, that there's never enough time—and that looking up isn't enough, looking up is never enough, you have to give too? You have to risk, and you have to give of yourself, or you'll never get anything back? I was so afraid to give him any part of me, Green, so afraid to give him my heart that I almost missed the chance to see what he could give me...."

Green and Adrian shared a look that broke my heart. Then Green's real, warm, and living arms were around her shoulders, and Adrian was a breath of a kiss on her brow and a fade of translucent pain into the trees.

"That's all I wanted to do...," Cory sobbed. "I wanted to give you peace, and your hill peace, because you've given me everything, and I just wanted to give you an end to this, to give you something, anything, to make you happy...."

"You want to give me something?" Green asked roughly, and if my feathers hadn't been sticking straight up already they would have ruffled up on their own, because his voice was angry and taut and urgent and throbbing with desire. Anything or anyone within a hundred-mile radius must have just flushed and swollen to simply be near the same air I was breathing.

"Anything...," she said, her voice equally rough, and all of a sudden I *really* needed to get the hell out of that garden.

"Then give me," he groaned and took her mouth with his own, and she returned the kiss fiercely, their rush potent and sensual and painful and all of the things I had never felt from either of them. Their kiss broke, and she trembled as he framed her face with his hands. "Give me," he said again, and their next kiss was even hotter, even more potent. Then she was kissing her way down his newly bared chest, and his shaking hands were both pushing on her head and trying to pull her up in that conflict of wants that I recognized but had never felt.

Cory wanted just as much as Green. She wanted to give and give and give, and she kissed her way down to his pale, soft stomach and bit sharply. His knees buckled, and he sat heavily on the marble bench behind him. Then his belt was undone, and then his slacks, and then his cock was bare and bright and palely jutting from his crotch in the moonlight, the head darker and glistening slickly.

"Give me...," he ordered roughly, and I couldn't remember him ever ordering me to do anything when we were together. The trust and the need would have made me weep if I had been human.

"Anything...," she promised around the head of his cock, and he groaned and knotted his hand in her hair and pushed, and she resisted. Instead, she licked and tasted and nibbled and then devoured, her lips burrowing in the golden hair at Green's groin and then riding up him to lick and taste and nibble again. My breathless silence, my terrible arousal, my shameful secret witness was interrupted by a soft, reproachful, birdlike sound. I looked up to see Mario in bird form, his head angrily cocked to one side and his beak gesturing imperatively to the night sky, which is where we should have been.

I nodded, dazed, and we both launched into the air, but for me there was no joy in flying, only desperate flight. I soared, I fled, I ran in flight, and Mario followed from a distance, powerful and calm on bigger wings and calmer wind.

Eventually I tired and turned back for home, touching down on the center lawn, the one you could see from Green's sitting room. It made me think human thoughts, and in a rush and a turn, I no longer wanted to be a bird. In a skin-shifting ruffle, I was standing barefoot in the garden.

"Aww, shit!" I said, trying to still my pounding emotions, my rushing heart. "I lost my shoes in trans." We did that sometimes—our clothes were carried in the oils from our feathers, and if we didn't concentrate, or if we taxed ourselves too severely, the oil got thin and something had to go.

"I wasn't wearing any in the first place," Mario said brightly. "So did you get to see enough, or should we put some fiber optics in their room?" he added, an edge of anger to his voice.

"I didn't mean to...," I choked, feeling infinitely stupid. "I went up to... I don't know, comfort her, after her thing with Green. I mean, she got into a *fight*, with *Green*, right? So Bracken's busy taking care of Green, and... I'm the third string, it's time for me to play, right?"

"I don't think she does birds," Mario said flatly, and I shook my head, wondering if I could justify my presence in that holy place to Mario or to anybody.

"Did you know Adrian haunts the garden?" I whispered.

He'd been pacing in front of me like an angry father, and that stopped him. "Adrian? Like Saint Adrian?"

I laughed, and it was the same sound I'd heard coming from Cory's throat. "The one and only. I was so goddamned surprised when I heard them talking that I turned."

And now Mario laughed, and unlike me, he was truly amused. "Well...," he said, gesturing helplessly. "I guess. Why not, right?" I nodded, but then he remembered he was outraged again. "But after that—why not fly away?"

I just looked at him, and he thought about it for a minute. Suddenly his anger faded, and he sank to ground, bare feet tucked under his knees— and as suddenly as we went from bird to human, he went from outraged father to good friend. "Yeah... a chance to see Saint Adrian himself. I guess I'd violate a little bit of privacy to see that."

Well, I might as well finish, I thought sadly. He knew how much I'd seen as it was. "And after that, I don't know. I guess I was just so hungry to see them, and...." My voice broke. I wondered if I had ever been a man. "They glowed," I rasped, sinking miserably down in the grass next to Mario.

"I know," Mario said, not surprised in the least. "If you go by her room when she's with Bracken, you can see a light show coming from under the door."

That so did not make me feel better. "She doesn't glow with me," I said painfully. "Green doesn't glow with me. Together, they practically set the sky on fire. But not with me."

Mario sighed. "Jesus," he said, and scrubbed his face with his hands. "Jesus, Nicky. Okay, we can't pretend we didn't see it, right? And I'll be honest, it was the most erotic thing... one of the most beautiful goddamned things I've ever seen. I can't even wish I could take it back, brother. I wish I could, but I can't. But what you've got to ask yourself, see, is what did you learn by being graced with something like that?"

"Learn?" I echoed stupidly. I heard another presence coming up beside us in the night, listening unashamedly from behind a tree nearby, but I was in no position to judge or be angry about eavesdroppers right now, so I let it be.

"It's like—I know your folks are still together, and still happy as far as you know, right?"

I nodded. They'd been writing, wanting to meet my mate. I'd put them off with one thing or another, because the situation was so beyond their understanding.

"Well, my dad raised me. I mean, my mom was still alive, but she was human—the whole bird thing freaked her out. So by the time I was old enough to figure it out, it was like, once a month my dad went by her place when her real husband was at work, and she lifted her housecoat, bent over the counter, and he threw her some money on the table and left."

My stomach turned. "Eww," I said quietly.

"Yeah. Eww. I waited a long goddamned time for Beth. I wasn't waiting for a female Avian, because the odds of that were... astrofuckinomical, right? So you can imagine my shock when I found one. But I was waiting for... someone. Someone special. And it's okay... well, not okay, but it's like, even though we didn't have that long together, I'm okay with waiting, because she was special and it was worth it, right?"

I nodded. I'd been waiting for someone special as well, and I'd thought I found her. When it turned out she didn't want me back, I thought I'd get over it and move on. Life didn't always work out like we planned.

"I know what happened to you. Being bound to Green and Cory when neither of them wanted you—I know it sucks. It was a... metafuckingphysical accident, and it sucked, and you're thinking there's nothing you can do about it." And here Mario turned to me, his brown eyes fathomless in the dark. "But the thing is, Nicky, you've got a lot to be thankful for, and you don't even seem to realize it."

I blinked. No one—not even Leah, whose entire presence on the trip had been brutally frank—had actually said this to me. "Yeah?" I asked.

Mario nodded. "Yeah." Rock solid and sure. "And not just because you get to lay anything with a pulse—although you'd better believe me when I tell you that's about all the rest of us are talking about now."

I flushed. "I didn't realize everybody knew," I said quietly.

"Are you kidding? After Leah got back, you're lucky she didn't take an ad out in the *Auburn Journal*."

I felt marginally better. Cory and Green hadn't been talking, at least.

"She said you were having a blast, and we were happy for you. I mean... half of the reason Green left the hill was to see if that whole binding thing with the sylphs would work. And I had a word with him before dinner, and he said it might—you know, Tommy and Dennis, LaMark—they might not have to, like, doom themselves in order to love the people they want, and I'm so goddamned overwhelmed with what Green has done for us that I can barely look at him, you know? We've got a leader here who will work to make us happy. Goddess—you remember Goshawk? We were so desperate for a leader that we followed that douche bag, and now we've got Green. That's luck in itself. And he's not just taking care of us as a people, he's taking care of you as an individual, and that's pretty fucking special. And on top of that, you get, like, every Avian's secret wet dream. You get to have your Twinkies and eat them too—with both kinds of cream filling. I mean, I'm seventy freaking years old and still in my sexual prime—don't think I haven't thought about it a time or two."

I looked at him in total shock. Mario looked twenty-five. We didn't age until we mated, which meant....

"Yeah—I was a sixty-five-year-old virgin before I found Beth." He was quiet then. "She was just barely past the age of maturity when we met. I never told her how old I was. I had just enrolled in college because I'd been a no-count chulo my whole long life, and I liked school so much I kept going even after she died. And I'm still going because I like the classes and I like the company, and I really like the idea of doing what Cory's doing and learning something that will help Green on the hill—and if you tell anyone that, I'll deny it."

"Of course," I said, feeling both humbled and miserable. Was everybody here a better human being than I was?

"So here's the deal. You get to live every bird-man's sexual fantasies, and you get to share the bed of a really good-looking man-god whenever he's feeling lonely—and he has his choice of bed partners, including his beloved whom he adores, so that's saying something. And once a month, this really pretty girl whom you love unrequitedly gets dressed up to go on the town. She smiles at you, dances with you, makes you feel special, and then she puts out to save your life. But she never rubs it in. She never makes you pay. She doesn't just hike up her housecoat and bend over. She treats you like a friend. She treats you like a lover, even. And just because she doesn't lie to you, you've forgotten how good your life is."

"Excellent," I said bitterly. "I'm an ungrateful shit—I get it."

"No, man—you really don't. What were you looking at out there tonight? What did you see that you don't see in the movies, or in bed with Leah or Willow or Ellis? What was it out there that broke our hearts?"

I thought about it. I thought about it so long that the silence lengthened, and my bird senses were still tuned to the night, so I heard our unseen companion sigh. It sounded sympathetic, and for some reason that made it easier for me to speak the truth.

"Giving," I said after a moment, "because they'd give anything for each other. Cory and Bracken and Green... all three of them... they're so bound together with love that it hurts them not to give."

Mario nodded. "So, brother—you've had a shitty deal, and I'm not here to dispute that. I'm not here to make you feel bad about it or to tell you to buck up because it could be worse, because you're a smart kid—you know it could be worse, and you know that what makes it worse is that you've got a front row seat to so much better. But what you've got to ask yourself is this—what do you have to give to these people?"

"I'm a human battery, Mario," I said, and I wasn't even bitter about this, because a small part of me thought it was sort of cool. "Doesn't that count?"

Mario sighed. "Nicky—is it raining here?"

"No...."

"Well, it's raining or sleeting or snowing all over the rest of fucking NorCal... but it's not raining on our heads. Why the hell is that?"

"Green controls the weather," I said. It felt silly to say it, even though we all knew it was true.

"It's what he does. It's his power, acting on his land. We don't even count that as giving, right? So, no—being a human battery doesn't count. What else can you give?"

I put my head in my hands. "I don't know, Mario. I don't have a fucking clue. That's half the problem—I don't have anything I can give to them. They don't love me like they love each other, and I don't have anything I can give to make that better...."

"Oh yes, you do, Nicky. Don't you see? The one thing you can give to them—to Cory, to Green, even to Bracken, who, I think, has shown a great deal of restraint in not strangling you for just breathing his woman's air—is your acceptance of the situation at hand, you know? Just accept. It will stop hurting you, and you will stop hurting them, and when all that hurt has gone away, it will just be you and the people you love and maybe a little joy left to spare, right?"

"Yeah," I whispered. "Yeah." Because he was right. He was wise and right, and I should know it by now, but what you tell your heart and what it tells you are not always the same thing. I sighed and looked around me.

On Green's hill, at least, it was a good night. Chilly, so I was glad for my sweater and quick metabolism, but only a little misty, so I thought maybe I could stay out there on the lawn near the little grove of trees and the pool for a while without freezing my ass off. As we sat there in the quiet, scenting the night, we heard the figure nearby in the grove of trees move just a little, in a way that spoke of great patience.

That seemed to be Mario's cue. He stood and gripped my shoulder. "Think about it, brother," he said softly. "I'm going to go flying, because Green's going to let it piss rain all day tomorrow, and I won't get too much of a chance." He took a few steps and then turned, nodding toward where our watcher sat waiting. "And Nicky—remember that of all the things they've given you, kindness is the most important."

"I never forget it," I said, but I nodded as well—because now I knew who was in the grove, and I knew what Mario was trying to tell me, and it shamed me that he'd think I would be such a self-involved prick as to be cruel to a guy who had only treated me with kindness since the four of us in the care package had all spilled into Green's hotel room a week ago, exhausted, charged, and giddy with our own sexual daring.

And then Mario was a bird—a much bigger bird than me, with a wingspan that defied the eyes and handsome mocha-colored wings. He was so strong and so beautiful in the night sky that it was just a pleasure to watch him lift gracefully into the air and disappear into the dark.

When Mario's last wing flutter had died, ghostlike, against the mist, I got up and moved to the little grove of trees, where Eric sat looking meditatively into the small clear pool of water in the middle. Deciding he'd been patient enough, I flopped down next to him with a grunt—sort of that all-American male greeting that we know and understand.

"Your friend is very wise," he said quietly.

"Yeah," I agreed. Mario and I had hardly said two words to each other while we'd served under Goshawk for nearly six months. Now he was my friend. "People surprise you that way."

"Mmm. Cory surprised me. I was kind of hoping I wouldn't like her, you know." I turned to him, eyebrows raised, hoping he'd go on. "I mean... I left the hill twenty years ago because I was falling in love with them—all of them. Bracken, Adrian, Green—I didn't want to be the only one not invited to the banquet table, right?"

Brother, did I know that. "Right."

"But then, Grace always cooks a little rich for my blood during banquet, anyway," he said with a sweet laugh. Maybe it just takes time for the bitter to fade from the sweet, I thought hopefully. Maybe Cory and I wouldn't always sound like we were eating our hearts with wormwood for salt.

"What would you rather eat?" I asked, not sure if the question was inane or profound.

"Rabbit," he said promptly, his boyish face alight with a coyote's glee.

"Me too! Cooked or raw?" I was laughing, because it was the first time it occurred to me that a predator was a predator whether it flew on wings or padded around on furry feet.

"That depends, now, doesn't it?" He looked at me slyly, sideways, as he laughed, and for maybe the first time in my life I realized that, when it wasn't a matter of life or death or mate or murder, flirting was fun.

"Yeah...." I trailed off because I didn't have a funny answer to that. Suddenly all my contact with Cory reared its brutally frank head, and I found that I badly wanted to talk honestly to this kind man. "Why did you come out here, Eric?" I asked, a painful longing in my voice. I wanted... I wanted this nice man to want me, I thought with a bump in my heart.

"Oh, Goddess...." He laughed, and although he was much older than me, his voice cracked like a teenager's. "I'm always so nervous at this part, you know?"

So was I. "It's weird...," I said, not able to look at him. I concentrated on the still pond in the moonlight instead, and was not altogether reassured when I was suddenly reminded of Bracken and Adrian. "I mean... all that time in the hotel room, and on the road... you'd think we could just... do this...." We had been naked together—had been *inside* each other, if it came to that. But the orgy had ended when we arrived home, and the others had gone their ways easily enough. Not Eric. He'd slept—truly slept—in my bed last night. We had both been exhausted from the trip, but we hadn't touched or spooned or even given any acknowledgment of the sexual frenzy we'd just spent our last week in. But Eric had said good morning to me as I'd left for school, and had been one of the first people I'd seen when I'd come home. Eric had been kind and funny, and he seemed to know firsthand what it was like to have a front row seat to the banquet but to not savor the taste.

"It's different," he said, and I could smell the nervousness in his voice. It made my desire stronger. "There's a difference between tumbling around naked like socks in a dryer, and…."

"And making a pass at someone you like," I finished for him.

"And making a pass at someone you want," he corrected from a gruff throat.

"It feels good to be wanted," I said, risking a look at him. He was nearly twenty years older than me, but he looked… he looked young. He looked vulnerable and afraid—and this, I realized, was what I had missed in my first foray into living my own life and not Green's and Cory's. He was putting a part of his heart out on the line in a way Leah and I had not done with each other—hell, in a way I hadn't ever even done with Cory. Cory's words from the garden, hysterical, self-recriminating, came back to haunt me.

"What do *you* want, Nick?" he asked, meeting my eyes with what looked to be a painful effort.

I moved closer to him, risked putting a hand on his thigh, moved my face in toward his, until we could see the actual color of each other's eyes in the moonlight and feel our breaths mingling in the chill. His eyes were blue-gray, and he had crinkles at the corners that I hadn't earned yet and a smallish, full-lipped mouth that puckered like a doll's when it was closed. I wanted to feel that mouth under my fingertip, but I kept my hand on his thigh because it was taut and muscled and real.

"I want to give," I said honestly. He smelled like warm animal and desire. He smelled like hunger. Beneath my hand his thigh muscles flexed, and I itched to touch the skin under his slacks. I itched to taste his body, to feel it arch and tighten under my hands, my lips, my tongue. "I want to give to someone who wants what I have to give. I want to give until I know how to laugh sweet, like you, and until I can make you laugh like that again."

He nodded, one tension flowing out of him, another, more wonderful kind taking its place. "Then give me," he whispered, and hands tangled in my hair and lips met mine, and I began my lesson and gave and gave and gave.

*Stay tuned for an
exclusive excerpt from*

Bound, Vol. 2

Little Goddess:
Book Three, Vol. 2

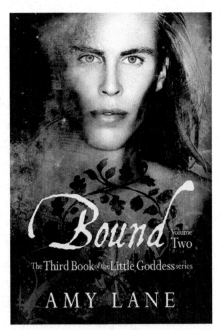

Cory's newly bound family is starting to find its footing, which is a good thing because danger after danger threatens, and Green can't be there nearly as often as he's needed. As Cory learns to face the challenges of ruling the hill alone, she's also juggling a menage relationship with three lovers—with mixed results.

But with each new challenge, one lesson becomes crystal clear: she can't be queen without each of the men who look to her, and the people she loves aren't safe unless she takes on that queendom with all of the intelligence and courage in her formidable heart.

But sometimes even intelligence, courage, and steadily increasing magic aren't enough to do the job, and suddenly the role of Cory's lovers becomes more crucial than ever. Nobody is strong enough to succeed in every task, and Cory finds that the most painful lesson she and her lovers can learn is not just how to deal with failure. Cory needs to learn that one woman is only so powerful, and she needs to choose wisely who sits outside her circle of family, and who is bound eternally in her heart.

www.dsppublications.com

I PULLED out my bag and situated myself in the deafening silence, then looked at Hallow expectantly. "So... any questions I can answer today, Professor Hallow?" I asked, feeling like I was eating my heart just to prompt the whole process that I had dreaded for weeks.

"A few," he said firmly, as though he was ready to get down to business. "Would it matter?"

"Well, I thought questions were the point," I said, confused.

"I meant, would it matter if everybody heard what you said about them?" he prompted, and I flushed.

"Yes," I said, shamed. "They rely on me. They *follow* me. Even..." I choked, because this truth was still painful. "Even Bracken. You don't... go off... on people who follow you."

Hallow nodded. His look of perpetual worry deepened, and I felt my stomach clench. This was totally going to suck. "You didn't say ex-lovers," he said, and it was such a non sequitur that now *I* was the one who was confused.

"I'm sorry?"

"You said 'ex-friends'—and as mad as you were, I knew you weren't serious. You didn't say 'ex-lovers.' Why not? It wouldn't have mattered—you were just 'going off,' as you said. You were going off in a totally safe place, with a totally safe person, and as upset as you were, you still didn't say 'ex-lovers.' Can you tell me why?"

I shrugged. "My love is a matter of life and death—to both of them." I shrugged again, my flush intensifying. "You don't say shit like that when it's that important. Not even when you're mad. Not even when it's safe."

"Not even in your own head?" he prompted gently, and I was instantly horrified.

"Goddess, no!" I gasped, the pain of even the thought too awful to contemplate. "No. Not even to think about." I wanted to make him even take the idea back, as childish as I knew that to be.

He nodded again, and I was starting to dread the slow, thoughtful incline of that noble head. "You're awfully controlled for someone so young, Lady Cory." He didn't miss my wince with the honorific, but he didn't say anything about it, either. "You didn't even lose control when you lost control. Can you remember the last time you completely lost your cool about something?"

Crap. It took me a minute to discipline my mouth and be sure my voice wouldn't betray me. "Of course I do," I said casually, working the cable needle deftly, knitting, knitting from the needle, knitting some more. "You couldn't have missed it. I was covered in Adrian's blood, I almost killed Bracken and Arturo, and a hundred vampires died." I swallowed, proud of how good I was getting at saying that without completely losing it. "I don't want to let that happen ever again."

"Which part?" he asked, an emotion in his voice that I couldn't define. I looked sharply at him, and he went on. "The part where you lost your lover, or the part where you killed the people responsible?"

Fucking hell. I looked him in the eyes and shook my head. "You know, Master Hallow, this whole therapy thing is sooooooo going to suck large," I said, so much feeling dripping from my voice that I was surprised it didn't melt the floor.

Hallow cocked his head sympathetically. "You owe me fifteen more minutes, my lady," he said gently, and I thought with a shocking jolt of venom that I could really hate this guy.

Fifteen minutes later, nothing had changed my mind. I felt like I had been put through the wringer, and my anger at my people hadn't dimmed one itty-bitty little teeny tiny bit. Hallow walked me to the door as promised and put his gentle hand on my stiff shoulder. Then he spoke in a voice meant to carry. "It was good talking to you, Lady Cory." He gave a little bow as he said it, which made my mortification complete. "I look forward to talking to you next week."

I smiled at him pleasantly and said, sotto voce, "If you think I'm ripping my soul open like that for you next week, you're high."

"If you don't," he said softly, "I'm going to insist to Green that you take a full hour at least twice a week." Then, louder, "So—next Tuesday, then?"

"If I don't eat your liver first," I smiled, and he smiled blandly back before gesturing Bracken inside his office. I glared at everyone left, and they all had the grace to look ashamed.

"I'm going running," I snapped. "If anyone tries to follow me, I'll fry them to the last grizzled pubic hair."

"Cory, it's not safe—" Nicky started, and I cut him off with a glare.

"Fuck you, Nicky, and the posse you're riding on." And with that I shouldered my backpack and took off, not even bothering to look behind me, because I was serious and I was pretty sure they were more afraid of me than they were of Bracken.

By the time Davy joined me on the track, I'd run half a mile on sheer pissed-offness. I'd run it too fast in the driving rain, and I was winded, sore, drenched, and irritated—but I was still angry, so when Davy came up beside me I didn't slacken my speed.

"Wow, Cory, you're going pretty fast," she said, surprised, and I just nodded, knowing that talking was beyond me right now. "Any particular reason?"

"I want my husband to live," I puffed out, and Davy, being a smart young woman, nodded and said nothing else for the rest of the run. It turned out to be pretty short, because in two more laps I had to slow down against my will, and we walked in silence for half a mile before my breathing slowed and she asked me if I wanted to talk about it. I shook my head.

"I just got blackmailed into therapy," I said sourly. "Ask me if I want to talk about anything else today."

Davy barked out a laugh. "That's harsh. What did he use as blackmail?"

I sighed, and it came out as a shudder. "My running time," I said, still blowing a little. It was pounding down frigid cloud-piss, but between my temper and the run, I was overheated. Frustrated, I pulled off my sweatshirt and my white T-shirt, leaving me in my black sports bra, walking faceup in the cleansing rain. Davy stopped suddenly, her yellow rain poncho making a whisking sound.

"Wow!" she breathed. "Cory, that is one hell of a tattoo on your back. Does it mean anything?"

I stopped, right there on the rubberized track. "Yes," I said through a suddenly rough throat. "It means a lot… but it's sort of hard to explain."

"Give it a try," she asked, lost in the weaving of leaves and blood that was written on my back.

"They're symbols," I said gruffly, "for people I love. It… it was sort of our way of binding ourselves to each other, so that… the world would know we belonged to each other."

"Which one is Bracken?" she asked.

"He's the sword with the red cap on it. And the blood." I shrugged. "It's sort of an ancestral thing for him."

"Who's the hawk?"

I shrugged again. "Nicky." She'd met him.

"But you two... you're like brother and sister...," she said, puzzled.

"Yeah. We should be, but... but our world is complicated."

Davy laughed. "It's the same world I live in."

"It is," I answered, and a wave of discomfort and worry suddenly crashed into me and broke. "You just don't know it. Look... Davy...." And at that moment, we both took a breath that we didn't finish.

"Holy crap, what is that stench...?" She choked, and as quick as that, we were wearing the shield I'd practiced two days before, and the fight with Hollow Man was on.

"Davy, we've got to get to Bracken and the others," I said breathlessly, calling silently for Green. "That smell is a bad thing, and we don't want to be here when it pounces."

I'd left my backpack in the locker room today, and I fleetingly mourned it as I grabbed Davy's hand and pulled her at a dead run toward the gate at the far side of the field from us. She was reluctant to go, and my shoulder twisted backward as I jerked her body forward and she finally took the hint and joined me. *A hundred meters*, I thought with fractured logic. We were both runners—we could make a hundred meters in a fairly brief amount of time.

And then something hit the shield with a ring like a marshmallow church bell, sending Davy and me flying in my cushioned bubble of power, bouncing us off the ground like kids in one of those big inflatable playpens. And the smell.... *Why couldn't my shields ward off the smell?* I thought dismally, but there was no time, no goddamned time to figure it out.

"What in the hell...." Davy pulled herself to her feet, and I grabbed her hand and dragged her back into our full-out run.

"Shut up and keep running," I panted. "And if I go down, go get Bracken."

"What's after...?" And we were hit again. It was moving too fast to see, and it didn't shatter my shield, but the invisible wall did get weak on the bottom, and we both went down face first. My nose exploded in white pain, and between that and the stench, my stomach cramped—

but it wasn't just me out here, it was Davy and me, and I needed to get her to safety. Both of us came up wiping blood from our knees, hands, and mouths, but I was the one who bounded to my feet again and went lurching for the end of the field.

"Shit!" I spat, reinforcing my goddamned shield and taking up that dead run one more time. I'd done something serious to my face when we went down, and not only could I not clear the stars from my vision, but my first breath had me choking on blood. *Twenty-five meters*, I thought, gasping from my mouth. We had twenty-five fucking meters and my mad was on.

Little Goddess: Book One

Working graveyards in a gas station seems a small price for Cory to pay to get her degree and get the hell out of her tiny town. She's terrified of disappearing into the aimless masses of the lost and the young who haunt her neck of the woods. Until the night she actually stops looking at her books and looks up. What awaits her is a world she has only read about—one filled with fantastical creatures that she's sure she could never be.

And then Adrian walks in, bearing a wealth of pain, an agonizing secret, and a hundred and fifty years with a lover he's afraid she won't understand. In one breathless kiss, her entire understanding of her own worth and destiny is turned completely upside down. When her newfound world explodes into violence and Adrian's lover—and prince—walks into the picture, she's forced to explore feelings and abilities she's never dreamed of. The first thing she discovers is that love doesn't fit into nice neat little boxes. The second thing is that risking your life is nothing compared to facing who you really are—and who you'll kill to protect.

www.dsppublications.com

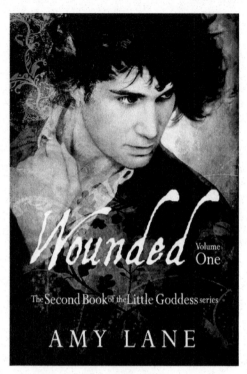

Little Goddess: Book Two, Vol. 1

Cory fled the foothills to deal with the pain of losing Adrian, and Green watched her go. Separately, they could easily grieve themselves to death, but when an old enemy of Green's brings them back together, they can no longer hide from their grief—or their love for each other.

But Cory's grieving has cut her off from the emotional stability that's the source of her power, and Green's worry for her has left them both weak. Cory's strength comes from love, and she finds that when she's in the presence of Adrian's best friend, Bracken, she feels stronger still.

But defeating their enemy is by no means a sure thing. As the attacks against Cory and her lovers keep coming, it becomes clear that their love might not be enough if they can't heal each other—and themselves—from the wounds that almost killed them all.

www.dsppublications.com

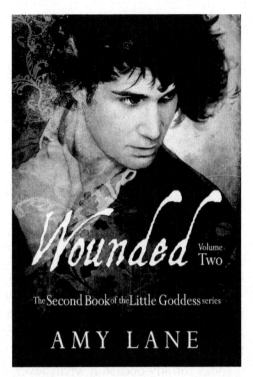

Little Goddess: Book Two, Vol. 2

Green and Bracken's beloved survived their enemy's worst—with unexpected vampiric help.

But survival is a long way from recovery, and even further from safety. Green's people want badly to return to the Sierra Foothills, but they're not going with their tails between their legs. Before they go home, they have to make sure they're free from attack—and that they administer a healthy dose of revenge as well.

As Cory negotiates a fragile peace between her new and unexpected lovers, Green negotiates the unexpected power that comes from being a beloved leader of the paranormal population. Together, they might heal their own wounds and lead their people to an unprecedented place at the top of the supernatural food chain—a place that will allow them to return home a better, stronger whole.

www.dsppublications.com

AMY LANE is a mother of two college students, two grade-schoolers, and two small dogs. She is also a compulsive knitter who writes because she can't silence the voices in her head. She adores fur-babies, knitting socks, and hawt menz, and she dislikes moths, cat boxes, and knuckle-headed macspazzmatrons. She is rarely found cooking, cleaning, or doing domestic chores, but she has been known to knit up an emergency hat/blanket/pair of socks for any occasion whatsoever, or sometimes for no reason at all. Her award-winning writing has three flavors: twisty-purple alternative universe, angsty-orange contemporary, and sunshine-yellow happy. By necessity, she has learned to type like the wind. She's been married for twenty-plus years to her beloved Mate and still believes in Twu Wuv, with a capital Twu and a capital Wuv, and she doesn't see any reason at all for that to change.

Website: www.greenshill.com
Blog: www.writerslane.blogspot.com
E-mail: amylane@greenshill.com
Facebook: www.facebook.com/amy.lane.167
Twitter: @amymaclane

Also from DSP Publications

EVOLUTION: GENESIS
LISSA KASEY

www.dsppublications.com

For more
great fiction
from

DSP PUBLICATIONS

visit us online.
WWW.DSPPUBLICATIONS.COM

CPSIA information can be obtained
at www.ICGtesting.com
Printed in the USA
LVOW01s2242020216
473427LV00027B/887/P

9 781634 761192